OPTION TO
KILL

D0963945

Also by Andrew Peterson

First to Kill
Forced to Kill

OPTION TO KILL

ANDREW PETERSON

THOMAS & MERCER

The characters and events portrayed in this book are fictitious. Any similarity to real persons, living or dead, is coincidental and not intended by the author.

Text copyright © 2012 Andrew Peterson

Published by Thomas & Mercer
PO Box 400818
Las Vegas, NV 89140

ISBN-13: 9781612187068
ISBN-10: 1612187064

Library of Congress Control Number: 2012945776

To my parents: Paul and Cindy Peterson

CHAPTER 1

A text tone interrupted Nathan's movie. He pressed pause and grabbed his cell from the coffee table.

echo five sierra charlie

He sat up and squinted at the message. Someone had just used his operative name, and he didn't like it. Only a handful of people knew his former company designation, and none of them would text him like this. In fact, anyone from his inner circle would've called, not texted. He wanted to ignore it, but that was wishful thinking. You can't uncook a steak, and this one was burned.

"Sierra Charlie"—the military designators for the letters *S* and *C*—had only one meaning: "situation critical." Someone was in a life-or-death struggle. It carried the same urgency as a "cover now" call over a police radio—drop everything and respond.

It could be a fishing expedition or an outright trap. He and Harv had enemies all over the world, and one of them could be baiting him. He'd delete this cellular account right away. Tonight. Nathan always kept his cell's GPS tracking capability disabled, but there were still methods of tracing a cell phone's location.

But on second thought, it seemed unlikely this text originated from a former enemy. If it had, he'd already be dead—or worse.

One thing was certain: whoever managed to obtain his cell number had to be resourceful. Maybe he could turn this around and get some info on the sender.

He tapped the screen.

who are you?

Nathan didn't consider himself a paranoid man, but now he felt vulnerable. He went upstairs to his bedroom and changed into 5.11 Tactical clothing, before punching a six-digit combination into his handgun safe. He grabbed his SIG and pocketed the suppressor and four spare magazines. He jacked a round into the chamber and lowered the hammer using the weapon's decocking lever. Gun in hand, he returned to the living room and turned off the Blu-ray player.

His cell chimed again, showing a single name.

lauren

Okay, fair enough, but not very useful. A first name didn't tell him squat.

how do you know about echo five?

Nathan waited through fifteen seconds of silence.

my mom

What mom? Besides Harv's wife, he didn't know any moms who would or should know his old CIA call sign. In fact, he didn't know any other moms, period. He turned off all the lights, cracked the blinds, and scanned the front yard. Sensing his change in behavior, his two giant schnauzers studied his every move. He took them to the kitchen door and pressed a forefinger against the capacitance scanner of the security keypad. The red LED turned green.

"Grant. Sherman. Search!" The dogs bounded out the door.

Nathan tapped another question.

where are you?

The messages originated from a phone with a local 858 area code, but "Lauren" could be anywhere. For one crazy moment, he toyed with the idea that Harv could be using someone to play a prank on him. Today *was* April Fools' Day, but he knew Harv would never do this, not even as a gag.

la jolla

Nathan's radar sprang up three notches. He was in La Jolla as well, his house no more than a seven-minute drive from any location within the community. Was there another La Jolla, in a different part of the country? He needed more info.

la jolla san diego? where in la jolla?

The answer arrived a few seconds later.

exxon lj shores blk suv

Nathan stared at the text. Exxon gas station at La Jolla Shores…in a black SUV? Depending on the signal at La Jolla Parkway, this person was no more than a three-minute drive away. Coincidence? Not in this marine's world. Time to get mobile. He grabbed his emergency travel bag from the hall closet, unzipped it, and secured the handgun, spare mags, and suppressor next to his folding Predator knife. He felt an adrenaline surge build as he laced his boots, so he slowed his breathing.

Whoever was sending these messages now had his full attention. If this was someone's twisted idea of a prank, there'd be hell to pay.

In the garage, he belted himself into his Mustang. He always kept the vehicle backed in so he could exit straight out, but more importantly, he also faced the door when it opened. Seeing the driveway was clear, he took a few seconds to send another text.

what kind of trouble are you in?

He started the engine, pulled forward only enough to allow the garage door to close, and pressed the button. He never left his house without watching the door finish its descent. Old habits died hard. He opened the home security app on his phone and rearmed the system with a six-digit code.

kidn

Kidn? "Kidding"? Was this Lauren person now telling him she was only kidding around? Then why use the "echo five" reference? It didn't make sense.

Nathan didn't text often but knew there were all kinds of abbreviations. Did she mean "kidnapped"?

He sent another text.

you still there?

Without waiting for an answer, Nathan started down the driveway. A few seconds later, his phone rang. He answered it, but didn't say anything.

"...me that phone, you little slut! Who are you calling?"

He heard a rustling sound, then a long silence ensued. Nathan sensed a malevolent presence on the other end, like the draft from a slaughterhouse.

"Whoever you are, this is none of your business. Stay away from her, or you're dead. I'll do you...*slowly.*"

The call went dark.

CHAPTER 2

Nathan braked hard at the bottom of his driveway as the privacy gate rolled open, then sped away, driving as fast as possible without being reckless. This area of Mt. Soledad was residential, with steep, curvy roads, and he didn't want to plow into anyone.

He no longer doubted the messages. There was hatred in the man's voice, vicious and deep. Nathan had no illusions about the danger of jumping into this situation, but someone named Lauren knew his CIA call sign and also knew the "Sierra Charlie" reference. During their time as an operative team, Harv and he hadn't interacted with many female operations officers, so it was unlikely Lauren was one of them. Besides, no trained spook would initiate contact like this, especially after fourteen years.

This definitely smelled like a trap. Nathan was many things, but naive didn't make the list. At this point, he fully expected the situation to turn ugly.

Nathan ran a stop sign and turned left on a busier street. This was a well-traveled route, so he didn't feel as concerned about speeding. People who lived along this road knew the score. He estimated no more than three minutes had elapsed since Lauren's first text. Pushing the limits of his Mustang, he raced down the mountain until a model citizen forced him to drive the speed limit. He couldn't pass, so he had to endure a painfully slow pace. At the bottom of the road, the signal to cross La Jolla Parkway was red. With a little luck, the delay wouldn't be long.

He pulled into the line of waiting cars and replayed the call in his head. The voice had a Hispanic accent. He guessed the man's age to be somewhere between thirty and fifty. The guy was obviously a bully by nature, and maybe worse, given the "die slowly" threat. Nathan knew about bullies—all too well—and if possible, he intended to properly introduce himself. We'll see who dies slowly.

He assumed Lauren was fairly young because of her reference to "my mom," which only made the situation more urgent.

The light changed and he followed the line of vehicles onto westbound Torrey Pines. The Exxon that Lauren had mentioned stood in a small retail center about two hundred yards ahead. As he approached, he scanned the area for a black SUV or any dark SUV but didn't see one. He turned into the driveway and coasted past the gas pumps on the left. The absence of a black SUV meant he faced two options: wait or leave. He favored leaving. At the driveway abutting La Jolla Shores Drive, he'd have to turn right— a median curb prevented a left.

Nathan looked both directions and saw something to his right. Two blocks north, a black SUV made a screeching illegal U-turn. He focused on the vehicle as it approached from the north, heading to the light at Torrey Pines. Someone behind him honked, an annoying *beep*. He ignored it and studied the Cadillac Escalade as it sped past. The male driver had been trying to make the green light at Torrey Pines, but the car in front him had stopped at the yellow. A girl sat in the passenger seat, and she appeared to be fairly young.

Nathan cut off a Lexus and accelerated to the same illegal U-turn location. In a somewhat reckless move, he whipped his Mustang around and ended up about ten cars behind the SUV. From this position, he shouldn't have any trouble staying with it.

He considered calling Harv and bringing him up to speed, but dismissed the thought. His friend was on vacation on the other side of the world, and this would only alarm him pointlessly. Depending on how ugly this turned, though, he'd have to get in touch with Harv soon.

After the light changed, the Escalade gained some separation, but he couldn't do much about it. From its current lane, the Escalade could peel left to stay on Torrey Pines or continue straight onto eastbound La Jolla Parkway. Ten seconds later, he had his answer. It went straight, heading for the intersection of I-5 and Highway 52. Without making abrupt lane changes, he closed the gap and settled into a slot five cars back.

Nathan thought about the texts the girl had sent. The man had grabbed her cell phone midcall, that much was obvious, and if he'd taken a minute to scroll through her messages he would've seen her reference to a black SUV at the La Jolla Shores Exxon. If so, the driver might be looking for a tail. But even if the driver had looked at the messages, he might not have thought anyone could get to the Exxon in time. There was no way to gauge the driver's level of situational awareness, so for now Nathan would play it safe and observe from a distance.

At the top of the grade, the Escalade continued east and merged into the flow of Highway 52. Nathan kept the same margin until he saw an opportunity to make a move. If the driver suspected he was being followed, Nathan would know soon enough. He eased into the right lane and passed a few cars. The motorcycle in front of him moved over to exit the freeway, which left his lane clear. He closed the distance, paralleled the Escalade, and glanced left.

Now that he had a closer look, he guessed the girl's age to be twelve, plus or minus a year.

The girl looked at him, and for the briefest instant, he sensed recognition on her face. She mouthed four words in an exaggerated manner.

Kidnapped, please help me.

Nathan learned to read lips long ago, and there was no mistaking what he'd just seen. He felt his body tighten and loosened his grip on the steering wheel. This was unquestionably the black SUV from the texts. Everything fit. Instinctively, Nathan committed the girl's face to memory. She looked Eurasian, with strong cheekbones and a few freckles. Her black hair was pulled back in a ponytail.

He glanced at his speedometer—seventy miles per hour—and eased off the gas. The Escalade advanced into his ten o'clock position. At least the eastbound lanes on Highway 52 weren't heavy with traffic. Rush hour had already come and gone.

Nathan retrieved a small notepad and pen from the glove compartment and assessed the ambient light. Not great. Most of the vehicles had their headlights on as the final traces of twilight stretched across San Diego. He wondered if the girl would be able to read his note. He thought so. Kids tended to have sharp vision.

Holding the notepad against the steering wheel, he wrote two words in large block letters: ECHO FIVE.

Nathan pulled forward again but kept his driver's-side window just shy of the Escalade's passenger window. If this girl truly was in trouble, he didn't want the driver to see the note. He hugged the left side of his lane and brought the note up, keeping it low in his window.

The girl looked over, and this time there was no doubt. Her expression told all.

Nathan nodded and fell back again, faking the appearance of a distracted driver who couldn't decide how fast he wanted to go. To complete the act, he grabbed his cell phone and brought it up to his ear.

Now what?

He'd just received a desperate plea for help from a kidnapped girl whose mother clearly had classified information. Some big questions needed answers. He inched forward again, matched the

SUV's speed, and looked left. The girl's expression worsened and she mouthed, *No police. Please, no police.*

No police? What did she mean by that? If she was being kidnapped, why wouldn't she want the police involved?

He dropped back into the Escalade's blind spot.

Options began forming. Should he follow the Escalade and call the police anyway?

Nathan looked at his gas gauge: less than a quarter tank.

His SIG and Predator knife were in the emergency travel bag, but engaging an unknown adversary in gun or knife play didn't seem like a solid option. And there could be more than one kidnapper involved, or more children. The tinted rear windows of the Escalade hid any occupants. If there *were* additional people back there, they might've seen the notes. Nathan supposed the closeness of the two side-by-side vehicles, combined with the fading light, could've made it difficult for anyone sitting in the back to see, but he wasn't sure. Strike that. If anyone were seated behind the girl, they definitely would've seen the note. Since the kidnapper hadn't changed speed or done anything out of the ordinary, Nathan believed no one else rode in back.

He felt naked in his Mustang. His six-foot-five frame barely fit into the custom seat he'd installed and his windows weren't tinted. He needed to turn disadvantage into an advantage, but how? How did being visually unprotected become an asset? His cell phone. He'd pretend to be texting against the steering wheel and drift into the Escalade. Just a bump. Nothing serious, but enough to warrant an exchange of insurance information. But what if the driver overreacted and lost control? The Escalade might roll, or cause a multivehicle accident. And what would happen if it didn't stop? What if it sped away? Nathan didn't want to endanger innocent people by engaging in a high-speed pursuit.

He needed more information and decided to risk another exchange. All he'd gleaned at the Exxon station was the image of a clean-shaven man with short dark hair and a pronounced chin who looked to be in his late thirties or early forties. He also appeared to be wearing a business suit. How many kidnappers wore business suits?

Assuming the girl could respond only one more time, he'd ask a tactical yes-or-no question. He wrote a new note, inched forward, and waited until he was just ahead of her window so she wouldn't have to turn her head as far. Riskier, though—from this position, the driver might be able see it. Without looking over, Nathan brought the pad up and held it low against his window. After several seconds, he lowered the note and glanced left. Keeping her head straight, the girl offered a barely perceptible nod. Whoever this child was, she was poised and smart. Nathan dropped back and thought about the question he'd just asked.

JUST YOU + DRIVER?

Answer: yes.

The big question returned. Now what?

The I-805 interchange was just ahead, and the kidnapper moved into the right lane. Nathan opened up some distance and followed the Escalade up the sweeping on-ramp. He began to feel a building pressure to do something. Come on, Nate. Think. What are you going to do? Taking the wrong course of action could backfire and cause more harm than good. Patience, he told himself. Sometimes no action was the best action. As long as he kept the Escalade in sight, he had options. On the other hand, it would take multiple assets to tail a vehicle effectively through surface streets. If the driver possessed countersurveillance training, he'd likely initiate a surveillance detection route. And if he did that, Nathan couldn't avoid being discovered. A single asset couldn't beat a properly executed SDR.

Ahead on the freeway, something caught Nathan's attention: the Amber Alert sign at Clairemont Mesa Boulevard displayed three bright lines of text. Set against the cobalt sky, the message demanded to be seen:

CHILD ABDUCTION

BLACK SUV

CA LICENSE UNKNOWN

There were few times when Nathan experienced a chill, but this was one of them. He moved over a lane to the west and slowly inched forward. The girl was no longer visible. The driver must've seen the Amber Alert and ordered her to crouch down.

The complexity and risk of his situation had just skyrocketed. Ironically, the Amber Alert hindered his efforts. Anything he did to interdict, even an "accidental" fender bender, would no longer be interpreted as a coincidence. The smallest act out of the ordinary would raise red flags with the kidnapper. On the flip side, the alert reaffirmed the immediate danger to the girl, and he now felt confident that any action he took would be justified.

The Escalade changed lanes and slowed to sixty-five. Several car lengths back, Nathan matched its pace as it made an additional lane change. The SUV was now directly in front of him. Anticipating the driver's next move, he eased into the slow lane, checked his rearview mirror, and dropped back farther.

As predicted, the kidnapper signaled and moved into the exit-only lane. He obviously wanted off this freeway, probably because there weren't any Amber Alert signs on surface streets. The center-divide sign indicated that the Balboa Avenue exit lay one-quarter mile ahead. Nathan maintained his distance as the Escalade slowed to fifty-five. Would the driver go east or west on Balboa? Playing it safe, Nathan didn't use his turn signal. The Escalade peeled right, heading for the westbound lanes.

At the traffic light, Nathan ended up directly behind the Escalade, a mere ten feet away. Okay, he told himself, there's a kidnapped girl named Lauren in the Escalade, and the Amber Alert system's activated. The kidnapper's edgy, wondering if anyone saw the girl and dropped a dime.

If Nathan were driving that Escalade, he'd execute an SDR, but he doubted many people had his level of countersurveillance training. If the abductor planned to try one, it would probably happen within the next mile or so. At least Nathan had the speed and maneuverability advantage. If this turned into a high-speed chase, the Cadillac could never outrun his Mustang.

At Genesee Avenue, the Escalade moved into the inside, left-turn-only lane and stopped at the red light. Nathan maintained a single-car buffer between himself and the target. Several vehicles had lined up in front of the SUV, also waiting for the light to change.

What do most kidnappers want? Privacy. If this were a ransom, the abductor would want seclusion, at least initially. The same would apply to an abductor bent on committing a sex crime. But what if this involved something else altogether? Something related to the mother who knew Nathan's former CIA call sign, who'd also taught her daughter operative code words? In that case, the kidnapper could be headed to a predetermined location to make a vehicle switch. He could have accomplices. Fellow professionals. But no professional would allow his victim to keep or use a cell phone.

Assuming the kidnapper didn't execute an SDR, he figured he could only keep this tail going for ten to fifteen minutes before being spotted.

The left-turn arrow at Genesee turned green, and the dual column of cars started forward. From this inside lane, the SUV could make a U-turn. If it did that, there was a good chance the U-turn was one of many to come designed to expose a tail. Nathan felt some measure of relief when the Escalade settled into the right lane of Genesee.

He pictured this area of San Diego in his mind. Assuming freeways were out of the equation, staying on major surface streets would be the fastest way to the kidnapper's destination, but doing that also ran the highest risk of crossing paths with an SDPD cruiser. Nathan didn't know for sure but believed Amber Alerts were broadcast to all law enforcement units within a certain radius of the abduction, which meant every cop in the area would now have the info. Unfortunately, in a city this size, there were literally hundreds, if not thousands, of black SUVs on the road at any given time. Would police start randomly pulling over black SUVs? He wasn't sure.

Genesee Avenue started down into a branch of Tecolote Canyon, where it would cross only a couple of roads before reaching Linda Vista. Nathan increased his separation to five hundred yards and accelerated to fifty miles per hour to stay with the Escalade. He decided to up the stakes. Since the kidnapper had been going south on 805 before seeing the Amber Alert, he believed that was the general direction the driver wanted to go. And the best way to do that was to make a right turn onto Linda Vista Road.

He moved into the fast lane.

At the bottom of the canyon, he passed the Escalade and returned to the right lane again. He didn't use his signal because he didn't want to draw any unnecessary attention. He was just another early-evening commuter on his way home from work. Twilight was in full effect now. Every vehicle had its headlights on. He looked in his rearview mirror, calculating. If he guessed wrong about this, he'd likely lose all stealth.

Linda Vista lay just ahead, and he slowed to make the turn. The light stayed green as he rounded the corner. The moment of truth arrived. If the kidnapper didn't turn right, Nathan would have to make an illegal U-turn and possibly blow a tire jumping the median curb.

He looked over his shoulder and saw the Escalade slowing for the right-hand turn. The kidnapper used his turn signal, probably to avoid making any kind of traffic violation. Nathan slowed to allow the SUV to catch up. In his side mirror, he saw the kidnapper signal and move into the left lane. He also watched for any sudden changes of speed.

The right side of Linda Vista Road hosted several fast-food joints; the left side was mostly residential. Since the Escalade immediately changed lanes to the inside, Nathan believed its next move would be a left turn onto Ulric to head down to Friars Road. He needed to keep the Escalade in front of him for this leg of the pursuit. But how?

An idea formed. Most drivers resented being cut off, and if Nathan timed his lane change just right, the kidnapper might feel a little irritation and the need to race ahead of him. It was a fine line. He didn't want to create suspicion, only annoyance.

Nathan slowed and waited until the Escalade was only twenty-five feet behind, and changed lanes without signaling. He saw its front end dip when the driver applied the brakes. Perfect. He moved into the left-turn-only lane and looked for a median curb on Ulric Street. Good—there wasn't one. If he had to make a U-turn because the Escalade continued west on Linda Vista, it wouldn't be a issue turning around. Come on, pull in behind....

Perfect. The kidnapper accelerated into Nathan's lane, turned on his high beams, and stopped three feet back. A feeling of relief mixed with anxiety from the blinding headlights behind him. He didn't think the driver would get out and offer a challenge, but if he did, that might create an ideal opportunity to "introduce" himself to the girl's kidnapper. Nathan reached up and casually made the high-beam adjustment on his rearview mirror.

Did the creep have a gun? He didn't like the idea of being in front, but it seemed the best way to continue the tail without being detected. Nathan doubted he'd be able to anticipate the SUV's move at Friars Road. At the bottom of Ulric, continuing south would be impossible without an east or west detour to cross the San Diego River and I-8.

Unless the kidnapper was totally inept, Nathan felt he couldn't continue this charade for more than two or three more turns, and he was beginning to feel the early signs of decision paralysis. The longer he waited to act, the more difficult acting became. At some point he'd have to force the issue. The question became, when?

To reel the kidnapper in, Nathan crept through the intersection when the light turned green, purposely going slower than necessary. Once on Ulric, the kidnapper swerved into the left lane and accelerated. He didn't look but felt the driver's malignant glare as the Escalade sped past. Nathan allowed it to get several hundred yards ahead before matching its speed again. He didn't believe his cover was blown, but one more stunt like that, and all bets were off.

Ulric began a gradual descent through a narrow canyon. Nathan formulated a plan. He had no illusions it would be simple, but it was time to act. A girl's life was at stake, and every passing minute represented increasing danger to her. He closed the distance to one hundred yards and knew the kidnapper would see the change in separation. Up ahead, the traffic light glowed red. The kidnapper slowed as several cars turned left at the light and started up Ulric toward them.

Now was his chance. There wouldn't be another like it. Nathan noticed multiple headlights in his rearview mirror but couldn't worry about them. He reached into the emergency bag and retrieved his SIG. He turned the laser sight on and tucked the weapon into his right pocket. The suppressor, folded Predator knife, cell phone, and spare magazines went into his thigh pockets. Everything you need in life: A knife. A gun. And a cell phone.

Nathan saw the light for the cross-traffic turn yellow and moved into the left lane.

Up ahead, the light turned green.

Nathan hit the gas.

CHAPTER 3

Even if the kidnapper had seen him coming, it was too late. Before the Escalade reached the intersection, Nathan pulled alongside and jerked the steering wheel to the right. Just before the impact, he exhaled, tightened his abs, and forced himself against the back of his seat.

The Mustang's airbag control unit did its job.

For an instant, Nathan felt stunned and unable to move. He thought his heart might actually fail. Son of a bitch!

He'd never experienced an airbag deployment and was damn sure he never wanted to again. Out his right window, he saw the Escalade jerk to a sudden stop. Nathan started a mental stopwatch, figuring he had fewer than sixty seconds to secure the girl and clear the area on foot.

The airbag had already deflated. A noxious chemical smell—like burned electrical wiring—filled the compartment, and for an instant, he thought his Mustang had caught fire.

Three seconds after impact, he had his seat belt unbuckled and his door open.

Five seconds after the crash, he was out of his wrecked Mustang.

His plan worked.

The front end of the Escalade was wrapped around the signal pole, steam gushing from its grille. The headlights he'd seen earlier arrived, but not in the way he expected. The arriving vehicle didn't slow down and gradually pull over to the side of the road. Instead, its front end dipped as the vehicle stopped with the unmistakable high-speed pulses of antilock brakes.

Armed with compact machine guns, two men in business suits jumped out and ran directly toward him. One of them already had his gun lined up. Cops? No way. Cops would immediately identify themselves as such. These guys weren't saying anything.

Nathan cursed. He'd been so focused on the Escalade, he hadn't detected a vehicle following him.

Pulling his SIG, he circled his wrecked Mustang and sprinted toward the SUV, believing the new arrivals would be momentarily confused and hold their fire.

All he needed was a second or two.

Behind the gunmen's car, he saw a second vehicle approach and its driver didn't appear to be paying attention. The driver attempted to stop and nearly succeeded but the car smacked the rear end of the gunmen's sedan with a loud, metallic *bang*. The impact wasn't hard enough to trigger any airbags, but the two gunmen turned, giving Nathan the precious seconds he needed.

He toggled the weapon's laser, painted the red dot on the lead gunman's chest, and fired two quick shots. Unsuppressed, the discharges hammered his ears. The gunman grunted and spun but didn't go down. Body armor? Under a business suit? He lined up on the second gunman, adjusted his aim below the belt, and fired twice more. The machine gun clattered away as the wounded man tumbled onto the asphalt. Before the first guy could recover, Nathan sent two more bullets, also lower. Both slammed home. The gunman dropped his weapon and cupped his groin. The guy fell to his knees and keeled over, cursing in Spanish.

Within four seconds, Nathan had popped off six shots and scored six hits. He considered finishing them but decided killing men while they were down wouldn't sit right with his conscience. And there was still a remote possibility they could be police or feds working undercover. He hustled over to the wounded men, gave them a pat-down for additional weapons, and picked up their MP5s. Ignoring their obscene protests, he tossed the weapons into the landscaping behind a low stucco wall.

Whoever had plowed the gunmen's vehicle was leaving. The driver backed up, made a screeching U-turn, and sped away up the hill—no doubt frightened by the gunfire.

Nathan hurried to the passenger side of the Escalade and found the girl screaming incoherently, her shrieks muffled by the glass.

Other than a steady stream of blood flowing from the driver's nose, he seemed physically unharmed. Although clearly dazed from the impact, the man held on to the girl's wrist tightly. Nathan didn't see a weapon, but stayed alert as he tried the girl's door. Locked.

Nathan banged the window with his gun. "Let go of her!"

No response. The driver was trying to free himself one-handed from his seat belt and the deflated airbags surrounding him.

Nathan circled to the shattered driver's-side window and swung his pistol through it like a club, clocking the kidnapper on the side of the head. That did the trick. The girl pulled free and cringed against her door. Nathan returned to the passenger side.

In his best command tone, he yelled, "You're okay, stop screaming."

The girl's expression showed recognition. He saw her eyes then—unmistakably blue, and startling in combination with her Eurasian face and black hair.

"We need to get out of here!"

She stopped crying but didn't move.

"Fine, stay with him. I'm leaving,"

She unbuckled her seat belt.

"Unlock the door."

She fumbled with the armrest, looking for the button.

He didn't have time for this. "Get back."

She looked over at the driver and didn't move.

"I'm going to break the window. Get back!"

She leaned toward the driver and turned her head away. He struck the tempered glass with his SIG and broke away the pieces clinging to the corners. He secured his gun in his pocket, grabbed the girl under her arms, and pulled her out. Wearing blue jeans, a lavender T-shirt, and white sneakers, she felt like eighty pounds of trouble.

A car approached from the south, its headlights illuminating the canyon's eastern slope.

"Hey!"

Nathan looked at the driver.

The guy spat blood onto the airbag. "You stupid son of a bitch, you have no idea who you're fucking with."

"Likewise." He pulled his SIG and thrust it into the Escalade's interior.

The driver held his hands up in a useless gesture.

Aiming at the driver's thigh, Nathan pulled the trigger.

CHAPTER 4

Nathan's Mustang wasn't drivable. The collision had collapsed the entire right fender into the wheel well. He considered using the gunmen's black sedan, but dismissed the thought. There were too many variables, including the possibility of a tracking bug. Instead, he took the girl across the street intersecting Ulric and began running up the sidewalk. He stole a look over his shoulder. The second gunman from the sedan had gained his feet and was limping toward the wrecked SUV, but he didn't make it. Halfway there, his legs quit.

Nathan noticed a stinging pain on the side of his hand and wondered what was causing it.

"We need to clear the area. Take my hand and don't look back."

"I won't." The girl's voice was soft but laced with fear.

He needed her functioning and coherent, not thinking about the violence she'd just witnessed. Distraction time.

"Is your name really Lauren?"

"Yes."

"That's a beautiful name. I'm Nathan. How old are you?"

"You aren't supposed to ask girls that."

"Thirteen?"

"Twelve and a half. What happened to your face?"

"It happened a long time ago. Are you injured? Does anything hurt?"

"My back."

Nathan hoped she didn't have a spinal injury from the impact. "Your back hurts?"

"The airbag felt really hot."

"You were leaning forward? With your chest on your legs? The airbag burned your back?"

"Uh-huh. Are they supposed to be hot like that?"

"I'm afraid so." He realized that the stinging on his hand must also have been caused by the airbag's heat. "Does your back hurt really badly?"

Nathan sensed her hesitate, as if she were trying to compare it with something else. "Not really."

They continued running up the sidewalk.

"Give me a number from one to ten, one being really mild pain and ten being the worst you could ever imagine."

"Maybe a three."

"Who's your mom?"

"I don't know...she's just my mom."

"I mean, what's her name?"

"Jin."

"Is that short for Jennifer?"

"No, it's just Jin. *J-i-n.*"

"What's her...your last name?"

"Marchand."

"With a *c*?"

"Uh-huh."

"Does she have a middle name?"

"Elizabeth."

Nathan was impressed by Lauren's stamina. She didn't seem the slightest bit out of breath from their running. "Where is she?"

"I don't know."

"Where does she work?"

"She doesn't have a job. She's a full-time mom."

"Lauren, being a mom *is* a full-time job."

"I guess."

"Are you okay? Can you keep running a little longer?"

"I'm on the cross-country track team."

"That's a pretty ring you're wearing."

"You don't have to distract me anymore. I've seen lots of violent movies."

"Well, that's reassuring."

Back at the corner, Nathan had seen a green street sign saying they were on Fashion Hills Boulevard, but it didn't seem like much of a boulevard. The only cars present were parallel-parked against its curbs.

"Lauren, are you wearing contact lenses to make your eyes blue?"

"No, they're just blue like that. Everyone stares at me. It's so rude."

"I know the feeling."

"My mom has one brown eye and one blue eye. She wears contacts to hide it. It's kinda freaky looking. It's called heterochromia iridis."

"I'm impressed." He knew of the condition but hadn't known its medical name. He really wanted to ask more questions about her mother—like, if she had Nathan's old CIA moniker, what *else* did she know? This rift in his personal security had to be dealt with—otherwise he'd spend the rest of his life looking over his shoulder. Harv and his family could be at risk, too. But now wasn't the time. At least the police wouldn't be able to trace his Mustang back to him. It was listed as belonging to the US Department of State. That would set off all kinds of bells and whistles in DC, but he couldn't worry about it. The emergency travel bag he'd left in the Mustang didn't contain any ID, but it did have a change of clothes, a toiletry kit, and fifteen hundred bucks in twenties.

Lauren broke the silence. "You shot the man in the car."

Nathan didn't say anything.

"Did you kill him?"

"No, I only neutralized him so he couldn't come after us."

"Did you want to?"

"There was a time in my life when I would've...but I'm not that person anymore. But to answer your question, yes, I wanted to kill him."

"Me too. He looked at me in a bad way."

"You mean the way a grown man looks at a grown woman? Like that?"

"He was creepy."

"You're a brave girl. What you did took guts—I mean the way you handled yourself when I was following you on the freeway."

"I was really scared."

"You did fine. Trust me."

"You seem like a soldier. Were you a soldier?"

"A long time ago. Marines."

"My stepdad was a marine. Did you ever kill anyone?"

"Yes."

"Was it hard, you know, like...Did you feel bad about it?"

"Shh. There's someone up ahead. Stop running."

"Where?" she whispered. "I don't see anyone."

"Shh."

On both sides of the street, landscaped embankments sloped up from the sidewalks. Nathan looked toward the sound he'd heard. On the opposite side of the street, an elderly man with a small dog descended some narrow concrete stairs. The stairs looked to connect to the street above them to the north. He'd heard the jingle of the dog's collar.

The man looked at them. "Did you guys hear gunshots?"

Nathan stopped. "Yeah, it sounded like it, but it could've been firecrackers. Hard to tell."

"Are you new to the neighborhood?"

"Yeah," Lauren said. "We live about a mile from here."

"Well, it's a good neighborhood. Must've been kids."

"Probably," Nathan said. "Have a nice evening."

"You too."

When they were out of earshot, Nathan said, "Why don't you want the police involved? I saw you say 'no police.'"

"The man had a badge."

"The man in the Escalade, the man I just shot?"

"He showed it to me."

"Can you describe it? Did it have a star, anything like that?"

"I think so."

He reevaluated his earlier assessment. This girl wasn't eighty pounds of trouble, she was eighty pounds of *pure* trouble. Had he just shot a police officer? And what about the other two? The suits from the sedan—suits wearing body armor. They were carrying Heckler & Koch MP5s, the weapon of choice for many federal agencies. He needed more info, but first things first. They needed to keep moving.

"We need to start running again."

They hustled past a private clubhouse with a pool and tennis courts.

"Where're we going?" she asked.

"Trolley."

"Trolley? What trolley?"

"Are you from San Diego?"

"No, I'm from Boston."

"You don't sound like you're from Boston."

"I'm not supposed to tell anyone where I'm from."

"Why is that?"

"I'm in the witness security program 'cause I saw something I wasn't supposed to."

Nathan stopped running and faced her. "Are you talking about the federal witness security program run by US marshals?"

"Uh-huh."

He stared at her. Eighty pounds of trouble just turned into several tons. "Lauren, are you telling me I just shot three federal law enforcement officers? You said you'd been kidnapped. Federal agents don't kidnap people!"

"Please don't be mad at me." She started to cry.

Had the Amber Alert been wrong? He knew the system wasn't perfect. Mistakes happened. Why hadn't the driver or the two gunmen identified themselves? The Escalade's driver hadn't acted like a federal agent, he'd acted more like a crime-family thug or sexual predator.

He knelt and took her hand. "I'm sorry. We both need to calm down. Look, I'm sorry for snapping at you. But try to understand the kind of trouble I'm in. *We're* in."

"You want to get rid of me."

"Lauren, listen to me very carefully. I'm not trying to get rid of you." He put a hand over his heart. "I give you my word as a marine. Soldier's honor."

"Promise?"

"I promise. We're in this together. We need to keep moving. Do you hear the siren?"

She nodded.

"I know this may be difficult, given everything you've been through, but you need to trust me, okay?"

"Okay."

The siren came from the southwest, probably down on Friars Road. If the man walking his dog kept going, he'd discover the accident scene and probably tell the arriving officer he'd seen a man and a girl walking away from the accident. Nathan estimated the SDPD cruiser would be at the wrecked SUV in ninety seconds. Within ten minutes, this entire neighborhood could be crawling with cops. He didn't plan on being around for the party.

They turned south on a street just west of the tennis courts. The street's surface changed from asphalt to concrete.

"Are you okay?"

"I didn't mean to make you mad."

"I wasn't mad. You know, like, angry mad. Don't worry about it." He gave her hand a squeeze. "We need to blend in and look like a father-daughter team. It's really important. If you see a cop, don't react at all. Pretend like we haven't done anything wrong. A little farther ahead, we're going to hike down a small canyon and head across the street into the mall."

"Are you sure you're not mad at me?"

"I'm sure."

"I made the man in the black car mad at me. I told him since I was just a kid, he should disable the passenger-side airbag."

"What did he say?"

"He told me I was stupid and to shut up."

Nathan didn't respond.

"I'm not stupid," she said loudly.

"Hey, I didn't say you were. Keep your voice down."

"I don't like being called stupid."

"Nobody does." He surveyed their surroundings. "Let's stop running and walk quickly."

"The man said he was going to teach me to be smart."

Nathan didn't like the sound of that.

"What happened to your face?" Lauren asked after a short silence.

"I'd rather not talk about it."

"Why not? It's no big deal."

"If you say so."

"You don't have any children, do you." It wasn't a question.

"What makes you say that?"

"I can just tell."

"Are we going to walk or talk?"

"We can do both, you know."

"No, I don't have any children."

"Why not?"

"It's complicated."

"It's okay, you don't have to talk to me."

He did his best R. Lee Ermey imitation. "Well, thank you very much. May I be in charge for a while?"

"I don't like that movie."

"You've seen *Full Metal Jacket*? And you remember that line? You're not old enough to watch that movie."

"My stepdad liked it. He watched it a bunch of times. I don't like the bathroom scene."

"Yeah, that's hard to watch. Who's your stepdad?"

"He's dead."

"I'm sorry."

"I didn't know him very well."

"How did he die?"

"I'm not supposed to talk about it, but he was murdered."

"Murdered?" Once more, Nathan wondered what he was getting himself into. Too many things didn't make sense. "How long ago?"

"Last night."

Nathan stopped and faced her. "Last night?"

"Uh-huh."

"I'm really sorry, Lauren."

This poor kid had been through the wringer. He toyed with the idea that she could be a pathological liar playing some elaborate mind game, but his instincts said no. The men with the machine guns weren't lies, nor was her abductor.

"You promise you won't ditch me?"

"I promise."

On the south side of the street, a short hedge followed the contour of the canyon's rim. Below that, Friars Road and the Fashion Valley Mall awaited.

One hundred feet lower on Friars Road, the siren they'd heard materialized from the west in the form of a police cruiser. Its blue-and-red flashing light bar stood out among the cars pulling to the curb. It raced below their position on its way to the crash site.

Nathan found a narrow trail weaving its way through the sagebrush. It wasn't difficult going, but Lauren lost her footing in several places. He kept her from falling. "You're doing fine. We're almost there."

"How do you know about this?"

"I've seen it from the road. I think people use it as a shortcut."

The bottom of the path dumped them into a small parking lot serving a three-story office building. Nathan stopped and put a finger to his lips. He inhaled through his nose and held still. As far as he could tell, no one was around. The fading siren and rush of cars along Friars Road were the only sounds.

"We're going to head out to the street and cross at the signal."

They walked down a steep driveway leading to Friars Road and turned west along the sidewalk. Nathan pushed the pedestrian button on the signal's standard and looked to his left.

A familiar-looking sedan barreled toward them.

What the hell?

How could this be the same black sedan from Ulric Street?

Its passenger-side window was already down.

Nathan made eye contact with the driver. The same driver who'd kidnapped Lauren.

Behind a rising MP5, a smile formed on the kidnapper's bloody face.

Nathan had to protect Lauren and draw his gun, but there wasn't time for both.

He made the decision.

Rather than reach for the SIG, he picked Lauren up and literally hurled her over a chest-high retaining wall beside the sidewalk. As best he could tell, she had about two feet of protective cover on the other side.

Nathan yelled for her to stay down and made a move for his gun, but too late.

Its antilock brakes thumping, the sedan arrived like a harbinger of death.

CHAPTER 5

After all he'd been through in the marines and the CIA, his life would end like this?

Right here? Right now? It seemed so random and pointless.

Then things happened fast.

Just as the kidnapper pulled the trigger, the sedan jumped forward from being rear-ended by a pickup truck. The sedan's airbags deployed in simultaneous claps. The distinctive crunch of metal on metal was followed by the thunderous percussion of the machine gun.

The shooter's arm jerked. The slugs shattered the rear passenger window and careened off the retaining wall.

Nathan crouched and shielded his eyes against the explosion of tempered glass. He looked up and saw fresh blood spatter on the rear window. The two men he shot on Ulric must've been in the backseat, and the collision had forced the driver's arm in their direction.

Time to move.

"Come on!"

Lauren didn't respond, she was clearly frozen from shock and disbelief.

"Lauren!" he yelled. "Let's go."

She sat up and reached for him. Two seconds later, they sprinted into the slowing traffic on Friars Road, heading for the mall. Nathan glanced over his shoulder and saw the kidnapper fighting the airbag. Well, he's two for two, Nathan thought. There's nothing like a second airbag to the chops to ruin a guy's evening.

Two more sirens rang out, probably fire and medical.

Nathan and Lauren kept running as the smashed sedan sped away from the scene, its plastic rear bumper dragging along the asphalt.

"He tried to kill us!"

"Come on, we have to clear the area." They hurried down the street leading into the Fashion Valley Mall. The parking garage on their left was fairly quiet, only a few shoppers looking for spaces. Nathan looked over his shoulder, relieved to see no one had focused on them. Several people were out of their vehicles, approaching the wrecked pickup.

Nathan took a deep breath and let it out slowly. He needed to quash the adrenaline coursing through his body. Those 9-millimeter slugs hadn't missed by more than a few feet. Luck favors the well prepared, although he knew more than luck had been involved. Nathan didn't consider himself a deeply religious man, but offered a silent thank-you for the fortunate outcome just the same.

Something didn't track, though. That sedan should've been miles away by now. Assuming the kidnapper could get his wounded comrades into the sedan in about a minute, that left plenty of time to leave the area. Why had Lauren's kidnapper been driving along Friars Road right then? Maybe he'd stayed in the area hoping to gun them down as he'd just attempted to. But with a banged-up car, a gunshot to his leg, and two wounded in the backseat, why risk cruising the area? The guy should've been concerned about bleeding to death, never mind the danger of being seen by police. Unless he *was* police. Lauren said they had badges. Would any law enforcement officer—federal or otherwise—execute a drive-by shooting? It seemed outrageous unless they were dirty, which might explain a lot. But if they weren't cops, and weren't dirty, what was so important? If Lauren was a protected witness and her kidnapper wanted her eliminated, why leave her alive at all? Why didn't he just kill her and stuff her body into the back of the SUV for disposal?

Her kidnapper obviously wanted her alive, and Nathan didn't like the potential reasons. She said he'd looked at her in a bad way. Anger flared at the thought of this little girl being brutalized by the creep. Maybe Lauren had information and her kidnapper planned to wring it out of her and pleasure himself in the process? Maybe he intended to use her as leverage to keep someone silent, or the reverse—to make someone talk. Whatever the case, Nathan intended to find out.

For now, they needed to merge with the mall's patrons. They were just another father-daughter combo out for a little shopping. Fashion Valley Mall had a two-story, open-air design. Retail stores occupied a central walkway with smaller branches connecting to it. It shouldn't be difficult to disappear in there.

Nathan swept the immediate area for security guards and didn't see any, but that could change. The unmistakable clatter of automatic-weapon fire would draw anyone with military, police, or security guard training over here to investigate. Nathan didn't intend to be around when they arrived. As far as the authorities were concerned, he was a wanted man. If anyone had witnessed the first collision at Ulric, they would've reported seeing a tall man purposely sideswipe another vehicle, shoot two men in the street, grab a little girl, shoot the driver of the wrecked vehicle, and then flee the scene on foot. Quite a nasty little cocktail he'd created for himself tonight. Pour in a shot of felony hit-and-run, add some attempted murder, and top it off with a twist of kidnapping.

A perfect time to enter the controlled environment of Nordstrom.

"We're going in here."

"What're we doing?" Lauren whispered as they walked in.

"We need to change our appearance. You know where to go?"

"Well, yeah."

"We also need to work on our communication skills."

She rolled her eyes. "Yes, I know where to go."

He gestured with his arm. "Be my guest."

This place assaulted the senses: glass and glitter were everywhere. He followed Lauren onto an escalator located in the middle of the store. At the top landing, they made a U-turn, proceeded to the opposite side, and ascended another escalator.

"What can I get?"

"Anything you want."

"This isn't a discount store."

"Don't worry about that, just pick something different from what you're wearing."

"Are you rich?"

"*Rich* is a relative term."

"My stepdad was rich. He drove a Porsche. I think it cost like a hundred thousand dollars."

"What did he do?"

"You mean like work? He made furniture."

"What kind of furniture?"

"Mostly patio stuff."

"He must've made a boatload of furniture to be driving around in a Porsche."

"He owned two factories."

They entered the girls' section, and Lauren began leafing through the clothes racks. Nathan wondered if shopping came naturally to kids her age. She looked like a pro.

"Anything?" she asked again.

"Yes, but we're a little pressed for time. I'm gonna head down to the men's department. Are you okay up here for a while?"

Her expression went blank, then changed. "I don't want any clothes."

He took a knee in front of her. "Lauren, I gave you my word. I only suggested it to save some time. If you want to stay together, that's okay, but we can't spend a lot of time in here."

Nathan scanned the area. A mother and her daughter were watching from across the aisle. He offered a smile and received two forced smiles in return. He used his eyes to point at the onlookers. Lauren looked at them and wiped her face. He felt bad for making her cry and knew she was embarrassed. He should have known better. Was this parenthood? Walking on eggshells all the time? Weren't kids supposed to be tough? He cursed inwardly and felt like an idiot. After what this girl had just been through, it was a wonder she could function at all. Lauren was plenty tough, but everyone—especially children—had a breaking point, and she'd just come close.

He spoke loud enough to be overheard. "Do you see anything you like?"

The mother and daughter resumed their browsing.

"I'm sorry I cried."

"I shouldn't have suggested we split up."

He felt it. Magnetic and strong. This girl needed a hug. He stayed on one knee and opened his arms. She practically fell into him. He held her head against his shoulder and caught a scent of strawberry. He felt her shudder from another spasm of tears.

"Lauren, I'm a jerk. I'm not used to being around kids. I'm really sorry about everything."

"You're not a jerk. I think you're a nice man."

"We're in this together. Just you and me against the world, kiddo."

He couldn't remember the last time he'd hugged a child. Maybe one of Harv's sons? How long ago was that? Five years?

"I don't have anywhere to go. I can't go home."

"We'll stay together until we sort this out."

Lauren looked behind him and tensed.

A male voice said, "Is everything okay here?"

Nathan released her and turned.

A security guard.

Nathan had asked her not to react, but her instinct was too strong. He couldn't fault her. He doubted this security guard knew of the Amber Alert or the wreck at Ulric Street, but it was a good bet he knew about the attempted drive-by shooting on Friars Road. Maybe a store employee had summoned this guard. Nathan's scarred face made him look hard and mean and often drew unwanted attention. What was wrong with people? Hadn't they ever seen anyone with a giant N carved across his face?

Nathan held Lauren protectively under his arm.

"Is everything okay here?" the guard asked again.

"Yes, we're both just really tired," he said.

"We can't afford this." Lauren held out a pantsuit and put on a sad face.

"Bekka, I didn't say that, exactly. I just said it's expensive." He made eye contact with the guard. "I've recently been laid off. We have to be careful what we spend."

"I hear ya. Y'all have a nice night, folks."

"Thank you, sir. We'll try."

The guard turned and walked back toward the escalator. The mother and her teenage daughter had resumed their surveillance. Time to go. The change in clothes would have to wait. He should've thought about the consequences of entering a public place like a mall, should've thought about all the security cameras. He also should've kept a better perimeter and seen the security guard coming.

He lowered his voice. "Change in plans. We're leaving, but not quickly. We don't want to look like we've been spooked. Good job with the security guard. Smart thinking."

"I forgot I wasn't supposed to react."

"You did fine."

Nathan had been in here only a few times but knew there was an exit out to an elevated walkway on the east side of the building. They'd head that way.

At the landing of the second-floor escalator, he spotted what he needed. "Lauren, see that mannequin up ahead on the right? I want you to pretend to look at the dress it's wearing, but look for the security guard we just saw. If you see him, form a fist with your right hand for a second."

She approached the mannequin, circled it, and touched the material. Her right hand formed a fist, then released.

Nathan kept his back to the escalator and whispered, "What's he doing?"

"He's talking on a radio."

His SIG. The guard must've seen the handgun's outline when Nathan knelt in front of Lauren. How could he have been so careless and sloppy? Every security guard in the mall was probably converging toward Nordstrom. He knew guards weren't allowed to take direct action against an armed assailant, but they could definitely call for reinforcements in the form of San Diego's finest.

How long did they have? Two or three minutes? They could run for it and take their chances, but sprinting through a crowded mall with a security guard pursuing them wouldn't work. An idea formed—the guard's handcuffs. If he could remove the flow of information, the rest of the mall's security guards would be blind.

He kept his voice low. "Lauren, we're going to run toward the exit. Stay close."

"I'm scared."

"Ready?"

CHAPTER 6

It all boiled down to timing. Nathan needed to execute a series of precise moves if his plan was going to work. He couldn't do anything about all the customers present, but he figured their desire to remain uninvolved would render them inert.

Nathan and Lauren made an all-out sprint toward the east exit.

"Stop! You're under arrest!"

Nathan pretended to lose his footing. He sprawled out on the ground and acted like he'd twisted an ankle.

"Stay on the ground! Keep your hands away from your body!"

"Don't shoot!" Nathan knew the guard didn't have a gun, but he needed to make his act believable. He assumed a facedown spread-eagle position on the floor.

Lauren stopped running and turned around. With the guard still behind him, he gave her a wink. Her expression changed, but he wasn't sure if she'd play along. She might bolt for the exit without him.

The guard ran forward and repeated his command to stay on the ground. Nathan turned his head and watched the guard remove the handcuffs. Perfect. In a quick move, he swept his foot and brought the security guard down. An elbow to the guard's jaw ended the struggle. Nathan hoped he hadn't broken anything, but he'd clocked the guy pretty hard. Within seconds, he had the guard's wrists secured around the chrome support of a clothing rack. He grabbed the guard's radio and tossed it aside.

Everyone in the immediate area looked startled and frightened. A heavyset man with lousy tattoos looked to be a potential threat, and Nathan decided to keep an eye on him.

He grabbed Lauren's hand and ran toward the exit, inwardly cursing at all the cameras that had just recorded his assault on the guard. How long before his and Lauren's faces were plastered on every television in the city?

Tattoo Man also moved toward the same exit, paralleling their pace. Just what Nathan needed, a frigging hero. He didn't want one surveillance source replaced with a new one. He'd have to deal with this. When the guy closed to within ten feet, Nathan pulled his SIG and pointed it at the man's chest.

The man raised his inked-up arms. "Hey, man, I don't want no trouble."

"Then get on the ground."

"Okay, take it easy."

"Please do it now."

The big man grunted as he dropped to his knees and flopped onto his belly.

Without looking back, Nathan tucked his SIG back into his pocket and did his best to cover it with his shirt. Outside the store, he had several options. Going left into the parking garage was out, as that would take them in the wrong direction. An escalator leading down to the first level was directly ahead. So was the entrance to Neiman Marcus, but they couldn't enter the retailer or go down the escalator without being seen by people inside Nordstrom—including Tattoo Man. Nathan made the decision to stay on the second level and head south along the stores lining the open-air walkway.

"We're going to hurry but not run."

Nathan spotted the new threat immediately. At the far end of the walkway, another security guard crested the mall's central escalator and began sprinting toward them. It was a woman.

"Follow my lead." He crouched down at a store window and covered the outline of his SIG with his right hand. He lowered his voice to a whisper. "Ignore her, Lauren. We're just window shopping."

There was no mistaking the hard-soled footfalls as the female guard approached. Nathan used the glass to study the shoppers behind him. In the reflection, he saw people on both sides of the elevated walkways freeze and watch the guard race toward Nordstrom. Time seemed to slow as the guard passed directly behind them. Nathan straightened up and watched with the rest of the people until the guard disappeared into Nordstrom. Tattoo Man would tell the newly arriving guard what had happened. He estimated they had less than half a minute to clear the area, unless the new guard took a few seconds to check on her downed comrade. Even that wouldn't give them much added time.

"Let's go."

Nathan and Lauren hurried along the walkway toward the central escalator. Along the way, Nathan overheard people talking about what they'd just seen. At every opportunity, he used the glass facades to check for the female guard's reappearance. So far, so good.

They hadn't walked more than halfway to the central escalator when a high-pitched voice echoed down the gauntlet of retail shops.

"Everyone freeze. Nobody moves!"

Nathan looked back toward Nordstrom and saw Tattoo Man standing next to the female guard. He stepped away from the glass, made eye contact with Lauren, and nodded toward the right. His message was clear: we're leaving in that direction. He looked over his shoulder and saw Tattoo Man point at them. Nathan couldn't hear what was said, but the guard immediately focused on them.

"You two! Don't move. You're both under arrest."

CHAPTER 7

They sprinted toward the central escalator.

"Stop! You're under arrest!"

Lauren couldn't run as fast as he could, so they'd never lose the second guard, even with all the people present. He formulated another plan.

At the top of the escalator, he said, "Stay behind me."

He bounded down the steps, pushing past a father holding his son's hand. He heard Lauren's footfalls as she followed. At the bottom, he made a U-turn to the right. Staying out of sight from above, he hugged the support wall and listened for the female guard's arrival.

When she stomped down the escalator, Nathan advanced to the landing and caught her by surprise. He could almost read the guard's thoughts, her expression registering shock at seeing a six foot five, 240-pound man with menacing scars appear out of nowhere. Within seconds, Nathan had her facedown on the concrete with her hands pinned behind her back.

He started another mental stopwatch, this one for sixty seconds. The guard tried to roll free, so Nathan forced the woman's arms up, straining her shoulders.

"Stop resisting. I'm not dangerous, and I'm not going to hurt anyone."

"You're in a world of trouble, buddy."

"Tell me about it. I'm going to cuff you. Please don't resist, or I'll use stronger force. I have no desire to tear your rotator cuffs. Order everyone to back away and not interfere."

"What?"

Nathan forced the guard's hands up a little and received a grunt of pain.

"Okay!" The guard raised her voice. "Everyone back off and don't interfere."

"Bekka, grab the handcuffs from her utility belt." He didn't want to use her real name.

"Where? I don't see them."

"That rounded pouch on her right hip. Unsnap the cover."

Lauren pried the holster open and pulled the handcuffs free.

Twenty seconds.

Nathan scanned the main walkway. No other guards appeared, but several dozen people had taken notice of the action. Hopefully there weren't any off-duty cops or service members among them. The sooner Lauren and he got out of here, the better.

Nathan was skilled in the proper use of handcuffs. In a quick motion, he slapped the sawtoothed side of one bracelet onto the guard's right wrist. He secured the handcuff snugly but made sure not to overtighten it. He kept a knee on the guard's back and repeated the procedure on her opposite wrist.

He kept his voice low to avoid embarrassing the woman. "We're leaving. If you try to pursue us, I'll take you down. Without the use of your arms, you'll go down ugly and lose some teeth, or worse. Do we have an agreement here?"

The guard nodded tightly.

Thirty seconds.

"Order everyone to stay where they are and not to follow us."

She took a deep breath and yelled, "Everyone stay where you are! Don't follow them!"

Nathan rolled the guard over and unbuckled her utility belt. The belt didn't have a gun, but it held other nonlethal weapons, plus a radio. It might come in handy, so he took the belt and put it on. Flipping his shirt over it, he heard a disturbance on the second-level walkway. The first guard might've recovered enough to reenter the fray. Another giant retail store stood just across the courtyard. Macy's. Holding Lauren's hand again, he ran for its entrance.

Just inside, they almost collided with an elderly woman who must've witnessed the takedown. Her face reflected fear.

Nathan made eye contact and said, "Evening, ma'am."

The woman backed up a step as they strode past. As far as he could tell, she was the only person in here who'd seen his restraint of the guard. Nathan knew she'd remain motionless in indecision for a few seconds, possibly longer. Her next move would be to exit the store.

Nathan spoke quietly to Lauren. "We're going to walk quickly. Follow my pace." He detoured to the right through a maze of clothes racks, glass counters, and featureless mannequins. The place looked a lot like Nordstrom, and he hoped its escalator would be in a similar location. Nathan knew it was best to use all three dimensions when evading capture. He looked over his shoulder and didn't see the elderly woman. A quick scan of his surroundings confirmed no one had focused on them.

Lauren spoke just above a whisper. "You moved super fast. How do you know all that stuff?"

He didn't want to ignore her question, but now wasn't the time. "We need to find the escalator." He hadn't been in here before, but knew the opposite side of the store connected to several multistory parking garages.

"It's probably in the middle of the store," she said.

"I agree. Good job with the guard back there."

"I'm glad you didn't hurt her."

He stole another look behind. All calm. He doubted this window of escape would remain open more than two or three minutes. If SDPD units were closing, they'd surround Macy's with as many officers as possible, which meant he and Lauren needed to get through here quickly. Everyone in the courtyard had seen them come in here. This isn't over, he told himself, not by a long shot. Stay focused.

He spotted the escalator. "There's our ride."

"I see it."

He thought about the questions he planned to ask Lauren. Too many things didn't add up. The three goons he'd shot at Ulric weren't federal law enforcement officers—unless they were dirty. No respectable deputy US marshal would attempt a drive-by shooting. Come to think of it, Nathan didn't believe *any* deputy US marshals were dirty. How could the WSP function otherwise?

So where did that leave things? If they weren't feds, who were they? And why did they want Lauren alive? But that no longer tracked. If they wanted Lauren alive, why try to gun her down? Maybe losing possession of her had made her worthless, a loose end in need of elimination. Whatever the case, escaping their immediate situation was only the beginning. This would be over only when Nathan decided it was over. Anyone who tried to murder a young girl was the worst kind of pond scum imaginable, and Nathan planned to sanitize that scum with prejudice.

They were halfway up the escalator when a loud, high-pitched voice roared through the ground floor. "Everyone freeze! Don't move!"

Nathan couldn't see her, but he recognized the unmistakable voice of the female guard he'd just cuffed. So much for their agreement.

A few steps above, a pair of college-age women turned, their expressions confused. They both looked at him.

"Sounds like a robbery," Nathan said. "Let's get outta here."

The two women hurried up the escalator and ran toward the south exit. He saw other people stare at the running women, but, like so many others tonight, they remained frozen, uncertain what to do. Nathan kept a normal pace, following the building's exit signs.

He heard yelling from the ground floor but couldn't distinguish any intelligible words. The guard was probably asking customers if they'd seen anyone fitting his and Lauren's descriptions. Since no one had taken any notice of them, he doubted the guard would get any useful info. Still, it wouldn't be long before the SDPD dispatcher had every available unit converging on this location. They needed to leave this building in a hurry, but not just this building—the entire area.

Ten seconds later, they were outside the store and mall, crossing a pedestrian bridge toward the parking garage. From every direction, Nathan heard multiple sirens. He couldn't distinguish the difference between fire, medical, and police, but he knew they would arrive within minutes, maybe seconds.

Just ahead, a second bridge would take them in the direction of the trolley station, Nathan's original destination. They hadn't gone ten steps when he heard the female guard's voice directly below them.

"Did anyone see a man and a girl come out here?"

Nathan lowered his voice to a whisper. "Lie down. She won't be able to see us."

In the middle of the bridge, they both assumed a facedown position.

A loud crackling startled him. The radio! He hadn't turned down its volume. He reached down to the utility belt and twisted the volume knob until it clicked off. He knew his saving grace was that the guard's radio had also crackled at the same time, masking the sound.

The guard repeated her question, not as forcefully. "Did anyone see anything?"

No one responded. The guard cursed, and Nathan heard her footsteps move laterally below them. Supporting the wrought-iron handrail, the bridge's curb didn't measure more than twelve inches, but the guard wouldn't be able to see their prone forms. Until the guard left, they couldn't traverse the bridge over to the parking structure without risking being seen from below. He didn't think the guard would hang around long. She'd likely return to Macy's to search the ground floor. With a little luck, they'd be clear of the parking structure before any SDPD units arrived.

A few seconds later, the guard's steps receded back to Macy's entrance. He stood and helped Lauren to her feet.

"Come on," he said. "We're going to walk fast."

Waiting for a trolley was now out of the question. Perhaps if he hadn't "introduced" himself to the security guards, the trolley might've worked, but the police were going to focus on Macy's, and the close proximity of the station meant they couldn't linger there. There might be a taxi nearby, but this wasn't the Vegas strip. Taxis were a rarity outside the downtown area of San Diego, especially at this hour.

The connecting bridge led them onto the second level of a brightly lit three-story parking structure. There weren't many cars present, maybe a couple dozen or so. The outer reaches were completely void of vehicles, and therefore void of cover as well. There was no sign of the college women. They must've gone down or up a level.

Since he and Lauren had entered Macy's on the ground level, Nathan decided to stay on the second level. Most fugitives wouldn't climb higher in buildings while being pursued, so staying on this level made tactical sense.

Fugitives? Was that what they were? In the eyes of the law, that was *exactly* what they were. They weren't only fugitives, they were armed and dangerous fugitives.

Every arriving police officer would be informed a handgun was involved. Nathan shook his head, thinking he should be at home, finishing his movie. He added the assault of two security guards to his cocktail. What was next, armed robbery? Fortunately, he didn't need money—he carried close to two grand in his wallet at any given time, and tonight he just might need it. He reflected back on his decision to enter Nordstrom for a change of clothes. Anyone who'd witnessed the drive-by shooting on Friars Road would describe them as a tall man dressed in khaki-colored pants with a dark long-sleeved shirt, and a young girl in jeans and a light purple T-shirt. Nathan wasn't just tall, he towered over Lauren by at least eighteen inches. They'd be hard to miss. A change of clothes had been tactically sound, and since he believed no one on the street had tracked their movements into Nordstrom, they should've been in and out of there in under five minutes. Encountering the security guard had been bad luck, nothing more. For now, he needed to stay focused on getting out of here without drawing any more attention. He also needed to extract information from Lauren without stressing her. Aside from her mother's role in all of this, he needed to know how she had ended up in the custody of her kidnappers.

They stayed on the north side of the parking garage and worked their way west until they arrived at a stairwell. Down to street level or up to the top? Nathan chose up. He knew there was a pedestrian bridge at the southwest corner of the structure, connecting to the elevated trolley station. He and Harv had once parked up there for a Chargers game and taken the trolley over to Qualcomm Stadium. Given their current predicament, waiting for the trolley was still out of the question, but they could take the stairs down to street level and slip away.

A siren closed on their position. He looked west toward its source and saw the red-and-blue flashes of an SDPD cruiser. It turned into the mall's parking lot and accelerated straight toward them.

CHAPTER 8

"What do we do?" Lauren asked.

"Stay calm. He doesn't know where we are." Mixed with the siren, Nathan heard the cruiser's engine roar. "Stay behind me." They ducked deeper into the stairwell's shaft and hugged the wall.

Ten feet below, the cruiser sped past, its howling scream reverberating off every building in the area. Nathan had to admit he was feeling a strong sense of urgency take hold, but he needed to stay calm for Lauren's sake. The cruiser's siren went silent as it stopped a mere thirty yards to the east. He hoped the arriving officer believed they were still inside Macy's. He thought most SDPD cruisers were single-officer units, so if the cop went into Macy's, they'd have a chance.

"Come on. We're going up another level."

They hustled up the stairs and were greeted by a vast expanse of concrete. Trellises with high-intensity lights marched along its length. It was damned bright up here. There weren't any cars present. Zero.

"Let's see how fast you really are. Ready?"

"Uh-huh."

"Here we go."

They began an all-out sprint to the far corner. It looked to be about a football field distant. He heard another siren closing and believed it was coming from the south end of Fashion Valley Road. He couldn't see its source, because the Town & Country Resort Hotel's tower and convention center blocked his view. But if he couldn't see it, at least the reverse was also true. They arrived at the bridge just as the second cruiser came into view on Fashion Valley Road. It turned onto the road paralleling the trolley station, and for the second time in twenty seconds, they found themselves with an SDPD cruiser barreling toward them.

Nathan saw what they needed to his left and didn't have to tell Lauren what to do. They hurried over to the structure's perimeter wall and hunkered down. Its three-foot barrier offered them visual protection from the street below. He made eye contact with Lauren and took her hand. He knew there were a few people waiting at the elevated trolley station, he'd checked during their sprint over. Right now, the intrusive cruiser had everyone's attention. He hoped no one noticed them. He stood with Lauren a little early so anyone who did see them wouldn't think they were hiding from the cruiser. It screamed underneath and kept going.

The elevated station was lower than the top level of the parking structure, so the pedestrian bridge sloped slightly downhill. He looked east along the trolley's tracks, saw the twin headlights of an approaching train, and changed his strategy. It was about time they had some good luck. Waiting for a trolley wouldn't have worked, but the arriving train provided a good opportunity to clear the area. From where they were, they shouldn't have any problem making it aboard. Running would now look perfectly natural—a father and daughter hurrying toward an approaching train.

They began a medium-paced jog.

Entering the platform, Nathan smelled it right away: a homeless stench for the record books. Its source was an elderly woman sitting on the bench. She looked to be trouble, her eyes narrowed and accusatory.

She spoke loudly. "You runnin' from the po-lice."

Several bystanders on the platform looked at them.

Nathan lowered his voice to a whisper. "Ignore her." He led Lauren a few steps away.

"Hey, I'm talkin' at you!"

He knew from the angle of her voice that she'd stood up.

Of all the cardboard-carrying fakes and frauds, why did they have to encounter the genuine article? And why now, of all times?

Lauren pivoted and faced the woman. "Leave my dad alone!"

"Is that what he tell you to say? You can tell me the truth, child."

"It *is* the truth."

"If he your dad, then why you runnin' from the po-lice?"

Nathan raised his voice a little so everyone would hear. "We weren't running from the police, we were running to catch the trolley." He pointed down the tracks to the oncoming headlights.

"You runnin' from the po-lice! I saw you."

"Believe whatever you want—please, just leave us alone." He turned his back and willed the train to speed up.

"Hey, I'm talkin' at you."

The trolley was still a good half minute away.

"Look, we don't want any trouble."

The woman was now yelling. "I'm making it my trouble. Look at your face. You're a monster! You got no right to steal this innocent child!"

Hopeless. This woman saw demons around every corner, lived in a disconnected world without rules of etiquette or conduct, and acted purely on impulse. Ironically, she was actually close to the mark. Maybe she had some sixth sense or a finely honed intuition, but whatever the case, she'd created exactly what he didn't want.

Nathan considered his options. Ignoring her wouldn't work. They'd already become the singular focus of her deluded reality. This woman would likely follow them onto the trolley and continue her tirade. What then? They sure as hell couldn't sit through

OPTION TO KILL

five minutes of verbal assault without every passenger focusing on them. Rendering her unconscious—tempting as that was—would only make things worse. Nathan looked beyond the woman and saw a middle-aged man tap the keypad of his phone three times. No doubt the man thought he was doing them a favor. Just the opposite.

Time to go.

They hurried over to the steps leading down to the street. The woman continued her rant, screaming at the top of her lungs while sirens howled in the distance. Nathan felt his stress level skyrocket and consciously relaxed his hands and jaw. Deal with it. React and overcome.

They couldn't go west toward Fashion Valley Road, because every arriving police cruiser came from that direction. Going back into the mall was out of the question. They were essentially trapped. He wanted to head south into the Town & Country Resort Hotel complex, but the San Diego River blocked their way. They could swim or wade across, but immersing themselves in the collective runoff of a major city wasn't at the top of his bucket list, not to mention that being soaking wet in their clothes would draw attention.

Despite his best efforts, it seemed likely they would end up in police custody. What a can of worms, he thought. No good deed goes unpunished.

Descending the stairs, he saw a godsend. Fifty yards to the south, a narrow pedestrian bridge stretched across the San Diego River. Outstanding! He hadn't known it was there. "Come on," he said quietly. "We're going across." Their bad luck had just turned.

Above them, the woman's tirade trailed off. Without a visible enemy, she probably felt less threatened. Despite the hassle she'd caused, he actually felt sorry for her.

The 911 caller on the platform would describe him and Lauren, so it wouldn't be long before the police connected the dots and focused their pursuit on this location. Their descriptions would

51

match with the security-guard incidents in the mall. Nathan had also seen security cameras on the trolley's platform. With some luck, they'd find a taxi near the front of the hotel and clear the area for good.

The trolley pulled onto the platform just as they stepped onto the bridge. The opposite side dumped them into a three-acre parking lot serving the convention center and hotel tower. Nathan believed the hotel's registration desk was on the south side of the property, so they'd head in that direction. Looking over his shoulder toward the trolley station, he saw a police cruiser's flashing lights. The newly arriving officer would undoubtedly head up to the platform to investigate the disturbance call. Nathan didn't think anyone had seen them cross the bridge, but if he were a cop, that's where he'd start looking. Fortunately, the green belt along the San Diego River screened them from view from the elevated station. If they could make it into the Town & Country Resort Hotel complex, disappearing would be relatively easy.

"All the police? They're because of us?" Lauren asked.

"Yes."

"Where are we going?"

"To find a taxi."

"I saw one back at the trolley station."

Impressive. Lauren had a good sense of her surroundings. How many stressed-out kids her age would have the presence of mind to notice a waiting taxi?

"I saw it."

"But the homeless woman wrecked things."

"Exactly. Are you up to answering some questions?"

"I guess."

"You guess?"

"It depends on what you're going to ask."

"It isn't negotiable."

"What's that supposed to mean?"

"It means you'll have to answer my questions. You can't hold anything back."

"But what about the witness security program?"

"What about it?"

"I'm not supposed to talk about it."

They continued south across the parking lot. He diverted to an adjacent aisle to avoid a businessman who was pulling a suitcase from the trunk of his car.

"Lauren, let's recap the last thirty minutes. On the freeway, you asked for my help because you said you'd been kidnapped. I followed your kidnapper and rammed my fifty-thousand-dollar Mustang into the side of his seventy-thousand-dollar Cadillac. I shot two men who may or may not be federal law enforcement officers, then put a bullet into your abductor's thigh just for sport. Minutes later, the very same man I shot attempted to gun us down in cold blood on a crowded public street with a fully automatic machine gun. I then assaulted two security guards, restrained them with their own handcuffs, and stole their equipment. I also threatened an unarmed civilian by pointing a gun at his chest. Have I missed anything?"

"It's not my fault."

"I didn't say it was. I'm just telling you what kind of trouble I'm in for helping you. I hear the food is lousy in prison."

In reality, Nathan wasn't worried about doing time, but he wanted Lauren to understand the depth of this mess. As a reminder, sirens continued to wail, seemingly from everywhere. The entrance to the north tower loomed just ahead. Set in the middle of the ten-story building, the entry foyer should take them into the interior of the hotel complex.

"But you were helping me," Lauren said. "Doesn't that count?"

"Afraid not. In the eyes of the police, I'm an armed and dangerous gunman who's taken a girl hostage. The police will shoot first and ask questions later."

"The police will shoot you?"

"In a heartbeat."

Nathan sensed her stiffen a little. He didn't like manipulating her like this, but he needed information. Come to think of it, turning Lauren over and ending this before anyone else got seriously injured or killed didn't seem like an altogether bad idea, but he'd already given his word he wouldn't do that, and threatening her would undermine his credibility. Besides, he never broke his word. Ever.

"So what's it going to be?" Nathan sensed her reluctance, but he knew she wanted to open up and tell him more. The trick was not pushing too hard.

"Are you sure it's okay to tell you?"

"Lauren, I have the highest security clearance available. Technically, I could sit in on presidential briefings. So, yes, it's okay to tell me."

"You mean like the president of the United States?"

"Yes."

She cocked her head to the side and hesitated again. "Tell me something secret about you first."

"I like taking bubble baths."

"Come on—I mean like really secret."

"You want some dirt? Okay, I've killed sixty-two people."

"*No way.*"

"Way. Now, you tell me how you ended up being kidnapped by those men."

"They came to my house."

Lauren and Nathan passed through the tower and proceeded into a landscaped area. A young couple nodded hello as they walked past an oval pool.

Looking over his shoulder, he lowered his voice. "Step by step, what happened?"

"The guy you shot in the SUV came to my door and said he needed to ask me some questions. He said he was with the witness security program and would protect me."

"Is that when he showed you his badge?"

"Uh-huh."

"Had you ever seen him before that?"

She thought for a moment. "I think so, in my stepdad's office."

"How long ago?"

"Maybe a month."

"What did he want to ask you about?"

"The dead girl."

"What dead girl?"

"I saw a dead girl in my stepdad's warehouse."

CHAPTER 9

Nathan pulled her aside, just off the main walkway. "You saw a dead girl? When?"

"Last night."

Nathan tried to absorb what Lauren had just said. "Did you see her before your stepdad was murdered?"

She nodded.

"What did the girl look like?"

"It was horrible. Her stomach was all cut up. There was blood everywhere."

"Was it a young Hispanic girl about your age?"

"Uh-huh."

The border murders. Nathan had been following the front-page story for months. A psychopath was stalking young girls along the San Diego border with Mexico, murdering them, and mutilating their torsos. Had Lauren seen the latest victim in that string of slayings? It seemed likely. Could her kidnapper be involved? Worse than that, could he *be* the serial murderer of seven girls? If so, Lauren was fortunate to be alive. She could've been victim number eight. Nathan didn't know too much about serial killers but believed they selected their victims based on certain physical criteria. Lauren wasn't Hispanic, but that didn't mean she couldn't have been chosen.

"Did you tell your mom?"

"I called her right away."

"What did she say?"

"She said she'd come pick me up." Her face clouded. "But she never came."

Nathan stowed that for now, he wanted to stay on the current string. "You said you saw the dead girl last night. Doesn't it strike you as odd that they waited nearly an entire day to ask you about it, and that US marshals asked, not the police?"

"I guess."

"Trust me, it's not normal. The police, not US marshals, should've talked to you last night. Unless no one reported it."

"You mean my mom never called the police?"

"That's what I'm thinking."

"I don't understand."

"Neither do I, but I'm sure she had her reasons. What else did she say when you called?"

"She was really freaked and told me to wait in my stepdad's office."

"Do you know where she was when you called?"

She thought for a second. "In her car. It automatically connects with her Bluetooth. I can tell."

"Was she alone?"

"I didn't hear anyone else."

"Let's back up a little. How did you get to the warehouse that day?"

"My stepdad dropped me off."

"Is that what usually happens? He drops you off and leaves?"

"Sometimes he stays and works in his office."

"Why were you at the warehouse?"

"Sometimes I hang out there. Nobody bugs me."

"Let's keep walking." They hurried past a gazebo-type building toward a small water feature, maybe a reflection pond. Another building, probably a restaurant, lay directly ahead. He led Lauren in that direction.

"What about school? Aren't you supposed to be in school during the day?"

"I don't go to regular school anymore."

Nathan waited. He wasn't sure she was going to say anything.

"I kept getting in trouble," she said. "Everyone hates me."

"Everyone doesn't hate you."

"It's okay. You don't have to say that."

"I'm serious. *I* don't hate you."

"You haven't known me very long."

"Maybe you want everyone to hate you." That hit a little too close to home. He wished he hadn't said it.

"Whatever."

"Did anyone see you when you found the dead girl?"

"I don't want to talk about it anymore."

"Lauren, look, I'm sorry. I shouldn't have said that."

"It's okay. Don't worry about it."

"It's not okay. I was out of line. It's just that you seem like such a nice girl, I can't imagine anyone hating you."

"You're just like me. You want people to hate you, too."

Ouch. This girl had just carved into his soul with a fillet knife. He tried to think of a way to change the subject. But he'd brought it up, not her. It seemed unfair not to come clean.

"Okay, Lauren...the truth. You're right—I don't want friends. Having friends means you have to trust them."

"And you don't trust people."

"Generally, no."

"Me either."

They followed a landscaped walkway lined with white benches and rosebush hedges. Up ahead, he was pretty sure a linear-shaped parking lot would take them to the main driveway of the hotel. They'd head that way and, with some luck, find a cab. Somewhere behind them, a siren wailed. It served as a reminder that the police were still pursuing them. They weren't out of this yet.

"When you think about it, we have no reason to trust each other. But look at all we've been through together. Is there any doubt I could've ditched you if I'd wanted to?"

"So why didn't you?"

"You asked for my help."

"Is that the only reason?"

He stopped walking and faced her. "What's that supposed to mean?"

She crossed her arms and stared him in the eyes.

What was she implying? Was she suggesting he had impure intentions? He supposed she was old enough to know about such things, and she said the driver of the SUV had looked at her in a bad way. "Lauren, I would *never* do anything to hurt you. It's important you understand that."

"Promise?"

"Yes, absolutely. Marine's honor. Cut me some slack here. You're only twelve years old, almost thirteen. Are there bad people in the world? Yes. Are there creeps who might try to take advantage of you? Sadly, yes. I'm just not one of them." He smiled. "Besides, I have a girlfriend. She's an FBI agent."

"No way. Seriously?"

"Yep. She's in charge of the Sacramento field office."

"Is she pretty?"

"Yes. But that's not the point. The point is, we're in this together. I'm not going to ditch you or try to take advantage of you."

"So we need to trust each other, like real friends would."

"That's right."

"So are we?"

"Yes." They started walking again.

"Do you really take bubble baths?"

"Yes, *without* a rubber duck."

She smiled, and it suddenly occurred to him that he no longer thought of her as a liability. What had he thought of her as? Eighty pounds of pure trouble? He supposed that was still true, but she felt more real now, more human. Lauren was also plenty smart, bordering on brilliant. Except for the slipup with the guard inside Nordstrom, she'd been remarkably poised tonight. Though he hadn't been around kids much, something told him Lauren was exceptional. Of course, most parents thought their kids were special, but Lauren wasn't his kid. They barely knew each other. Granted, they'd shared some harrowing moments tonight, but there was something else beyond that, something he found hard to label. He felt comfortable with her, similar to when he'd first met Holly. He didn't know how or why, but he knew Lauren felt it, too.

As they walked, Nathan tried to turn their conversation back to the chain of events that had led to her seeing the dead girl and what happened after that.

"Let's get back to the warehouse. Walk me through it. How did you see her? What were you doing?"

"I was Rollerblading and a forklift almost hit me."

"Rollerblading?"

"The aisles are really long and straight. It's perfect, except I ran over some cardboard and fell. I saw something through the slots under the pallets. You know, where the forklift blades go?"

"I know how they work. What did you see?"

"I went around to the other side, but I couldn't see well enough, so I crawled on my hands and knees, looking under the pallets, until I found the right spot."

"So, there was a secret hollow place inside all the stacked pallets?"

"Yeah, but the pallets were stacked really high, so I couldn't climb up to look."

"Then how did you see her? You know, her cut-up stomach?"

"I hid under the desk in my stepdad's office until everyone left and then moved the pallets."

"Lauren, I may not be the brightest bulb in the closet, but you can't move pallets of patio furniture."

"I used a forklift."

"You can operate a forklift?"

"It's easy. My stepdad taught me. He taught me to drive, too."

"Drive? You mean cars?"

"It's no big deal. Kids fly airplanes at my age."

He conceded the point. "Well, aren't you full of surprises. Why couldn't you just look between the pallets? Aren't pallets usually stacked with gaps between them?"

"That's what was kinda weird. Someone taped sheets of cardboard around the inside."

"So the cardboard prevented you from seeing through the gaps?"

"Uh-huh."

"So you moved the pallets out of the way, and that's when you found the dead girl hidden in there?"

She nodded. "It was horrible."

"What did you do next?"

"I ran into my stepdad's office and called my mom."

"You didn't have a cell phone? I thought all kids your age had cell phones."

"I didn't have it with me yesterday. My stepdad took it away as punishment."

"But you had it earlier to send me the texts."

"I know where he hides it in the house. My mom showed me."

There seemed to be some big holes in her story. For every question she answered, five more sprang up. Should he press harder for more info? At the moment, she didn't seem too upset talking about it, but that could change.

"All of this happened after-hours, right? How did you get home?"

Her face clouded again.

He took her hand and pulled her aside again. She looked as if she was about to lose control. "You drove yourself home."

"I took one of the vans. My stepdad keeps the keys in his office."

"You never called the police?"

"No."

"Who told you your stepdad had been murdered?"

"The man in the black car."

"When did he tell you?"

"He called me this morning. He said to stay in the house and not talk to anyone. He said he'd pick me up later. I was really scared."

"I can imagine. When was the last time your mom contacted you?"

"Right before I sent you the texts."

"How did she contact you?"

"A text. She sent our code word."

"What code word?"

"We've had this code word ever since I was really young. She made me memorize a phone number. If she ever sent me the code word, I was supposed to text the secret words to the phone number right away."

"The 'echo five sierra charlie' words?"

"Uh-huh."

"What was the code word?"

"Werty."

"*W-e-r-t-y*? Spelled like that?"

She nodded.

Nathan pulled out his phone and opened a text window. The letters were in a straight row along the top of the keyboard. It made sense—they'd be easy and fast to enter.

"Do you know what 'echo five sierra charlie' means?"

"No."

"So your mom never mentioned me by name, ever? You had no idea who you were texting?"

"She just said someone would come and help me."

"Looks like that someone is me. Now, about that warehouse... You said you were in there after-hours. Isn't there a security system?"

"I know the security code."

"So you disarmed the system and left the warehouse in a company van. Did you rearm it?"

"No. I guess I should've."

"Don't worry about that. I want to see it."

"The warehouse?"

"Are you okay going back in there?"

"I guess...We'll be together, right?"

"Yes, but I need to get some things from my house first. Are you hungry? When was the last time you ate anything?"

"This morning. I had a bowl of cereal."

"We'll grab a bite on the way over. Let's find a cab first." They continued toward the front of the hotel complex.

"Does everyone stare at your face?"

"I've gotten used to it over the years."

"Does it bug you?"

"Depends on my mood."

"What happened?"

He lowered his voice. "I was interrogated by a very sadistic man."

"Seriously? You mean like tortured?"

"Yes."

"Do you have nightmares about it?"

"Yes. Let's find a cab."

That's when he saw it, directly ahead: the black sedan, its wrecked rear end unmistakable. It cruised past the main driveway from right to left and braked to a stop.

Had the driver seen them? Even though the sedan was several hundred feet away and their immediate area wasn't well lit, he wasn't sure. How could that sedan be here? There was no way the driver could possibly know they were in this hotel complex...

unless he had a police scanner. Someone from the trolley station could have seen them cross the river and reported it, but if that were true, where were the police?

He grabbed Lauren's hand and backtracked along the landscaped path with the white benches. "Stay close."

"What are we doing?"

"The guy who took you is back."

"How does he know where we are?"

Nathan watched the brake lights wink out as the sedan moved out of his line of sight. He took Lauren off the path into a dark area of landscaping where he could watch the parking lot.

"I'm scared."

He gave her hand a reassuring squeeze. "He can't see us."

Bleed light from the sedan's headlights grew brighter as it cruised down the opposite side of the U-shaped parking lot. It slowly rounded the corner like a predatory cat.

"Lauren, don't make a sound." He crouched next to her, reached into his pocket, and pulled the SIG. Forty feet away, the sedan rolled to a stop.

CHAPTER 10

Lauren leaned against him.

The tinted passenger window rolled down, revealing a pale smile.

Nathan sensed a malevolent presence reach for them. He squinted and held perfectly still.

The driver stared, also unmoving. When he spoke, it sent a shiver across Nathan's shoulders.

"You can't hide forever, sweet Lauren. I'll find you, and when I do, we're going to party all…night…long…"

The window rolled back up, and the sedan pulled away.

Nathan put an arm around her. "I won't let him hurt you, Lauren. Don't be afraid."

"How did he find us?"

A sound—the sharp crackle of a police radio—shattered the night silence from somewhere behind. Nathan thought it might have come from the water-feature area. A flashlight beam sweeping the concrete walkway confirmed it.

"Shh…don't say anything," he whispered. "Stay close." They hugged the wall of the building and worked their way deeper into the landscaping. The officer from the trolley station must've followed them into the hotel complex.

They couldn't go out to the parking lot. Lauren's kidnapper could still be lurking, and he'd already demonstrated his disregard for collateral damage. The approaching cop became Nathan's immediate concern. From their current position, they were discoverable. They needed to find solid visual cover in a big hurry. A flashlight beam would easily penetrate the landscaping and nail them.

Scanning his surroundings, Nathan saw an opportunity, but it involved some risk. The flashlight came nearer. No choice. He took Lauren's hand and led her toward the entrance to a restaurant. If the cop swept his flashlight in their direction, they'd be seen. All they needed was a few more seconds.

Just as they reached the restaurant's entrance, the cop's radio crackled again. Nathan thought the narrowness of the walkway offered them some visual cover. He looked over his shoulder and pulled the door open.

They passed an empty hostess station. Just ahead, he saw an exit out to a pool area. He hoped they'd find a way over to the registration desk by going that direction. Nathan felt a slight case of claustrophobia; he didn't like being surrounded by structures. Single-story hotel rooms lined both sides of the pool. He angled toward the far side and picked up their pace a little.

They entered the hotel lobby to find a few people standing in line at the registration desk. He took Lauren out the front door and saw a parked taxi, but its driver was gone. Back inside, Nathan saw a clean-cut man who might fit the bill. Wearing a Chargers ball cap, he sat in a chair near the entrance.

"Is that your cab out front?" Nathan asked in Arabic.

The man's expression betrayed surprise. Nathan wondered if the reaction was from seeing the scars on his face or from his knowledge of Arabic. Probably both.

Nathan pulled out his wallet and removed a $100 bill. He continued in Arabic, "We need a ride."

The driver responded in kind. "I'm not available. I'm waiting for someone."

Nathan pulled two more bills and handed all three to the driver. "We don't need change."

The driver nodded and took the money.

Outside, Nathan skimmed the immediate area again but didn't see the sedan. The siren he'd heard earlier was louder and seemed to be coming from the direction of the mall. He knew the police had a description of the sedan from the drive-by shooting. Nathan also believed Lauren's kidnapper had to know that every cop in the area was looking for a dark sedan with a smashed rear end. Even if the presence of police in the area didn't concern the guy, the bullet wound to his leg had to be distressing at best and downright life-threatening at worst. Nathan didn't think Lauren's kidnapper would hang around the area, but that was what he'd believed earlier, just before they were nearly gunned down on Friars Road.

They slid into the cab, and Nathan thought they just might make it out of here in one piece. Lauren sat close as the cabbie turned the meter on. Nathan saw a small Garmin or TomTom navigation unit attached the windshield but couldn't tell which brand.

"What language is that?" Lauren asked.

"Arabic."

"You speak Arabic?"

"Yes. Please head for La Jolla," he told the driver. "Take eight west to five north."

He removed the utility belt he'd taken from the security guard. Nathan craned his neck and looked behind as the cabbie pulled onto Hotel Circle North. All clear. No sign of the sedan.

He felt his cell phone vibrate and removed it from his pocket. It was Harvey.

"Sierra charlie."

"Understood," Harv said.

"Ten minutes."

"You got it."

Nathan ended the call.

"What does that mean?" Lauren asked.

He lowered his voice and looked around for the black sedan. "I'll tell you later. Do you have anything in your pockets? Anything electronic?"

"No, just a piece of paper. My mom told me to take it from my stepdad's office. It was hidden. She told me where to find it."

"Let me see it."

Nathan unfolded it and held it up in the bleed light from the streetlamps. Below a single name, a list of numbers stared back at him.

Hernandez:			
1.53	90	50	(4871)
1.64	95	60	
1.85	90	55	(37)
2.07	95	70	(116)
2.14	95	70	
2.39	95	80	
2.42	90	80	(4702)
2.78	85	85	
2.96	90	110	(34)
3.02	95	150	(32)

"This was in your stepdad's office?"

"Yes."

"When did you take this?"

She looked at the driver.

"Last night?" he asked.

"Uh-huh."

"After the forklift business?"

She nodded.

"Why didn't you mention this earlier?"

"I don't know. I forgot."

"Don't worry about it. Do you have any idea what these numbers mean?"

"No."

He studied it a moment longer and came to only the most rudimentary conclusions. The left column was arranged in ascending order, but the other three weren't. The left-middle column ranged from eighty-five to ninety-five and didn't seem to have any discernible pattern. The right-middle column started at fifty and increased in value, with one exception—the third row. And the fourth column's parenthetical numbers looked completely random.

"Where are we going?" Lauren asked.

"My Clairemont house."

"Can we get something to eat first?"

"Yes."

Nathan knew a break in conversation would give Lauren a chance to process some of tonight's action. It had to be tearing her up. She'd seen a crazy amount of violence over the last twenty-four hours.

He thought back to her abductor. The tone of his voice had given Nathan a chill—not an easy thing to do. The guy had sounded like embodied evil. The reference to partying with Lauren "all night long" couldn't be mistaken for anything other than his intent to sexually assault her. That would fit at least part of the MO of a serial killer like the one who'd been murdering the girls. But serial killers tended to be careful control freaks, more prone to ambushes using overwhelming power than to public confrontation. What kind of serial killer would face down his victim *and* her protector? Much less bring along armed backup? No, this guy might be a sick creep, but he had a larger agenda than simply assaulting and killing Lauren.

The cabbie drove the speed limit as he took the I-5 north-bound on-ramp. Nathan checked again and didn't see any sign of a tail. The closest vehicle was a white Nissan or Toyota, and there weren't any dark sedans in sight.

"Nobody is following us," the driver said in English.

"Where are you from?"

"Lebanon."

"Is your family here?"

"No, my wife and daughters are still there. They're living with my parents. I'm saving money to bring them all over. It is very expensive."

"No doubt. I admire what you're doing. I hope you're reunited with them soon."

"I miss my girls. Your daughter's very beautiful. She has your eyes."

"Thank you. That's kind of you to say. Please take the Clairemont Drive exit and head east."

The driver nodded.

If the driver's compliment had embarrassed Lauren or made her feel uneasy, she didn't show it.

"There's a grocery store about a mile off the freeway on the right," Nathan said to Lauren. "We'll grab a sandwich and some other stuff we might need."

"Can we get pastrami?"

"Absolutely."

The cab pulled into the retail center, and Nathan asked him to park in the middle of the lot and wait—he didn't want any other vehicles near their cab.

"Give us five minutes," he told the cabbie. "Would you like anything?"

"Black coffee, please."

Nathan looked around the parking lot as they walked toward the entrance. "My house isn't far from here. We'll head over there next." Thinking ahead, he'd ask their driver to drop them off several blocks away. He didn't like the idea of taking the cab all the way to his front door. Nathan owned two homes in San Diego, one in Clairemont, where he spent the majority of his time, the other in La Jolla, where he'd received Lauren's text. He felt more comfortable in the Clairemont residence's low-key environment.

The deli was closed, but they found a refrigerator with pre-made sandwiches and grabbed a pastrami. Lauren seemed rather subdued. The reality of her situation was probably sinking in. She had to be exhausted, mentally and physically. Overall, he had no complaints about her and again wondered how many kids her age would be as resilient. Before the cabdriver had mentioned her eyes, Nathan hadn't noticed the similarity to his own. But now, as he looked at her, he had to admit they did look eerily identical. He didn't know how many people with Asian lineage had blue eyes but believed it to be extremely rare. He couldn't recall seeing any-one like Lauren before, but if he had, he would've remembered. Without a doubt, Lauren was beautiful.

As uncomfortable as the thought was, he had to consider the possibility that Lauren could be his daughter. The similarity of their eyes couldn't be dismissed. He thought back thirteen years, trying to recall if he'd been with any Asian women, and came up blank. At that point in his life, he'd still been recovering from the botched mission that had resulted in his capture and subsequent torture. He hadn't slept with *any* women during that turbulent time. In fact, he hadn't slept much at all. He'd been heavily medi-cated, drifting in and out of chronic depression and despair. There was simply no way Lauren could be his. None. Besides, he didn't think she was tall enough. He hadn't been around many kids her age, but if she'd inherited half his genes, she ought to be taller.

Figuring they needed more than just a sandwich, he went back to the registers and grabbed a handheld shopping basket. Lauren asked for an apple juice, saying it was her favorite drink.

He thought back to her question at the Town & Country Resort Hotel: *How does he know where we are?* It seemed as though her abductor knew precisely where she was. A lucky guess? Not likely. The police scanner was the most reasonable explanation. The cop who followed them into the complex would've reported his location to dispatch, and the cop could've also said he was heading toward the front of the hotel where Nathan had spotted the sedan. The other possibility—an inside source—didn't sit well with him. Lauren said she didn't trust the police, maybe for good reason.

But if her abductor had no law enforcement credentials, it seemed crazy for him to remain in the area with all the cops converging. Maybe if the guy was twisted enough, he'd risk hanging around to recapture Lauren—but with a life-threatening gunshot wound? Nathan had purposely avoided shooting the man's femoral artery, but his destroyed quadriceps muscles had to be crippling. Yet the man persisted. Why was capturing or killing Lauren so important?

The border murders. She'd seen the dead girl. But if her kidnapper was behind the murders, he could've killed her in seclusion when he came to her house. Did she know something he wanted? Did he plan to use her as leverage? Against whom? Her mom? Too many questions with no answers.

When Lauren put the bottle of apple juice into the basket, he got a good look at her ring. It was really quite beautiful, with a heavy gold setting. It didn't look like costume jewelry, but hadn't the stone been red inside Nordstrom? Now that he thought about it, he was certain it had shone bright red.

"Lauren, wasn't your ring red inside Nordstrom?"

"It changes color."

"It changes from red to green?"

"Yeah, it's really cool. In the daytime it's green, and sometimes it's green inside, like now, but mostly it's red, like in my room."

"May I see it?"

"My mom said I'm never supposed to take it off, but I guess it's okay."

She handed it to him, and he took a closer look. It was an oval cut and looked to be about three carats in size. Nice quality. The setting was almost certainly fourteen-karat gold. "Follow me. We need to find an incandescent light."

"What kind of light?"

"A regular lightbulb." He led her to the rear of the store and found the restrooms. A quick glance over his shoulder confirmed no one was watching. Nathan nodded to the women's restroom. "See if anyone's in there and tell me what kind of lighting it is. Are there long fluorescent tubes, like out here, or regular lightbulbs, like in your bedroom? Here, take your ring and tell me if it turns red in there."

She gave him a look.

"Don't worry, I'll be right here. You can hold the door open if you like."

She disappeared inside. A few seconds later, she came back out.

"No one's in there. It turned red."

"I want to see it."

"You're going in the girls' bathroom?"

"Yeah, I do it all the time." He held his hand out.

She rolled her eyes and gave him the ring.

"Be right back."

At the threshold of the women's restroom, Nathan watched an amazing phenomenon occur: the ring seemed to sparkle with two different colors. Once inside, he examined it under the bulb over the sink. If this thing's real, it's worth a small fortune. This was one of the rarest gemstones in the world. Alexandrite. Green by day, red by night. Nathan was no expert but knew something about the stone. Last year, Harv had bought his wife alexandrite earrings, and they displayed a nice color change—from bluish green to light purple—but they didn't come close to the quality or pure spectral transition of this stone. This little beauty went from emerald green to bright pinkish red. Nathan didn't know what it was worth, but he knew how to find out. No wonder Lauren's mom didn't want her taking it off.

He left the restroom and gave her the ring. "It's an alexandrite. If it's real, it could cost as much as your stepdad's Porsche."

"Seriously?"

"Don't lose it—you can cash it in for a college education someday."

"The man you shot tried to take it."

"Is that why he grabbed your wrist?"

"Uh-huh."

"It could be synthetic, but something tells me it's real." He looked at his watch. "We'd better get back to our cab."

Nathan paid for their items and led Lauren outside. The cab was still there. He assessed the parking lot's lighting as they walked toward their ride.

"Lauren, is there anything else you can tell me about your mom? Did she ever talk to you about her life before you were born?"

"A little."

"Where was she born?"

"Korea, I think."

"Where was she raised?"

"In an orphanage. I think she had a pretty bad childhood."

"I can imagine." Nathan looked at the cab. He'd forgotten the coffee. He was about to turn around when he noticed that the driver had his head tilted down, but there was wasn't any bleed light from a cell phone illuminating his face. Maybe the bill of his Chargers hat concealed it, but Nathan didn't think so. Something rubbed him wrong. When they were twenty feet from the cab, the driver dipped his head lower, as if trying to hide his face. Why would he do that, unless—

He dropped the grocery bag and shoved Lauren to his right, hard enough to send her sprawling. "Stay down!"

The cab's door flew open.

Nathan pulled his SIG.

A much taller man burst from the cab, crouched behind its open door, and pointed a handgun at him.

Nathan sidestepped away from Lauren and toggled the SIG's laser. He put the red dot on the man's chest.

His opponent fired first.

Shit! The discharge's flare ruined his vision, but at least the bullet missed. Aiming on pure instinct, Nathan double-tapped the trigger and simultaneously closed his eyes. The rapid reports hammered his ears and cracked off every building in the area. The cab's window shattered.

"Lauren, stay down!"

Aiming lower, he sent a third bullet through the sheet metal. The man jerked but didn't go down.

Before the gunman could recover, Nathan sprinted forward, grabbed the man's arm, and dislocated his shoulder with an upward thrust. His opponent grunted and dropped the weapon. Nathan drove his forehead into the man's nose and felt cartilage collapse. He kicked the handgun aside and swept his leg, taking the gunman down. Nathan used the butt of his weapon on the gunman's jaw and watched the man's eyes roll up for a few seconds, before refocusing.

Even though this guy was out of the fight, Nathan patted him down, confirming the presence of a ballistic vest. He didn't find a wallet but felt the outline of a cell phone in the guy's coat pocket. He'd take that before leaving.

Tires screeched nearby. Nathan looked up, seeking the source. Fifty yards distant, a familiar black sedan barreled toward them.

Nathan squared with the new threat and painted his laser onto the windshield.

The vehicle braked to a sudden stop.

For several seconds, nothing happened. The sedan just sat there, motionless.

Nathan felt a malevolent presence again and knew it was the same man who'd taunted Lauren at the hotel. He squinted and kept the red dot glued on the windshield.

Then, with measured precision, the sedan slowly backed away.

Nathan wanted to shoot, but he knew a stray ricochet could injure or kill an innocent.

"Lauren, form up!"

"What?"

"Come over here."

Blood streaming from his nose, the man at his feet moaned and tried to roll over. Nathan put a boot on the guy's neck and applied half his weight. "I'll crush your windpipe if you try anything cute."

"*No hablo inglés.*"

Nathan repeated the threat in Spanish and refocused the laser back onto the windshield of the retreating sedan. The man at his feet wasn't Hispanic. Like Lauren's abductor, he had fair skin and dark hair and looked to be in his early forties.

"*Quien es su jefe?*" *Who is your boss?* Nathan didn't expect an answer and didn't get one. "*Dónde está el taxista?*"

"*En el baúl.*"

"*Muerto?*"

"*No.*"

"Lauren, pop the trunk. The lever should be inside, on the lower left." He nodded toward the cab's interior.

She gave the downed man a wide berth and reached inside.

Nathan heard the trunk pop open. "See if the driver's okay."

"His forehead is bleeding."

"Is he breathing?"

"Yes, but his eyes are closed."

Nathan wanted to question the man at his feet, but he didn't have time. Any doubts they were being tracked were now dispelled. The presence of the sedan at the hotel could be explained, but not here. Even if Lauren's abductor had a police scanner, it wouldn't have led him to this location. Could *his* phone be the culprit? He didn't think so, but wasn't sure.

The black sedan stopped backing up and turned toward Clairemont Drive. Nathan glanced around the parking lot. Several people were watching from a distance. Time to go. He crouched down next to the gunman and told him to hold still. In a quick move, Nathan pistol-whipped him on the side of the head, rendering him unconscious. He didn't know if Lauren's abductor would return to get him, but he couldn't do anything about it. He wasn't willing to kill this man in cold blood, especially in front of Lauren.

Nathan had no doubt that someone had already called 911. They needed to clear the area, but he had to deal with the tracking problem or they'd face this scenario again. The black sedan turned right onto Clairemont Drive and accelerated away.

"Lauren, take off your shoes."

She looked confused but did it.

"Are you sure you don't have anything in your pockets?"

"Yes."

"Hold still. I'm going to pat you down. I think there's a transmitter on you somewhere."

She reached up and removed her hair tie. "The man you shot gave this to me."

"When?"

"When he picked me up at my house. He said not to take it off."

Nathan wanted to ask why she hadn't bothered to mention this little morsel of information earlier, but knew that would only upset her. He examined the hair tie. About an inch in diameter, it was shaped like a disk and looked to be veneered in stained wood. The elastic cord was secured on the back with two small brackets. He set the hair tie on edge and struck it with the butt of his gun. It shattered into several pieces. In the dim light from the open door, he saw a broken microchip and a watch-type battery. He pursed his lips and looked up at Lauren, his expression guarded.

"I didn't know about that!"

"Calm down. I didn't say you did."

"You believe me, don't you?"

"Of course I believe you. I'm just glad we found it." He stood up. "We're going to clear this area as fast as we can. Stay with me, okay?"

"What about my shoes?"

"Grab them. We'll stop and put them on later."

Nathan pulled a napkin from the grocery bag and carefully plucked the gunman's cell phone from his pocket, taking care not to smear any fingerprints. He put it in the bag and began running toward the southwest corner of the parking lot. Somewhere north of their position, a siren rang out, probably a fire department engine. He hoped most of the cruisers from this area were responding to the action at Fashion Valley Mall. It might buy them a few extra minutes.

At the corner of the shopping center, they hurried past a Hometown Buffet restaurant. No one was present outside, but several cars were waiting in a fast-food drive-through lane. He expected he and Lauren looked like a father and daughter fleeing a dangerous scene. Everyone in the area must've heard the handgun reports. The sooner they got out of here, the better. Nathan knew this neighborhood well, his second home was no more than half a mile distant.

He felt his phone vibrate. The number was blocked. He considered letting it go to voice mail but answered anyway. It could be Lauren's abductor.

"I don't like taking calls from blocked numbers."

"Keep Lauren safe. You're the only person I trust."

"Jin."

"Keep her safe, Nathan."

"How do you know about echo five? How do you know *me*?"

"You're her uncle."

The call ended.

CHAPTER 11

How could he be Lauren's uncle? He didn't have any brothers or sisters. Why would the woman lie about her identity? Was it just to create a phony familial bond in order to ensure his involvement? If so, it wasn't necessary. He'd already committed to protecting Lauren. Even if Jin believed she was his sister, that didn't make it true. People can believe anything they want. But if it were true, the repercussions were monumental, especially for his father. He tried to imagine the chairman of the Senate Committee on Domestic Terrorism possessing a long-lost illegitimate daughter.... Had Senator Stone McBride fathered a child during the Korean War? Lauren said her mom was from Korea. It wasn't a stretch to believe it could've happened. Did his dad know about Jin—and maybe Lauren too? And could he have intentionally buried it all these years? The press would have a field day if it leaked.

Under a streetlight he took a knee and looked at her, searching for the truth. The cabdriver's words returned: *Your daughter's very beautiful. She has your eyes.* There was no denying it. He'd seen Lauren's eyes inside Nordstrom, and they were a perfect match with his own—deep cobalt toward the pupil, surrounded by an even darker hue of blue.

"That was your mom."

"What did she say?"

"She said I'm your uncle."

"No way! Seriously?"

"That's what she said, but let's not jump to any conclusions. We have the same eyes, but that doesn't prove anything. If ever you needed to be totally honest with me, now's the time. Did your mom ever mention she had a half brother?"

"No, I'd remember that."

Nathan thought she was being honest. Further speculation seemed pointless, at least right now. He needed to avoid distraction and keep his head in the game. Hopefully they'd bought a little time by destroying the tracking bug. Maybe now Lauren's kidnapper would focus on getting medical attention—and he'd have to do it outside the normal EMS structure.

He looked over his shoulder. No one from the parking lot seemed to be watching them, but the 911 operators would be informed that a man and a girl had fled the scene on foot. Once the police arrived and found the Fashion Valley guard's utility belt in the backseat of the cab, they'd piece things together quickly. He was tempted to backtrack and watch from a safe distance to see if Lauren's abductor returned for his unconscious man, but exiting the area was clearly the best course of action.

"Come on," he told Lauren. Together they crossed a road and ran at a decent clip for a solid minute.

This neighborhood was laid out in a grid, with older single-family residences lining the streets. Nathan didn't see anyone out for a stroll, so he slowed their pace.

"Let's walk for a bit while I call my friend back."

Lauren took a long look behind them. He'd need to talk to her later about being more discreet.

Nathan entered the international code and tapped out Harvey's number.

"What's your situation?" Harv immediately asked.

Nathan relayed the chain of events from the beginning, including a description of Lauren's kidnapper and his Spanish-speaking friends. He also told Harv about Lauren's alexandrite ring and gave him Jin's full name—Jin Elizabeth Marchand. He didn't mention the big news yet.

"Got it," Harv said.

"There's someone else to look at," Nathan said. "Lauren's stepdad. He wasn't murdered by coincidence. The timing is highly suspect."

"What's his name?"

"Hang on. Lauren, what's your stepdad's first name?"

"Malcolm."

"Malcolm Marchand? Does he have a middle name?"

"I don't know what it is."

"What's his company's name?"

"I think it's Marchand Patio something. I'm not sure."

"Do you know the address?"

Lauren shook her head. "I know how to get there, though. It's in Otay Mesa."

"Did you catch that, Harv?"

"Yes. I'll relay all of this to Holly and follow through with what she can dig up."

"Lauren, what's your La Jolla Shores address?" Nathan held the phone out while she rattled it off. "Did you get that?"

"Got it," Harv said. "Quite a night you've had."

"It gets better," Nathan said. "Jin called a few minutes ago and said I'm Lauren's uncle."

Silence on the other end.

"You still there?"

"You don't have any brothers or sisters."

"Apparently I do."

"And you believe this woman?"

"I can't explain it, but yeah, I do."

"The complexity of your situation has just increased by a factor of ten."

"Tell me about it. We're heading over to the Clairemont house, ETA five minutes."

"Can you question Lauren deeper about her mom?"

"Yeah," said Nathan, with a glance at Lauren, "but it's a little delicate."

"You picked one hell of time to get in the shit."

"It picked me."

"Do I need to say it?"

"I guess I've been a little out of sorts." He looked at Lauren again. "Cut me some slack. I'm not used to being around kids."

"You have a gift for understatement. You should've suspected a tracking bug at the hotel. There's no sense beating yourself up over it now."

"No need—you're doing a fine job."

"I'm taking the first available flight to Los Angeles."

"Harv, you're in Istanbul. Assuming you find a nonstop, that's what…a fourteen-hour hop?"

"Thirteen and change. Depending on my departure, I can probably be in San Diego in eighteen hours, plus or minus."

"Don't do that. Seriously. I can handle this. Stay with your family and enjoy your vacation." As he said it, Nathan realized how absurd it sounded. If the situation were reversed, Nathan would drop everything and help his friend. "Can you forget I just said that?"

"Apology accepted. Is there any way I can convince you to lie low until I get there?"

"I'm dealing with a first-class turd. He needs to be neutralized."

Nathan heard Harv sigh. "Will you at least try to avoid more firefights?"

"*Try* being the operative word."

"Ask Holly about the reported kidnapping. It's within the FBI's jurisdiction. Maybe she'll have some additional info on it."

"Nate, from everything you've told me, Lauren's abduction smells like organized crime. And organized crime can have sources inside law enforcement. Stay mobile and off the grid. Put your cell on vibrate, and wait for me to get back to you. Text me if you need anything. I think it's safe to use your cell, but try to limit it. I want you alert and focused."

His friend was right, of course. "Sounds good. Thanks, Harv."

"You got it. I'll call Holly right after we hang up and relay everything you just told me. Depending on what she finds and how quickly, I'll get back to you."

"In case anything happens, my next stop's going to be the warehouse where Lauren took the list of numbers from Marchand's office."

"All right. Let me know when you have that address."

"I will, if the situation allows." Nathan paused. "Harv, don't tell Holly about Lauren."

"I won't, but you need to call your dad at some point."

"Yeah, I know. I'm just hoping he'll be as surprised as we are."

"May I suggest a certain amount of...discretion on your part."

"You can suggest..."

"Think about your mom. I'll call you soon."

He tucked his cell into a special hip pocket for phones. Still heading west, they crossed a busier street. Several new sirens wailed in the night. SDPD certainly had its hands full.

"Nathan?" Lauren had stopped.

"What?"

"Can I put my shoes on?"

Nathan gave her a nod.

While Lauren laced up, she asked, "Who's Harv?"

"He's my business partner. We own a private security company."

"Is that how you know about handcuffs and stuff?"

"I worked for the government after the marines."

"You were a spy, weren't you." It was a statement, not a question.

Nathan didn't respond.

"But you can't talk about it. How many languages do you speak?"

"Six, including English. But only four fluently."

"Seriously?"

"Yes. Does your stepdad's warehouse have skylights?"

"Uh-huh. There are solar panels too."

"Are there motion sensors inside?"

"I don't know. Probably not. The cats would set them off."

"Cats?"

"They catch mice. Only one lets you pet him, though."

"What kind of lock is on the door you normally use to get in?"

"You have to press buttons, like at airports."

"And you know the code?"

"Uh-huh. It's one-four-seven-eight-five-two. You have to use the same number on the inside to disarm the security system."

"We'll try that first."

"The man you shot in the parking lot didn't die. He wasn't even bleeding."

"Ballistic vest."

"Why are they trying to kill us?"

"We're loose ends. When we get to your stepdad's warehouse, you'll need to show me exactly where you found the piece of paper with the numbers."

A minute or two later, they arrived at Nathan's house. He glanced at his watch—2103 hours—and lowered his voice. "Stay behind me."

Lauren moved closer. He drew his SIG and led her to a side-yard gate. With his back to her, he held up a fist, but then realized she wouldn't know what it meant. He bent low, his face inches from her ear. "Don't make a sound. I'm going to clear the rear yard. I'll be back in fifteen seconds."

"But you promised—"

"It's okay," he whispered. "Just sit tight."

He set the grocery bag down and reached over the top of the gate to unlatch it. It swung silently. He inched forward to the corner of the house and peered around the corner. All quiet. His rear yard was small, defined by a seven-foot privacy fence. Mature jacaranda trees provided additional screening from his neighbors. The keypad next to the rear door showed a solid red light. No one had tripped the infrared beams crisscrossing the yard. Following a narrow trail of concrete pavers toward the sliding glass door, he approached the keypad, which was now blinking—he'd walked through a beam. He placed his forefinger on the small glass window of the security keypad. The capacitance scanner correctly identified the valleys and ridges of his fingerprint, and the LED turned green. He diverted over to the trunk of a Jacaranda, retrieved his hidden key, and went back for Lauren.

"We're good to go."

"Don't forget our sandwich." Lauren followed him through the yard into his house. "I can't see anything. It's too dark."

"We're going to keep the lights off. Your eyes will adjust."

"I need to use the bathroom."

"Me too. Ladies first."

"Where is it?"

Nathan pressed a dimmer switch near the door, activating half a dozen nightlights plugged into outlets around the room. He turned the knob to its lowest setting. "Better?"

"That's way cool."

"The bathroom's down the hall, first door on the right. Leave the light off." He smiled. "And you don't need to lock the door."

Lauren rolled her eyes.

"I'll get us a couple of plates. We aren't going to stay long."

Nathan watched her disappear down the hall. Lauren was a good kid, but he suspected she carried some kind of baggage that he couldn't quite pinpoint—like an elusive fish in an aquarium. He'd test her soon, but the timing had to be right. The trick would be not pushing too hard. He supposed all kids had issues of one kind or another. But Lauren's could be severe. She'd said she didn't trust people, and that tended to have its roots in betrayal.

He set plates on the coffee table and grabbed two bottled waters, plus the sandwich, from the bag. A moment later, he sensed her presence, watching from the corner of the hall.

Without looking over, he said, "Did everything come out okay?"

"You aren't supposed to ask that."

"Sorry. Couldn't resist. Let's eat."

"You have the coolest bathroom I've ever seen. It's so clean."

"Soap and water are cheap."

"Do you watch TV from the bathtub?"

"Hockey and football, mainly."

"That's *so* male."

"Well, last I looked…"

"I saw a Blu-ray player."

"I like movies. Sometimes I listen to music."

"What's your favorite song?"

"'Adagio for Strings,' by Samuel Barber. It's pure genius."

"I've never heard of that."

"Classical."

She sat a comfortable distance away on the couch. "You just prayed."

Again, Lauren amazed him with her level of awareness. She'd make a good operations officer someday.

He nodded. "I'm thankful for the things in my life."

"I've been to church a few times. Everyone's really nice."

"Goes with the territory."

They ate in silence for a moment.

"What was it like, you know…being tortured?"

He stopped midbite and looked at her. Be careful, there's a demon down there. "I can't speak for anyone else, but for me, the worst part isn't the pain. It's being powerless to stop it. It's an extremely infuriating experience. You just have to disconnect from it."

"What do you mean, 'disconnect'?"

"You pretend it's happening to someone else." He took another bite, hoping Lauren wouldn't pursue the subject further.

"People can be really cruel to each other. Kids are the worst."

"How's that?"

"I mean like bullies. They make other kids cry for no reason."

"Bullies are insecure, that's why they do it. If they had spiritual balance, they wouldn't feel the need to hurt anyone."

"You're pretty smart, I can tell."

"I'm just an ordinary guy."

"Ordinary guys don't know stuff like you do."

He took a swig of water. "Tell me about your mom. What's she like?"

"I don't know…she gets mad really easily. She cries a lot too. Like over small stuff. She accidentally broke a plate in the sink once, and then she broke every plate in the cabinet by throwing them on the floor. She sat on the floor crying for like an hour."

Nathan knew it well, built-up rage followed by depression.

"Has she ever been physical with you?"

"You mean like spankings? No, never. She gives me time-outs. Sometimes they're pretty long. I had to spend the entire weekend in my room once."

"Bread and water?"

"Huh?"

"You seem like a pretty good kid. She's done well raising you."

"I think she's a good mom, but sometimes she goes away for days without telling me where she went. She doesn't call, either. My stepdad got really mad whenever she did it."

"Maybe she just needs time alone. I do the same thing, but I always tell Harv where I'm going. He'd kill me otherwise. We need to stop at my security company to pick up some equipment. Have you ever been on a motorcycle?"

"No."

"He nodded toward the garage door. "It's in there."

"Can I see it?"

"Lauren, you haven't been completely honest with me."

"What do you mean?"

"When you first saw me on the freeway, you recognized me."

Her tone became defensive, on the verge of panic. "My mom made me promise not to tell!"

"Tell what?"

"That I knew it would be you who helped me."

Nathan wanted to lash out but held back. "How did you know it would be me?"

"I've seen you before."

"*When and where* have you seen me?"

"Last year, in the grocery store at La Jolla Shores. My mom wanted me to know what you looked like. Please don't be mad at me."

"*Mad* isn't the word. I'm disappointed."

"That's so much worse."

"I'm giving you a onetime 'get out of jail free' card. Remember when I said you couldn't hold anything back?"

"Uh-huh."

"I meant it. Is there anything else I should know?"

"The ring isn't mine. My stepdad gave it to my mom, but she never wears it."

"Why's that?"

"I think she's embarrassed. She doesn't want people to think she's rich."

"And?"

Lauren didn't respond right away. He hoped she'd be honest.

"Okay. I knew it was an alexandrite and that it's like really expensive."

"How expensive?"

"A hundred and ninety thousand dollars."

"Are you telling me you're wearing a ring worth nearly two hundred grand?"

"Uh-huh."

"And you aren't worried about losing it?"

"Not really. I never take it off when I'm not at home."

"Does your mom know you wear it?"

"She said it's okay. Since I'm just a kid, no one thinks it's real. It was too big for me, so she made it smaller."

"She took it to a jeweler and had it resized?"

"I guess."

"How long was she married to your stepdad?"

"Only about a year."

"How did they meet?"

"I think at a school meeting."

"Does your stepdad have children from a previous marriage?"

"Two boys, but they're total brats. They're mean to me."

"They just lost their father. It's going to be hard on them. Do they live with their mother?"

She nodded.

"Does your mom have friends she likes to hang out with?"

"She doesn't have any friends."

"Why's that?"

"I guess she doesn't trust people."

"Sounds familiar."

"What's that supposed to mean?"

"It means she's like us."

"She didn't love him."

"Your mom didn't love your stepdad? Why do you think that?"

"I could just tell."

They sat in silence while they finished off the sandwich. Nathan saw that she had good table manners. "I tried to kill another man tonight. Are you okay with that?"

"You mean at the grocery store? But he was trying to kill you. That makes it okay, right?"

"You know why I'm asking?"

"There might be more bad guys trying to kill us, and you'll have to kill them first."

"That's right."

"Are you really my uncle?"

"If you're asking me if I believe it without any proof, then yes. Our eyes are nearly identical. My father, your grandfather, is a US senator. He's a very important political figure."

"Seriously?"

"You said your mom is from Korea. My father was a marine. He served over there during the war."

"This is too weird. Why wouldn't she tell me about you? You seem like a nice man."

"I have my moments."

She didn't say anything.

"I'm sure your mom has her reasons. Hopefully we'll find out soon. But until then, don't tell anyone we're related unless I say it's okay. Never even mention it."

"I won't."

"Thank you for telling me the truth. Remember when I told you my girlfriend is a special agent in charge in the FBI? Her name's Holly Simpson. She runs the Sacramento field office. I'm telling you because she's going to help us figure out what's going on. So if you think of something important or remember anything else, no matter how small it seems, you tell me right away."

"I will."

"You've seen a lot of violence tonight."

"I'm not freaked out or anything, if that's what you mean."

"Things could get worse."

"We'll be together, right?"

"Yes, but you could slow me down, and that could put both of us in danger. So if I tell you to do something, you have to do it without question. It's like a marine following orders. Are you okay with that?"

"I guess."

"There's no room for guessing. It could be a life-or-death situation. I need to know you'll do exactly what I tell you without questioning it."

"I can do that."

"Good. Now take these plates to the sink!"

She threw her napkin at him.

"At least you haven't lost your sense of humor." He held out his hand, and she shook it, her expression sincere. "Let's take a look at that motorcycle."

CHAPTER 12

He opened the garage door and watched Lauren's eyes widen.

"OMG. We're riding that?"

"Holly's helmet will be a little big for you, but it should be okay. I'll be right back. I'm going to reload my SIG and stock up on ammo."

"Can I come with you?"

"I'm just going down the hall—" Nathan stopped when Lauren's face went blank. He'd seen this expression before, in Nordstrom. There was no harm in letting her tag along. She stayed close as he walked down the hall to the master bedroom.

"This house is really cool. I like your antique furniture."

"Holly told me the same thing, almost word for word. I'll have to show you my La Jolla home sometime. My giant schnauzers are going to love you. You're about the same size."

She put her hands on her hips. "I weigh eighty-three pounds."

"Like I said…"

In his bedroom, he reloaded the SIG's magazine and put three fifty-round boxes of subsonic ammo in his left thigh pocket. The right side still held the SIG's suppressor and spare magazines.

Lauren watched in silence. He knew she was evaluating his every move, looking for uncertainty or weakness. Understandable, given their circumstances.

"Lauren, your lavender shirt isn't dark enough for a night op. I need you in black, at least your top half."

He removed a black T-shirt from his dresser and asked her to put it on. It hung to her knees. She cocked her head to the side, pursed her lips, and stared at him. No words were necessary.

"What's wrong? It looks great."

"I can't be seen like this."

"Don't worry, that's our goal, remember? Come on, I'll cut the excess off in the kitchen with scissors."

"With scissors..."

Fighting a smile, he grabbed Holly's helmet from the hall closet and handed it to her. "Try it on." She fumbled with the chin strap, so he showed her how to fasten it.

"There's a microphone."

"Voice-activated Bluetooth."

"Okay, now I'm impressed. This is seriously cool."

"It's really important you don't lean while we're riding. Just stay upright behind me, okay?"

"I will."

"I need to check the front yard before I open the garage door. Don't worry, I'll be back in twenty seconds."

Nathan retraced his steps through the backyard and scanned the front of his house. All clear—no sign of the menacing black sedan. Feeling confident he'd destroyed the only tracking bug and his cell hadn't been the culprit, he went back inside. Lauren looked silly wearing the huge helmet and baggy shirt. Clearly, she was thinking the same thing.

"I must look like a total geek."

"If we crash, at least your noggin's protected."

"That's not very encouraging."

As promised, he trimmed about eight inches from the bottom of her T-shirt.

She looked down at herself. "At least let me tuck it in."

Nathan waited while she retreated to the bathroom to do it. He grabbed his keys to First Security and took her into the garage, where she approached his motorcycle in a manner resembling reverence.

She ran her hand along the gas tank. "This is a custom paint job, isn't it?"

"Our receptionist's husband does it for a living."

"I've never seen anything like this before."

The gas tank on his Harley went from pure white on the front end to pure black on the back, with a perfectly blended transition in the middle. The frame followed suit with a much longer blended area. Tons of chrome sealed the deal. He had to admit, it was an awesome-looking motorcycle.

"Wait until I fire her up. Remember, don't lean. I'll grab Holly's leather jacket for you. It's not too cold out, but riding creates a windchill." The jacket also prevented road rash in case of a spill, but he didn't need to share that.

Nathan put on his jacket, opened the garage door, and mounted the bike. When he turned the ignition, Lauren grinned at the deep-throated rumble. Out of respect for his neighbors, he didn't rev the motor in the traditional Harley-Davidson manner. It was also better to let the big twin warm up gradually. He pulled on his helmet and activated their Bluetooth units.

He spoke into the microphone boom at a normal conversational level. "Can you hear me okay?"

"Uh-huh, perfectly."

"Okay, climb on."

She immediately reached around his waist and bear-hugged him.

"Lauren, you don't have to hang on that tight. Just sit up, hold my sides, and don't fight it when the motorcycle leans into a turn."

Idling on his driveway, he pressed the remote on his key chain and waited until the garage door was all the way down. Using his iPhone, he rearmed the security system to his house.

A twist of the throttle sent them on their way.

"This is so cool!"

"Glad you're having fun back there." Nathan didn't know with certainty what caused it, but riding gave him a strong sense of security. Maybe it was the open air or the illusion of power, or something far more intangible, but this merging of flesh and machine felt good. It was as simple as that. He experienced the same sensation in his helicopter.

Following the same route they'd taken on foot ten minutes earlier, Nathan returned to the site of the shooting at the grocery store. As he'd suspected, several police cruisers were on scene, along with two fire department engines and an ambulance. He didn't see the gunman or the cabdriver. Maybe they were already secured in the ambulance. There was nothing to be gained by hanging around, so he took Mount Acadia Boulevard down through Tecolote Canyon.

They hadn't gone three miles when he felt his phone vibrate.

"Why are we stopping?"

"My phone. It's probably Harv." He pulled into a small retail center, killed the engine, and removed his helmet.

It was Harv. "What's your situation?"

"We're good."

"According to Holly, Lauren's kidnapping was reported by an anonymous source. A woman reported seeing a man abduct her from her front yard, kicking and screaming, and force her into a black SUV. The police activated the Amber Alert based on that report, and they reported it to the FBI."

"Jin probably made the call. Lauren's story doesn't agree with the report, though. She said the guy knocked on her door and claimed to be from the witness security program. She wasn't taken by force."

"Maybe Jin had to report it that way or the police wouldn't have activated the Amber Alert system."

"That sounds right. The question becomes, how did Jin know about the kidnapping? Lauren said she hadn't seen her mom in over twenty-four hours. If Jin witnessed it, why didn't she intervene?"

"Maybe she was outnumbered or wasn't armed."

"Probably both. Calling it in could've been her only option."

Nathan updated Harv on what Lauren had admitted about Jin's having pointed him out the year before so Lauren would know what he looked like.

"I don't like the sound of that at all."

"Me either. It's a colossal security breach. We're both careful, but neither of us has had any reason to believe we're under surveillance. Now I have to wonder."

"Unless we determine otherwise, we have to assume Jin knows everything about us. Where we live, where we work—everything."

"Agreed," Nathan said. "It's unsettling enough to find out I have a half sister. But this security issue?" He shook his head and imagined Harv doing the same.

"I hope your dad doesn't know about Jin. It'll be a lot easier to stomach. It's hard to image him hiding this from you all these years. Let's give him the benefit of the doubt. Don't spend a lot of time at your Clairemont house."

"We're already on our way to First Security to get a few things. I pulled over to take your call. We're on the Harley."

Harv half laughed. "You've got Lauren on the back of your hog?"

"My Mustang's out of commission. We're a little short on options."

"Switch over to a company Taurus at the office. The keys are in Gavin's desk drawer, right side."

"I'm planning to."

"Candace found me a nonstop to LAX on Turkish Air. It leaves in four hours. I didn't consider the customs delay when we spoke earlier, so count on me arriving in San Diego in about twenty-two hours."

"What about a chartered flight? You could land directly at Lindbergh."

"That's a good idea. A smaller jet will need to make additional stops, but it could be faster. I'll have Candace look into it right away. Oh, I also relayed your description of Lauren's kidnapper and his men to Holly. I told her to go up the chain of command to Director Lansing in Washington, if necessary."

"Harv, I'm not sure that level of involvement is warranted."

"This whole thing's bigger than just you and Lauren. Think about the border murders and the dead girl Lauren saw in Marchand's warehouse."

"Lauren's kidnapping may not be related."

"What does that finely honed intuition of yours tell you?"

Nathan didn't answer.

"Exactly," Harv said. "My gut still says it's some brand of organized crime. I think it's fair to assume the only reason Lauren's kidnapper didn't have her killed right away is that she has or knows something he needs."

"The piece of paper..."

"Can you scan it and send it to my cell phone?"

"Yeah, I'll do that from the office. If Lauren had it when she was kidnapped, why didn't her kidnapper just take it?"

"Good question."

"Harv, hang on. Lauren, that piece of paper...did your kidnapper ask about it?"

"No. My mom said not to tell anyone I had it."

"Harv, did you catch that?"

"Yes. Send it to me ASAP. I'll take a look. I think it's fair to assume he didn't know Lauren had it, or even suspect she did, or he would've taken it."

"Agreed."

"Well, hopefully Holly turns up something more about Lauren's kidnapper. She's also got her people all over the Marchand angle. I'll call you back once I hear from her."

"Make it a three-way. I've got a bunch of questions, starting with the unconscious bad guy I left in the grocery store parking lot. When you talk to her, ask if the police have him in custody."

"Will do. Now, keep your head down until I get there."

Nathan put away the phone and merged into the northbound traffic. "Lauren, are you sure you don't know what the numbers on the paper mean? Your mom never talked about it?"

"She said not to tell anyone I had it. I wasn't even supposed to tell you. She called it her insurance policy. Does that help?"

"I think your mom was speaking metaphorically. It's not an insurance document. When did she tell you about it?"

"Last night. Right after I saw the dead girl."

"So she told you to take it *after* you told her about the dead girl?"

"Uh-huh."

Unfortunately, Nathan wasn't getting any closer to learning the significance of the numbers. Harv was good with this sort of thing and had an uncanny ability to see order in chaos. Hopefully he'd see something.

"My security company is in Sorrento Valley, near the 805 freeway. How're you doing back there?"

"This is really fun."

"Are you cold?"

"A little, but I'm okay."

"We'll be there in about ten minutes."

"Can I call you Uncle Nate?"

"Absolutely not."

"Okay, Uncle Nate."

He gunned the engine, and she yelped in fear.

"Hey, that was mean!"

"Just letting you know who's in charge."

CHAPTER 13

Nathan kept their stop at First Security brief. Lauren asked tons of questions, mostly about all the "cool" equipment in the Bat Cave—First Security's high-tech countersurveillance garage. Kids never ceased to amaze him. They might not know how to use a pick and shovel, but they sure knew their way around computers. Lauren helped him scan and email the document to Harv's cell phone. Half a minute later, Harv sent a text saying he'd received it.

Nathan left his Harley in the Bat Cave, picked up a prepacked duffel bag, and was preparing to lock the place up when he realized that he'd forgotten something. He went back inside and found what he needed: a small plumber's torch.

Five minutes after arriving, they were back on the road in a company Ford Taurus, their destination Otay Mesa, near the Mexican border.

During the drive, Lauren went quiet again. Nathan didn't mind and actually preferred it. It gave him a chance to think about his plan of action at the warehouse. Gaining entry topped the list. In a nutshell, he intended to get in, learn as much as possible, and get out. He didn't want to be inside the building more than ten minutes. The warehouse might employ a silent alarm system or other security measures, and police response time was impossible to predict. It could be anywhere from thirty seconds to thirty minutes.

A glance in Lauren's direction confirmed that she was close to nodding off. He'd hoped to use the travel time to ask more questions about her mom, but he figured a little shut-eye wouldn't hurt her. With rush hour long gone, Otay Mesa ought to be a thirty-minute drive.

His cell vibrated.

"I've got Holly on the phone with us," Harv said.

Nathan kept his voice low. "Hi, Holly."

"Hi, Nathan. What's your situation? Are you and Lauren secure?"

"Yes, we're on our way to Marchand's warehouse."

"You might want to rethink that," said Holly. "I don't have anything conclusive yet, but we've started digging into Marchand Patio Supplies, and I don't like what we're seeing."

Nathan glanced at Lauren. She looked asleep. He kept his voice low. "Such as?"

"Lauren's stepfather was only part owner of his company. A minority owner."

"Okay...who owns his company, then?"

"Three separate corporations, which themselves are owned by a combination of other foreign companies. We've only begun to untangle this mess, but a couple of the shell companies have high-level flags associated with an internationally wanted criminal who's well known to the Bureau."

"Who's that?"

"Hans Voda, a Spanish-born man with a dozen or more aliases. He's connected with a couple of the major Mexican narco-trafficking cartels. Basically a freelancer, as far as I can tell. But he also does his own business on the side and cuts the cartels in on his action to keep them happy. He's wanted for murder—high-profile assassinations—in at least three countries. He's a nondescript dark-haired, fair-skinned forty-two-year-old man, but he's known to disguise himself and has obviously been very hard to track down."

Nathan replayed images of Lauren's abductor in his mind. "The kidnapper definitely fits the description. And he had a Spanish accent. Could be our guy."

"Hans Voda," Holly said, repeating the name, letting it sink in. "He's on Interpol's ten-most-wanted list. He's wanted for extortion, smuggling, drug trafficking, prostitution, and human trafficking, including along the US–Mexican border. And that's all in addition to the alleged murders. The Interpol profile indicates he's a high-functioning psychopath with...am I on speaker?"

"No." Another glance at Lauren showed her motionless and in the same position as before.

"He's got a thing for young girls, Nathan. If you hadn't rescued Lauren, it's a good bet he would've sexually assaulted her and killed her. He's not an armchair quarterback. He personally gets into the dirt because he likes violence."

"It could explain why he didn't clear the area. I spoiled his little party."

"I'm telling you, he's as vicious as they come. He makes your old friend Montez look like a choirboy. I'd sure feel better if you turned this over to us."

"I understand where you're coming from, but I'm not planning to take any unnecessary risks."

"Every minute you're with Lauren puts both of you at risk."

"Lauren's safe with me. I won't let anything happen to her."

"Well, I'm worried about both of you."

"What can you tell me about Jin?"

"It's what I *can't* tell you that concerns me. We've got nothing on her. I can't find any records at all. I ran her full name through every available database and came up with nothing. Sound familiar?"

"Yeah, she's invisible. Like Harv and me."

Harv jumped in. "Nate, she could be a spook, or worse."

"True, but my take is that she's a good guy in all this."

"You shouldn't assume that just because she's protective of Lauren."

"I can't explain it. You'll just have to trust that she's a white hat in this. But for some reason, she's unable to protect Lauren."

"You're speaking in present tense," said Harv. "What about her past? We don't know anything about her. All we really know is she's Marchand's wife and he seems to be neck deep in Voda's world."

"That's true, but if Jin knows as much as we suspect she does, we'd both be dead if she wasn't on our side. She pointed me out to Lauren last year. And if she knows about me, it's a good bet she knows about you."

"Okay, I'll grant you that. So where does this leave us?"

"I'll keep Lauren with me and stay mobile."

"I know you don't want direct help from us at this stage," said Holly, "but let me send Special Agent Grangeland in your direction. I'd feel a lot better if you had a second pair of eyes—and a second gun."

"That's a tempting offer, and she's a proven asset, but we're okay for now."

"Well, then legally we're on shaky ground," Holly said. "As a sworn law enforcement officer, I'm officially telling you to back off."

"I understand. I've officially been told to stand down. You're covered."

"That's not what I'm worried about," said Holly, with some frustration in her voice. "I want to hear from you after you've looked around the warehouse, and don't leave any trace of your entry. We may need evidence in court someday."

"I'll be wearing gloves. Lauren doesn't need them, she's already been all over the place. Her prints can be explained."

"Since Voda took Lauren's phone," Holly said, "he'll have your cell number from the texts you exchanged with her tonight. Is your cellular account secure?"

"Yes," Harv cut in. "Both our phones are hidden under a double-layered shell company with an eventual address in Delaware. It would be extremely difficult to trace our phone numbers back to First Security without direct access to Verizon's encrypted servers. Holly, don't get the wrong idea: our shell companies are legit and legal, they're just not doing any actual business."

"I wasn't worried. You've both got US government plates on your vehicles. So even if Voda noted the Mustang's plate, he can't trace you that way, either. I think you're okay. He'd need to have a pretty high-level informant to get anything useful on you guys."

"Right. If it's even Voda," Nathan said.

"True," said Holly. "We can't confirm it yet, but I still have to report his suspected presence up the chain of command right away."

"Understood." Nathan thought for a moment. "Assuming it's Voda, is there any way you can discreetly find out if the Bureau or any other law enforcement agencies have a man inside his operation?"

"I suppose. Why are you asking?"

"I'm not saying it will happen, but there could be more confrontations tonight, and I don't want to worry about a friendly-fire situation."

"Confrontations?" Harv asked. "What happened to lying low until I get there?"

"Look, I'm not planning to engage Voda or his men—I've got Lauren with me. But I need to know if I do face that situation, I won't be shooting at any undercover federal agents."

"Nathan, you don't have to go after him," Holly said.

"Under normal circumstances I would agree, but Jin's a wild card. She knows who I am, and until we figure out what her connection is, Voda's fair game. Maybe I'll just wring it out of him. I'd love to give him a taste of his own medicine."

"Holly," said Harv, "I'm with Nate on this. He needs to act as he sees fit until we understand who Jin is and why she's involved, especially given what she knows about us."

"Okay," Holly said. "I'll look into the undercover question. But remember, I'll only be able to speak for the FBI. What other law enforcement agencies may be doing..." She let the sentence hang.

"Understood. And if you have to talk to Director Lansing, tell him the truth, everything that's happened. Don't hold anything back. Tell him everything you know."

"I'm glad to hear you say that, Nathan. I was planning to. I can't withhold any of this from him."

"I wouldn't expect you to. Lansing and I have an unspoken understanding. Our trust in each other isn't absolute, but we have a proven history together. He knows the score."

"I'll be honest, Nathan. I'm uncomfortable with this. I know you're not indiscriminate, but if it's truly Voda, he's a gold mine. This could be an opportunity for us to collar him...."

Nathan knew she'd purposely omitted the word *alive*. He didn't say anything, didn't trust himself to.

"Of course," she added, "I won't second-guess any action you take to protect yourself and Lauren."

"Thanks, Holly. Harv, can you forward the list of numbers?"

"I already did. Holly, it should be in your inbox."

"What numbers are you talking about?"

Harv answered. "Lauren had a piece of paper in her pocket with columns of numbers."

"She took it from Marchand's office," Nathan added. "Jin told her it was important, an insurance policy of sorts."

"I'll take a look right away."

Nathan was about to sign off, when an idea struck him. "Wait a minute...if I call Lauren's phone, Voda might answer. He confiscated it from her. Holly, can you record the call and get a voice print?"

"Yes, but I'm on my cell. Can you write down a different number?"

"I'm pulling over. Hang on a sec."

"Nate, keep going," Harv said. "Ask Lauren to write the number down. There should be a notepad and pen in the glove box."

"Lauren, I know you're awake. Pop the glove. I need you to write down a number. Holly, I'm putting you on speaker. Okay, shoot."

"I'll give you my field office number. All incoming calls are recorded. After the recording, hit extension two-five-eight-seven. It'll ring straight through to my office. I'll pick up before you initiate the three-way call with Lauren's phone."

Lauren wrote the phone number and extension on the pad.

"Harv, we'll talk later. Look into the private charters."

"Candace is doing it as we speak."

"Okay, Holly, I'll make the call to your field office as soon as we hang up."

"I'll be waiting."

Nathan looked at Lauren. "I'm going to call your cell phone and see if your kidnapper picks up. I'm setting up a three-way call with Holly so she can record it. What's the number she just gave us?" Nathan keyed it in and tapped the call button. He waited until the recorded message ended before entering Holly's extension.

"I'm here," Holly said.

"Good," said Nathan. "Hang on. I'll make the other call." He pressed the symbol for adding a call and asked Lauren for her number. When it began ringing on Lauren's phone, he brought Holly back into the call. "Holly, are you there?"

"I'm here. I'll call you afterward."

A moment later, a voice Nathan recognized answered Lauren's phone. "Whoever you are, I'll give you credit. You've got some balls. Turn the girl over, and I'll let you keep them."

"Good evening, Mr. Voda."

A pause. "You think I can't find you?"

"How's the leg?"

"Give me the girl."

"I'm a businessman. How about a trade?" Nathan winked at Lauren. "Three hundred grand, and she's yours. I don't take checks."

"And if I say no?"

"It's been nice talking with you. Good-bye, Mr. Voda."

"When and where?"

"I'll get back to you." Nathan ended the call and waited for Holly. Fifteen seconds later, his cell vibrated. "Did you get that?"

"Yes. We'll do a voice-print analysis. I wish you'd kept him on the phone longer."

"I don't want him to think I have ties to law enforcement. Hopefully he guesses I'm horning in on his action—a rival cartel or some independent contractor. It's something he should be able to relate to."

"Smart thinking. We'll do another three-way on your next call. I'll get my people working on this right away."

"Sounds good. One more thing. I need you to find out if SDPD has my bad guy in custody from the grocery store."

"Will do," Holly said. "Harv already asked me about it."

Nathan also told her about the MP5s he'd stashed behind the stucco wall where he'd rammed Voda's Escalade. It was possible Voda and his goons had retrieved them, but he needed to mention it just in case. The only thing Nathan didn't tell Holly was that he'd seized a cell phone from one of Voda's men. He felt badly about not mentioning it, but if he had, Holly would want it right away and he needed to go through it first.

Holly's tone was firm. "No unnecessary risks, Nathan."

He agreed, thanked her, and ended the call, then looked over at Lauren. "If you're going to fake being asleep, you have to slow your breathing in half."

"You noticed my breathing? Seriously? You are *such* a spy."

"You watch too many movies."

"It's okay, you don't have to tell me the truth."

"Let's change the subject. I need to go over some stuff with you before we reach your stepdad's warehouse."

"Like what?"

"Like being very quiet during the operation. Don't say anything or make any noise unless I prompt you. We're invisible."

"Sounds cool."

"Lauren, this is serious. I mean it. Don't make a sound. I want you to think about your footsteps, your breathing, accidentally bumping into things. You need to be totally silent."

"I can do that."

"You also need to learn some basic hand signals." Nathan showed her the gesture for holding position, taking point, following, forming up, hunkering down, looking in certain directions, and several others. Lauren was a quick study and could emulate all of them within a minute. He also taught her directional indicators using the clock method. Twelve o'clock—straight ahead. Six o'clock—directly behind. Three o'clock—to the right. Nine o'clock—to the left. He tested her with a couple of landmarks, and she seemed to have a good command of the concept. Perhaps a little too good.

"A point of clarification. You are not taking an active part in tonight's operations. I am *not* giving you a gun to act as my backup. Your role is to be very quiet and stay out of my way. If I need something from you, I'll ask. Understood?"

She nodded agreement, but he saw her mind working behind those discerning blue eyes.

CHAPTER 14

After they exited the 905 interchange, Lauren directed Nathan east toward Otay Mesa for several miles, then had him turn left into a cluster of industrial buildings. A huge auto-wrecking complex dominated the right side of the road. Nathan was somewhat familiar with this area of South San Diego. First Security had installed a state-of-the-art system in a self-storage facility a little farther down 905.

Lauren sat forward and pointed to a side street. "Turn here. It's the next one on the right."

Nathan studied the huge building as he drove past, making a mental note of the security lights mounted on the walls. Many of the lights were dark, and it didn't take long to see the pattern. Along the loading dock, every third light was on. Marchand probably did it to save on the electric bill. He didn't see any security cameras, but that didn't mean there weren't any. He guessed the building's footprint to be roughly three hundred by five hundred feet, and it looked to be about twenty-five feet high. Whatever the case, Mr. Marchand probably stored a boatload of patio furniture in there. Several vans were parked about two-thirds of the way down the loading dock, under an illuminated security light.

"Are those the company vans?"

Lauren nodded.

"You used one of them to drive home last night?"

Another nod.

"You okay?"

"This place creeps me out. We'll be together, right?"

"Yes."

He made a U-turn and cruised past the south side, taking notice of the building's main entrance. Two cars were parked at the curb, but the amount of dust and grime on them suggested they hadn't been moved in some time. Just to be sure, he pulled alongside and had Lauren reach out and feel their hoods. She said they felt cold. The public streetlights weren't a huge concern, but if anybody drove past while they were on foot, they'd be seen. The low, fire-resistant landscaping offered no place to hide. Anyone seeing a man with a duffel bag would probably be more than a little suspicious. Nathan might as well wear a cardboard body sign with CAT BURGLAR in huge block letters.

He decided the loading dock offered the best option for visual cover. A ten-foot-high wall paralleled the sunken area where trucks backed up against the building to load and unload their cargo. If he parked the Taurus behind the wall, no one from the street could see it.

He was just about to turn into the driveway when he spotted bleed light from an approaching vehicle. He gunned the engine and made a quick left turn back toward the auto-wrecking yard. Ten seconds later, he saw the vehicle turn down the street where he'd just been. He also saw the unmistakable shield-type logo of a security company on the door panel. This complicated things and forced a change in plans. He didn't know the frequency of the patrol vehicle's rounds, so parking next to the loading dock was out. He'd need to find a parking place along the street, preferably with a few other cars present. Near the wrecking yard, he found a good location. It would make their approach to the warehouse longer and less stealthy, but it couldn't be helped. He made a U-turn, pulled up to the curb, and parked.

"What're we doing?"

Nathan nodded toward the warehouse. "Security patrol."

"What are we going to do?"

"We're going to wait."

Half a minute later, he watched the security vehicle exit the warehouse property on the far side of the building and turn directly toward them. Crap. He didn't know if the driver would recognize an additional vehicle parked on the curb since his last cruise-through.

"Lauren, climb into the back and lie down. I'll be right behind you. Hurry!"

She unbuckled her belt and scrambled over the center console. Nathan hit the door-lock button and heard all four locks clunk into place. He practically dived into the rear compartment and flattened himself out on the seat.

Lauren's head ended up against the small of his back.

The world outside grew brighter with each passing second as invasive light raided their hiding place. He felt Lauren's body shudder and reached back to give her arm a reassuring squeeze. The light reached a peak as the patrol car pulled alongside. The bleed light changed from white to red as the driver applied the brakes. Things got worse when a million-candlepower beam swept through the interior above them. The intensity hammered Nathan's eyes. He knew the driver was using the post-mounted spot to check their car. The beam moved back and forth in a jerky yet controlled manner.

"What do we do?" Lauren whispered.

"Don't move a muscle."

Then, as quickly as it had arrived, the blinding light vanished and red illumination filled the Taurus again. To Nathan's relief, the crimson glow ebbed as the patrol vehicle continued down the street. He lifted his head just enough to see the patrol car turn right at the corner and disappear from sight.

"He's gone, but this is a good example of what you're *not* supposed to do. I understand you were scared, but you have to be absolutely quiet at times like that. You broke my concentration."

"I'm sorry. Are you mad?"

"If I get mad, you'll know it. There was no harm done this time, but you have to control your fear. Pretend there's someone inside of you who's really tough and mean. She takes over when you're scared or worried."

"You mean like a multiple personality?"

"Yes."

"Are you speaking from experience?"

"I'll have to take the Fifth on that."

"The Fifth?"

"We're going to leave the car here and head to the warehouse on foot. We'll hold hands so we look like a father and daughter in case anyone sees us."

He grabbed the duffel from the trunk, locked the Taurus, and placed the keys on top of the right rear tire. Thankfully, the three-minute walk was uneventful and no one saw them. At the driveway to the loading dock he asked, "Which door do you use to get inside?"

"It's near the vans."

"We're going to run." They hustled over to a trio of roll-up doors. Nathan looked for a camera, but didn't see one. He approached a steel door with a punch button keypad. Above the door, a sign stated FIRE EXIT. DO NOT BLOCK. "Is this it?"

"Uh-huh."

"Go ahead and enter the combo, just like you did last night."

Lauren pushed the sequence of numbers and tried the handle. It didn't move.

She made a second attempt.

"Are you sure you're using the right code?"

"Yeah, positive." She tried again, with the same result.

She was about to punch the numbers a fourth time, but Nathan blocked the keypad with his hand. "Many security systems only allow three attempts before triggering the alarm. Someone changed the combo. We'll have to do it the hard way."

Nathan removed the grappling hook from the duffel and wound its rope into loose coils. He swung the hook over the top of the parapet and tested its anchor by gradually applying more and more weight until it supported his entire mass. He created a loop at knee height and tied the duffel to the end of the rope.

"Good to go. After I'm up there, put your foot into the loop and walk your hands along the wall as I pull you up."

"What are those doughnut-shaped things for?"

"They keep the rope away from the wall, which makes it easier to use near the top. Okay, I'm going up."

Climbing a grappling-hook rope close to a wall required power and dexterity, but Nathan had the technique down. Once on the roof, he felt exposed, but the three-foot-high parapet gave him some cover. He dropped to his knees and gave Lauren a nod. She stepped into the loop, and he began hoisting her up.

"Use your hands to steady yourself. It's like crawling on the ground, only you're doing it vertically. Don't look down." Lauren struggled as he pulled. She kept grabbing the rope with both hands to avoid falling. This wasn't going to work. Lauren didn't possess the dexterity or balance needed to form a stable triangle. "Hang on tight. I'm pulling you up in a hurry."

Nathan used sheer strength to hoist her and the duffel up the wall. When she was near the top, Nathan anchored his stomach against the parapet and wrapped the rope around his right forearm to keep the rope from slipping.

"Lauren, keep breathing. Don't hold your breath." He saw her face then, streaked with tears. Keeping the rope in one hand, he abandoned all sense of personal privacy, encircled her waist with his free arm, and hauled her over the top. Visibly trembling, she hugged herself.

Nathan kept his voice low. "You okay?"

She wiped her cheeks. "Sorry about crying."

"You did fine, trust me." He brushed her hair back from her face to get a better look. Other than being shaken, she seemed okay. He pulled the duffel up and took a moment to scan the immediate area. "Do you need a minute? Can you keep going?"

She nodded tightly.

"We're going silent. If you need to ask me something, poke me once. If you see something I should know about, poke me twice."

"Okay."

It was significantly darker up here. The bland illumination from the streetlights no longer reached them. Nathan removed a night-vision visor and secured it on his head. He turned the device on, lowered the gain, and pivoted the scope down to his left eye. He felt a single poke.

"What is that thing?"

"Night vision."

"Can I see?"

He was about to sigh, but realized her curiosity might take her mind off the stress of the ascent.

He took the device off and handed it to her. "Take a look, but make it quick."

"OMG! This is supercool. I can see everything."

"Lauren, keep your voice down."

"I want one of these," she whispered.

"You got five thousand bucks in your pocket?"

"No way!"

"Way. Take a quick look at the stars."

"Oh, wow, this is awesome. I can see the Milky Way. The Big Dipper is really bright. "

Nathan tested her with a spontaneous question. "What's the Big Dipper part of?"

"Ursa Major." She tensed as though she'd been tricked into revealing more than she wanted.

He logged a mental note. "I see you're up to speed with your astronomy, but we're a little pressed for time."

Figuring it wouldn't hurt to have her equally equipped, he removed the second visor and showed her how to turn it on and adjust the gain and focus. He tweaked the fit and secured it on her head. "Keep both eyes open. The scope pivots up and down like this. Stay low and follow me. Think about your footsteps. Walk quietly."

Hunched over, they worked their way west, staying close to the parapet. Although they could be seen from the loading dock, no one from the street could easily see them. If the security patrol returned, they could duck behind the parapet wall. As Lauren had mentioned, an impressive array of solar panels dominated the middle portion of the roof. Surrounding the solar array, dozens of four-foot square skylights dotted the roof's landscape. Some of them were dimly glowing with faint light from below, others were dark, but all had opaque covers, so he couldn't see into the warehouse. Nathan chose the darkest skylight, then peeked over the parapet to make sure there weren't any roll-up doors directly below it. He gave Lauren a hunker-down hand signal. She stopped walking and crouched. He smiled and knew she saw it through her NV scope. She smiled back and gave him a thumbs-up.

He set the bag down, removed his gun belt, and put it on. He knew she wanted to say something. "What?"

"You look like a cowboy," she whispered.

"Thanks, I think....I'll need your assistance with the next part." In reality, he didn't need help, but he wanted to keep Lauren's mind away from the horror she'd seen in the warehouse the night before.

"What are you gonna do?"

"Watch and learn."

He removed one of the folding USMC Predator knives and opened it. Keeping the torch away from the skylight, he ignited it with a lighter and adjusted the flame to a bluish color. It made a hissing sound as the flame formed a fine cone. "Hold the torch upright and keep it from falling over. We don't want to burn the place to the ground. Yet."

He took his left glove off and put it on his right hand upside-down. The insulated handle plus the double-glove protection would shield his skin from the heat. He moved the blade of the knife into the flame and turned it back and forth slowly. The trick was making the knife hot enough to cut the material, but not hot enough to re-fuse the plastic on the back side of the cut. He could've used a battery-powered grinder to cut an opening, but that would've made the devil's own noise. Although slower, this was a silent method. It took two test attempts to find the right temperature. He reheated the blade and pushed it into the opaque plastic of the skylight and began melting a cut line. He got six inches before the knife started to slow and get sticky. Just before the knife stuck in place, he pulled it out and repeated the process again. A noxious odor drifted.

"Don't breathe that in."

"How do you know about this stuff?"

"Books."

"Yeah, right."

It took multiple melts before he had a twenty-four-inch square ready to be removed. For the final cut, he grabbed the piece of plastic with his free hand so it wouldn't drop to the floor below. He made the final cut and placed the Plexiglas next to the skylight. Nathan had purposely made the opening directly along the skylight's frame so anchoring the grappling hook and dangling the rope wouldn't break any remaining Plexiglas.

He motioned for Lauren to follow and stepped away from the skylight.

"Once we're inside, I'll follow you to your stepdad's office. You'll have to go in first, unless you can safely climb down that rope. If not, I'll lower you to the floor."

"You'd better lower me. I have big-time acrophobia. I almost lost it coming up the wall."

"We need to be totally silent from now on. There could be acoustic alarms down there. Once your foot's in the loop, use your hands to guide yourself through the opening as I lower you. When you're below the skylight, grab the rope with both hands. Don't look down until you're close to the floor. The duffel bag will be below you, so watch out for it."

Lauren made it to the floor without incident. The only trouble she had was a scrape on her forearm from the edge of the opening. Ten seconds later, Nathan joined her on the concrete. He felt two taps on his arm and turned. Lauren pointed to a bright light on the perimeter wall near the fire exit door. In the green image of his NV scope, he saw the unmistakable intensity of an infrared beam's source. Invisible to the naked eye, the night vision picked it up easily. Had they entered through the fire exit door Lauren normally used, they would've broken the IR beam.

Nathan bent low and whispered, "Good work. Sit tight for a sec." Before proceeding, he needed to know where the beam went. He retrieved a plastic spray bottle from the duffel and turned the nozzle to a fine-mist setting. Aiming toward the IR beam's source, he pulled the trigger. At waist height, a bright line materialized in shimmering splendor. The beam ran from left to right, covering the fire exit door and the larger freight doors. It shouldn't be a problem.

Even with only every tenth ceiling light illuminated, their NV visors were too bright. Nathan turned Lauren's gain to its lowest setting before adjusting his own. He took a moment to orient himself. The warehouse contained long aisles of pallets stacked two and three high. Each pallet secured large cardboard boxes, presumably the patio furniture Marchand manufactured. If that were true, there was enough stock in here to supply the entire state.

Keeping his voice low, he asked, "Where's the office?"

She pointed. "That way."

"Remember, no sounds at all. Walk quietly. I've got our six. You lead the way."

Nathan trailed her down a long aisle. He wanted to see the location where she'd seen the mutilated Mexican girl, but figured it should wait until he finished searching the office. At the end of the aisle, parked forklifts were being charged. Next to the forklifts he saw a piece of white equipment. It had some kind of robotic-arm device above a wheeled cart. He tapped Lauren on the shoulder and pointed at it. She shrugged and followed him over. When they got closer, recognition came. This thing didn't belong in here. More than that, it seemed randomly out of place. Nathan stared at the unmistakable GE logo on its side and shook his head.

Keeping his voice low, he said, "This is a portable X-ray machine. Do you know why it's here?"

"No."

"Ever seen it before?" he whispered.

She nodded.

Holly had said Voda was into smuggling, so maybe this thing was somehow related. Nathan didn't know the price tag but believed it had to cost a small fortune. Something else caught his eye. Tossed aside near the corner of the building, several hundred empty one-gallon water bottles littered the warehouse floor. The sight of the bottles triggered something, but he couldn't pinpoint it. He'd either seen or heard something about plastic water bottles on the news. He stowed the thought. Right now, he needed to search the office, look at the crime scene, and bug out. Following Lauren along the south wall, Nathan saw some doors that probably led to ground-floor offices or storage rooms. One of them would lead to the building's main entrance.

He trailed her up a set of stairs into a short hallway. Lauren stopped at a closed door with a keypad like the one they'd tried outside. He tried the knob. Locked.

"Is it the same combo?"

"It's different."

After she entered a sequence of numbers, the LED on the key-pad turned green and he heard a soft *click*. They were in. Large, square windows occupied the exterior wall, their vertical blinds open. Overflow from the streetlights provided all the illumination they needed.

This office didn't look like it belonged in a warehouse. A granite-topped desk with an iMac computer dominated the center of the room. Stylish office furniture and accessories lined every available inch of wall space. The furnishings in here had to top one hundred grand. Whoever Marchand was, he'd done well for himself.

"Where did you find the piece of paper?"

"Under the desktop."

"Show me."

She pointed. "This piece lifts up, but you have to move the light first."

In the green image of the scope, he saw an ultrafine line between the right wing and the center portion of the desk. It was nearly undetectable—a clever hiding place. No one would think twice about it. The random pattern of the granite concealed the line. He slid the heavy brass lamp aside and hoisted the piece of granite. Plain particleboard greeted him.

He put the small slab on the carpet. "So, the piece of paper was right here? Sitting flat under the granite?"

"Uh-huh."

Nathan opened a few of the desk's drawers but didn't see anything out of the ordinary.

Based on the hiding place on the desk, Nathan began searching the office, looking for anything that might employ a similar method of concealment. He frowned at an antique typewriter sitting on a coffee table near the windows. It was hand-powered, not electric. He couldn't remember the last time he'd seen one of these things. Why was it here? It seemed out of place with this office's modern furniture. No other antiques were present. He thought about the piece of paper and removed it from his pocket. He placed the paper facedown on the desk, ran his fingers along its surface, and felt the embossing of the stamped numbers. In this day and age of printers, why would someone hand-type the information, unless it was the only copy and whoever typed it didn't want any digital record whatsoever?

"Lauren, did you ever see your dad use this typewriter?"

"No."

"What about your mom? Has she been in here?"

"I don't know."

"But she knew about the hiding place on the desk."

"I guess."

"You guess? She told you where it was, right?"

"Uh-huh."

Nathan stared at the desk, concentrating. He put the piece of granite back, slid the desk lamp back into position, and heard a barely audible squeak of metal. He picked up the lamp and felt something move inside its brass base. He shook the lamp to confirm it. There was definitely something loose in there. It could be the power cord, but he didn't think so. He set the lamp on its side and examined its felt bottom. The felt appeared to be off-center by no more than an eighth of an inch. He tugged at a corner of the felt and was rewarded with the sound of Velcro tearing. The squeak he heard was from the tiny sliver of exposed brass rubbing along the smooth granite. He hadn't heard a squeak when he'd first slid it because the exposed sliver of brass was on the trailing side. He tore the felt free, and a bundle of Bolivian passports fell onto the desk. He removed the rubber band and opened one. The unsmiling face of a young Hispanic girl stared back. She looked to be around Lauren's age—twelve or thirteen. He checked the other passports and found similar photos.

A chilling thought struck him: Could he be looking at the border murder victims? Had a monster named Hans Voda snuffed out these innocent lives? It seemed likely. But if so, what was Marchand's role?

"Lauren, are you okay looking at these pass—" He stopped midword.

Cigar smoke.

It hadn't been there when they'd walked through the warehouse.

Smelling it now meant only one thing.

They weren't alone.

CHAPTER 15

"Lauren, stay close and don't make a sound!" He pocketed the passports, slung the duffel over his shoulder, and pulled his SIG. The cigar smell was much stronger at the top of the stairs. He peered around the corner and heard a voice coming from somewhere in the middle of the warehouse. From their current position on the south end of the warehouse floor, they'd need to traverse nearly five hundred feet to return to the rope.

"Aquí, gatito! Aquí, gatito gatito!"

Someone was calling to one of the cats. He pivoted his NV scope down to his eye. Several aisles to their left, about halfway down the warehouse, he saw the unmistakable glow of a cigar against the pallets of boxes. The powerful night-vision scope picked it up easily.

He bent low and whispered, "We're going down. Take off your shoes and leave them here. Hurry!"

Although Nathan was able to descend the stairs quietly, he couldn't risk it with Lauren. They had to make their way back to the rope without making any noise. Lacking the security code, they couldn't exit the building without setting off the alarm, which undoubtedly made a boatload of noise.

At the bottom of the stairs, he led Lauren back the way they'd come. In the green image of his night-vision scope, he looked at the X-ray machine again as they hurried past its strange form to the perimeter wall. Knowing his boots wouldn't be silent if they needed to run, he removed them. Nathan gave her the hand signal to follow and started down the aisle along the perimeter wall toward the rope. They'd made it only halfway down the warehouse when a cell phone trilled to life. He couldn't hear the conversation, but he *did* hear the footfalls of someone running in the direction they needed to go. This wasn't good at all. He stopped and held up a closed fist. Lauren bumped into him.

Near the place where they'd entered at the north wall, they heard the fire door open, followed by a grunt of pain.

In Spanish, a man's voice boomed through the warehouse. "I'm going to kill that stupid son of a bitch."

"Easy, boss."

"I'm going to cut his fucking nuts off!"

Nathan knew it was Voda then.

"We need to get the bullet out of your leg and close the wound. You've lost a lot of blood."

"He thinks he can make a move on me? We'll just see about that."

"Stay here, boss. I'm going to grab the medical bag and turn the lights on."

Nathan heard running footfalls recede toward the offices on the south wall.

They didn't have more than thirty seconds until the entire warehouse flooded with damning light. The rope might be seen— its dangling form was no more than one hundred feet from the fire-exit door where Voda had entered. They were trapped, and he didn't know how many men he faced. There were at least two— Voda and the man who'd called to the cat. How many more had come inside? Thugs like Voda tended to surround themselves with plenty of firepower.

Time to move, and the rope was no longer an option. They needed an alternate exit. He led Lauren back toward the X-ray machine and ground-floor doors on the south wall. He knew one of them would lead to the warehouse's main entrance, but which one? At the end of the aisle, he stopped short and put Lauren on hold again. He felt a trembling hand on his back and turned. In a barely audible whisper, he said, "Become the tough girl. She has no fear."

Nathan hoped she'd hold it together. If she panicked, he'd have a firefight on his hands, and without knowing his opponent's numbers, he didn't like the odds. By himself, he'd have a much better chance of neutralizing everyone in the warehouse, but Lauren's presence complicated things. He toyed with the idea of putting her on hold while he took care of business, but if he wasn't successful, Lauren would be at the mercy of Voda and his men—not acceptable.

One thing was certain: he'd never allow them to be captured by that nut job, even if it meant eating bullets. A quick death for Lauren would be infinitely preferable to what Voda had planned for her. He shoved the destructive thought aside.

After turning on the lights, Voda's man would likely return to the fire-exit door and tend to his wounded boss. Nathan hadn't seen a master set of light switches but doubted it would be upstairs where Lauren's shoes were. Since the grappling-hook rope was dark in color and motionless, they might have a few seconds or even minutes before anyone detected it after the lights came on. He also didn't think Voda would be looking for a rope. He turned off their NV scopes so the warehouse lights wouldn't ruin the photoelectric plates.

Then it happened.

Without warning, every overhead fixture snapped on.

Even though Nathan had known it was coming, it still chewed at his nerves. Sodium vapor light invaded every square inch of the place, making it look like broad daylight. He held position inside the perimeter aisle and used the pallets of boxes for cover. Peering around the corner of the aisle they were in, he saw Voda's man emerge through one of the ground-floor doors and hustle back toward the north wall where Voda had entered. He also heard multiple voices coming from Voda's direction, meaning there were at least three men in here, possibly more. They needed to reach the same doors where Voda's man had retrieved the medical bag and turned on the lights. But as they moved in that direction, they'd be visible from the far side of the warehouse floor. Voda and an unknown number of his men would have a clear view of them down the long-axis center aisle. Fortunately, they could traverse most of the south wall without being seen. The long rows of boxes screened them from view.

He took Lauren past the X-ray machine along the south wall and stopped short of the central aisle. Moving his head ultra-slowly, he looked around the edge of a large cardboard box and saw four men huddled around their leader with some sort of compact assault rifles slung over their shoulders. One of them looked in the direction of the rope and pointed. They all looked.

Voda used a hand signal Nathan recognized. Voda made a peace symbol, pointed at his eyes, and gestured right and left. Voda's men fanned out in both directions and disappeared from sight.

Seconds counted. With no other option, Nathan sprinted across the main aisle.

He heard Voda's voice boom through the cavernous space.

"The south wall! Get them!"

With surprising speed, Voda pulled a handgun, took aim, and fired two shots. The staccato reports blasted through the warehouse.

Nathan shoved Lauren forward as Voda's bullets smashed into the wall behind them and zinged away. Lauren lost her footing and sprawled on the floor.

Nathan fired three suppressed shots down the center aisle, purposely aiming low. He hoped to score a skipping shot off the concrete. Nearly five hundred feet distant, Voda cringed and limped to the left, seeking cover. Shooting at Voda also served to put his adversaries on notice. They now knew they were facing an armed intruder, which would slow them down a little.

Nathan tried the first door.

Locked!

The second door was also locked.

From the sound of their footfalls, Voda's men were already halfway down the aisles. In less than ten seconds, he'd be facing opponents armed with fully automatic machine guns. Surrender wasn't an option, and he couldn't engage Voda's men without putting Lauren at risk. If this next door was locked, he'd force it open and try to ambush his pursuers.

It opened!

Nathan kicked it closed behind them. Seeing nothing to brace the door, they ran through the entry foyer toward the glass doors leading out to the parking lot.

Nathan saw it right away. The doors were chained through the handles.

This was a one-way trip. They couldn't go back.

Nathan used the SIG's suppressor like a hammer to break the tempered pane. He reared back and kicked the aluminum handle. It broke free from its frame and dangled from the chained side. He recalled a nasty memory of cutting his feet on broken glass, but figured his socks would insulate him from the worst of it. He scooped Lauren up and carried her over the shards. Clear of the glass, he set her down and fired a single shot through the door he'd kicked closed after entering the foyer. They began an all-out sprint to the southeast corner of the warehouse.

When they reached the edge of the building, he heard yelling and knew his pursuers were outside. He had to slow them down.

"Stay behind the building!"

Nathan toggled the SIG's laser, painted the dot on the leading man, and pulled the trigger. He scored a hit. The man shuddered but didn't go down. Nathan had forgotten about the body armor. Two seconds later, a staccato blast of machine-gun fire forced Nathan to duck around the corner. Dozens of slugs careened off the sidewalk and slammed into the building across the street. Exposing only his left arm around the corner, he fired two more shots in the direction of the entrance. He risked a quick look and saw all four men lying prone for cover.

They couldn't continue toward the Taurus without being in the gun sights of Voda's men, so he angled across the street, heading for the loading dock of the adjacent warehouse to the east. Lauren remained silent during their sprint, but she was breathing too fast.

"Lauren, slow your breathing. One breath every five strides."

"Okay!"

While running, Nathan turned and sent two bullets toward the spot where he'd fired the blind shots around the corner. He figured it might slow Voda's men by a few extra seconds. If they could just make it to the next warehouse, he knew his pursuers would find an empty street when they reached the corner. They wouldn't know which way he and Lauren had gone. A few more yards, and they'd be out of sight.

When they reached the safety of the warehouse, he glanced over his shoulder and didn't see the gunmen. Nathan knew Voda's men would likely split up and continue the chase.

"Lauren, I want you to reach deep and run as fast as you possibly can."

"Okay!"

She surprised him with a sudden burst of speed, and he actually fell behind for a few seconds. Rather than continue east toward the wrecking yard, Nathan took Lauren north between two smaller buildings sharing a common loading dock. Without their shoes, they'd have a difficult time managing a prolonged footrace. Also, the machine-gun fire had likely generated 911 calls. The police would be converging on the area.

From somewhere on the opposite side of the building, Nathan heard a man yell and felt confident it was Voda. Would he call off his men and cut his losses or have them continue the pursuit? Nathan believed the former but wouldn't assume that. Voda had already shown his disregard for caution at the Fashion Valley Mall and in the grocery store parking lot. In Nathan's mind, this hunt was still active.

He felt his cell vibrate and ignored it.

At the far end of the loading dock, Nathan turned east toward the auto-wrecking yard. If only he could secure a different set of wheels. The problem with auto-wrecking yards was that all the damned autos were wrecked. He shoved the useless thought aside to stay focused.

Lauren seemed okay now. Earlier, she'd been on the verge of hyperventilating. Nathan planned to circle back to the Taurus, but without knowing if Voda's men were still in pursuit, he'd have to slow his pace and check every blind corner. He turned right at the street paralleling the wrecking yard and was surprised to see there weren't any cars parked along the curb. They'd have no cover if they ran its length back to the Taurus.

He knew what to do, but it involved some risk. They'd hop the fence and use all the junked cars for cover as they worked their way south. The risk would be from four-legged sentries. The term *junkyard dog* wasn't just a colloquialism. They existed, and there could be one or more of them in there. He didn't like the idea of shooting a dog, but it was vastly preferable to engaging Voda's men in a firefight.

A cheap, tattered canvas covered the fence of the wrecking yard. Although missing in places, the canvas would offer them additional concealment. He took Lauren across the street to where several nicer-looking cars were parked just inside a small U-shaped area of the fence. He was about to help Lauren scale the barrier when he felt two pokes.

Lauren pointed to a narrow opening in a vehicle gate where its locking chain didn't keep it tightly against the post.

"Good eye," he whispered. "Think you can fit?"

She nodded, turned sideways, and easily slipped through under the chain. Nathan would never make it. His profile was twice Lauren's. With the duffel still slung over his shoulder, he used the chain as a foothold and climbed over. The chain clinked, but it wasn't too loud. A noxious odor of motor oil, old tires, and gasoline hung in the air. He took a few seconds to watch the opposite side of the street for any sign of Voda's men. All quiet.

"Watch and listen for dogs."

Lauren visibly tensed at the comment and drew her arms against her chest.

"Don't worry, all they'll do is bark and raise hell. I won't let them get close."

They needed to traverse around a thousand feet to make it back to the Taurus.

Without their shoes, they had to be careful in here. "Use your night vision to look for glass and sharp objects on the ground."

"It's turned off."

He turned their units on. "Focus about three feet in front of you."

Nathan took them deeper into the yard, where he found a north–south corridor of cars parked hood-to-hood. All of them had varying degrees of accident damage, most of them looking totaled. There wasn't more than eighteen inches between the cars, but it allowed them to make decent progress. Every so often they had to scramble over a hood to continue. Both of them were rapidly growing filthy with grime and dirt. At roughly the halfway point, Nathan put Lauren on hold and climbed into the bed of a pickup. He eased up just far enough to look over the fence but saw no one.

"You okay?"

She nodded tightly.

"We'll get through this."

Thankfully, there didn't seem to be any dogs patrolling the yard. He saw no prints or scat. Thinking about it more, Nathan realized this place didn't lend itself well to dogs. It was too confined and would tear up their paws.

They both heard it at the same time. A distant siren.

"We're going to pick up the pace a little. We need to clear the area before the police get here." There was no point in telling her a canine unit would probably be coming—in this border area of San Diego, canine units were common.

Nathan abandoned all stealth and began running between the cars whenever possible. He snuck another peek over the fence and determined they were close enough to the street where the Taurus was parked. They climbed over several rows of cars before making it to the perimeter fence. Nathan saw a new problem right away. The top of the chain-link fencing employed sharp, forklike prongs. He worked his way over to a rear-ended SUV that would offer them a good platform for hopping the fence. He saw what he needed inside the vehicle, but he wouldn't be able to open the door. The SUV was sandwiched between its neighbors.

He kept his voice low. "We need a floor mat."

Scanning the immediate area, Nathan was amazed that every window of every vehicle was intact. Incredible. He didn't want to break any glass, because that would make a substantial amount of noise. They didn't have time for this.

"Lauren, I'm going to take my shirt off. Don't freak out."

"What do you mean?"

He scaled the hood of the SUV and looked across the street. There was no sign of Voda or his men. He removed his shirt, folded it half, and placed it on top of the sharp prongs lining the top of the fence.

"What happened to you? All those scars!"

"Come on. Up and over. I'll hand you the duffel."

She straddled the fence before dropping to the other side. He lowered the duffel into her arms and climbed over. Lauren gave him the bag, and they ran in a full sprint toward the Taurus. The police siren sounded much closer. They had less than a minute.

At the Taurus, he retrieved the keys from the top of the tire and used the remote to unlock the doors. The car made a damning *chirp*, and all the parking lights flashed. He'd have to talk to Harv about disabling that feature. He tossed his shirt and duffel into the back but left his NV on. Before starting the engine, he twisted the headlight switch from AUTO to OFF.

Nathan believed the police response would be coming from the west, so he backed onto the street paralleling the wrecking yard and accelerated toward Otay Mesa Road. The buildings on his right would screen them from any approaching police units.

"Lauren, look around. Let me know if you see any cars following us."

"I don't see anything."

"Keep looking."

"Are those scars from when you were tortured?"

"Yes."

"They're horrible…"

"Stay focused. Keep looking for cars following us."

"I will."

He hadn't planned on exposing his damaged skin to Lauren, but there'd been little choice. At Otay Mesa Road, he removed his NV, turned on his headlights, and accelerated into the light traffic. Up ahead, he saw the flashing light bar of the arriving SDPD unit.

He pulled his cell and handed it to Lauren. "Check the call log."

Lauren's voice held a softer tone. "There's one from Harvey Fontana."

"Put it on speaker and play the message."

Harv's deep baritone survived the tiny speaker. "*Call me back as soon as you can.*"

CHAPTER 16

"Should I press CALL BACK?"

"That won't work." He gave the international code for Turkey, then gave her Harv's number.

Harv answered on the third ring. "What's your status?"

"You're on speaker. Lauren's with me. We're just leaving the warehouse."

"What'd you find in there?"

He turned right on Otay Mesa and relayed what they'd seen: the portable X-ray machine, the typewriter, and the Bolivian passports.

"The X-ray machine's probably related to Voda's smuggling operations," Harv said. "The passports are a tougher call, but they might be connected to the border murders case. It sounds like all the passport photos fit the descriptions of the victims. The question becomes, why would he need them? Illegals are inherently untraceable."

"Yeah, I thought of that."

"Have you made heads or tails of those hand-typed numbers?"

"Not yet."

The police cruiser they'd heard earlier screamed by.

"Is that for you?" Harv asked.

"Voda's men aren't overly concerned about using automatic weapons in public."

"What happened to avoiding more firefights until I get there?"

"I feel a lecture coming."

"If I thought it would do any good..."

"We're heading to La Jolla for a change of clothes. We're both trashed."

"Last I checked, you don't have any twelve-year-old girls' attire in your closet, unless there's something you haven't told me."

Lauren smiled at the lighthearted comment.

"Cute, Harv. We'll wash them. There's something I didn't mention when we had Holly on the three-way call. I confiscated a cell phone from the gunman at the grocery store. I haven't had a chance to look through it, but I will once we arrive at the house."

"It might be a throwaway, but it might contain texts or other frequently called numbers we can trace."

"My thoughts exactly."

"Why didn't you tell Holly about it?"

"Because her people will want it right away. And I don't want to give it up until I've had a chance to go through it myself."

"I agree with you keeping it, at least for now."

"I'm still uncomfortable not telling her about it."

"Hey, the FBI doesn't tell us everything they're doing."

"The next time we talk, I'm telling her I have it."

"Put it in your mailbox at the street after you've looked through it. They can pick it up at their convenience. Update me when you get to La Jolla. My flight doesn't leave for...three more hours."

"Have you told Candace about Lauren?"

"Yes."

"What'd she say?"

"She said you'll make a good uncle. Now, will you *please* try to avoid more gunplay?"

"For you, Harv, anything…" Nathan signed off and pocketed his cell.

"I like Harv. He sounds like a nice man."

"He's superprotective of me, overly at times. Are you okay looking at the passports?"

"I guess."

He dug them out of his pocket. "See if you recognize any of the faces."

She stared at the fourth one. "This is the girl I saw."

"Are you sure?"

"Yes."

"What's her name?"

"Margarita Gutierrez."

Nathan wondered why Voda or Marchand had kept the girl's passport. The same question applied to all the others. Why keep them unless they planned to reuse them? Voda might choose girls based on their likeness to these photos. If so, how many additional girls did Voda plan to murder? Nathan felt something else was at play. If all Voda wanted were victims to feed his twisted habit, there was an endless supply of illegals coming across the border. Holly had mentioned Voda's ties with professional coyotes. He didn't think coyotes needed passports for anyone. Not only that, but the vast majority of illegals were men seeking work. He didn't know how many families attempted to cross the border together but believed it wasn't too commonplace. Maybe Voda had some kind of human-trafficking thing going and he skimmed off the top for his own pleasure. If so, there could be dozens of young girls at risk.

"Do you recognize any of the others? Look for someone with the last name of Hernandez." It was the surname atop the typed list of numbers.

"I don't see that name. They all look so sad. Are all of these girls dead?"

"I don't know."

"I wish there weren't bad people in the world."

"Me too."

Fifteen minutes later, Lauren was close to dozing off. Her comment about bad people wasn't naive, just reflective of her age. Nathan's resentment and anger flared at Voda for terrorizing her. She was just a kid and didn't deserve any of this. Again, he marveled at her resilience. Considering everything they'd been through, she seemed remarkably poised. He gave a tiny portion of the credit to himself, knowing she'd tapped into his composed nature. Overall, he had no complaints.

Without his shirt, Nathan felt a little chilled, so he adjusted the temperature. Scrolling through his cell's log, he found Jin's number and made the call. He hadn't expected an answer and didn't get one. He let it ring ten times before giving up. If Jin's call had originated from a cellular carrier, it should've forwarded to voice mail. He pictured an isolated pay phone ringing into the night somewhere. For now, it seemed she would have to be the one to initiate any additional contact.

Thinking about Jin was a stark reminder he needed to call his father. Sooner or later, he'd have to break the news. He glanced at his watch—just after 2300, making it 0200 in Washington. There was no sense calling his dad in the middle of the night. Although the startling news of a long-lost Korean daughter warranted a wake-up call, he thought it could wait. After sixty years, what was five more hours? Besides, Nathan knew how he'd feel if the situation were reversed. He wouldn't want a midnight call from his dad telling him he had a teenage son or daughter. Good luck falling back asleep after hearing that.

He also owed Voda another call. After their initial call, which Holly had recorded, Nathan had told Voda he'd call him back. Voda…What kind of person could murder a young girl like Lauren? Not only murder her, but do unspeakable evil first. Did he feel no guilt? No shame? Was it arrogance? Smug superiority? What drove the guy? It had to be insanity, but Nathan knew not all killers were technically insane. Some of them simply enjoyed violence, enjoyed torturing and killing. He'd had this discussion with Holly several times, and although she'd tried to explain it, he just didn't get it.

Despite what he used to do for a living, he didn't consider himself a cold-blooded killer. Yes, he'd been a sniper, but he'd always believed the kills he and Harv made were both supportable and warranted. They'd saved countless innocent lives. Was the death of one evil person worth the lives of ten good people? Was that a fair trade? Perhaps it defined what snipers do: trade lives.

"What are you thinking about?"

"Huh?"

"What were you thinking about?"

"It's kinda personal, but if you must know, I was thinking about killing Voda."

"I've thought about it too. Is that bad?"

"For someone your age, I'd have to say...maybe."

They drove in silence for a while.

"Nathan, do you believe in evil?"

"You mean theologically?"

"I guess."

"Then yes, I believe in evil. There are dark forces working in direct opposition to God."

"Is it hard being religious—you know, like being a Christian?"

"I can't speak for anyone else, but to answer your question...yes."

"Was Voda going to kill me?"

"Yes."

"And do other things too?"

He took a deep breath. "Yes."

"I'm glad you saved me."

"Try not to think about it."

"It's hard not to."

"Do you know what *intangible* means?"

"No."

"It refers to something we can't understand. The circumstances that brought you into my life, and me into yours, are intangible. Think about it. If you take one thing from our pasts and change it, a completely different outcome happens. Look at tonight's events. If I had waited one extra minute to respond to your texts, I may not have seen the black SUV leaving the Exxon station. I could've arrived after you were gone and just driven home. In truth, that's nearly what happened. Think about our close call with the security patrol at the warehouse. If he'd seen us hiding in the backseat, a new set of variables would've been in play. The security guard driving that vehicle didn't know our situation. All he would've seen was a grown man and a twelve-year-old girl lying down in the backseat of a car together. Since we didn't look homeless, he would've been suspicious and might've called the police. When you broke my concentration, I was formulating a plan based on what the security guard did or didn't do. I call them if-then scenarios. If the security guard does this, then I'll do that. And each if-then event triggers another, and another. It's a chain that contains a vast number of possibilities based on the original, triggering event. After you sent me the text, a chain of events unfolded that led to us being together. In a visual way, think about the shape of a pyramid. The triggering event is the top, and the base represents all the possible outcomes. The height of the pyramid represents the length of time since the triggering event."

"So if you'd been in the bathroom when I sent the text, you may not have seen it in time to rescue me?"

"Yes, that's exactly right. I usually take my cell in there, but I don't always. I could've been at my Clairemont house, rather than La Jolla, and I never would've arrived in time. I used the word *intangible* because it describes the concept of causation or causality from a human perspective. We'll never know why things unfold the way they do. Personally, I don't think we're meant to. Do you know where I'm going with this?"

"Perfectly—you're trying to distract me from thinking about Voda."

He tried not to smile. "Everything I said is true. A complex chain of events is fluid in nature and can't be predicted with certainty. Jeff Goldblum plays a character in *Jurassic Park* who talked about this."

"I like that movie."

"Me too. Changing the subject, I have a live-in housekeeper who takes care of my La Jolla home. Her name's Angelica. She stays in a separate area of the house. We don't want to wake her, so we'll need to be kinda quiet once we arrive. I'll need to imprint you to my dogs."

"Imprint me?"

"My two giant schnauzers are personal protection dogs."

"You mean, like guard dogs?"

"Yes."

"They won't bite?"

"No. Since we'll be driving up in an unfamiliar vehicle, they won't let us get out until they identify me. They'll also bark, which reminds me—I'd better call Angelica and let her know we're coming."

"Why do you need guard dogs?"

"Let's just say I have a colorful past."

"With lots of red."

"Time to change the subject again."

"I won't tell anyone."

"Especially if you have nothing to tell."

"I thought we trusted each other."

"Lauren, it's not an issue of trust."

"Your past is supersecret? You could get in trouble if you told?"

"I'm sorry, Senator, I have no recollection of that."

"What's that mean?"

"It means you're asking me something I'm not going to answer."

"Okay, okay. I get it."

"Thank you."

CHAPTER 17

At the privacy gate to his La Jolla home, Nathan pressed a forefinger onto the security keypad and the gate rolled open. Halfway up the steep driveway, two dark forms bounded toward them and challenged their intrusion. The dogs barked and snarled, blocking their way.

Nathan rolled the window down a few inches and yelled his command word. "Cope!"

They stopped barking and cautiously approached the driver's-side door. He rolled the window down the rest of the way and extended his arm. "Good boys. I'm really glad to see you guys." Their docked tails wagging, both dogs approached and sniffed his hand.

That's when he saw it.

A tightly folded piece of paper was stapled to Grant's collar. "What the hell…"

He put the Taurus in park, grabbed his SIG, and slid out. He pulled the paper free and said, "Grant, Sherman. Search!"

The giant schnauzers ran up the driveway and disappeared from sight.

"What's going on? What's that piece of paper?"

"Shh…" He pocketed the note and crouched next to the open door. "Hand me one of the NV scopes. They're in the duffel. Backseat." A few seconds later, he had the device secured on his head with maximum gain. "Wait here. Don't make a sound."

Scanning the landscaping along his driveway, he hustled toward the house but stopped short of losing sight of the Taurus. One thing was certain: Angelica hadn't attached the note to Grant's collar. She'd never done that, and never would. He ducked behind an oleander and waited. The stapled piece of paper worried him. His dogs were well trained. Grant and Sherman would never allow anyone to approach them without issuing the command word, *cope*, and no one besides Harv or Angelica should know that word. Restraining poles wouldn't work, because the dogs were conditioned not to approach strangers for just that reason. They also wouldn't eat anything strangers offered them, so they couldn't have been drugged. Someone either knew his command word or had used a tranquilizer gun. Nothing else short of killing them would've worked. At this point, he felt relieved they weren't dead.

Nathan wanted to read the note, but right now he needed to stay alert until his dogs finished their reconnaissance. If they detected anyone inside the property, they wouldn't attack, but they'd raise hell. So far, all was silent. He'd give them a little more time before whistling them back to his position. He looked down the driveway and saw Lauren sitting in the Taurus. Not surprisingly, she had an NV scope up to her eye. He gave her a wave and she waved back. He also gave her the "hold position" hand signal. Until he knew his property was clear, he didn't want her out of the vehicle.

In the green image of his NV, he saw them appear at the top of the driveway and trot down. "Good boys."

Confident there weren't any intruders present, he returned to the Taurus.

Lauren looked concerned. "What's that folded paper?"

"I don't know yet."

"Aren't you curious?"

He was, intensely. "It can wait. Let's get situated inside first."

When they crested the driveway, Lauren said, "Oh, no way! You *do not* live here!"

"You're right. I spend most of my time at the Clairemont house."

His multistory home looked like it was carved into the hillside. Designed to take maximum advantage of the view overlooking La Jolla Shores, it featured wedge-shaped elements that were stacked atop one another in a random yet structured way. Low roof angles and extended overhangs gave it a Frank Lloyd Wright feel.

"This house is awesome. You're rich, aren't you?"

"To quote someone I know, 'you're not supposed to ask that.'"

"Are those cannons real?"

"The barrels are real. They're working replicas of Napoleon twelve-pounders used during the Civil War." Mounted on square pedestals, the two cannons held flanking positions on either side of the front door and appeared to be guarding the entrance.

He killed the engine.

Grant and Sherman stood next to the Taurus, tails wagging.

"You can get out. They won't hurt you."

"Are you sure?"

"I'm sure."

They approached her cautiously. She drew her arms against her chest.

"You haven't been around dogs much."

"We never had a dog. My mom doesn't like them."

"Why's that?"

"I don't know. She just doesn't."

"They aren't going to bite. Hold your hand out, palm up."

They both sniffed her. She smiled and petted Grant's head.

"See, you still have all your fingers."

"They seem nice."

Nathan was about to reach for his keys but realized he didn't have them. "Wait here. I need to grab my spare key. I'll be back in under a minute. Grant. Sherman. Stay." He felt confident they were alone, but kept alert anyway. He jogged across the driveway toward the garage. He stole a look over his shoulder. Lauren seemed intrigued by the dogs and was using both hands to pet them. Dogs and kids were a good match.

Once out of sight, he pulled the folded piece of paper from his pocket and held it under a solar-powered landscaping light. He felt something taped to the back and found an old, tarnished dog tag. He'd look at it later.

Nathan:

This must seem unfair, but I don't apologize for placing Lauren in your care. She's no longer safe with me. Voda's back in town, but at least if he captures me, I won't be able to tell him where she is, even under duress. I'm going after him. Either he lives or I do, but not both. As long as Voda's alive, Lauren will never be safe. I can't tell you more, but I'm paying back an old debt. I could run, but it's not the life I want for Lauren. She's a good kid with a kind heart. She deserves a structured and stable life. You have no children, so she's the last of our family's bloodline. Only one other person in the world knew about our father, and he took the secret to his grave. He was a powerful yet kind man who cared for my mother over the years and reunited us just before she died. Lauren is his child, but she has her grandfather's eyes, and yours. This dog tag is the only evidence my mother ever existed. I want you to have it. The proof of my identity is on the back. I never knew my mother. I was taken at birth as a GI baby and grew up in a North Korean orphanage. Her name was Han Choon-Hee. She loved our father, and it broke her heart never seeing him again. Our father doesn't know about me. My mother had no way to contact him. You'll have to decide if you tell him or not, but if you do, it must be kept secret. If Voda ever discovers Lauren's true identity, he'll use her to create a scandal, or worse.

The piece of paper Lauren has is somehow crucial to Voda's operations, and he'll stop at nothing to recover it. Voda thinks I have it, and I'm going to use that to bait a trap. Before Voda murdered him, Malcolm told me another young girl is in immediate danger, but I don't know more than that. Malcolm wasn't a bad man. He loved Lauren and was a good stepdad. The lure of easy money and a life of luxury sucked Malcolm into Voda's world, and before he knew it, Voda owned him. Many times he wanted out, but Voda threatened to kill me and Lauren. There's only one way out of Voda's world. After Lauren told me about the murdered girl, I told Malcolm to run and never look back, but Voda already had him. He tortured Malcolm for hours before killing him. I won't be able to help you again. As long as Voda's pursuing me, you and Lauren will be safe. Keep her with you and never let her out of your sight. She's headstrong and stubborn, so you'll have to be firm with her.

If Voda prevails, you'll have to step up. As long as Voda's alive, Lauren will be in mortal danger. I had hoped to be a part of your life someday, but that would put you and Lauren at risk from more than just Voda. True heroism is selfless. No one knows that better than you.

Han Jin-Kyong (Jin Elizabeth Marchand)

"You said you were getting the spare key."

He whipped around, aiming his SIG. Adrenaline coursed through his body like acid. "Lauren, don't ever do that again! I almost shot you. Never ever sneak up on me!"

"What does it say?"

He took a few deep breaths to quash the rush. "It's from your mom."

"Can I read it?"

He considered the ramifications but decided Lauren deserved the truth. He nodded her over, and she sat down cross-legged to read it. Nathan watched her eyes move back and forth. Her expression went blank before a single tear formed.

He put a hand on her shoulder. "Lauren, you'll see your mom again."

"You promise?"

He knew he couldn't guarantee it, but said it anyway. "Yes, I promise."

"What are we going to do?"

"We're going to find the girl who's in trouble and save her."

"But what about my mom?"

"There's not much we can do until she contacts us again. When she does, I'll tell her not to go after Voda alone and that I'll help her."

"But what if she doesn't call, like before?"

"I know how to make her call."

She sounded on the verge of panic. "How? How will you make her call?

"Patience, Lauren. A good marine knows when to lay low and wait. It may not seem like it right now, but we've got the advantage. Everything's going to be okay."

"You're just saying that to make me feel better."

"I won't deny that's partially true."

She didn't respond. He wondered when he'd find a chink in her armor. She'd been remarkably poised until now. He chalked it up to frayed nerves and fatigue.

"Your mom's going to be okay. She's a survivor."

"Do you think she was a spy too?"

"Lauren, I never said I was a spy. *You* said it. Come on, we need to wash your clothes. You can use one of my shirts. It'll fit you like a tent, but it should be okay. I think Angelica's shoes will work, but they might be a tad loose. You can wear two pairs of socks."

"Can we stay for a while? I'm really tired."

"We have to think about the girl your mom mentioned. There's someone just like you out there, and she needs our help. We have to find her."

"How? Do you think she's on one of those passports?"

"I don't know."

"We should help her."

"We will. Come on, let's go inside."

He moved some bark under the solar light and grabbed his hide-a-key. The entrance foyer to his home was no less stunning than the outside. A life-size bronze sculpture of a Civil War soldier was surrounded by a spiral staircase leading to the upper floors. The artist had captured the soldier's expression perfectly— part determination, part fear.

"Looks like Grant and Sherman like you. Want to score some points? Say the word t-r-e-a-t."

"Treat."

Two sets of ears perked up simultaneously.

He nodded toward the kitchen. "There's a jar with dog snacks on the island. When you open it, they'll sit down. Tell them they're good dogs and give them two or three each. I'm going upstairs to change. I'll bring you a shirt."

"Is that a library?"

"I've been collecting books for a long time. I'll be right back." He hustled up the stairs to his bedroom, thinking about Jin's note. Several things jumped out at him. She'd mentioned a debt and something about running. She also said she wouldn't be able to help him again. She didn't just say *help him*, she said *help him again*. As far as he knew, he hadn't received any help tonight. Maybe she was talking about the initial texts she told Lauren to send, but they didn't qualify as help, they qualified as get-your-ass-moving commands.

He wondered about her life in North Korea, what it must've been like—growing up in a DPRK orphanage as a GI baby had to be rough. He knew something of Korean society, and it wasn't tolerant of mixed-race people. People thought America was bad? American prejudice paled in comparison with Asian cultures'. A half-white child, especially from that era, would've been ridiculed and shunned. What had she said about her mom's guardian? He read the note again. *He was a powerful yet kind man who cared for my mother over the years and reunited us just before she died. Lauren is his child, but she has her grandfather's eyes, and yours.* *Powerful* could mean anything from political to military. From the sound of things, this mysterious official was significantly older than Jin if he'd cared for her mother. He hoped Lauren was the result of a consensual union.

Nathan removed the dog tag from the note and peeled the Scotch tape. His father's name, MCBRIDE, MATTHEW A., along with his serial number, was stamped deeply into its surface. They don't make dog tags like they used to, Nathan thought. A small notch occupied the nine o'clock area of its edge. Some other stamps were also present. He turned it over, found a single drop of dried blood, and shook his head. It was amazing that this tiny piece of history had survived through the years. It reminded him he needed to call his dad at some point. At least Jin had confirmed that he was unaware of having fathered her. This was going to rattle the senior senator from New Mexico to his core. Scandal would be high on his dad's concern list. Nathan regretted the thought, knowing it was unkind and shallow. Yes, his father held an important political position, and yes, he'd be concerned about a scandal, but this would tear him up emotionally. Learning about a long-lost daughter after nearly sixty years was going to cause emotional pain. Jin had said her mom loved his dad. Nathan wondered if that love had gone both directions—and maybe still did. Harv was right: he needed to think about his mom. This wouldn't be easy for her.

Nathan emptied his pockets onto the bed. The piece of paper from the warehouse loomed large. So did the gunman's cell phone from the grocery store attack. He unfolded the paper from

Marchand's office and looked at the numbers again. It was obviously a list of some sort, but for what? Probably drugs. He turned on the nightstand light and used his iPhone to take pictures of Jin's handwritten note and both sides of the dog tag. He texted all three images to Harv's cell.

He changed into a fresh set of black 5.11 Tactical clothes, grabbed a spare shirt for Lauren, and reloaded his pockets with everything from the bed.

Downstairs, he found her in the library, holding a book.

"This is an old book."

He winced, thinking about her dirty fingers.

As if reading his mind, she said. "I washed my hands. I've read this."

"It's a classic, and it's also a first edition, so don't drop it."

"What's that mean?"

"It means you're holding the very first printing ever made of that book."

"Seriously?"

"Harv gave it to me for my fortieth birthday."

She smiled. "That must've been a *long* time ago."

"Hey, watch it. Can you name any other titles from the author?"

"*Dr. Jekyll and Mr. Hyde.*"

"Well, I see your education is well rounded. I'm impressed." He returned *Treasure Island* to its shelf. "Something's got me curious, though. When I asked you what the Big Dipper was part of, you knew the answer. I don't think many twelve-year-olds would know about Ursa Major. Care to enlighten me?"

"My mom taught me the constellations. Other stuff too."

"Like directional vectors? Is that how you understood them so well?"

"Uh-huh."

"What about basic survival skills? Would you be able to make a fire from scratch out in the wild?"

ANDREW PETERSON

"Depends on if there's any dry material suitable for fraying."

Nathan's eyes narrowed. "Let me guess: you've got a dragon tattoo on your back."

She rolled her eyes. Although the expression was designed to convey, *Give me a break*, he found it charming—one of several traits he liked about her.

He handed her the shirt. "You can change in the bathroom near the laundry room. It's that way, through the kitchen. Throw your clothes into the washer and use the quick-wash setting. The house has soft water, so you don't need much detergent. Holler if you need help getting it going. You'll see a pair of tennis shoes. They're Angelica's. Go ahead and try them on."

"I'm worried about my mom."

"You deserve the truth—that's why I let you read the note. Your mom is going against a dangerous and cunning man. I'm planning to help her, and you can help me by staying calm. The calmer we are, the stronger we are. We'll get through this. Together."

She gave him a hug. "I'm glad you're my uncle."

For the second time tonight, he found himself hugging a kid. "Are you hungry?"

"Maybe a little. Where does Angelica live?"

He pointed to a door on the far side of the library. "It's like a separate home, but it's connected by a glass hallway."

"She's like a maid that lives here?"

"Not at all. I think of her as my adopted mom. Her family was killed in Nicaragua during the civil war."

"That's terrible."

"Yeah, war tends to do that."

After Lauren changed into his shirt, he could see from her body language she felt a little insecure. She must be at that age when kids become self-conscious about their appearance. Maybe it happened at an earlier stage, probably did, but Nathan had no experience with it. He'd just act like she looked perfectly normal, despite what a good-looking kid she actually was.

"Help yourself to something to eat. Grab anything you like."

"Okay, but I'll make it for both of us."

"Sounds good." He turned her loose in the kitchen and settled onto the living room sofa. Since he didn't know if the gunman from the grocery store was in police custody, he handled the battered cell phone carefully, trying to avoid smearing any potential prints. It was a fairly cheap model that didn't look like it had smartphone capabilities. He found the call logs and scrolled through them. One number was used frequently—could be Voda's cell. On the voice mail screen, he saw one unplayed message, from 8:47 p.m. He tapped the button, hoping he wouldn't need a password—most phones kept it in their memory. He'd know soon enough.

In Spanish, Voda's voice came out of the tiny speaker. Nathan turned the volume down. *"I want both of them alive."*

Nathan thought this message must've been just before the grocery store shoot-out. He tapped a message with a time stamp of 8:21 p.m.

"Marcus is dead. Antonio and I are both wounded. Call me right away."

One final message was from 7:40 p.m.

"I have the girl. I'll be there in thirty minutes."

Starting with Lauren's kidnapping, the voice mails spanned just under an hour. Nathan believed the second message came from Voda, right after the attempted drive-by shooting on Friars Road. Antonio and Marcus were likely the two gunmen from the wreck who'd arrived in the black sedan. Nathan had been forced to shoot below the belt because of their ballistic vests. Marcus had died either from Nathan's bullets or from Voda's. Nathan believed the latter. Antonio was likely sitting in the back of the sedan when Voda's arm got jarred on Friars Road.

Nathan used the dictation app on his iPhone to record all three messages and inserted the time of each message with his own voice. Next, he found the text messaging screen and saw an entire string of texts to the phone number he'd seen most frequently in the call logs. Almost certainly, this was Voda's cell number. He went into the kitchen.

"It's not ready yet," Lauren said.

"I'm just getting a pad and pen."

Nathan returned to the living room and wrote the most frequently used number on the notepad. He used his iPhone to take photos of all the remaining numbers stored in the call log. He checked the camera roll of his phone, making sure the phone numbers he'd just photographed could be read. He repeated the same procedure on the text threads. It took about twenty-five photos to capture everything. Not surprisingly, there weren't any contacts stored in the phone. Based on the short call log and text string, Nathan felt reasonably confident Voda's man had been careful to delete the earlier entries, but it hadn't been done within the last hour before he'd lost the phone. He went back and reread the texts, looking for anything specific, and found a potential candidate. In the middle of a string, Nathan zeroed in on:

make sure s delivers the opus xas tonight

Nathan didn't know what an "opus xas" was, but it looked promising. The text had a time stamp of 7:44 p.m., four minutes after the voice mail message from Voda that he had Lauren. He went into the kitchen again and asked Lauren if Voda had been texting after he picked her up. Lauren said he had been, until he'd caught her doing the same. When Nathan didn't leave the kitchen, she put her hands on her hips.

Nathan smiled and returned to the living room, where he opened a web browser on his phone and typed "opus xas" into the search box. None of the listings looked encouraging. The first reference was to some kind of bistro—a bar and grill in Texas. The next five listings looked equally useless. Maybe *opus xa* was singular and the *s* made it plural. Nathan removed the *s*, searched again, and was rewarded with new listings.

Opus X As were premium cigars made by Arturo Fuente. They were also expensive and rare. From what Nathan initially found, they ranged in price from $70 to $100 per stick. He checked a few listings and saw they were out of stock. Cigars like these probably had to be special-ordered. Many online cigar retailers claimed they were the most coveted cigars in the world. This definitely sounded like a viable lead, especially given that Voda's man in Marchand's warehouse had been smoking a cigar. Nathan hadn't known what brand, but it had been cigar smoke, not cigarette.

Other than this Opus reference and Voda's cell number, the phone didn't appear to have much usable info, but he knew the FBI would be able to dissect it more thoroughly. He'd research the Opus cigar business more deeply, but right now he wanted to concentrate on the paper from Marchand's office. He unfolded it and placed it on the coffee table.

Hernandez:

1.53	90	50	(4871)
1.64	95	60	
1.85	90	55	(37)
2.07	95	70	(116)
2.14	95	70	
2.39	95	80	
2.42	90	80	(4702)
2.78	85	85	
2.96	90	110	(34)
3.02	95	150	(32)

Staring at the columns of numbers, he tried to see a pattern, but nothing jumped out. The parenthetical column seemed the most random. Three of its numbers were in the thirties, two were close to five thousand, but the third number down, 116, didn't seem to have anything in common with the others. Since none of the Bolivian passports had the name Hernandez on it, the list became even more cryptic. There were no dollar signs, but that didn't mean anything.

It sounded like Lauren was working on a gourmet meal. Whatever the case, she seemed to know her way around a kitchen. He heard drawers opening and closing and a few pots and pans clanking. It could've been louder, though—she was making an effort to minimize the noise.

He closed his eyes and leaned back. A little sleep wouldn't hurt, but he couldn't dismiss the image of another girl being in danger...

CHAPTER 18

Wearing a white nightgown, a young girl sits on a bed, her hands balled into fists. Her crying is soft but sounds forced. A mass of black hair hides her face. Without warning, she whips her head, revealing a beautiful but intense expression—like an angel on a mission. Her hair waves as if blown by an invisible source. He looks more closely. One eye is blue, the other is gone—its empty socket weeps black fluid. She stands and takes a step forward, bringing a pale hand up, pointing at him...

"To the dryer."

Nathan awoke to Lauren's startled face.

"Are you okay?"

He whipped his head around, orienting himself. "How long?"

She finished his question. "Were you asleep?"

He nodded.

"About ten minutes. You were having a nightmare, weren't you?"

He nodded again. "Not too bad, though. Lauren, in the future, it's best to wake me from a distance, okay? Just yell my name, but don't ever touch me while I'm sleeping."

She sounded a little irritated. "Well, okay…I said I made some mac and cheese for us and moved my clothes to the dryer."

The girl on the bed still haunting him, Nathan sat up and ran a hand over his face. "You made mac and cheese from scratch?"

"It's easy. Come on."

To his surprise, she had two place settings arranged on the dining room table. "You keep this up, and Angelica might be out of a job."

"I didn't add a lot of butter. It's not good for your arteries."

"Amen to that."

"I had to use jack. You didn't have any cheddar."

He tried a bite. "This is really good. Thank you for making it."

"You're welcome."

"Tell me something. Why did you pick *Treasure Island*? There are several thousand books in there. Why that one?"

"I'm not sure. I guess I was thinking about my ring."

"What about it?"

"I don't know. I guess it's kinda like pirate treasure, only modern."

"Treasure…"

Nathan got up from the table and hurried into the living room.

"What's wrong?"

He looked at the typed list of numbers, focusing on the fourth column, but didn't see what he was after. "When you said *treasure*, I thought about a map. I thought there might be coordinates, but the numbers don't work."

"Why don't the numbers work?" she asked.

"Because GPS coordinates don't look like this."

"What are they supposed to look like?"

"Latitude and longitude numbers are followed by minutes and seconds, but these numbers don't work and there're no decimals for the seconds."

Lauren seemed confused, but he didn't feel like explaining it further.

"San Diego has a latitude of thirty-two degrees," he said slowly. "That's one of the numbers, but its longitude is one-seventeen west." He smiled when he saw it. "They're reversed."

"What?"

The answer had been staring at him the entire time. Using the grocery pad, he wrote the oddball column of numbers in reverse. Starting with 32, he ended with 4871.

32 34 4702
116 37 4871

He inserted the symbols for degrees, minutes, and seconds and then added decimals to 4701 and 4871 and found himself looking at a beautiful set of GPS coordinates.

32° 34' 47.02"
116° 37' 48.71"

"The numbers work now?"

"Yes. San Diego's at thirty-two degrees latitude, but it's one-seventeen west longitude, so these coordinates are east of us. Not too far, though. Grab your plate and follow me." He took her into his study, turned on the computer, and opened the Google Earth program. Zooming in on the San Diego area, he moved the mouse east. He watched the longitude side of the GPS coordinates increase until it reached 116 west, then kept going until it read thirty-seven minutes.

"How do you know where to go?"

"See those numbers at the bottom of the screen? See how they change as I move the mouse?"

"Uh-huh."

"All I have to do is move the mouse until both the latitude and longitude numbers match the numbers on the paper. If you move off the satellite image, you can drag it using the mouse, like this."

He showed her how to scroll across the picture and use the directional and angle features in the upper-right corner. "To zoom in or out, use the wheel on the mouse."

"This is supercool. Can you spy on people?"

"It's not a live feed. You're looking at an older compilation of pieced-together photos."

"Can I do it?"

He leaned over her shoulder after she sat down. "Keep going south until you see the number next to thirty-two switch to thirty-four. Then move east until the longitude numbers start to align." He ate a few more bites.

She was a quick study, but he had to remind her to zoom with the mouse wheel. Within thirty seconds, she had the coordinates located.

"They don't match perfectly."

"Don't worry about that. I have a GPS reader that's accurate to under one meter."

"What is this building?"

"Judging from the size and shape, I'm guessing it's a motel. Only one way to find out. You up for a little road trip to Tecate?"

"I'm not going like this."

"Do you know how to use MapQuest? I need to check the dryer."

"Not really."

"Type 'mapquest dot com' in the address bar. Hit 'get directions,' then type in 'La Jolla, California,' in the first box and 'Tecate, California,' in the second box. I'll be right back."

He opened the dryer and felt Lauren's pants. They were still damp, so he closed the door, added five minutes to the timer, and returned to his office.

"It says it takes an hour and five minutes."

"Good job. We'll make it there a little faster than that."

"Can I drive?"

He half laughed but realized she was serious.

"I have no doubt you could do it, but your presence behind the wheel would be difficult to explain to a CHP officer. 'I'm sorry, Officer, but my daughter wanted to drive' isn't going to be an adequate explanation."

She looked disappointed.

"Trust me."

"Can you really get my mom to call?"

"With absolute certainty? No."

"What are you going to do?"

"I don't want you worrying about that right now. We'll be facing a big set of unknowns in Tecate. I want you to think about everything I've taught you tonight."

"Like being superquiet."

"Yes. I may ask you to stay in the car when we get there. If I do, don't argue about it, okay?"

"I won't. If you were going to ditch me, you would've done it already."

"That's right. So there's no need to worry about that anymore. Your mom wants us to stay together. And thanks for making the chow."

"I thought you liked it."

"*Chow* isn't a derogatory term."

"Oh, it made me think of dog-food ads on TV."

"Lauren, honestly, it was the best mac and cheese I've ever had."

She crossed her arms and smiled.

"Did you wash a towel? I saw one in the dryer."

"If you put a dry towel in with a small load, it speeds up the drying process."

"I didn't know that trick, but it makes perfect sense."

They ate the rest in silence. He liked that about her—she didn't fill their conversational voids with small talk.

Nathan nodded toward the laundry room. "Why don't you try on Angelica's shoes and check on your clothes. I'll take care of the dishes."

Before leaving the house, Nathan checked the duffel for the GPS reader and found it next to the handheld thermal imager. He'd show Lauren how to use them during the drive to Tecate. He hoped she'd get some sleep. Sooner or later she'd hit a wall, especially after being physically drained from multiple adrenaline rushes. They'd run for their lives more than once, and the evening was far from over. Nathan didn't like retreating from danger—he'd prefer to face threats head-on—but Lauren's presence forced a change in tactics.

He thought about leaving her with Angelica, but based on everything he'd learned about Lauren's personality, she'd never accept it and would probably leave, even if it meant being alone on foot with no place to go. She might even walk down to her La Jolla Shores home—right into Voda's hands. Besides, Jin had made it clear she didn't want Lauren out of his sight.

Fully dressed, Lauren walked into the living room wearing Angelica's shoes. "They're a little loose, but I don't think they'll come off."

"Are you sure?"

She nodded.

"I need to make another stop at First Security to pick something up. You can wait in the car. It shouldn't take more than two minutes once we get there."

"Okay."

"I meant to tell you this earlier, but you did a good job at your stepdad's warehouse. You handled yourself well, didn't panic."

"I was really scared."

"You did fine."

"It's weird—I thought about myself like you said. You know, like, having a tough girl inside me?"

"Works, doesn't it?"

"Sort of. I think it takes some practice."

"That's one thing we'll try *not* to practice too much."

CHAPTER 19

Nathan made the detour to First Security brief. Figuring it wouldn't hurt for Lauren to be similarly protected, he grabbed a smaller ballistic vest. She asked about the big case he placed in the backseat. He told her it was for surveillance once they arrived in Tecate.

When he thought back to the GPS coordinates, the way they were listed on the piece of paper wasn't initially obvious, but they also weren't concealed all that well. Nathan was reasonably sure the reverse order was a simple stopgap measure to disguise the coordinates from prying eyes, nothing more. Guys like Voda often didn't trust their own people. Betrayal from within was always a concern.

Nathan had no idea what awaited them in Tecate. The columns of numbers could mean anything. But what if the numbers weren't columns? What if they were rows? Thinking about them as line items made more sense. If that were the case, he could reasonably expect to find ten objects at the coordinates. Ten objects covered a lot of ground. They could be anything from trash bags full of illegal drugs to who knows what. Depending on what Nathan found, he might be able to use it as leverage against Voda.

He also couldn't dismiss the idea that the GPS numbers could already be disguised with a mathematical cipher. They could be chasing a proverbial wild goose and find nothing at all. Even though Google Earth pointed them toward their current destination, he knew accuracy could be an issue. The coordinates on the paper might take them to a completely different destination than Google Earth indicated. He should've confirmed that before leaving the house.

"Lauren, do you know how to access the Internet on an iPhone?"

"Well, yeah."

"Okay, I want you to check something for me." He handed her his phone. Type 'Wikipedia dot org'—that's o-r-g—into the address bar." He had to spell Wikipedia for her. "Then type 'Tecate, California,' into the Wikipedia search box." He also gave her Tecate's spelling.

"Okay...hang on. It's loading."

"Let me know if you see any GPS coordinates. There should be a little map."

"It's still loading. Okay, it shows a picture...I see the map."

"Does it list coordinates?"

"Yes."

He handed her the pad. "Do the degrees and minutes match?"

"Yes, but the last numbers aren't the same."

"Don't worry about that." At least this confirmed they were going to Tecate's general locale. "Now, open a new Safari page and type this into the search box: 'Google Earth a-c-c.' You should get a dropdown line that says 'Google Earth accuracy.' Start there and check out a few entries. Let me know what you find."

"Okay."

That ought to keep her busy for a few minutes. He wanted to know the general margin of error. He glanced in her direction and saw she had the phone about twelve inches from her face. Give it thirty years, he thought, and she'll be holding it at arm's length.

If the general location was a motel, as Google Earth indicated, the coordinates on the paper would most likely lead to a specific room. It made sense. Nathan tapped his knowledge of GPS. At the equator, one second of longitude was just over one hundred feet in length, so, at their current latitude of thirty-two minutes, one second of longitude ought to be around sixty feet, which meant one-hundredth of a second would be just over half a foot. Having coordinates showing hundredths of a second should take them to a specific motel-room door. He wouldn't know with certainty until they arrived. A drive by the motel would tell him if he had the right building, but he'd need to determine the precise coordinates on foot.

He had to consider the strong possibility that the room was already under surveillance by either good guys or bad guys—or possibly even both. If he was wrong about the piece of paper being the only copy, all bets were off. There could be a small army of Voda's thugs waiting to ambush him, or a squad of federal agents waiting to intercept him.

"Okay, it says accuracy can vary a lot, depending on a bunch of stuff."

"I figured as much."

"It can be really accurate down to one meter, or it could be way off by, like, a hundred meters or more."

"Good work."

"Your phone's vibrating. It's Harvey Fontana." She handed it to him.

"Harv."

"I'm boarding a nonstop flight in thirty minutes. It's the fastest way to get there." Harv's tone lightened. "I booked a business-class seat. If I'm going to be miserable, I may as well be miserable in style."

"Well said."

"What's your status?"

"We're on our way to Tecate. The piece of paper Lauren had contained GPS coordinates."

"I saw them too. That's why I'm calling."

He told Harv about the note from Jin attached to Grant's collar.

"Do I need to say it?"

"We'll be careful, but this definitely confirms your suspicion about Jin. She knows where I live. Not only that, she managed to staple a note to Grant's collar."

"That's no easy trick without knowing the stand-down command. You do practice with your dogs in the yard. It's possible she got it that way."

"That's the most reasonable explanation."

"Are we on speaker?" Harv asked.

"No."

"We have to be concerned about something else as well. She said she's going after Voda. If he bags her, she could give us up under torture."

"Yeah, I thought of that, but there's nothing we can do about it right now."

"She hasn't called you back?"

"No."

"Then he might already have her."

"You're raining on my parade again."

"What are friends for? How's Lauren doing? Has she been asking about her mom?"

"Not too much, which is a little surprising."

"What do you think?"

He glanced at Lauren and winked. "Lauren said her mom disappears for days at a time, so our current situation isn't especially alarming to her."

"It should be alarming to *you*. I also feel compelled to remind you you're heading to a Mexican border town in the middle of the night with no backup, and Holly said Voda has known ties with coyotes."

"Why doesn't that make me feel good?"

"Nate, this is serious. You need me for this operation."

"There is no operation. I'm just gonna have a look around."

"Like you did at the warehouse? I seem to recall you mentioning being shot at. *Again*."

"I appreciate your concern."

"I'm seriously considering pulling executive override."

"Harv, don't do that." Executive override was a blood oath between them. If either of them ever felt what they were doing was downright reckless, he could use executive override to call things off. To date, neither of them had ever invoked it.

"Give me a good reason."

"Every minute Voda's loose, innocent lives are at stake. He might already have his next victim."

"Then again, he might not."

"Suppose it was Lucas or Dillon?"

"I can't believe you just said that."

He didn't respond. Didn't need to. Harv was a father and knew the score.

"Dammit, Nate."

"I promise, no unnecessary risks."

"If you get your ass killed, I'm going to kill you again in heaven."

"I stopped by the office and grabbed a vest, if that makes you feel better."

"It doesn't. What's your ETA to Tecate?"

"About an hour."

"At least I have the exact coordinates of where you're going. I'll be able to tell the authorities where to collect your bodies."

"You sure know how to boost a guy's confidence."

"Use the radios. Lauren can keep an eye on your back."

"I was planning to. Thanks for not pulling EO. I would've honored it."

"Don't make me regret this decision for the rest of my life. I expect to hear your cheerful voice again right after you *look* around at the motel. No firefights."

Nathan signed off and tucked his phone away.

"He really cares about you," Lauren said.

"He cares about both of us."

"I don't have any friends like that."

"Some friendships take a lifetime to develop. Others can happen in a few hours." He smiled. "Try to get some sleep."

An hour later, they arrived on the outskirts of Tecate. Harv was right. Without bona fide backup, reconnoitering the motel was dangerous. If he didn't see any bad guys before they saw him, the situation could get ugly in a big hurry. He'd have to play this cat-and-mouse game carefully. If anything happened to him, Lauren's fate would fall into someone else's hands—not acceptable. Until he had a better idea of what was going on, he'd move cautiously at the motel and thoroughly assess the situation before taking any action.

But first things first. He needed to determine where the GPS coordinates led. If Holly's people had also discovered the coordinates, this might be over already. There could be FBI or ICE agents in play, which added a layer of complexity and brought the potential for friendly fire into the equation. A quick call to Holly could remove that variable, but it would also tip his hand. He decided to call *after* conducting a reconnaissance.

He didn't know a lot about coyotes but knew they weren't model citizens. The very nature of what they did made them human traffickers, and their core motivation was the pursuit of money. Human rights meant nothing to them, and that made them fair game in Nathan's eyes. Anyone willing to sell human beings or aid in that practice was morally bankrupt at best, downright evil at worst.

"Lauren?"

She blinked a couple of times.

"We're coming into Tecate. I need to go over some stuff with you."

"How long was I asleep?"

"About forty-five minutes. I'm going to show you how to work the radio and the handheld thermal imager. They're both easy to use. I'll handle the GPS reader. According to Google Earth, our coordinates should be on the left side of the road."

Before driving into Tecate, Nathan pulled to the shoulder. The city lights on the south side of the border were clearly defined by a straight line—the international boundary. He gave Lauren a quick lesson with the radio and HHTI. "To talk, all you do is press this button. Press it to talk, then let go. Don't say anything unless you see something I should know about. If I say something to you but don't ask a question, press the button and let go. I'll hear a click, which means you heard me. It's called an acknowledgment click."

"What am I looking for?"

"We'll go over that in a little bit."

Nathan held the GPS reader in his left hand and continued south along the road. He slowed to a crawl at the motel and confirmed that this was the location. It was an L-shaped single-story building with a small office on the corner near the road. The neon sign indicated VACANCY. He kept going south, turned onto a side street, and made a U-turn. No traffic was present—a double-edged sword. He liked the lack of activity, but if anyone were watching the motel, he couldn't cruise past more than twice without raising suspicion. He scanned for a place to park where Lauren would have a clear view of the motel's parking lot. A good tactical location looked to be across the street on a vacant lot. He could park among several unconnected semi trailers. It also allowed for a quick exit, should it become necessary.

He turned left and went far enough down a side street to make a U-turn without being seen from the motel. He turned off the lights, crept into the vacant lot to avoid raising dust, and killed the engine. This was a good spot, but it had drawbacks. The disconnected trailers offered them visual cover laterally but also prevented them from seeing laterally. They had a clear view forward and behind, but not sideways. Nathan decided it was a good trade-off.

He reached into the backseat and grabbed the case. Inside was a bowl-shaped device with a handle, similar to a radar gun.

"What is that?"

"Parabolic microphone for eavesdropping. It reflects and focuses sound waves from very narrow angles. At this distance, I can isolate a single motel window or door. If anyone's inside talking, I should be able to hear them, but I need to know which room. The only way to do that is on foot with the coordinate reader. I need you to sit tight while I conduct a foot reconnaissance. We'll be able to communicate using the radios, but the same rule applies as it did at the warehouse. Don't talk to me unless you see a vehicle or person approach the motel. Keep the doors locked. I'm leaving the key in the ignition. If someone sees you or approaches the car, let me know by radio. If that doesn't work, turn the key and honk the horn. I'll be here in no time."

"I don't want to be alone."

"I know it's hard, but try to relax."

"If I go with you, we'll look like a father and daughter again. My mom said you shouldn't let me out of your sight."

"Lauren, we had this discussion."

She crossed her arms and didn't respond. He knew this was tough on her, but he wanted to do foot reconnaissance alone.

"I need to put on my ballistic vest and wire the radio."

He sensed an emotional withdrawal from her and hoped it wouldn't become a major problem. Since he'd first rescued her from Voda, they'd been together constantly. This would be their first separation, and she'd just have to deal with it. Before donning the vest, he clipped the radio to his belt and connected the earpiece and transmit mike wires. He covered everything with a black sweatshirt and attached the small microphone to the collar.

He turned their radios on and locked the channel settings so Lauren couldn't inadvertently change frequencies.

"Are you okay?"

She looked straight ahead.

"Lauren, I need you focused and alert. Stop thinking whatever you're thinking. We're a team and I need your help. I'll tell you about one of my missions. I promise."

"You're just saying that."

"Have I lied to you tonight?"

"I guess not."

"I need you to watch my back while I'm out there. Let's do a radio check."

He reached down to his hip and pressed the transmit button. "Test." He heard his voice through Lauren's radio. "Okay, give me a *test* back."

She brought the radio up. "*Test.*"

He adjusted the volume. "One more, please."

"*Test.*"

"You're five by five. Loud and clear. Take turns using the NV and TI. Remember to keep both of them pressed against your face so there's no bleed light. Turn both their gains down so your eyes will adjust faster when you're not using them. This won't take long. I'll be right back."

CHAPTER 20

With its suppressor attached, Nathan's SIG wouldn't fit into his front pocket, so he tucked it into his waist and used the sweatshirt to cover it.

He didn't like leaving Lauren behind, but this wasn't like the warehouse operation. He figured he could sprint back to the Taurus in under fifteen seconds from anywhere across the street. At Marchand's warehouse, it would've taken several minutes to return to the car.

He slid out, closed the door with gradual pressure to minimize the sound, and pressed the transmit button. "Lock the doors." He heard his radio click just before the *clunk* of the doors being locked. "You won't see me for about thirty seconds. I'm going to cross the street north of our position. Keep an eye out for anyone on foot. I'll see a vehicle if it enters the motel's parking lot, so you don't need to report that." He received another click. Again, she impressed him. He'd expected her to say something. "You're doing great, Lauren. Take a look with the NV and let me know if anyone's sitting in any of the cars. Do you see anyone?"

A soft *no* came through his ear speaker.

"Turn on the TI and tell me how many of the cars have warm signatures." He didn't need the info but knew it would keep her involved.

"*Four of them.*"

"Stay on the TI. I'll be crossing the street in fifteen seconds. Are we still clear? Is anyone on foot in the parking lot?"

"*No.*"

Nathan angled toward the motel and glanced to his right where the Taurus was parked. He couldn't see it yet. "Give me two clicks when you have me in sight."

With his head slightly bowed, Nathan held the coordinate reader like a cell phone and pretended to be texting while walking. He heard two clicks.

"Copy. I'm going to traverse the sidewalk along the rooms. I'll stop and act like I'm sneezing at the coordinates." He received another click. Lauren was coming through like a champ. She was no substitute for an experienced operations officer like Harv, but she provided a layer of security he wouldn't otherwise have.

This place looked like a thousand other fleabags. Cheap lighting fixtures covered with cobwebs flanked every door, half of them dark. He kept the cell phone ruse going as he advanced along the gauntlet of doors. From many of the rooms, a bluish glow from televisions bled through gaps in the curtains. A few windows were open. To his right, a fenced pool looked like it hadn't been used in years. He continued to the inside corner of the motel and turned south. The GPS coordinates continued to align. Each step altered the longitude readout by several hundredths of a second.

A little farther...

Here.

Room 127.

He went two steps past the door, turned away from the building, and pretended to sneeze. If anyone was staking out this room, he felt confident he hadn't given himself away. He saw another opportunity to further enhance his act. At the south end of the motel, he stopped at a vending machine and reached for his wallet. Acting frustrated, he patted down his other pockets, before issuing a dismissive wave at the machine. With more purpose, he walked back the way he'd come.

Barely moving his lips, he said, "Lauren, do you copy?"

"*I'm here.*"

"I'm on my way back. ETA one minute."

"*Okay.*"

Her first slip-up. She should've only clicked, but he wouldn't hold it against her. She was probably confused by his vending-machine ploy. She had to be wondering why he'd done it.

At the motel's office, he turned north and went fifty yards before crossing the street. He circled around the vacant lot and approached the Taurus from behind. "I'll be there in ten seconds. Unlock the doors." Good—she clicked the radio without responding. Had she said something, he'd need to remind her about acknowledgment clicks only.

Getting in the sedan, he said, "That wasn't so bad, was it?"

"You faked wanting a soda, right?"

"Good call."

"In case anyone's watching."

"Right again. Now that we know which room it is, we're going to use the parabolic mike. I didn't hear anyone, but I'm pretty sure the TV's on in there." He grabbed the NV scope. Sure enough, a telltale glow leaked from the edges of the curtains.

"Sit tight. I need a minute to set up the directional mike." He retrieved the case from the backseat and removed the dish and its hardware from their foam protection. He assembled the parabolic mike, connected the wires and power source, and rolled his window down. Before putting on the headphones, he turned the volume to zero. Even though the Taurus was well concealed between two semi trailers, Nathan opted to forgo setting up the tripod to mount the dish. Using it inside the Taurus wasn't ideal, but he preferred to remain concealed. It wouldn't be a problem—the parabolic mike's twenty-inch diameter would allow him to hold it just inside the driver's-side window and steady it against the jamb. He felt a tap from Lauren and took off the headphones.

"How do you aim it?"

"You amaze me, Lauren. That's an intelligent question. See this thing attached to the microphone's boom inside the dish? Harv installed it for night use. It's a low-power ultraviolet laser, nearly invisible to the naked eye, but the NV can see it easily. By using the mike in tandem with the NV, I can see exactly where it's pointing."

"You have the coolest stuff. Can I listen?"

"Yes, but in a minute. Stay on the TI and keep looking for any movement. Besides," he said under his breath, "there could be age-inappropriate sounds inside that room."

"Do you mean—"

"Don't ask."

"That's *totally gross*."

"Just stay on the TI and look for movement." After putting on the headphones, he turned the volume up and pointed the dish low to pick up the laser's dot in the NV. He slowly tilted the dish up until the bright dot hit the motel's wall. Adjusting the dish slightly to the right, he painted the laser on room 127's door. The world outside came to life. The low drone of the TV sounded perfectly clear, but for an instant, he thought he heard something else. "Lauren, turn up the volume. The knob is on the control unit next to me. Turn it clockwise until it stops."

The TV grew louder. There it was again, muffled but unmistakable. A young woman or girl was crying. He heard a toilet flush and then water running in a sink.

"What do you hear?"

"Shh…" The weeping got louder for a few seconds, then went silent. "Someone's crying."

"Crying?"

He kept the dish pointed at the door but heard only the television.

He thought about his options. They boiled down to two. One, do nothing and observe the room for an undetermined amount of time, or two, find out who was in there. He hadn't felt the pressure of time until now. There was a desperate and forlorn sound to the girl's crying from either physical or emotional pain. Nathan didn't favor sitting on his hands while someone suffered, but gaining entry into that room involved severe risk. He needed more information. An idea formed.

"Lauren, grab my cell and call 411. When the automated voice asks for a city, say Tecate, California. Wait for the operator and then ask for the number of the Tecate Palms Inn. The operator will connect you. When the manager answers, tell him you're in room 126 and the TV's too loud in 127. You got that?"

"Yes."

Nathan kept the dish pointed at the door while Lauren made the call. He moved it to the motel's office and painted the laser on a window.

"It's asking if I want a text of the number."

"Choose yes."

"Okay, it's ringing."

"I can hear it in there."

In his headphones, Nathan heard a man with a Hispanic accent say, *"Tecate Palms."*

Lauren relayed the phony noise complaint.

The man said, *"I'll take care of it."*

"He hung up," Lauren said.

Nathan reacquired the door to 127 and heard the phone ring inside. An unfriendly male voice answered in Spanish, *"Bueno."*

He couldn't hear the manager but knew Lauren's complaint was relayed.

"My television isn't loud."

He waited through several seconds of silence.

"*I said it's not loud, you dumbass!*"

Nathan heard the phone slam into its cradle with a bang.

A second voice, also in Spanish, asked, "*Who was it?*"

"*The manager. He said our television's too loud.*"

"*It's not loud.*"

"*No kidding! That's what I told him.*"

Nathan heard pounding on the wall. Then the man who had answered the phone yelled, "*It's not us, you dumbasses!*"

Nathan now knew there were at least two men in the room, plus one female in distress who sounded young. Not a good combo, especially given the rude and dismissive attitude of the man who had answered the phone. How many people would pound on a wall and curse the occupants on the other side after a request for quiet? The guy didn't even care if he had the right wall. Their accents were local, Tijuana or Mexicali. They clearly weren't Spaniards from Europe. Voda and his men spoke quite differently, so if these guys weren't Voda's, who were they? Coyotes. It fit. Holly had said Voda had ties to coyotes, and Nathan believed coyotes tended to be criminal thugs who'd act just like the man in the motel room. Coyotes were also armed, often heavily. Jin's note referred to another young girl in danger. The pieces fit, but not with absolute certainty. Nathan weighed the evidence.

The coordinates led to this exact room.

Jin had said there was a girl in danger.

He heard a young girl crying in there.

And the occupants of that room sounded rude and arrogant.

What if the two men in the room were undercover federal agents? There could be a stakeout going. If that were true, Nathan knew any action he took could have catastrophic results. Months, if not years, of surveillance and planning could go down the drain. He thought about Lauren's description of the dead girl in her stepdad's warehouse—a perfect match to the border murders. He couldn't live with himself if he didn't do something and another dead girl turned up in the mountains. He doubted federal agents randomly pounded walls and cursed the occupants on the other side. But if they *were* feds, the entire motel could be under surveillance and his trip to the vending machine and back had just been recorded. Not only that, but the location of their Taurus might now be known and it too might be under surveillance. If so, he should've been intercepted by now. His use of the parabolic mike on the hotel room would raise red flags, and any potential stakeout team would be wondering who he was and why he was here. All they'd know was that he wasn't part of the stakeout team, and if he wasn't part of the team, he'd be considered a wild card who could potentially wreck everything.

"What are you thinking about?"

"Huh?"

"You looked lost in thought."

"I'm considering all kinds of variables and weighing my options." He spoke a little louder. "If anyone's watching me, you have three minutes to make your presence known."

"Who are you talking to?"

"To anyone who's listening."

"Someone's listening to us?"

"We're going to find out." Given their position between the trailers, he doubted anyone was listening, but it didn't hurt to make sure.

Lauren looked around. "What do we do?"

"Wait until three minutes has expired."

"Then what?"

"*We* aren't going to do anything. I need you to watch my back, just like before."

"You're going over there again?"

"Yes, and I could be coming back in a big hurry, so be ready. When you see me enter the motel room, start the engine."

Verifying the headlight knob was in the off position—not auto—he got out, tucked the suppressed SIG into his belt, and covered it with the sweatshirt.

"Lauren, maintain radio silence unless you see anyone approach the motel on foot." He silently closed the Taurus's door and heard Lauren lock it.

Taking the same route, he angled across the street, began a brisk walk along the motel's sidewalk, and consciously slowed his breathing.

He turned right at the inside corner of the motel.

When he reached room 127, he reared back and kicked the door with all his strength.

CHAPTER 21

What Nathan saw caused rage, feral and deep.

Lying naked on the bed, a young Hispanic girl was blind-folded and gagged, with her wrists bound together. She'd obviously been assaulted—multiple times.

The right side of her abdomen showed a fresh incision, secured by surgical staples.

Sitting on the bed next to her, a shirtless man held a can of beer, his face reflecting shock at the sudden intrusion. He dropped the can and reached for a nickel-plated .45, but not in time.

Nathan double-tapped him in the chest.

Suppressed, the subsonic rounds sounded like muffled firecrackers.

The guy grimaced and looked down at the raw holes before his head lolled to the side.

Nathan swung his SIG to the left.

The creep at the table dropped his food and held out his hands. "Voda said it was okay!"

"It's not *okay*." Nathan shot him in the throat.

The back of the guy's neck exploded, spraying the wall beyond. His spinal cord severed, he fell forward and cracked his chin on the table.

Nathan tucked the SIG into his belt, pulled his Predator knife from its ankle sheath, and cut the rope binding the girl's wrists. Pulling the bandanna from her mouth, he removed the blindfold.

She cringed away from him at the same time he heard movement in the bathroom.

Aiming a huge handgun, a third man appeared.

Nathan dived for cover beside the bed as the gun boomed. He sensed the bullet miss his head by inches.

The girl screamed.

The window shattered.

Lying on his side, he pulled his SIG and toggled the laser. From underneath the bed, he lined up on the man's ankle and squeezed off a shot.

The man howled and cursed in Spanish.

Nathan fired again, destroying the guy's other ankle.

His opponent collapsed to the floor, and for a brief instant, they locked eyes.

Nathan sent two bullets into the man's rib cage before shooting his gun hand. Splattered with blood, the handgun slid across the bathroom's linoleum and thumped against the wall.

Still screaming, the girl ran for the open door.

Nathan stuck out his foot and tripped her.

With no other choice, he wrapped his left arm around her waist. "I'm not going to hurt you!" he said in Spanish. "You're safe now."

Eyes wild, she struggled like a panicked cat, trying to twist free. When she attempted to bite his arm, he dropped his gun and locked her in a nelson.

"I'm here to rescue you!"

She stopped struggling and held still.

"That's right, you're safe now. Calm down." This poor girl had been hysterical with fear, understandable given what she'd just endured. "I need you to get dressed as quickly as you can. Do you understand me?"

She nodded tightly.

He released her from the nelson but kept a firm grip on her arm. He didn't want her bolting from the room.

"Do you speak English?" he asked, still in Spanish.

"No."

Nathan pointed at the dead men. "They'll never hurt you again." He knew that telling her this would be an important step in her recovery. With the girl in tow, he hurried around the bed to assess the third man's condition and check him for ID. Red-faced and coughing blood, the thug was fully dressed in nice clothes, probably the ringleader. Questioning him was pointless—this guy couldn't speak even if he wanted to. And he didn't look like one of Voda's men. Although Hispanic like the coyotes, he was clean-cut.

Nathan was about to pat the guy down, when Lauren's voice screamed through his earpiece.

"Nathan!"

He looked toward the open door but didn't see anything. "Get dressed," he told the girl. "Quickly."

Nathan peered around the doorjamb. From the direction of the motel's office, two men ran toward the room, wielding compact Kalashnikovs.

Across the street, the Taurus's engine roared as it shot out from between the trailers.

Shit! They had Lauren!

He directed the SIG's laser onto the lead gunman and fired.

The man spun and tumbled to the asphalt.

A deafening roar ripped across the parking lot as the other gunman opened fire.

In a starlike pattern, white fire spit from the AK's flash suppressor.

Again Nathan dived for cover, this time behind the brick wall that supported the shattered window. He felt the masonry vibrate as dozens of slugs slammed into the other side. To his right, the bedsheets jumped as bullets tore through the open door.

The girl!

She was okay. She'd been directly behind him in a bent-over position, putting on her underwear, during the AK's barrage. The brick wall had shielded her.

He had to disable the Taurus before it got away.

From carpet level, he peered around the corner and placed the SIG's laser on the Taurus's right front tire. He was about to shoot, but to his surprise, it didn't speed away.

It hopped the curb and barreled straight toward him.

The remaining gunman turned.

Nathan watched in awe as the Taurus plowed the guy down like a bowling pin.

The AK clattered away as the man cartwheeled over the hood and crashed into the windshield. Nathan's mind registered a wiper blade breaking free at the same instant he understood what was happening.

Lauren was driving!

Its antilocks engaging, the Taurus thumped to a stop forty feet from the room.

Nathan turned back to the girl. "Grab the rest of your clothes. We're leaving!" He gripped her by the arm above her abraded wrist and hurried out the door.

The man Lauren had rammed was attempting to crawl toward his weapon. Nathan lined up on his hip and sent a bullet.

The man yelled something foul and covered the wound.

Keeping a tight grasp on the girl, Nathan ran for the Taurus.

In the dim light of the parking lot, he watched Lauren climb across the center console and open the passenger door. Since

Lauren and the girl were small enough to share the seat, he pushed the girl inside and slammed the door closed. In a fluid motion, he hopped across the Taurus's hood and got behind the wheel.

Nathan tucked the SIG under his leg and smoked the tires, executing a perfect half doughnut. Three seconds later, he made a screeching turn out of the motel's parking lot and stomped on the gas.

"Lauren, see if you can get the seat belt around both of you, then search her clothes. You're looking for a tracking bug. Anything electronic, okay?"

"Okay!"

"Lauren, slow your breathing again."

Nathan noticed it right away: a front-end shimmy.

The steering got spongy, and the Taurus lurched to the left.

Lauren must've blown a tire jumping the curb. It was immediately obvious this vehicle didn't have run-flats. Its front-end slant was too severe.

In his rearview mirror, he saw a set of headlights bounce out of the motel's parking lot. The headlights straightened as the vehicle accelerated in pursuit.

With a wrecked tire, he'd never outrun this new threat.

He pulled a fresh magazine from his pocket. "Lauren, reload the SIG." He had only six shots left in the gun.

"I don't know how!"

He silently cursed himself for not having shown her earlier how to do it. Scanning both sides of the road, he looked for a place to pull over. He needed a tactical location and saw an opportunity. Ahead on the right, a small truck park held several dozen semis.

Without hitting the brake, he rammed the chain-link gate. It came completely free from its hinges and slammed into the side of a semi's trailer. Using the same truck to shield them from view, he brought the Taurus to a stop. A dust cloud swirled as he climbed out. He left the door open and reloaded the SIG. From the direction of the motel, he heard the roar of the pursuing vehicle's engine.

"Stay in the car," he said in Spanish. "Lauren, don't let her get out."

"She's freaked! What do I do?"

"Hit the door-lock button. Help her get dressed. And search her clothes!"

Nathan ran to the cab of the semi and steadied his SIG on the approaching vehicle. It appeared to be a Hummer H2. He looked for a light bar or post-mounted spot indicating a law enforcement vehicle. Seeing neither, he painted the laser on the windshield and walked five shots low across its width. The glass went opaque.

The H2 veered into the truck park's fence, taking out several posts before coming to a stop. Nathan sent two more bullets into its front tires and waited several seconds. Detecting no movement, he ran back to the Taurus and put a bullet in its other front tire. With both tires deflated, the Taurus would be easier to control, but he knew they wouldn't get far before driving on the rims.

He climbed back in, reloaded the SIG with his last full magazine, and hit the gas.

The girl had her pants on.

"Her stomach's bleeding," said Lauren. "What are those metal things?"

"Surgical staples. We'll check her in a few minutes, but we need to clear the area first."

Nathan rammed a closed gate on the opposite side of the truck park. It flew open and banged against its stop. He turned east on a street intersecting the main road.

"Lauren, zoom the nav out and locate the road that goes north, to the left." He remembered seeing it on the Google Earth map. "It should be about a mile straight ahead."

Nathan had to drive at a painfully slow pace to preserve the rubber for as long as possible. Once the rims were exposed, they'd make a terrible racket and create a fireworks display. Crawling along this road became a double-edged sword, but it couldn't be helped. Driving slowly wouldn't draw much attention, but it also wouldn't put much distance between them and the motel. He didn't hear any sirens but knew that wouldn't last long. The burst of AK fire had been nothing short of deafening. U.S. Border Patrol agents were all over the place.

The girl leaned toward Lauren and began crying again.

"What did they do to her? Did they—"

"Yes."

"Did you kill them?"

He didn't respond.

"Good. They deserved it."

"Lauren, there's nothing good about killing."

"How can you say that after what they did?"

"Get it out of your head."

She went silent.

"I'm sorry. I didn't mean to snap at you."

"It's okay. I know you're not mad at me. She can't stop crying."

"Help her get her shirt on."

Maintaining twenty miles an hour, Nathan looked at the nav and saw the road they needed. He resisted the urge to stomp gas and slowed his breathing.

He wanted to ask the girl some questions but knew she was in no condition for that. He decided to risk an icebreaker. As softly as he could, he asked for her name.

She didn't answer and leaned closer to Lauren.

"Is your last name Hernandez?"

He heard a barely audible "*sí.*"

"What's your first name?"

"Abrille." She pronounced it *Ah-breel.*

"That's a beautiful name. You're safe now, Abrille. No one's going to hurt you anymore. I'm Nathan, that's Lauren."

He no longer believed there'd been a stakeout at the motel, which meant he'd just saved this girl from a protracted death—humanity at its worst. Nathan had seen his share of violence and torture during his time with the marines and CIA. He'd been on both sides of the equation and knew what Abrille was feeling all too well. Lauren's presence had a calming effect on the girl. She stopped crying, but she was still trembling.

"Lauren, grab a water from the duffel and give it to her. It's okay to take your seat belt off."

Abrille downed the entire bottle. He wondered how long she'd gone without food or drink.

"*Más?*" Nathan asked.

"*Sí, por favor.*"

Lauren caught the meaning and grabbed another.

According to the nav, they were now about halfway to the turn. Fortunately, a hill on the south side of the road screened them from being seen from the motel. Nathan knew arriving law enforcement would start there and have their hands full with a violent and bloody crime scene. The man Lauren had plowed into might or might not be able to escape in time. The first man he'd shot in the parking lot wasn't going anywhere and would probably die. Nathan hadn't taken a wounding shot, he'd nailed the center of the man's chest. He doubted coyotes wore body armor, like Voda's men. Including the men from motel and the H2 driver, the world now had five fewer dirtbags.

Thinking back to this evening's earlier action, he hadn't killed anyone, but not from a lack of effort. His initial shots at the Ulric crash site would've been fatal had it not been for the body armor the gunmen had worn. The same could be said about the gunman from the grocery store. Ironically, the only man he hadn't tried to kill tonight had been Voda. But at that moment in time, killing Voda hadn't been warranted. Right after the Ulric Street crash, he hadn't known anything about the man. He could've been Lauren's disgruntled father. Had Nathan known who Voda really was, he would've shot him in the head, not the thigh. Hindsight was always like that.

In a soft voice in Spanish, Abrille said, "Thank you for rescuing me."

The words sliced into his soul, and he struggled to maintain control. Now wasn't the time to show anything other than steadfast confidence. His passengers needed to know their rescuer was in command and mentally stable. It also didn't hurt to tell himself the same thing.

He couldn't say for sure, but Abrille's Spanish didn't sound local, which meant her Bolivian passport was likely authentic.

"My stomach hurts," she said.

"What happened to you?" Nathan asked.

"A doctor operated on me."

"How long ago?"

"Three days."

He shook his head at what this child must've endured. It was bad enough being brutalized, but after abdominal surgery? Killing those assholes had been more than justified. In fact, they'd died too well.

"Lauren, was there anything in her pockets?"

"Just a passport like we saw in my stepdad's office."

"Does she feel hot, like she's got a fever? Check her forehead."

"It feels really warm."

Likely an infection. This made things more urgent. Abrille didn't appear to be in dire trouble yet, but that could change quickly. She needed antibiotics and possibly more surgery. If the doctor had botched the job, she could become septic—if she wasn't already. He knew what to do, but they needed a vehicle.

The turn was just ahead. "Lauren, give Abrille some air. Roll your window down."

They all heard it, the whine of a siren, probably a fire engine—they were usually first to respond—but it would have to stage away until law enforcement secured the scene. The shot-up H2 was a good quarter of a mile from the motel. With a little luck, it wouldn't be discovered for several more minutes, especially if no one had witnessed Nathan's pistol skills.

"Lauren, do you know any songs? I want you to sing to Abrille."

"Sing? You mean like a song?"

"Just pick anything, but sing softly."

"I don't understand…"

"Please, just do it."

Lauren began the "Itsy Bitsy Spider" song.

Out of the corner of his eye, he saw Abrille huddle closer to Lauren, almost hugging her.

"I think she likes it."

"Keep going."

Lauren's soft singing created a stark dichotomy. Here they were, fleeing a scene of unspeakable human depravity and violence to the soft melody of a children's nursery rhyme. Nathan thought back to what the man sitting at the table had said: *Voda said it was okay!* He had experienced a moment of pure clairvoyance and knew exactly what the creep meant. *If Voda's gonna kill her, why should he care if we do her first?* The sickos were simply taking advantage of an opportunity. Including the driver of the H2, there'd been at least six of them. Even as he shook his head in disgust, Nathan found his logical side asking a question: Why six men? It didn't take that many thugs to guard one twelve-year-old girl. Nathan could envision two men, but six?

He fought the Taurus onto the northbound road and looked over his shoulder. The hill still offered them cover from the motel. He'd need to start looking for an opportunity soon. From the sound of the tires, he didn't have much time left. He slowed to fifteen miles an hour. The terrain remained flat, but up ahead, it looked to begin a gradual ascent.

Lauren finished a second rendition of the song.

"Good job," he said.

"I can't believe what they did to her."

"Try not to think about it. The important thing is, she's safe now."

"What are you going to do?"

"I'm going to procure alternate transportation."

"You're going to steal a car."

"Yeah, that's the general idea."

"Can't you just ask to borrow someone's car?"

He glanced at the dashboard clock. Knocking on a complete stranger's door at 0220 and asking to "borrow" his or her car had a snowball's chance. Worse than that, the odds of finding a car with the keys in it were even more remote, and even if he did manage to find one, starting its engine would probably alert its owner, and if its owner had a gun, things could turn ugly. He wasn't willing to engage anyone in a firefight over a vehicle. But his circumstances were bordering on desperate. He had to think about Abrille. How long did she have?

"I can help you," Lauren said.

"How's that?"

"We can ask together, you know, like a father and daughter. We can say we ran over something and got flat tires, but we have to take Abrille to a hospital 'cause she's like really sick."

Nathan went over the pros and cons and decided it was worth the risk. The biggest con involved law enforcement. At this moment, their location wasn't known, but that would change if more violence ensued over a vehicle. "Okay, we'll try it your way. First."

He spotted a small house on the left side. All its windows were dark, and several cars were parked in the yard, a few of them not looking roadworthy. Maybe no one would be home and they'd find keys inside the house.

Nathan turned on his headlights, but they were broken from ramming the gates in the truck park. He crawled down the gravel driveway and asked Lauren to steer while he pulled off his sweatshirt and ballistic vest. Along with his radio, he tossed them into the backseat.

Whoever lived here took care of the place. The mowed lawn and modest landscaping were free of any weeds. He expected to be challenged by one or more dogs, but surprisingly, none was present. Near the front door, he stopped at an angle so the home's owner could see the passenger side. Nathan left the engine running and opened his door. Before climbing out, he tucked the SIG into the small of his back. Was he really doing this? It would be just their luck to encounter a paranoid nutcase.

"Lauren, get out and leave the door open. I'll do the talking."

A porch light snapped on, and the front door opened. Wearing a faded black T-shirt and blue jeans, a medium-built man in his fifties stood in the open door. With a pump-action shotgun in his right hand, he looked all business. Nathan focused on a tattoo imprinted on the man's shoulder.

"Who are you and what do you want?"

Nathan stopped midstep. "We have an emergency and need help."

"What kind of emergency?"

Nathan pointed to the tires."

"Call Triple A."

"I have a very sick girl in the car. She needs a doctor."

"Call nine-one-one."

"You're Airborne Ranger. Eighty-second."

"Knowing my tat don't mean shit."

"Can't deny it."

The man motioned with the gun. "What's wrong with the girl?"

"Coyotes."

Nathan waited while the man processed the info.

"What unit were *you* with?"

"First Recon, Delta Company."

The man leveled his shotgun and stepped down from the porch. "What does *semper fidelis* mean?"

"Always faithful."

"Are those sirens because of you?"

"Yes."

"Tell me the truth, and I'll help you. What's your situation?"

Nathan started from his surveillance of the motel and briefly recounted everything that had happened. He omitted the part about killing five men and shooting up the H2.

"That's one hell of a fish story."

Nathan backed away from the Taurus. "Have a look—the parabolic mike's in the back."

The man raised his gun a little and walked with a slight limp. He peered inside. "Your windows are tinted."

"It's not locked."

The guy looked at Lauren and motioned with the shotgun. "You open it." He stepped back and assumed a tactical position from which he could look inside the sedan's door when it opened but use it for cover if needed.

This guy was definitely a trained combat soldier. Nathan would've taken the same position had their situations been reversed.

Nathan issued Lauren a nod. When the man was distracted looking inside, Nathan pulled the SIG from behind his back, rotated it in his hand, and held it out in surrender. It took less than two seconds.

The guy refocused on Nathan. "Whoa! That's some trick. I didn't even see you make a move."

"Take it. We aren't here to rob you."

"All right, Marine, you just convinced me."

Nathan tossed the SIG into the backseat.

The man lowered the alley sweeper and extended his hand. "Gerry Hanson."

"Nathan McBride. This is Lauren."

"Sorry about the greeting, but you can't be too careful around these parts. We see some unsavory types wander through."

"No doubt. I would've played it the same way. Bad jump?"

He shook his head. "Drunk driver broadsided me. Rode a desk for eight years after that."

"Sorry to hear it."

"Shit happens. Is the girl okay? What happened to her?"

"She's got a fever, probably from infection. She's had a rough night." He motioned with his eyes toward Lauren.

"*Fucking* coyotes." He looked at Lauren. "Pardon my language, ma'am."

Holding a small dog, a woman in a sweatshirt appeared at the door. "Who is it, Gerry? Should I call the sheriff?"

"Everything's okay—it's just some folks who broke down on the road."

"Evening, ma'am. How about an even trade," Nathan said to Gerry. "The Explorer for the Taurus."

"That Taurus looks brand-new."

"She's got some fresh damage to her front end, but she's yours. I'll sign the pink slip."

"That's a mighty kind offer, but I can't accept it. It ain't a fair trade, even with them broken headlights. My Explorer's fifteen years old. Just return it when you're finished."

"That's a promise, Gerry."

"You recons are a tight-knit bunch. I bet you could tell a few campfire stories."

"Maybe we'll exchange a few when I come back. Is there any way you can conceal the Taurus?"

"I'll swap it out with my wife's car in the garage."

"I wish we could stay, but Abrille's in an urgent situation."

"I'll get the keys. Do you need anything for the road, coffee or chow?"

"We're okay, thanks."

"Be right back."

Gerry disappeared inside.

"What did he mean by *tight-knit bunch*?" Lauren asked.

"I'll tell you later. This turned out well. Good call, Lauren. To be honest, I wouldn't have tried it without your suggestion."

He thought about changing the license plates, but that would take time, and the Taurus's government plates couldn't be removed easily. He weighed the risk-versus-reward aspect of doing it and decided it was marginally acceptable leaving the plates as is. Besides, if they were pulled over or had to stop at a checkpoint, the government plates wouldn't do much good and might actually raise additional suspicion. This Explorer wasn't in great shape. It didn't look like an official government vehicle.

Gerry reappeared. "She runs good, but you're gonna need gas soon. I think she's got just over a quarter tank."

"I'll bring her back full. I want to give you something as a thank-you. Might come in handy out here." Nathan pulled one of the night-vision visors from the duffel and handed it to Gerry.

"Oh, man, this is a fourteen. I can't accept it. I know how much these little babies cost."

"Please, take it. It's the least I can do. Honestly, it's yours."

"You're a stand-up guy, Nathan. I wasn't going to ask, but what happened to you?"

Nathan knew he was referring to the scars on his face. "Botched mission."

Gerry slowly nodded. "Let's exchange those stories when you come back."

"That's a promise."

Gerry helped them transfer everything into the Explorer. Abrille hesitated but got out. Lauren put an arm around her and helped her into the backseat.

"She don't look so good," Gerry said.

"She'll be in good hands soon."

"You were never here."

"Copy that. One thing you need to know. There's a first-class turd behind all this action tonight. You been following the border murders case?"

"Yeah, I have. A real wacko."

"I think this girl would've been the next victim."

"No shit?"

Nathan nodded. "I'm ninety-nine-point-nine percent certain no one saw us drive down your driveway, but I can't say it with absolute certainty."

Gerry's eyes narrowed again.

"You'll need to be extra alert for the next twenty-four hours or so. It will be a 'shoot first and ask questions later' situation, and you'll know it when it happens. Spanish nationals. They could be wearing body armor. Aim low or make head shots. We're talking about multiple threats with MP5s."

"If any Spanish nationals mosey down my driveway, I'll say hello for you."

"Does your wife have someplace she can go? Right now, like, tonight?"

"That's affirmative."

Nathan asked for the shortest way back to Highway 94, and Gerry gave him the directions.

"Safe travels, Marine. Thanks for the NV."

They shook hands once more, then Nathan climbed into the Explorer and hit the road.

CHAPTER 22

Nathan pulled away and couldn't help but wonder how differently it would've turned out if anyone other than Gerry had appeared at the door. He didn't like the idea of taking someone's vehicle by force, but he would've had it been necessary. Nathan said a silent thank-you to the Big Man upstairs and turned left out of the driveway. If they were going to hit any roadblocks, they'd probably be set up within the first few miles along Highway 94. He figured fewer than five minutes had passed since he'd arrived at Gerry's house, and he doubted law enforcement could get anything set up that quickly.

If Voda's coyotes had seen them enter Gerry's property, they should've attacked by now. But, as Nathan had told Gerry, he couldn't assume anything, and revealing the potential threat was the right thing to do. He had little doubt Gerry could kick some ass if it came to it. Rangers were a tough bunch. Interservice rivalries aside, recons and rangers were close cousins.

"How's Abrille doing?"

"She's crying again."

Nathan asked the girl how her stomach felt, and she said it stung, which surprised him a little. He'd expected her to say it ached, like a cramp. He reassured her they were taking her to a doctor who'd take good care of her. He also told her nothing would happen to her without her permission, figuring the statement would restore some feeling of security. He didn't know a lot about rape victims, but he'd learned from his own experience being tortured that part of the recovery process involved reestablishing a sense of being in control.

"Lauren, I need you to make another four-one-one call. For the city, say Rancho Bernardo, California, then ask for Dr. Douglas Reavie's office. That's Reavie, R-e-a-v-i-e. You got that?"

"Uh-huh."

"When you get the doctor's answering service, say it's a medical emergency and you're calling for Nathan McBride, and that you need to be connected to the doctor immediately. When the answering service puts you on hold, hand me the phone."

"Okay."

Nathan checked his mirrors and saw no other cars on the road. He was about to pass his phone back to Lauren, but it vibrated. He showed Lauren the number. "Is that your cell number?"

"Yes."

He asked Abrille to be very quiet and took the call. "I'm a little busy right now, Mr. Voda. May I call you back?"

"Do you have the piece of paper from the warehouse?"

"What paper are you talking about?"

"Don't play games. The lamp on the desk wasn't precisely where it was supposed to be."

"Are you talking about the lamp that used to contain the Bolivian passports? That lamp?"

Silence on the other end. He sensed Voda's rage and frustration. "Give me the paper, and I'll double your fee."

Given what Voda had just confirmed, Nathan thought he sounded remarkably poised and confident. Perhaps overly so. Nathan decided to razz him a little. "I think you should make a list of the items you want. I fear the list may grow as the evening progresses, and I wouldn't want you to forget anything."

"That's cute."

"I noticed an old typewriter in Marchand's office. This wouldn't be the only copy of your list, would it?"

"You said it yourself: you're a businessman. I see no reason we can't come to some sort of agreement."

"I'm certain we can, but I'm a little pressed for time at the moment. Thank you for calling, Mr. Voda. I'll get back to you soon." Nathan ended the call.

"Was that him?" Lauren asked. "Why were you so nice?"

"It's part of the game. He wants the paper from your stepdad's office."

"But my mom's note said Voda thinks she has it."

Lauren was right, and he didn't like the potential ramifications. What would Voda have assumed upon finding the paper missing? Since he and Lauren had been in the warehouse when Voda and his goons had arrived, Voda might conclude Nathan took it. But, as Lauren pointed out, her mom was under the impression that Voda thought Jin had it. Yet Voda hadn't implied that. Instead, he'd sounded certain Nathan possessed the paper. The question became: Why? How could Voda know with absolute certainty that Jin didn't have the paper? The answer chilled him. He needed to keep Lauren from pursuing this train of thought.

"You're right. Voda thinks your mom has the paper, which tells us something very interesting. Voda doesn't know about our little raid out here. If he did, he wouldn't have asked if I have it— he'd already know. And that in turn tells us something else. No one from the motel contacted him with the news. And if no one from the motel contacted him, it's a good bet that his contact person is dead, which gives us the advantage. As long as Voda thinks Abrille is still available, we can use it against him."

"How?"

"I'm not sure yet."

"What if he hears about the motel on the news?"

"I think it's fair to assume that since he doesn't know the location of the girl, it will be just another news story to him. Gang shootings happen all the time. On the other hand, if that location has been used before, it would definitely raise some suspicion. But think about it: If Voda were using the same location over and over, he wouldn't need GPS coordinates. He or one of his men would just go to room 127 at the Tecate Palms Motel. There'd be no need for coordinates. Thugs like Voda are paranoid and untrusting, especially of their own people. He's constantly worried one of his men will betray him. He probably uses a different location each time to avoid establishing a pattern."

"Do you think he was going to kill Abrille like the others?"

Nathan took a deep breath. He didn't want to blow smoke with Lauren. She deserved the truth. "Yes. Almost certainly."

"Then we just saved her life."

"Yeah, we did, but she's going to have deep psychological scars for the rest of her life. She'll have to find a way to deal with it. She'll need counseling. Look in her eyes, Lauren. See the pain she's feeling. She isn't just some toy for amusement—she's a human being with feelings, just like you and me. She doesn't speak English, but that doesn't make her any less important."

"People are so cruel."

"I know it's hard after all we've been through, but try not to dwell on the negatives. As a perfect example, look at what Gerry just did for us. He gave us this vehicle on nothing more than my word I'd bring it back. Keep your faith in humanity."

"But you were both soldiers. Maybe he wouldn't have done it if you weren't a soldier."

"That's true, but I was also willing to trade the Taurus for it. I suppose somebody else might've suspected the Taurus was stolen, and the outcome could've been completely different."

"It's that causal pyramid, right?"

"Causality. But yes. Again, a very specific chain of events is unfolding. Now that we have Abrille, the base of the pyramid just got a whole lot bigger."

"Maybe *your* faith in humanity is a little better too."

"How's that?"

"You were going to just steal a car."

Nathan didn't respond right away. She was right. Asking to borrow someone's car hadn't even occurred to him until she'd suggested it. He supposed his desire to save the girl played a role in his train of thought, but he wasn't sure anymore. Again, Lauren's sense of intuition amazed him. Maybe it was a family trait. There'd been times during his childhood when he could've sworn his father knew exactly what he was thinking. He supposed all parents got to know their kids like that, but his dad's ability seemed uncanny at times. Speaking of, he'd need to call his father soon. Washington was three hours ahead, making it just after 0530 there.

"You're absolutely right," he said. "It's easy to forget there are genuinely good people in the world. I'd like to believe that most people aren't purposely cruel to one another. I think a lot of people tend to be mistrusting in general, but very few are downright cruel."

"Did I kill the man at the motel?"

"No, but he's going to need orthopedic surgery. Go ahead and make the four-one-one call. You know what to say?"

"Yes."

He listened to Lauren talk to the operator as he turned west on a road that would take them back toward the highway they'd used to enter Tecate. From there, they'd make a right turn onto Highway 94.

"Okay, the lady said to wait on the line." She passed the phone to him.

Nathan waited through a brief period of silence. "This is Dr. Reavie."

"It's Nathan McBride, Doctor. Thank you for taking my call."

"Do you need me to head over to my surgical suite again?"

"Yes."

"Can you tell me what's going on?"

"I've got a Hispanic female around age twelve. She's got a small incision on the lower-right portion of her abdomen. It's stapled closed. The incision is inflamed and leaking, and she might have a fever. She said she had a surgical procedure three days ago."

"It would be useful to know what was done to her."

"Hang on, Doctor. I'll ask." Abrille told him she didn't know.

"She says she doesn't know."

"What's her condition? Is her heart rate elevated, and is she breathing in short, shallow breaths?"

"Just a sec. I'm putting you on speaker. We aren't being recorded, are we?"

"No."

"Lauren, put your fingers over her wrist near her thumb. Let me know if her pulse seems high."

"She won't let me touch her hand."

"Abrille, we need to know how fast your heart is beating. Please let Lauren touch your wrist, okay? She's not going to hurt you."

Nathan wanted to pull over, but he couldn't risk any delay right now. They needed to clear this area before any roadblocks went up.

"Is she letting you do it?"

"Yeah. It feels kinda fast."

"Is she breathing quickly? And shallow?"

"Yes."

"Did you catch that, Doctor?"

"Yes. Can you see any mottling on her skin?"

"Yes, I saw that earlier, on her abdomen, around the incision."

"Does she seem restless or agitated?"

"Yes, but it could be a result of her trauma. She's also fatigued. Her agitation comes and goes."

"Bring her in as soon as you can. When was the last time she had anything to eat or drink? Anything in her stomach increases her anesthesia risk."

"She drank about sixteen ounces of water a few minutes ago. Other than that, I don't know."

"If she needs surgery, we'll do a rapid-sequence technique of inducing anesthesia to reduce the risk, but it's better if she doesn't have anything more than water in her stomach. She's got four symptoms of sepsis. If she's in full septic shock, her life's at risk and she'll need intensive care. It's more than I can provide here. Since you haven't taken her to an urgent-care facility, may I assume you'd like to keep all of this confidential?"

"Yes."

"I can do that, but at my discretion, I'll transfer her to Pomerado. Agreed?"

"Agreed. She doesn't speak English, though."

"That won't be an issue. I speak Spanish."

Nathan lowered his voice. "She's been assaulted, multiple assailants."

There was silence on the other end for a few seconds. "Before or after her surgery?"

"After for sure, but I don't know about before."

"Again, I'll treat her, but I'm not set up for this sort of thing. I don't have a rape kit, and she'll need immediate counseling."

"The rape kit won't be necessary."

"Do I want to know?"

"I think it's best if you don't."

"What's your ETA?"

"If all goes well, around an hour. Can you give me your address again?" Nathan committed it to memory. "Thank you, Doctor. I really appreciate this."

"I'm glad to help," said the doctor. "But I need to disclose something you might not be aware of. The girl's treatment can start off as emergency care, and I can help with that, but as I mentioned, if she has a life-threatening infection, she'll need admission to Pomerado, and because she's a minor, she'll need legal consent. If she doesn't have a legal guardian available, the courts will get involved. There's no way around it."

"I hadn't considered that. What can we do?"

"If her identity's at risk, a pseudonym can be used, like they do for gang risk or prominent public figures. The assault also triggers the involvement of Child Protective Services. I am legally—and morally—required to report even the slightest suspicion of child abuse, and if I don't, I could see license suspension or revocation, and even jail time."

"I won't put you or your career at risk, Doctor. I'll take her straight to Pomerado."

"You don't need to do that yet. For now, this is an emergency treatment. We'll deal with the other issues later. I just wanted to make you aware of what's involved with a minor."

"Does her citizenship matter?"

"Not when it comes to emergency treatment. I can't say for sure, but if she was brought into the US illegally, ICE will probably get involved."

"Let's try to delay that for as long as we can. She's in the best possible hands in your care."

"That's kind of you to say. I'll do everything I can to insulate her. I have an ace up my sleeve, but we'll talk about that later. Right now, my only concern is treating her condition and making sure she makes a full recovery."

"I agree. We'll see you in about an hour."

"I'll be ready."

"Thank you, Doctor." Nathan ended the call.

Lauren asked, "What did you say? I couldn't hear you."

"I wanted to spare you from certain details."

"I already know what they did. They raped her."

"Lauren, *rape* isn't just a word. Short of murder, it's one of the worst offenses committed. It's a form of torture. Try not to dwell on it. Abrille is safe now. Dr. Reavie said she shouldn't drink or eat anything in case she needs surgery."

Nathan told Abrille she couldn't drink any more water until the doctor said it was okay. He made the turn onto Highway 94 and accelerated to the safest speed he could maintain. Until they reached the Dulzura area, the highway remained laced with dangerous curves and steep canyons.

Something about Voda's operation wasn't making sense. If he were behind the border murders, raping and killing these girls after his men had their way with them, then why did he want the list so desperately? The female victims didn't have any intrinsic value to Voda that Nathan was aware of. Something else didn't make sense. The man sitting at the table in the motel had said, *Voda said it was okay.* But it was plainly evident Voda hadn't known Abrille's location. Maybe it was common knowledge that Abrille's captors could do whatever they wanted as long as the girl was delivered alive. Common knowledge...the sick bastards.

A new thought arose: What if Abrille hadn't been the primary target in the motel room? Nathan realized now that a quick look through the room would've been best, but there hadn't been time. Even if the additional gunmen from the parking lot hadn't been there, Nathan had needed to leave in a hurry.

In his mind's eye, he reexamined the motel room. Nothing jumped out. There hadn't been any crates, boxes, or plastic bags, but he'd noticed several empty one-gallon water bottles tossed in the corner. Actually, he'd seen something similar at Marchand's warehouse...

Nathan didn't think the motel room was a stepping-stone in a chain of locations that ultimately led to a "pot of gold." It seemed unlikely the room held instructions leading to a subsequent location. One thing *was* certain: if Abrille had been the only asset in the motel room, Voda considered her extremely valuable. *Why?*

In her note, Jin said Marchand didn't know Voda was involved with murder, but that seemed a little naive. The border murders case was a front-page story. Marchand obviously knew Voda was complicit in various criminal activities—Jin's note said as much—but a giant chasm separated smuggling from murder. Whatever the case, it seemed as though Marchand had withheld the paper containing the coordinates from Voda and gotten himself killed in the process.

But that only raised more questions. Obviously Voda hadn't been the person who hand-typed the list of numbers, or he would've simply taken the paper with him. Why risk leaving it in Marchand's office? And if Marchand had hidden the list under the granite desktop for safekeeping, maybe even to use it as leverage against Voda, how did Voda know about the hiding place? In her note, Jin had said Voda bragged about torturing Marchand for hours. Marchand must've given it up. Voda had probably wrung the secret hiding place out of him. The timing was a little suspect, though. If Voda knew about the piece of paper the night he captured Marchand, why not head over there right away and get it? Since Jin had relayed the hiding place to Lauren, Marchand must've told Jin about it first. Marchand could've endured Voda's brutality in order to buy time for Jin and Lauren—or himself—knowing that once he gave up the hiding place, he'd be killed.

Something else Jin had written stuck in Nathan's memory. She'd mentioned paying back an old debt. What debt, and to whom? He wondered if there was a tie-in with North Korea. Clearly, she'd been born there, so how did she get out? Escaping North Korea wasn't easy without inside help. She'd referred to a powerful man helping her mother over the years. Maybe the same man had arranged her exit and smuggled her out. Could that be the debt? If so, how did it relate to their current situation? Maybe Voda had ties with North Korea. It was common knowledge that DPRK was essentially a giant criminal enterprise with tentacles all over the world, and counterfeiting US currency was one of its key operations. Nathan didn't think the piece of paper was about counterfeit money. He'd read an online news story recently about DPRK and counterfeit pharmaceuticals and cigarettes. DPRK also manufactured and exported meth, crack, and heroin. You name it, they were into it. If Voda had ties to DPRK, it might explain Jin's involvement.

"Lauren, do you remember your mom ever meeting with someone who looked Korean or Asian?"

"No, I don't remember anyone like that."

"What about phone calls? Did you ever hear her speak Korean to anyone?"

"Just French."

"French? Your mom speaks French?"

"Uh-huh, she said she learned it a long time ago. I think she was my age, but I'm not sure."

"Did you ever ask her about it?"

"I remember asking her what language it was. She said it was French and that she learned it in school."

"That's all she said—she learned it in school? Is that why you think she was young?"

"I guess."

Nathan didn't know much about DPRK schools, but they sure as hell didn't teach French as part of their standard curricula. Excepting its criminal enterprises, DPRK was perhaps the world's most xenophobic state. Secrecy wasn't merely a word in DPRK, it was a lifestyle. North Korea would never teach French in its schools, which were strictly controlled by the government.

On nothing more than a pure hunch, Nathan asked, "Abrille?"

"*Digame*," she answered. *What?*

"*Parlez-vous français?*"

In a soft voice she said, "*Oui.*"

This couldn't be a coincidence. No possible way. Since Abrille seemed to be okay talking a little, he stayed in French and asked where and when she had learned to speak it. She said she was from Bolivia and a private tutor had been coming to her orphanage and teaching her French. Abrille didn't speak French fluently, but she spoke it well enough to have a conversation. Nathan asked if other girls were being taught French. She said yes, and that they were also being adopted.

The base of Nathan's pyramid had just grown tenfold. Not only did Abrille speak French, but Jin did as well, and they were both raised in orphanages *and*, apparently, had both learned to speak French around the same age.

"Did you just speak French to Abrille?" asked Lauren.

"Yes."

"Abrille knows French?"

"Yes."

"That's weird."

"It's definitely a surprise. I think it's fair to assume that not one in ten thousand Bolivian girls her age would know French. How's she doing? Is she restless? Does she seem agitated?"

"No, but she's still breathing kinda fast."

Nathan pressed the gas a little harder. Thankfully, they hadn't encountered any law enforcement roadblocks. But if they were stopped, Abrille's presence couldn't be easily explained. On the other hand, most kids her age didn't have bona fide ID, but her lack of English might raise red flags. She had a passport, but Nathan didn't know if that would help or hurt their situation. If the Explorer's plate were run, Nathan wouldn't come back as the owner and a link to Gerry would be created—something he didn't want. He considered going over what Abrille should say if they were stopped, but that would only serve to frighten her more. Right now, she seemed somewhat calm.

Overall, Nathan couldn't complain about the way things had unfolded tonight. Although he and Lauren had endured some tough moments, they'd been counterbalanced with good moments—like encountering the pedestrian bridge across the San Diego River, finding a waiting cabdriver at the Town & Country Resort Hotel, and now Gerry. Rescuing Abrille was at the top of the good-moment list. With a little luck, they'd be clear of any roadblock danger within the next ten minutes.

He checked his cell and had two bars showing. He'd wait until he had a better connection to call Holly with an update. Harv was at thirty thousand feet for the next twelve hours or so. Most commercial carriers offered air-phone service, but Harv wouldn't call unless he thought of something crucial. Also, the air-phone connection wouldn't be secure.

When he thought about it more, maybe he shouldn't call Holly. He felt pulled in two different directions. Because of his personal relationship with her, he felt obligated to give her updates so she wouldn't worry, but in doing so, she'd need to report his activities, and he didn't want that. He'd asked her about potential undercover agents inside Voda's operation, but he didn't plan to ask Holly for more help than that. He'd initially thought he might need her to track down Voda, but he now had the ability to force Voda to come to him.

The trick would be keeping Lauren safe through any future confrontations. Confrontations? That was a gross understatement. Nathan fully expected things to turn even uglier than they had been, and there may come a point where leaving Lauren in a secure location would be his only option. He didn't know how she'd deal with it. Lauren was strong-willed, a trait he admired, but it might prove to be a problem. So far, she'd been reliable and inventive. Watching her plow the gunman in the motel's parking lot had been nothing short of astonishing, and if she was capable of doing that, what else could she do? Again, he couldn't help but wonder how many kids her age had her guts and willpower.

One thing remained certain: he wouldn't involve Lauren in any direct action against Voda. She could continue to be his eyes and ears, but that was as far as it went. Although Nathan didn't know anything about parenting, he knew being consistent was essential. Before the warehouse raid he'd told Lauren he wasn't handing her a gun to act as his backup, and that wasn't going to change—plowed gunman or not.

He concentrated on driving and gauged his operational readiness at 80 percent. Not great, but nothing a catnap at Dr. Reavie's office wouldn't cure. Sleep deprivation took a gradual toll, becoming cumulatively worse and worse. Maybe Harv was right. Waiting until his friend arrived from Istanbul didn't sound too bad right now. But Nathan had Voda on the defensive, and allowing too much time to pass might undermine that. A catnap would have to do. During one mission in Nicaragua, he and Harv had lasted an entire week on nothing more than two-hour catnaps. It wasn't ideal, but he'd do it again to protect Lauren if that was what it took.

"Abrille stopped crying, but she's shivering a little."

"Okay. Try to keep her calm, and don't let her drink any more water."

"I won't. What were you just thinking about?"

"I was thinking about the motel, how you ran that guy over."

"Are you mad about that?"

"Just amazed. I couldn't believe you did it."

"It looked like you needed some help 'cause you didn't see the men with the guns."

"That's what the radios are for. When you yelled my name, I thought they had you. I felt sick to my stomach about it."

"That's nice of you to say."

"I felt empty, like I'd lost someone…like…hell, I guess I don't know what I'm saying."

"You're saying you care about me."

Nailed again. What was Lauren's spell over him? There'd been times tonight when he'd made mistakes he wouldn't normally have made. He supposed it might have something to do with a lack of experience with kids, but he doubted he would've had the same issue with anyone else. He knew he possessed a conflicted nature, and it wasn't entirely from his botched mission in Nicaragua. He'd always been guarded. Maybe Lauren acted like an amplifier, or, more accurately, a prism, and she'd revealed a new color in him.

Had she activated some kind of dormant paternal instinct? How could this happen? It seemed crazy. He wasn't Lauren's dad—far from it. But he knew he'd do anything to protect her.

Lauren spoke softly. "Remember when I asked you why you didn't have any children? You told me it was complicated."

"I was avoiding the question."

"Does it bother you to talk about it?"

"Let's just say it's outside of my comfort zone."

"I'm sorry for mentioning it."

"No need to apologize."

"I think you'd make a good dad."

"Thank you for saying so. Truthfully, settling down and having a family isn't complicated. People do it all the time. It's more an issue of opportunity with me."

Lauren didn't respond right away. "Opportunity?"

Nathan lightened his tone. "For one, it would be good to be married first."

"Well, yeah."

"Holly once told me I would've been a good dad. Harv has mixed feelings on the subject. There are times when Harv agrees with Holly, and other times he's thanked heaven I haven't reproduced."

"I'm sure he was just teasing you."

"We can only hope…"

Not having children wasn't a selfish indulgence. Nathan was as unselfish as people came. Like he'd told Lauren, it was a lack of opportunity. He'd never found anyone compatible until he met Holly… Well, he knew that wasn't entirely honest. He'd never really sought a meaningful relationship, and his past career as a marine sniper and CIA operative had certainly gotten in the way. But Harv had moved beyond it—he had a wife and two sons. Nathan was a loner by nature, and he'd resigned himself to never being able to share his life intimately with anyone. He'd been honest with Holly and told her as much.

"It's okay to care about someone," she said.

"Sorry, I wasn't…you know, dodging what you said, but I can't help but wonder how all of this came down tonight. It's crazy. I was sitting at home, watching a movie, and here I am, transporting a sick and injured Bolivian girl who speaks French to a plastic surgeon."

"But you made decisions that led to this, didn't you?"

"I was thinking in more general terms."

"Abrille's still shaking."

"Chills are a common symptom of an infection. She'll be in good hands soon. I think we're past any potential law enforcement roadblocks at this point. I know it may be difficult, but see if you can get some sleep. If you sleep, it might help Abrille sleep too. When we get close to the doctor's office, I'll wake you up."

"I don't think I can sleep right now. I feel wide awake."

"Yeah, me too."

"Well, you *are* driving."

"Point taken. Try to get some sleep."

CHAPTER 23

Nathan drove the next fifteen minutes in silence, hoping Lauren would doze off. He thought about Holly, how to tell her about the most recent events, how to explain his lie of omission about the cell phone he'd taken from Voda's man at the grocery store. Telling the whole truth was probably the best approach, but frankly, he didn't want the FBI entangled in his pursuit of Voda. Especially now, in case Voda had indeed captured Jin.

On the other hand, Holly's people had tremendous resources at their disposal. And Holly would want to help, despite his reluctance.

It's okay to care about someone, Lauren had told him, speaking with the wisdom of the ages. And it was a mutual feeling between Holly and him.

It was time to call her... His phone showed a strong connection, so he tapped Holly's cell number.

"Hi, Nathan. Is everything okay?"

He gave a Holly a complete update, starting with the GPS coordinates he'd found embedded in the list of numbers and ending with the raid at the motel and his possession of Abrille.

"Holly, I executed those two men in the motel room. There's no way to sugarcoat what I did. They weren't armed when I shot them. The third guy in the bathroom was self-defense. So was the man in the parking lot."

"Nathan, nothing you just said goes any further than me. Tell me what you saw when you kicked in the door."

He glanced into the backseat. Lauren was asleep, but Abrille wasn't. He lowered his voice and described how Abrille had been naked, bound, and gagged with a greasy slob sitting next to her with a beer in his hand. "Something snapped. My safety catch didn't engage."

"I wasn't there," said Holly. "I didn't see the girl. As a law enforcement officer, I wouldn't have shot them, but I'm damned sure I would've wanted to. I'm not going to condemn you, and you shouldn't either. You're the most honest and honorable man I've ever known. I'm glad you told me."

"There's something I *haven't* told you, and I don't feel good about it. I confiscated a cell phone from Voda's gunman after the grocery store shooting. I didn't tell you because I wanted it for myself."

"Does it have any useful information?"

"To me, not really. To your people and their resources, almost certainly. The gunman hadn't deleted the call logs within the last hour of its use. There's also a text string, probably to Voda's cell. All I can do is apologize and offer no excuses."

"Thank you for telling me."

"You deserve the truth."

"Will you turn it over to us?"

"Yes, right away, but we need to talk about something you touched on when we last spoke. I need to handle Voda in my own way, and you know I don't always work within the strict confines of the law. I don't want to compromise your position within the Bureau. If you feel obliged to relay everything I report to you, then

I don't know where that leaves us. I can't have Big Brother looking over my shoulder—I don't operate that way."

"I understand what you're telling me. Here's what I suggest. From now on, you'll have to decide what you do and don't tell me. This won't work any other way. If you don't want Director Lansing to know what you're doing, then don't tell me."

"That doesn't sound like you. You've always had some discretion. Something's changed."

"I wanted to tell you in person."

"Tell me what?"

"I've been offered a job in Washington. It's not official yet, but it would be a significant promotion."

"Holly, that's terrific news! Congratulations. I'm not happy about you being farther away, but we've talked about this. We both knew it could happen. When?"

"Next month. I haven't decided to accept it yet. I wanted to talk to you first."

"Holly, your career's important. You've earned this."

"What about us?"

Nathan knew he needed to choose his words carefully. "Nothing needs to change. We can still be together. Military couples make it through deployments. We can too. I don't see a difference."

"Thanks. I didn't know how you'd feel about it."

"We both have careers, separate lives. It doesn't have to be complicated."

"I'm glad to hear you say that. I feel the same way, but let's talk about this later. What's your next move?"

"I'm taking Abrille to Dr. Reavie."

"The same doctor from last year?"

"Yes."

"Have you thought about aftercare for Abrille? It sounds like she's going to need it."

"I haven't figured that out yet."

"What about Special Agent Grangeland? I know you don't want our direct help, but I started her in your direction a few hours ago. I figured it couldn't hurt to have her standing by, you know, just in case."

"Holly, I don't want to put you in an awkward situation again. Involving Grangeland does that."

"Abrille's a material witness in a rapidly expanding federal case, and you've already got your hands full with Lauren."

Holly was right—he couldn't take care of both Abrille and Lauren. Abrille needed more than he could provide, especially the counseling.

"Okay. Tell Grangeland she's in. Again, you'll be obliged to share everything we've discussed with Director Lansing, but I have one request. I'd like Dr. Reavie's involvement with Abrille to remain as anonymous as possible. I spoke with Dr. Reavie a few minutes ago, and he pointed out there are significant legal and moral issues involved because she's a minor. Even if he doesn't treat Abrille, he's obliged to inform CPS of her assault. To make matters worse, Abrille doesn't have a legal guardian for consent purposes. It's a can of worms. Do you think there's anything the Bureau can do?"

"I'll look into this right away and give it top priority. Since Abrille's a material witness against Voda and his operation, I'm sure we'll be able to solve the legal-guardian issue and protect her."

"Depending on what Dr. Reavie finds, he might have to transfer Abrille to a local hospital's ER, which means the legal-guardian and consent issue becomes immediate. Can Grangeland assume that role on a temporary basis if needed?"

"I honestly don't know. We're talking about signing legal documents, hospital admission forms. There's no way to explain Grangeland's role without tracing her involvement back to Dr. Reavie, and ultimately to you. All roads lead to Nathan McBride."

"Isn't that the truth. Well, if Abrille needs to be hospitalized, I'll step up and sign her admission papers and act as her legal guardian. It could be the only way to make sure she doesn't end up in foster care today. She needs counseling, not day care. I'm already facing jail time for my actions tonight—what's a little fraud and forgery added into the fray? Holly, there's something else I haven't told you."

"Okay..."

"Jin is my sister."

There was a pause on the other end. "Your sister? You don't have any sisters."

Nathan told her about the call from Jin and the note stapled to Grant's collar along with his father's dog tag and the dried drop of blood.

"Nathan, this whole thing could be some sort of elaborate ruse to flush you out."

"I've thought about that, but Jin already knows who we are, Harv and me. If she wanted to expose us or damage the US, she could've done it already. She could've created a scandal with my dad or given us to the Iranians. They'd love to parade our heads through the streets of Tehran. There are countless ways she could've ruined our lives, but she hasn't."

"If Jin's truly your sister, then it changes everything. I sensed you were holding something back, but I didn't want to say anything. I figured you had enough on your plate without worrying about me. This has to be tearing you up, not knowing what Jin's role is in all of this."

"It's extremely unsettling, to say the least."

"No wonder you're reluctant to involve us. Do you think your dad knows about Jin?"

"I've been debating it all night, but my gut says no. Jin's note says he doesn't. When I get time, I'll send you everything in my iPhone. I took photos of all the text strings and call logs. I also recorded the verbal messages with my dictation app."

"Send that to me as soon as you can. Of course, I won't tell a soul about Jin being your sister."

"The only thing I'm certain about at this point is that Jin *isn't* involved in some elaborate sting designed to expose Harv and me. I'm also fairly certain Jin is more than just a stay-at-home mom. She's been teaching Lauren basic survival and tactical skills, and she speaks fluent French. Now, get this: so does Abrille. And they both learned French around the same age. And they were both raised in orphanages."

"I seriously doubt any of this is a coincidence."

"My thoughts exactly. I tried calling the number Jin used, but it rings without being answered. It's probably a pay phone. A pay phone..." he said slowly. "Hang on, I'm going to check my cell's call log and see if the number Jin used appears in the gunman's cell. I'm driving, so I can't do this quickly. Hang on..."

Being careful not to take his eyes off the road for more than two seconds at a time, he located the call from Jin in his own phone and looked for the same phone number in the gunman's call log. It wasn't there. "The number Jin used isn't logged in the gunman's cell. I was hoping to catch a break."

"It's possible she can't call because of her situation. I know you don't want to think about it, but Harv could be right. Jin may be integrally involved in Voda's operation, but she's being torn in opposite directions because of Lauren."

"If that's true, it's inconsistent with her note. She said she was taking Voda down at all costs."

"And now that she's gone silent, you have to consider that she might have failed, right?"

Nathan glanced at Lauren, who seemed genuinely asleep. "Right. Look, I won't ask you to withhold anything permanently from Lansing, but I might ask for a delay in passing certain information along."

"Based on everything you just told me, I think that's a fair compromise, but any delays need to be a few hours, no more than that. Agreed?"

"That's more than reasonable. Thanks, Holly. Can you track down the phone number Jin used?"

"Yes."

Nathan gave her the number.

"Let me know what you find, but please keep it between us for now."

"No problem. I'll send you a text, then delete it from my phone."

"I'm sorry I didn't tell you about Jin or the gunman's cell phone. I wish I had a good excuse, but I don't."

"You know I'll never betray your confidence. Ever."

"Thanks, Holly. I've been feeling terrible about it."

"For now, I'll just say I haven't heard anything more from you. If push comes to shove, Lansing could find out we've talked from my cell phone records, but I don't think he'll go that far, and even if he does, he won't know what we talked about."

"Could this compromise your new job? I can't live with that."

"Nathan, we're talking about your sister, Senator Stone McBride's daughter. My new job doesn't take precedence over that. When are you going to tell him?"

"I could've called already. I guess I'm stalling."

"Nathan, he's chairman of the Senate Committee on Domestic Terrorism. He's one of the most powerful political figures in Washington, not to mention he's friends with Director Lansing and the president. Remember those other friends in high places CIA director Cantrell said you have? Need I say more?"

"I don't know why I didn't think of all this sooner."

"You're too close to it."

"I'll call him."

"What you're doing—protecting Lauren and Abrille—I think it's extremely selfless and honorable. Don't ever forget you're a good guy through all of this, okay?"

"Thanks, Holly. I needed to hear that."

"You have an unbelievable ability to handle stressful situations—it's one of your most valuable assets—but it takes a toll. You don't show it, but I know this Jin business is tearing you up.

I've heard this tone in your voice before. You need sleep. Can you drop off for a spell at Dr. Reavie's office?"

"I think so."

"I'll update Grangeland on Abrille's situation. You've got enough on your plate. And, Nathan? You aren't doing any jail time—that's a promise."

"Thanks. I needed to hear that too."

"Get some sleep. Count on seeing Grangeland arrive at Dr. Reavie's office around oh-five-hundred or so. Give her that cell phone, and she'll get it to us."

"Thanks, Holly. You're the best."

Half an hour later, Nathan arrived on the outskirts of Rancho Bernardo. Despite Lauren's comment about being wide-awake, she'd managed to doze off. Slumped in the backseat, she and Abrille looked innocent and peaceful.

Nathan pulled into the parking lot of a small retail center and stopped in front of Dr. Reavie's office. It looked as though Dr. Reavie's workplace shared a wall with a small restaurant. At this early-morning hour, few cars were present. A few seconds later, Dr. Reavie stepped through his front door and approached the Explorer. Nathan couldn't recall ever having actually met him. In his mid-fifties, he was tall and lean and appeared to be in great physical shape. Despite the circumstances of having been called in the middle of the night, Dr. Reavie wore a friendly expression. Nathan believed it to be genuine, but he knew it was for Abrille's sake as well.

Nathan asked Lauren to sit tight. He climbed out, made eye contact, and offered his hand. "It's nice to finally meet you, Doctor. Please accept my apology for this."

"There's no need to apologize. It's nice to meet you too. Let's check on our patient."

Nathan opened the passenger door, and Abrille sat perfectly still. She looked so tiny. In Spanish, Nathan said, "Abrille, this is Dr. Reavie. He's going to look at your stomach. He's not going to hurt you, and he won't do anything without your permission. Okay?"

Abrille said, "Okay."

Also in Spanish, Dr. Reavie said, "Hi, Abrille. How are you feeling?"

"A little sleepy."

"You were asleep. You woke up just now?"

Abrille nodded.

"Do you think you can walk okay?"

Another nod.

Dr. Reavie offered his hand, and, surprisingly, she took it. Nathan had fully expected her to cringe away from him or act apprehensive, but Abrille did neither.

Hand in hand, Dr. Reavie and Abrille walked toward the entrance. Abrille was hunched slightly, probably from pain. Nathan motioned with his head to Lauren. She climbed out and took his hand. Just inside the door to the right was a small waiting area. Nathan closed the front door and sat down. Lauren took a seat next to him.

"Is Abrille going to be okay?" Lauren asked.

"I think so, but let's see what Dr. Reavie says."

The moment of truth would arrive soon. Nathan's situation would either become significantly more complicated or remain relatively stable. Everything hinged on whether Abrille needed emergency treatment at a hospital. Nathan leaned his head back and tried to remain optimistic. If Abrille had to be admitted for emergency care, someone would have to assume the legal-guardian role, and it looked as though that someone was him. A horrible crime had been committed against Abrille, and Nathan knew the police would get involved. If an SDPD unit arrived to take a report, would Nathan be recognized? His face had been recorded on video at several different locations tonight. The best images probably came from Nordstrom, where the lighting was brightest. He didn't know how fast the SDPD ballistics lab processed evidence, but his shell casings and any recovered slugs from the initial crash site at Ulric would match the shell casings from the grocery store shooting, and now the Tecate Palms Motel as well. It was a good bet Nathan's photo had been circulated to every law enforcement agency in San Diego County.

Nathan didn't think Abrille's condition looked life-threatening, but he wasn't making the assessment. Dr. Reavie was. Either way, once Special Agent Mary Grangeland arrived, she'd become a tremendous asset. As a material witness and organized-crime victim, Abrille would benefit from the protection and resources of the FBI. She'd likely be placed in the witness security program. Ironically, that was the same program Lauren had thought she was entering when Voda first kidnapped her.

Dr. Reavie entered the waiting area.

"Jane and Linda are getting Abrille prepped."

"Dr. Reavie, this is Lauren."

In a formal manner, Lauren shook hands.

"It's nice to meet you, Lauren."

"Nice to meet you too. Are you going to operate on Abrille?"

"I hope we won't need to, but we better have a look and see."

"Thank you again for doing this," Nathan said. "It's very generous of you."

"I'm just glad to be able to help. Hopefully she's got a localized infection on the abdominal wall or just under the skin that I can treat here."

"I hope so too. First names?" Nathan asked.

"Doug."

"Nathan." They shook hands again. "I forget when, but I think Harv mentioned you work with your wife as a team?"

"Yes, Jane is a CRNA and does a great job as a nurse anesthetist. We work together well. Jane also participates on our trips to Mexico, where we repair cleft lips and palates in children."

"You do that pro bono." It wasn't a question.

Doug nodded. "Since I wasn't sure what we'd be facing, I asked Linda, my surgical nurse, to be present as well."

"I'm sorry. I guess I hadn't realized what was involved."

"Again, there's no need to apologize. Emergencies happen. I'm glad to help. Regarding the ace I mentioned on the phone, I have a good friend in charge of the juvenile division of the district attorney's office who could help us with reporting this discreetly. I've done some free plastic-surgery treatment for some of her victims, and I think she'll help us."

"Report what?" Lauren asked.

Nathan answered for the doctor. "What happened to Abrille has to be reported to Child Protective Services. She's a victim of a violent crime, and she needs to be protected. I'm sure Doug needs to do some pre-op work, so let's allow him to get started." He looked at Dr. Reavie. "May I tell you something with doctor-patient privilege?"

"If it's about tonight's activities, it's probably better if you don't."

"Lauren is my niece. I just found out tonight that I have a half sister I never knew about."

Doug's expression remained somewhat guarded. "That's got to be quite a shocker."

"To put it mildly. Harv's never actually said it, but I know he thinks of you like family, and Harv's like a brother to me. I guess that makes our connection like family too."

"That's very kind of you to say."

"I never properly thanked you for helping us last year. You were more than generous."

"Thank you for sending the flowers."

Nathan and Lauren took seats in the waiting room while Doug locked the front door.

"Would you like something to drink? There's a refrigerator in the back—help yourselves. If you need it, the bathroom's right around the corner."

"Thanks, Doug."

"This may not take long."

"Can I watch?" Lauren asked.

"I think that's a question for your uncle." Doug looked at Nathan. "If Lauren's presence has a comforting effect, she could stay until Abrille is sedated, but not after that."

"I think it's best if we let Doug do his job without him having to worry about us."

Doug turned, then stopped. "Abrille will need follow-up care. Do you have something arranged?"

"Yes. Special Agent Grangeland's on her way."

"I remember her."

Nathan smiled. "Most people do."

He leaned his head back and closed his eyes again. Holly was right, he needed some rack time, but dozing off in front of Lauren wasn't a good idea. His recurring nightmares could be a problem. She'd have to be formally warned about the danger of waking him. At his La Jolla home, she'd awakened him from a light sleep, so it hadn't been dangerous. Harv often joked about using a ten-foot pole to wake him, and unfortunately, that humor had roots in the truth. If Nathan were to enter REM sleep, waking him suddenly could have catastrophic results. Before he'd met Holly, one of his first attempts at having a relationship with a girlfriend had ended badly. Even though Nathan had warned her to wake him from a safe distance, she'd given him a little shake and ended up in the hospital with a dislocated shoulder and two broken fingers. The emergency-room scene had been awkward at best, downright humiliating at worst. Despite his girlfriend's insistence that Nathan hadn't done it on purpose, no one believed her explanation. They just assumed she was another battered victim who was protecting her abuser. And Nathan's scarred face only made things worse. He'd never forget the looks of contempt from the emergency room's staff. Despite pressure from the attending ER doctor, his girlfriend hadn't pressed charges because she knew

Nathan hadn't intended to hurt her. A week later, he'd gotten a "Dear John" email.

Holly had said she'd take care of the call to Grangeland, but he tapped her number from his contacts list and got dumped into voice mail—she was probably on the phone. He left her a message supplying her with Doug's address and also told her he was lying down for a catnap. She'd know not to call.

"I'm going to get some shut-eye in one of Doug's examination rooms. Are you okay out here for a spell?"

"You can't sleep out here?"

"Again, let's just say it's complicated."

"It's your nightmares, isn't it?"

He nodded. "Just knock on the door and make sure I'm awake before anyone comes in. Tell Doug to knock, okay?"

"Why hasn't my mom called?"

"I'm sure she's okay. Try not to think about it."

He left the waiting room for some much-needed rest...

And awoke with a start. What the hell was that sound? There it was again. Knocking. He looked around, quickly orienting himself.

"I'm awake."

He glanced at his watch. Only twenty-five minutes had passed. He got up from the floor, stretched, and opened the door. Dr. Reavie greeted him.

"How's Abrille? Is she okay?"

"Yes, she doesn't have sepsis, like I suspected, but she does have an infection in her abdominal wall. I've got her on sulfa antibiotics, and I don't think she'll have any problem recovering, so at this point she doesn't need to be transferred to Pomerado."

"Well, that's good news."

Doug's expression remained serious.

"What is it?" Nathan asked.

"You aren't going to believe what we found."

CHAPTER 24

Doug handed Nathan a small Ziploc bag.

"Tell me you're kidding," Nathan said.

Ten beautifully cut gemstones sparkled in the fluorescent light.

"Alexandrites," Doug said. "And nice quality."

"Incredible."

"I found them just beneath her Scarpa's fascia, a fibrous layer in the fat. They were probably aligned along the length of the incision to look less obvious."

"That makes sense. I hadn't noticed anything other than the staples."

"The swelling helped hide them as well. Abrille has low body fat on her abdomen, which could explain why they were under the fascia but not as deep as the muscle. But anyone with medical knowledge would've been able to feel them just like I did when I palpated the area. Linda's putting on the bandages right now. I had to close the wound loosely because the infected tissues may need to drain, but if the scar doesn't heal nicely, I can revise it later."

"So you think Abrille's going to be okay?"

Doug nodded. "Even though the wound was purulent and inflamed, the infection was localized to the subcutaneous fat and Scarpa's fascia. It didn't extend to the deep fascia. I irrigated it with antiseptic solution, and it looks pretty good. I think with the combination of cleansing it well, the antibiotics, and her youth, Abrille should make a full recovery."

"That's great news. Do you think this wound was created solely for the purpose of implanting these gemstones?"

"In my opinion, yes. She probably got the infection because one or more of the alexandrites wasn't properly sterilized."

"She's a human courier," Nathan said under his breath. He poured the gemstones out of the Ziploc onto the examination table and removed the paper from his pocket.

Hernandez:

1.53	90	50	(4871)
1.64	95	60	
1.85	90	55	(37)
2.07	95	70	(116)
2.14	95	70	
2.39	95	80	
2.42	90	80	(4702)
2.78	85	85	
2.96	90	110	(34)
3.02	95	150	(32)

"Doug, help me out here. Take a look and tell me what you think." As he spoke, Lauren entered the room and stood near the door. "We can ignore the fourth column—it's a set of GPS coordinates. If we assume each line represents one of these alexandrites, what do the numbers mean?"

"Maybe the carat weight for each stone?" Doug asked. "They look like they range in size with the list."

"Agreed," Nathan said. "What about the second number?"

"I'm not sure. Diamonds are graded with the four Cs. It might have something to do with grading."

"Are alexandrites graded like diamonds?"

"I don't know, but I suppose they could be."

Nathan tapped his memory. "Cut, clarity, carats...and...I can't remember the last one."

"Color," Doug said.

"Can I see?" Lauren asked.

Nathan motioned her over. "We're trying to figure out what the second numbers mean."

She pointed at the gemstones. "Those were inside Abrille?"

"Yeah." Nathan handed Lauren his phone. "Could you look online for a short description of alexandrite, something that gives us an overview?"

She began tapping away.

"Their color changes," said Doug. "Under the OR lights, they were a bright reddish orange. In here, under the fluorescents, they're a dark emerald green. It's a beautiful color."

"Lauren, can we see your ring?"

She pried it off her finger and handed it to him. Next to the others, its emerald color appeared to be a flawless match. It was a good bet the stone in Lauren's ring came from the same mine.

"I'm certainly no expert on the subject," Doug said, "but I bet the amount of color change is the primary factor in determining value. Size, cut, and clarity would be considered, but color change is probably the most important."

"Okay," said Nathan, looking back at the list. "So what do you think?"

"The number next to the weight could be the percentage change in color."

Nathan thought about it for a second. "So if the number was one hundred, the stone would turn from pure green to pure red?"

"Yes. If I'm not mistaken, red and green are complementary colors."

"They are." Lauren looked up from Nathan's phone. "We learned the color wheel in school. The other pairs are purple and yellow, and blue and orange. If you try to mix them, they turn an ugly gray color."

Doug nodded. "It could explain why the same number appears on more than one line. If that's the case, then these alexandrites come pretty close to a complete spectral change in color. The lowest number is eighty-five percent. That probably makes them very rare and expensive."

"Okay, I found something," Lauren said. "Should I read it to you? It isn't, like, real long or anything."

Nathan made eye contact with Doug and offered a barely perceptible smile. "Sure," he said.

"Okay, here goes. Chromium gives alexandrite its color. In most minerals, a trace element like chromium would provide only one color to the mineral, but in alexandrite it produces two. Coloring agents are dependent on the wavelength of light and the chemical bonds in the crystal to determine the color that they will cause. An element like copper in normal light causes a green color, like in mal-ah...ch—?"

Nathan helped her. "Malachite."

"Oh, thanks." She continued: "...and a blue color in...ah-zur-ite. Did I say it right?"

"You were close. It's azurite."

"Okay...and a blue color in azurite. It all depends on the character of the chemical bonding. In a single specimen of alexandrite, the chromium is in such a balanced state that the color of the specimen depends on the character of light that hits the crystal. If the light is natural sunlight or fluorescent light, the crystal will be green; however, if the light is incandescent light from a common indoor lightbulb, then the crystal will appear red."

"I'm impressed," Doug said. "You read very well."

Lauren smiled. "I practice with my mom a lot." Her face clouded for a few seconds.

Nathan knew she didn't want to cry in front of Doug, so he reached out and held her hand. "What about the third number?" Nathan asked.

"Tougher call, but I'd guess it's the fifth C."

"The fifth C?"

"Cost. All four Cs determine cost."

"Are you thinking what I'm thinking?"

Doug nodded.

"Then the third number is probably the dollar amount in thousands. So the biggest alexandrite is worth $150,000?"

"I don't think so," Lauren said.

"Why not?"

"Because my mom said this ring is worth $290,000, and it's about the same size as those bigger ones."

"Cost per carat," Doug said slowly.

"Oh, man, then we're looking at a small fortune. Doug, can you get a calculator?"

"Your cell phone has one," Lauren said.

"We'll need a running tab."

"I'll get a pen and paper." Doug left the examination room and returned momentarily.

"I'll give you the numbers," Nathan said. He multiplied 1.53 by 50,000 and said, "76,500." He did the same thing on the next line: "98,400."

Half a minute later, Doug read back all the numbers so Nathan could total them.

"If we're right about this, then Abrille had $1,872,650 worth of gemstones embedded in her body."

"Seriously?" Lauren asked.

"The evidence doesn't lie. Lauren, it's really important you never mention anything about Abrille or Dr. Reavie to anyone. I don't want anyone to know we were ever here."

"I promise I won't."

"I'd better go see how our patient's doing," Doug said, and left the examination room.

"Lauren, it's fairly obvious Voda's been using these girls to smuggle alexandrites. Did you ever hear your mom talk about Bolivia?"

"No, never."

"Why would Abrille need to speak French?" Nathan asked, more of himself. Abrille had told him the other girls were also being taught French because they thought they were being adopted as well. Maybe their final destination was France or a French-speaking country. If that were true, then why were the border murder victims found in the mountains of East San Diego? It didn't make sense. Why teach the girls French if they weren't going to use it? The most reasonable explanation seemed to point toward a horrible deception—that the girls were being adopted, rather than used as human couriers and then discarded. Nathan wondered why Voda would use them like this in the first place. Couldn't a smuggler simply carry the gemstones through airport security in a carry-on? It probably had to do with passenger screening. If a carry-on bag were searched, the gemstones might be discovered. And if an attempt were made to hide them—like in the lining of the bag—it would cause suspicion among airport security and might even lead to the smuggler's being detained for questioning.

Having filled out US customs paperwork many times, Nathan knew that items over a certain dollar value had to be declared. Using the girls as couriers, Voda left no paperwork trail, paid no duties or taxes, and eliminated the need to trust adult couriers with his precious cargo.

It seemed unlikely that the coyotes had known about Abrille's payload, with the possible exception of the third man, who'd appeared from the bathroom. He'd looked different from the coyotes, more formal and measured. Clearly, he hadn't been one of Voda's men, because if he had, there would've been no need for the paper containing the GPS coordinates. If true, that meant that

Voda's actual possession of the alexandrites started once the gemstones arrived in the United States. If the coordinates were used to protect whoever was supplying the gemstones, then Abrille's location was probably released upon receipt of a payment—likely the final payment. That might also explain why Voda was willing to pay so much to recover the paper containing Abrille's location—he'd already made the final payment for his purchase.

The more Nathan thought about this human-courier scheme, the more perfect it seemed. A nondescript man traveling with a young girl wouldn't draw any unwanted attention, especially if they both possessed a valid passport and shared a last name. The metal detectors might discover the staples, but signs of recent surgery wouldn't look suspicious and might even elicit sympathy. And the gemstones wouldn't trigger metal detectors. Transporting the alexandrites inside the girls also ensured absolute possession and control—a cruel but effective smuggling technique. And even more cruel, when the gems had been extracted, the girls would be murdered and discarded—known only as the latest border murder victims.

Nathan made a mental note to mention to Holly: the previous border murder victims should be examined for an incision like Abrille's—if they hadn't been already. The San Diego medical examiner's office was operated by top-notch professionals who were unlikely to miss something like that. Of course, if the other victims were Bolivian orphans like Abrille, then their torsos might have been slashed to mask the cargo wounds. Voda or his henchmen would've removed the staples, but there'd be tiny puncture marks present. If the entire area surrounding the wound were cut away, there wouldn't be any puncture marks left, but the corpse would be missing about a quarter-inch sliver of skin on both margins.

"What are you thinking about?" Lauren asked.

"I was thinking about Voda's smuggling operation, how cruel it is to use the girls like this."

"It's pretty bad. But you saved Abrille."

"*We* saved her. You were there, remember?"

Lauren beamed at the compliment and gave him a hug. "We're a team."

"Right—a team."

Nathan had a few calls to make, especially the big one to Voda. He'd have to determine the best way to use Abrille and the cache of alexandrites against the guy. He looked at his watch— 0337 hours. His dad would be up and dressed by now, but Nathan wasn't quite ready to make the call. He also needed more shut-eye. Although he could keep going for another eighteen hours or so, it wouldn't be tactically sound. He'd lived much of his adult life according to the military adage "Sleep when you can."

He checked with Doug, who confirmed that Abrille would need several more hours to recover from the anesthetics. Special Agent Grangeland was still ninety minutes away, so Nathan decided to use the time to get more sleep. The call to Voda would have to wait. Nathan programmed his phone to wake him at 0450 hours, which gave him ten minutes to splash some water on his face before Grangeland arrived. Maybe Doug had an extra toothbrush lying around somewhere.

Despite everything on his mind, Nathan managed to nod off.

The iPhone's alarm did its job. He checked the time and sat up.

Coffee.

He ached for a fresh cup, knowing full well it was a quasi-addiction. He didn't drink, didn't gamble, and didn't smoke, but he *did* consume coffee. He found Doug around the corner in a small office.

"Did you get some sleep?"

"About an hour," Nathan said. "Thanks for letting us crash."

"It's no trouble. I've been catching up on some dictation."

"How's Abrille?"

"She's doing well."

"Special Agent Grangeland should be arriving any minute. Thanks again for everything, Doug."

"I'm happy to help. I've got a small safe embedded in the slab if you need a secure place to store the alexandrites."

"I appreciate the offer, and it's not a matter of trust, but I think it's best to distance ourselves from you as much as possible."

Doug nodded. "You look like a man in need of coffee."

"Indeed I am."

"Follow me."

Grangeland arrived a few minutes later. With Doug in tow, Nathan and Lauren went out front to meet her. Emerging from a nondescript sedan and walking toward them in tan tactical pants and a dark polo shirt with the FBI seal embroidered above the left pocket, Grangeland looked stunning. Her blond hair was pulled back in a ponytail. Closing the deal, her Glock service piece occupied her right hip in a compact holster. Although Nathan had never asked how old she was, he guessed mid-thirties.

"Grangeland, if we keep meeting like this, people will say we're in love."

"You're unlovable."

"It's damn good to see you."

They embraced tightly.

Lauren interrupted them. "Well, aren't you going to introduce me to your...*friend*?"

Nathan winked at Grangeland. "Special Agent Grangeland, meet Lauren Marchand."

They shook hands. "It's nice to meet you, Lauren."

"It's nice to meet you too. Is your gun loaded?"

"Yes, all FBI special agents are required to carry loaded weapons in public."

"Are you a good shot, like Nathan?"

Nathan kept a straight face and crossed his arms, as if asking Grangeland: *Well, are you?*

"I think I can hold my own."

"Let's go check on Abrille," Nathan said, ending Lauren's interrogation. He sensed a *Have you ever shot anyone?* question coming.

Grangeland said hello to Dr. Reavie and gave him a hug—a good one.

"Easy, Grangeland," Nathan said. "Doug's a married man."

In the small recovery room, Linda had Abrille in a semi-upright position in a large recliner. Dressed in a light blue surgical gown, Abrille looked groggy, barely awake. After what she'd been through, it was probably for the best.

Doug returned to his office while Nathan got Grangeland a cup of coffee.

"I need to give you a thorough update on everything that's happened," Nathan said. "I'd like your input in planning my next move."

"Sounds good," Grangeland said.

With Lauren in tow, Nathan and Grangeland returned to the waiting area. Five minutes later, Grangeland knew the whole story.

Nathan handed the confiscated cell phone to Grangeland. "I want to pursue the Opus X A cigar reference from the text string in there. If we can determine where Voda or his men purchased the cigars, it might give us a good starting place."

"Okay, I'll see what I can dig up. How much of this am I sharing with Holly?"

"She talked to you about that?"

"While I was driving. She said to let you decide."

"Let's see what you find first."

"You got it."

"As I understand it," Nathan said, "Holly's working on Abrille's situation. Since Abrille's a material witness against Voda, I'm pretty sure she's trying to get Abrille into the witness security program as soon as possible. But for now, she stays with us. Since she didn't need to be admitted to the hospital, we've got some extra time. We'll get her situated in the same hotel we used last year and make sure she's as comfortable as possible. I appreciate you helping me out." He looked at Lauren and winked. "As you can see, I've already got an eighty-three-pound ball and chain."

Lauren poked his arm. "Hey, don't be mean."

"You'll live. We're both gonna get some rack time while Grangeland does some homework."

"But I'm not tired."

"Suit yourself. I'm crashing for a couple more hours." Nathan looked at Grangeland. "I'm not sure what time Doug's office opens for business, but we need to be out of here before it does. I'm setting my alarm for oh–seven hundred. See you in about two hours."

Nathan awoke to the electronic buzzer and again had to orient himself. He left the examination room and found Grangeland and Lauren sitting in the waiting area.

"Did you find anything useful in the cell phone?"

"I think so. One of the phone numbers in the call log belongs to a retail tobacco shop called Samantha's. It's in Del Mar. The text with the Opus X A reference mentioned having the cigars delivered. Guess what? Samantha's does deliveries. I checked the website."

"Good work. We'll head over there as soon as the doors open. Do we know what time that is?"

"I'll check the website again."

"I'd like you with me for this, which means Abrille has to be with us as well. I'm sure Samantha's isn't open this early, so let's do this: let's get checked in and give Abrille a chance to get more rest. We'll order room service. Lauren and I haven't eaten anything in a while."

"Sounds good," Grangeland said.

Although sleepy, Abrille could walk, and Grangeland helped her into the FBI sedan. Lauren sat next to her and held her hand. Doug offered a few pillows to make Abrille's ride more comfortable, saying they didn't need to be returned. After moving Gerry's Explorer to a remote area of the parking lot, Nathan stuffed all the loose equipment into the duffel bag but left the parabolic mike behind. He slung the bag over his shoulder and hustled back to the front door. They exchanged good-byes with Doug and Jane, and they went on their way.

CHAPTER 25

With Abrille and Lauren secured in the backseat, Grangeland drove out of the Rancho Bernardo Inn's parking lot while Nathan entered Samantha's address into the nav. Grangeland had determined the place opened at 0900. The tobacco shop was located in a small retail center off I-5 in Del Mar. According to the map, it ought to take around twenty-five minutes to get there, but rush-hour traffic would probably add some extra time to their drive. It was just after 0830 hours, so the timing should work okay.

"Lauren, I'm going to tell Grangeland about us. I think of her like family. Several years ago, she helped Harv and me in Montana. You don't need to know the details, but she nearly died during the mission."

"Seriously?" Lauren asked.

"I think Nathan's exaggerating a bit."

"It's no exaggeration. Now, just because *I'm* telling Grangeland about us doesn't mean it's okay for *you* to tell anyone."

Grangeland glanced into the backseat at Lauren, before looking at Nathan. "Tell me what?" she asked.

"Lauren's my niece."

"Your niece? But you don't have any brothers or sisters. Do you?"

"Jin is my half sister. While my father was stationed in Korea during the war, he had a brief relationship with a young woman."

"Does he know about Jin?"

"No."

"Given who your father is, someone might be trying to create a scandal."

"Yeah, I thought about that, but I don't think that's Jin's motivation. She has classified information on Harv and me. If she wanted to harm either my father or me, she could've done it long ago. Jin wrote me a lengthy note and said my father doesn't know about her. She taped his Korean War dog tag to the note. There was a dried drop of blood on the back of it. I'm sure Jin included the blood so we could do a DNA analysis. But at this point, I don't have any reason to doubt her. Lauren and I have nearly identical eyes. It's been a dominant family trait for generations."

"This is going to be a real shocker for him."

"True, and we still don't have any idea how Jin ran afoul of Voda's operation. On the one hand, it may have been the bad luck of marrying Marchand, who was doing some business with Voda. But given what little I do know about Jin, I think it could be more than a coincidence."

Grangeland nodded. "Yeah, most moms don't vow to go after criminals, even if the bad guys kill their husband. Plus"—Grangeland looked over at Nathan—"she *is* related to you. I've never known with certainty what you and Harv did for a living, but it doesn't take a giant leap to conclude it involved covert ops."

"Let's just say we worked for the government in a discreet way."

"Nathan was a spy," Lauren interrupted with conviction. "I'm going to be a spy too."

"Lauren, we've had this discussion. I never said I was a spy."

Grangeland smiled, then grew serious. "Maybe Jin has a covert background as well?"

"That's what Harv thinks, and I'm beginning to agree. She's been teaching Lauren basic survival and tactical skills."

"I know how to make a fire from scratch," Lauren said.

"Impressive," Grangeland said.

"I know other stuff too, like how to work radios and night-vision scopes and thermal imagers."

Grangeland glanced at Nathan with a puzzled expression.

"Let's stay focused here," Nathan said. "Lauren, when we get to the tobacco shop, I want you to remain in the car with Abrille. She's still sleepy, but I want you to keep a close eye on her anyway."

Lauren didn't respond.

"Okay?"

"Okay…"

"Thank you. Trust me, if it's what I think, you won't like it in there."

Samantha's occupied a prominent location just inside the main driveway leading into a retail center. Grangeland parked as close to the front door as possible. Even though it was a cool morning, she rolled the windows down a bit to keep the sedan from getting overly warm in the sun.

Nathan pivoted in his seat. "Okay, Lauren. We'll be right back. Sit tight. This shouldn't take long."

Lauren looked like she wanted to protest, but remained silent.

"Grangeland, I know it's against Bureau policy, but we don't want to look like cops. Do you have a different shirt?"

"Yeah, I have a change of clothes in the trunk."

"Do you mind changing your shirt and leaving your service piece behind?"

"I suppose that's okay." She popped the trunk and climbed out. She returned with a white button-down shirt and got back in. Without hesitating, she pulled her FBI shirt off.

Black bra.

The visual burned into Nathan's brain before he could stop it.

"Hey, you aren't supposed to look," Lauren said with a slap to his shoulder.

"Well, I didn't look, *exactly*."

Grangeland buttoned her blouse. "It's okay, Lauren—he's seen me before."

"For cryin' out loud, Grangeland, you're gonna give this innocent child the wrong idea."

"I thought Holly was your girlfriend," Lauren said.

"She is. Grangeland's referring to something that happened… Oh, forget it—there's no use trying to explain."

"What's wrong, Nathan? You look kinda red."

He stared straight ahead and shook his head.

There was something about the smell of a tobacco shop that appealed to Nathan. It didn't smell noxious or bad. It had a seasoned aroma that he knew took years to create.

Just inside the door, Grangeland whispered, "That's Samantha, over by the register. I recognize her from the photos on the website."

"Let's go say hello."

Like caged gorillas, the handful of male customers stared at Grangeland. Nathan couldn't blame them, but good grief, a little discretion was in order. "These clowns are acting like they've been on a deserted island for the last twenty years," he whispered.

"I've tried to get used to it, but I don't think I ever will."

Nathan and Grangeland walked up to Samantha, who held up her hands like a robbery victim. "Whatever it is, I didn't do it."

Nathan faked a bewildered expression. "We'd like to get some Opus X As and heard this is the place to buy them."

"Then you heard right. How many would you like? I only have five in stock. They have to be special-ordered from Fuente."

"We'd like fifty. Delivered…"

Samantha's eyes grew a little. "I see. You *do* know how much they cost, right?"

"Indeed we do."

"Follow me."

They followed Samantha past the walk-in humidor and into the stockroom. They entered a small office embellished with all kinds of cigar posters, most them featuring beautiful women in alluring poses. Samantha sat down behind her desk and sighed. She waved to a couple of chairs. "All right, you two. Why are you really here?"

Nathan exchanged a glance with Grangeland.

"Come on. I had you guys pegged as cops the moment you walked in."

"What gave us away?" Nathan asked.

"Instinct. I see a lot of people walk through my door, and I can usually nail cops within the first few steps."

"I'm impressed, but you're only half right."

"She's the cop, not you. If you're after information on my Opus X A buyer, don't bother asking unless you can produce some paper."

"We're hoping to avoid that," Nathan said.

"No doubt you are, but I'm protective of my clients, especially the one you're interested in. For one, he tips like a champ."

"I'm really more interested in you," Nathan said.

Samantha's expression changed.

"You may have us nailed, but I've got you nailed as well."

"I'm intrigued. Do tell."

"You don't like men much, except as customers. You have one or more cats. You're left-handed, you like to vacation in Mexico, and your favorite color is blue. Oh, and you've got a rocking plastic surgeon."

After a few seconds, Samantha said, "To quote someone I just met, what gave it away?"

"A couple of things," Nathan said with a straight face. He saw Grangeland roll her eyes.

Now Samantha smiled a genuine, gleaming grin. "Well, big guy, you just earned my undivided attention."

"There's a very traumatized young girl in our car, and we think the man who buys your Opus X As is responsible for hurting her. We think he's a serial. We're talking about half a dozen girls."

Samantha paused, and Nathan saw he'd scored a direct hit. "Then why no paper?"

"I'm working independently."

"With a cop? Did this girl's father hire you?"

"She's an orphan."

"How do I know this won't come back to bite me?"

"You don't."

Samantha lit a cigarette and squinted. After a few seconds she reached down, opened a drawer, and placed a file on her desk. "If you'll excuse me for a minute, I need to check on some inventory in the humidor."

Without looking back, Samantha walked out of her office and closed the door behind her.

"You want to tell me what just happened?" Grangeland asked.

Nathan opened the file. "We communicated."

"Yeah, I gathered that. How did you know all that stuff about her?"

"I presume you mean the not-so-obvious things? See those eight-by-ten photos on the wall behind her desk? I gambled on the woman in both of them being more than just a friend." He nodded toward the door. "She's working the register out there. This is a mom-and-mom establishment."

"That was a big gamble."

"Look at the photos. What else do you see? The photo on the left is in Cancún. The one on the right's in Cabo. Both picture frames are blue. So is her coffee cup, and her hair tie's also blue."

"What about the cat reference?"

"Hair on her blue blouse."

"You saw all of that?"

"You're forgetting what I used to do for a living."

"I can't forget something you haven't told me."

"Point taken. Trust me, if we'd tried to strong-arm Samantha, she would've clammed up."

"I'm amazed."

"At what?"

"You got the information without having to break anyone's arms."

"Thanks…I think."

"Well, we've got what we came for. Now what?"

"It's time to cull Voda's herd."

"I'm a special agent in the FBI. I didn't hear that."

On the return walk through the shop, Nathan spotted Samantha inside the walk-in humidor. "I'll be right back," he told Grangeland.

"You find what you needed?" Samantha asked as he approached.

"Yes, thank you."

"The place is near Montgomery Field. Some kind of furniture retailer."

Nathan thought that sounded promising. Marchand manufactured patio furniture.

"Was it a big building? Like a warehouse?"

"It wasn't really big, you know, like a Costco, but it was pretty good-size. I told the guy on the phone we don't deliver that far south, but since he bought one hundred Opus X As, I told him I'd make an exception. I handled the delivery personally. The guy paid cash, just under ten grand, then threw in a five-hundred-buck tip."

"Can you describe him? Was he fair-skinned? European-looking, with a Spanish accent?"

"I'm no expert, but yeah, I'd say he looked Spanish. He definitely spoke with an accent."

"How about his build, hair color?"

"Tall guy, good-looking." She smiled. "Not as tall or as good-looking as you, but he was definitely over six feet. I don't remember the exact color of his hair, but yeah, it was darkish."

That didn't fit Voda, because he wasn't tall, but it could have been one of his men. "Anything else you can tell me about the place?"

"Not really. To be honest, I wasn't paying a whole lot of attention. They wanted me to deliver the cigars at the back of the building, though. I remember feeling a little nervous about it. I thought maybe I'd get ripped off, or worse."

"Why did you think that?"

"It was the way the guy talked to me on the phone. He sounded…I don't know…arrogant, like a jerk. He made me feel like I was nothing more than a delivery girl, even though he knew I owned the store."

"Yeah, that sounds like our guys. How many men did you see?"

"Just the tall guy who bought the cigars."

"Thanks again, Samantha. You're a stand-up woman. Sadly, it's an uncommon trait these days. I honestly don't think you have anything to worry about. Besides, I have a feeling some of your best customers are law enforcement, and I'm willing to bet they're quite protective of you."

"Right on both counts. I'm a pretty good judge of character. Despite your hardened look, you're actually quite personable."

Nathan didn't respond.

"I'm being serious. What you said to me in my office? It took some manhood, if you catch my drift." She lowered her voice. "Tell Ms. Ice Water to lighten up a little."

"We are who we are, Samantha."

"Amen to that. Get some payback for the girl."

"That's the general idea."

Nathan left the humidor and found Grangeland near the entrance with her back against the wall, watching the door. It was no wonder Samantha had her pegged as a cop. No doubt Grangeland didn't like being unarmed, probably felt naked without her service piece.

Back at Grangeland's sedan, Lauren looked a little peeved at having been delegated to babysitting duty. Still under the influence of the anesthetic drugs, Abrille slept with her head propped against a pillow.

Nathan slid into the front passenger seat while Grangeland retrieved her Glock from the trunk. He pivoted toward Lauren and asked, "That wasn't so bad, was it?"

With crossed arms, she said, "I don't like being left in the car. *I* could've helped you."

"Trust me, you wouldn't have liked it in there." Nathan told a white lie. "The place was lousy with smoke."

"You aren't kidding," Grangeland said, supporting his exaggeration. "My eyes are burning,"

"Mine too. Let's get back to the RB Inn."

"I'm staying with you," Lauren said in a matter-of-fact tone.

Nathan didn't respond. In her note, Jin had mentioned Lauren's stubborn personality, and some of it seemed to be showing. He had little doubt Lauren would strongly resist staying with Grangeland and Abrille. But rather than challenge her statement, he kept quiet and thought about his next move: a little visit to the furniture store. He needed to properly introduce himself to the tall Spaniard.

Back at the Rancho Bernardo Inn, Nathan parked as close to the entrance as possible to minimize Abrille's walk.

He needed to call his father. Further delay would serve only to distract him, but he didn't want to make the call until he was alone. He looked at his watch—his father would already be on the Senate floor. Nathan decided to send a text and tapped the message in capital letters.

SITUATION CRITICAL: CALL ME BACK ASAP

That ought to get his dad's undivided attention.

Everyone in the sedan waited until he was finished texting. Nathan pivoted to face Lauren. "I know you don't want to stay with Grangeland and Abrille, but I really need you to. I promise I'm not ditching you—you have my word. I won't be gone long, a couple of hours at most."

"But I want to come with you."

"Please don't make this difficult for Grangeland, okay?"

She sounded dejected but said, "Okay."

He felt some surprise at her reaction. He'd expected an argument. "Try to get some sleep. You haven't had much in the last thirty-six hours."

Lauren nodded slightly. "I will."

"Thank you." He knew Lauren didn't have his stamina, so he chalked up some of her compliance to fatigue.

He looked at Grangeland. "This could be a dead end. Give me two hours, max. Understood?"

Nathan knew she'd gathered his meaning—her expression confirmed it.

After Grangeland retrieved her overnight bag and briefcase from the trunk, Nathan waved good-bye and drove out of the parking lot.

CHAPTER 26

Without Lauren, Nathan felt tremendous freedom, as if a giant burden had been lifted. He knew it wasn't fair to think of her in that light, but facts were facts. Lauren complicated things. Not only would her absence allow him complete independence, it would also free him from constantly worrying about her safety. Nathan wasn't overly concerned about his own safety, but if anything happened to him—like death—at least Lauren would be secure with Grangeland. Lauren's long-term future remained in question, but at the very least, being Senator Stone McBride's granddaughter would afford her a solid future.

Nathan preferred not to use Grangeland's Crown Vic for the drive to the furniture store. She might need it later, and if things turned ugly, he didn't want to create a solid link to the FBI and Holly, at least not yet. Since he'd left Gerry's Explorer at Dr. Reavie's office, he made a quick detour to First Security for a vehicle change. Montgomery Field wasn't far from First Security, so the delay was minimal.

Thirty minutes later, he arrived at the address he'd acquired from Samantha's office. As she'd described, the building was fairly large—about the size of a big grocery store.

Staying in his vehicle, he circled the building, making a note of all the emergency exits. The loading dock looked similar to the one at Marchand's warehouse, but smaller in scale. He didn't see any security cameras, but that didn't surprise him. This wasn't a bad area of San Diego, and this building didn't have a research or high-tech purpose like many of its neighbors did. There didn't appear to be a need for enhanced security, at least none that he could see.

He considered his options for gaining entry. A glass facade dominated the middle portion of the storefront along the main street. The landscaping along the perimeter of the parking lot didn't offer much visual cover. Fortunately, this wasn't a busy thoroughfare. It terminated at the boundary of Montgomery Field. Any traffic around here would be limited to the immediate businesses.

At the end of the street, he turned around and cruised past the store in the opposite direction. He pulled up to the curb, opened a browser in his iPhone, and typed "Domino's San Diego" into the search box. A few seconds later, he had a listing of five Domino's locations and chose the closest one. He tapped the GET DIRECTIONS button and watched the route appear.

Four minutes later, he was walking up to the counter and smiling at the young woman behind the register.

"I have an unusual request. It's my niece's birthday. She just turned twelve, and she loves Domino's." He lowered his voice. "I'll pay you twenty bucks for your hat. She'll absolutely love it."

The woman spent a little too long studying his face. "Seriously? All you want is my hat?"

"Twenty bucks."

She looked around and took it off. "Here. You don't have to pay me."

He winked at her. "Can I get one of your boxes to put it in?"

She disappeared into the back and returned with a box.

Nathan fished his wallet out and put a twenty in the tip jar.

"Thanks! But you didn't have to do that."

"It's my pleasure. You're a lifesaver."

He diverted to the alley along the rear of the building and spotted what he needed. In a quick move that took no more than ten seconds, he threw the sedan in park, climbed out, and removed the magnetic sign from the top of a delivery car. He didn't feel right about stealing the sign, but he justified the theft as an emergency. Compared with his actions over the last fourteen hours, this qualified as a mere hiccup in the larger scheme of things.

Nathan returned to the furniture store and pulled up to the curb. He put on his ballistic vest and covered it with the black sweatshirt he'd used at the Tecate motel. It wouldn't look terribly out of place, since the temperature hadn't climbed yet. He got out, placed the Domino's sign atop the sedan, and donned his twenty-buck hat.

He cruised into the furniture store's driveway and parked directly in front of the double glass doors, where his sedan couldn't be missed. He placed his suppressed SIG in the box and took a deep breath to ease the tension.

Holding the pizza box with both hands, he approached the entrance.

He knocked on the door and waited.

After half a minute, he banged on it forcefully.

A tall man with dark hair appeared, and he didn't look real happy. This guy stood several inches north of six feet and fit Samantha's description. Nathan saw the black gloves right away, and his radar went up several notches. The gloves had a sheen, as though wet.

The man's voice sounded muffled behind the glass. "We're closed."

"I can't find an address. Can you help me?"

"Are you deaf? I said we're closed." He spoke in a Spanish accent, perfectly audible through the door.

Nathan waved toward the sedan. "Come on, man. I need a good Samaritan. I'm looking for a place called Startronics. I've got an extra combination pizza from a botched order. My manager said to just give it away. It's yours."

Nathan slipped his left thumb under the box's lid and eased it up half an inch.

Responding to a query, the man looked toward the interior and yelled in Spanish, "Some pizza asshole wants directions." The man listened for a few seconds and turned back to Nathan. Switching back to English, the guy said, "Take a hike."

"I'm truly disappointed," Nathan answered in Spanish.

The man's face slackened in surprise.

In one fluid move, Nathan flipped the box open and pulled out the SIG.

The man yelled something unintelligible and turned to run.

Nathan shot him in the back of the thigh.

The suppressed shot shattered the tempered glass. Thousands of tiny pieces fell in a sparkling shower.

The wounded man dropped to the floor and yelled, "It's him!"

Nathan kicked the door's aluminum handle like he'd done at Marchand's warehouse. It broke free and clattered on the floor.

In Spanish, someone from the back of the showroom floor yelled, "Franco, what's happening!" It wasn't Voda's voice.

Before the downed man could answer, Nathan stepped inside and kicked him in the face. Hard. The guy's nose exploded.

He saw it then: the unmistakable smear of blood on the floor from the man's gloves.

Semiconscious, the man moaned and rolled into the fetal position. Not caring if his kick was fatal, Nathan patted the guy down for weapons, removed a knife from the guy's ankle sheath, and hurled it across the room. He also found a box of wooden matches. Not surprisingly, it had some kind of cigar maker's logo. He squinted at the words: MADE IN NICARAGUA. A grisly flashback threatened to invade his thoughts, but he slammed the door on it.

He was about to toss the matches aside, but decided to keep them. Inside, above the door, a security camera eyed the entrance foyer. Using the SIG to screen his face, Nathan shot the camera. Chunks rained onto the floor.

Were these guys expecting him? It seemed likely. The man he'd kicked in the face had yelled, "It's him." If this was a trap, he'd just sprung it. Fighting a strong desire to leave, Nathan advanced deeper into the store and ducked behind a leather sofa combo. He peered above its form and saw a man running toward the entrance.

"Franco!"

Halfway down the showroom floor, the man stopped when he spotted his downed comrade. Nathan didn't see a gun in the guy's hands, but that would change soon enough.

He took aim to shoot the guy, when the sound of a roaring engine forced his attention outside.

A pickup screeched to a stop ten feet from the front door.

Three men armed with AKs ran toward the entrance.

This was *definitely* a trap.

And these clowns were packing some serious firepower.

They didn't look like clean-cut Spaniards—they looked more like hardened mercenaries or coyotes—and they were probably looking to get some payback for their dead friends at the Tecate Palms Motel. Nathan didn't relish being captured by these guys.

It was time to kick some ass without taking any numbers.

He subconsciously patted for the SIG's spare magazines in his thigh pockets, confirming their presence.

What happened next was driven by pure skill and experience.

Peering just over the top of the sofa, Nathan let the first gunman enter the building, which allowed his two comrades to follow suit. The lead gunman focused on the unconscious man, before whipping his head around, looking for a threat. Nathan burst up from the cover of the couch and activated the SIG's laser.

He lined up on the second gunman's chest and fired twice. Before that man hit the floor, he sent two more bullets into the third man, center mass. Both of their expressions registered shock and disbelief, likely from being dispatched so easily. The first man he had shot dropped his AK and clutched his chest, blood oozing between his fingers.

The lead gunman attempted to duck for cover, but not in time. Nathan double-tapped him in the rib cage.

At close range—in just under four seconds—Nathan had fired six shots and recorded six hits. All three men were dead or dying, and they hadn't returned a single shot. He ejected the SIG's magazine and inserted a fully loaded one.

He needed to deal with the retreating man in the back of the store before more reinforcements arrived, but this showroom held numerous hiding places. An ambush could come from anywhere. On the flip side, all the furniture could be used as visual cover for his advance. The safest way to advance would be along the perimeter. If he stayed close to the wall, he'd reduce his threat area by half.

Nathan looked toward the rear of the store for any sign of movement but detected none. In a crouch, he sidestepped along the length of the sofa and checked the men he'd just neutralized. Obviously, they hadn't been well trained. After entering, they should've immediately fanned out in different directions, but they'd been momentarily distracted by the unconscious man lying on the floor. Nathan didn't relish killing these men, as he had in Tecate, but he didn't feel guilty either. It was just business, and these poor saps were on the wrong end of it.

Two of the mercenaries weren't breathing, and the third would be joining his friends soon.

A radio crackled to life. *"Franco, can you hear me? Franco!"*

To avoid exposing himself on the main aisle of the showroom floor, Nathan reached out and grabbed the man he'd kicked by the ankle. He yanked the guy over to the corner of the sofa and removed the radio from his hip.

In Spanish, Nathan said, "Franco's not feeling well right now."

"*Who is this?*"

"I'll be asking the questions from now on."

"*Whoever you are, you should leave while you still can.*"

"But I have unfinished business."

Radio Man didn't respond.

"I'm afraid your mercenary friends aren't feeling well either." Nathan waited a few seconds. "I'm really looking forward to meeting you."

Watching for motion at the rear of the store, he turned the radio off and hurled it across the showroom floor. It thumped twice before going silent. He tested the man he'd kicked in the nose by dislocating the guy's trigger finger. It gave with a sickening *crunch*, similar to that of a knuckle being cracked. When Nathan got no reaction, he felt confident the man was down for the count.

Keeping his head up as much as possible, Nathan ran in a crouch through the maze of furniture to the wall on his right. From there, he kept his attention focused on the rear wall and worked his way deeper into the store. Twenty-five yards distant, he spotted a security camera mounted on the rear wall near the roll-up door. It looked to be covering a zone adjacent to the receiving area. Nathan toggled the SIG's laser and bench-rested the handgun on a dining room table. Adjusting for the increased distance, he aimed slightly above the camera and gently squeezed the trigger. The bullet slammed home, and once again, pieces of plastic, metal, and glass rained down. The camera's destruction echoed through the interior, louder than his suppressed shot. If Radio Man had been using the camera to track his movements, that gig was over. At least they were even now.

Watching the last known location of Radio Man, he wove his way through the displays of furniture and stopped behind an artificial ficus tree anchored in a huge ceramic pot. It was a good place to assess his next move. Underneath the second camera he'd destroyed, he saw the entrance to a receiving area. A wide roll-up door was currently open. Since no one else had challenged him up to this point, he felt reasonably confident Radio Man was alone, but he wouldn't assume that. Until he determined otherwise, he'd proceed as though this place were filled with armed men.

Before continuing, he took a few seconds to scan the upper reaches of the surrounding walls for additional security cameras but didn't see any. Holding his SIG with both hands, he kept it tight against his chest and eased toward the roll-up door. To get there, he had to work his way through a two-walled mock bedroom set adorned with pastel-colored furniture. Because his clothes contrasted so starkly with his surroundings, he made a dash for the corner of the roll-up door and stopped next to its jamb. Camera fragments were strewn across the concrete. He peered around the corner at knee level and studied the receiving area. All quiet.

He spotted another camera, on the perimeter wall above the receiving-bay doors, and switched the SIG to his left hand. Steadying his aim against the jamb, he sent a bullet through its lens. He looked around the corner to his right, keeping his body low. Several dozen large cardboard boxes were stacked in the middle of the floor, along with a forklift. The sight of the vehicle made him think of Lauren. On the far side of the room, three add-on rooms had been built against the west wall. Nathan figured one of them was an office. The other two would probably be a janitor's closet and a break room. All the doors were closed.

He pivoted around the corner and sprinted for the cover of the oversize boxes.

So far, so good. No one had shot at him.

The area directly behind him didn't offer an effective place to hide. Excluding the forklift, it was unused open space. If Radio Man had come in here, he'd probably bolted for the far side of the receiving bay, toward the add-on rooms. Nathan supposed his mark could've run straight through and left through the fire-exit door, but he hadn't heard anything to support that.

He sensed the man's presence lurking.

It was too bright in here.

Knowing it created a double-edged sword, Nathan began systematically shooting the overhead fluorescent tubes. With each discharge of his handgun, the tubes made a popping sound and flashed like fireworks. Cylindrical pieces of glass crashed to the floor as the bulbs broke in half and fell from their fixtures. He destroyed all but a single pair behind him, creating the condition of having the sun at his back. He gave his eyes a few seconds to adjust to the lower light level while he loaded a fresh magazine into the SIG.

From this location, he had a good view of the receiving bay. It looked to be about forty feet in depth and ran the entire length of the building. A cardboard-baling machine, along with several pallets of wire-bound cardboard, dominated the wall adjoining the showroom floor. The perimeter wall leading out to the loading dock looked similar to that of Marchand's warehouse. A fire-exit door flanked two roll-up doors for moving furniture into and out of the receiving area. Packing peanuts, plastic wrap, twine, and various other kinds of trash littered the floor. A musty odor hung in the air. Nathan didn't see a Dumpster but expected to find some kind of trash container near the add-on rooms.

Keeping his SIG level, he advanced to the pallets of baled cardboard and crouched. Tactically, this environment favored the defender, offering multiple places to hide. Psychologically, he held the advantage. If Radio Man was alone, the guy would be acutely aware that he faced a competent and deadly enemy. Putting himself into the guy's shoes, Nathan believed he'd hide in a location where he could see the entire receiving bay and wait for an opportunity to ambush his opponent.

That's when he saw it. Pay dirt. A sliver of light emanating from beneath the leftmost door of the add-on rooms winked out. Whoever was in there had just turned off the light.

Taking advantage of the situation, Nathan sprinted the length of the receiving bay because the man in the room wouldn't be able to see his approach until his eyes adjusted to the darkness. In the dim light coming from behind, Nathan saw that the door's handle was on the right side and angled in that direction. He flattened himself against the perimeter wall of the receiving bay and saw the source of the smell he'd detected earlier—a three- or four-yard Dumpster.

He stopped behind its rectangular form, held perfectly still for a few seconds, and heard nothing.

The door to Radio Man's hiding place stood ten feet away. If the guy cracked the door, he wouldn't be able to see Nathan because the door opened inward. In order to see the Dumpster, he would have to open the door fairly wide.

Without knowing how long he had until reinforcements arrived, Nathan needed to act quickly to flush the guy out.

He reached over the Dumpster's rim and felt for what he needed.

Without making a sound, he slowly approached the door and crouched next to the wall. As best he could see in the near-darkness, the door appeared to be closed, not cracked open. He knew the guy would be feeling a substantial amount of fear at this point. When a man was being hunted, silence, coupled with darkness, was extremely unnerving.

Nathan removed the box of matches from his pocket.

Facing the wall, he lowered himself to the deck and pivoted onto his right hip. In a risky move, he gently placed his SIG on the concrete and struck a match. The sound was damning, but probably not detectable from the other side of the door. He ignited the paper plate he'd grabbed from the Dumpster. Staying on his hip, he kicked the door with all his strength.

It crashed open with a loud *bang*.

Radio Man sprayed the empty doorway with a fully automatic weapon. The sound was deafening. Nathan closed his eyes to preserve his low-light vision. When the maelstrom stopped, he tossed the flaming plate into the room like a Frisbee.

He heard the unmistakable sound of a magazine being ejected. A second later, it clinked on the floor. Nathan grabbed his SIG, gained his feet, and rushed through the door.

In the orange glow of the burning plate, Nathan saw a panicked man attempting to load a fresh magazine.

They locked eyes.

In a desperate move, his opponent lowered his head and charged.

Nathan shot him through the top of his skull.

The man went down in an ungraceful swan dive. His chin cracked on the concrete at the same time he landed on the plate.

The orange light vanished, and Nathan found himself engulfed in darkness.

He slipped out of the room and hurried over to the Dumpster. Using it for cover, he peered over its rim and looked for any kind of movement in the receiving bay. The faint glow from the single fluorescent fixture cast long shadows across the floor, but none of them moved. Again, he held perfectly still, listening for any sound. All he heard was Radio Man's last breath, a gurgling exhalation. He waited ten seconds before reentering the room.

Nathan felt for the light switch, flipped it on, and squinted at the sudden brightness. The smell of burned paper and gun smoke hung in the air. Spent 9-millimeter shell casings littered the floor. Next to Radio Man's open mouth, a tiny pool of blood had formed, probably from biting his own tongue. It's just business, Nathan told himself, but the sight of the dead man triggered a sense of loss. This was someone's son and maybe someone's father. He dismissed the useless thought and surveyed the small room. As he'd suspected, it was an office.

Although Nathan believed this man had been alone, he didn't know it with absolute certainty. And someone might've heard the automatic gunfire. The roll-up doors leading outside were made of thin metal, probably aluminum. The sound would've been hard to miss.

He approached the second of the three add-on doors. Again, the knob was on the right side. He crouched and silently bypassed the door. If anyone was in there, he'd probably be expecting his opponent to check the doors in linear order. By skipping the middle door, he made himself less predictable.

At the third door, he saw that the knob lay in the same place. Staying in a low stance, he reached up, turned the knob, and pushed the door open.

He inhaled through his nose and caught a sour smell, like a homeless stench. He held still and waited. All quiet. He slowly reached around the jamb, feeling for the light switch, and froze when he heard a soft voice.

"Please...help me."

CHAPTER 27

What Nathan saw tore at his soul.

A shirtless man was strapped to a chair with duct tape. Bruises covered his face from forehead to chin. Graying black hair plastered his skull. The flesh around his eye sockets was inflamed and swollen, and his lips were a mess. Whoever this poor sap was, he'd been put through a Mob-style interrogation.

Nathan needed to check the remaining room. He kicked its door open and found the light switch. Seeing only a storage room full of boxes, he ran back to the bound man.

The man slowly raised his head and blinked a few times. Although Nathan didn't recognize him, some degree of recognition seemed to show in the captive's eyes.

"You're going to be okay. Don't try to move." Nathan cut the tape tethering the man's wrists and ankles to the chair.

"How...long...?"

"Have you been here? I don't know. Who are you?"

The man cleared his throat with obvious difficulty. "Marchand."

"Malcolm Marchand? You're Malcolm Marchand?"

The man nodded.

"Jin thinks Voda killed you."

Marchand didn't respond.

"I'm gonna get you outta here. More of Voda's men might be coming."

Nathan cut the duct tape around Marchand's rib cage, then tore the strips from his skin in quick pulls. Nathan was ready and caught him as he slumped forward, then gently laid him on the concrete. "I need to do a quick check for spinal injury. Can you feel this?" He squeezed an untouched area of Marchand's lower leg.

"Yes. Where's Lauren?"

"She's safe. Don't worry about her." That's when he saw Marchand's bare feet. Most of his toes had been smashed, the nails split and caked with dried blood. Whatever wrongs Marchand had committed with or against Voda, he'd paid dearly for them. Jin's note said Marchand had wanted out of Voda's operation, so he couldn't be all bad.

Nathan squeezed Marchand's other leg. "Feel that?"

"Yes."

Nathan tucked the suppressed SIG into his waist. "This is going to hurt. Sorry."

Marchand howled in agony as Nathan scooped him off the floor and stood him up.

"Can you walk?" Nathan asked.

"I think so." Marchand took a step and nearly fell.

Nathan steadied him, realizing that walking him out of here would take too much time. Fortunately, Marchand wasn't a big man. At five foot seven, he probably weighed 175 pounds or so. Without asking, Nathan slung Marchand over his shoulder in a fireman's carry. Marchand cried out again. Nathan couldn't fault the guy—his ribs weren't firm like they should be. Hauling Marchand, he ran from the receiving-bay office toward the roll-up door leading to the showroom floor.

He stopped at the corner and peered around the jamb. Abandoning all stealth, he ran through the maze of furniture and took Marchand out the shattered glass door. He had to brace Marchand's body against the Taurus to open the rear door. After laying him down, Nathan hurried to the other side of the vehicle. As gently as possible, he pulled Marchand across the seat, then reached across and tucked his legs inside.

"Be right back," Nathan said.

He reentered the store, pulled his SIG, and approached the man with the bloody gloves—the thug who'd been torturing Marchand. The guy had regained consciousness, but he was clearly lethargic and unable to get up. When Nathan pointed his gun, the man held up a hand in defense.

"I ought to kill you, but I'm not going to." Nathan shot the man through the shoulder—a serious but not life-threatening wound. He'd purposely aimed high to avoid opening the guy's brachial artery.

The man cursed and clutched the wound.

"Tell Voda I'm willing to make a deal, but it will be on my terms. You got that?"

The man winced and nodded.

Five seconds later, Nathan pulled away from the furniture store and drove as fast as possible without jarring his passenger too much. Marchand was in pretty bad shape, but Voda's men had clearly avoided deadly force, wanting Marchand alive. The question was: Why?

"Voda has my wife," Marchand said. "Your half sister."

Nathan shot a glance at Marchand, disturbed by the man's knowledge of Jin's relationship with him.

"He may have already killed her." Marchand stopped to cough. It sounded like gravel in a plastic bucket.

Nathan turned his head again and saw Marchand wipe blood from his mouth. Probably a perforated lung. Not severe, or he'd already be dead.

"How do you know Voda has Jin? And what makes you think she's my sister?"

"When they first took me," said Marchand, "Voda was looking for Jin. They asked me all kinds of things about her: her properties, her cars, her habits. All her friends. Her personal history." He coughed again. "They beat the crap out of me. I couldn't take it. I told them everything I know, which really wasn't all that much. I'd never realized until then how little I actually knew about my wife."

"Keep going."

"Late last night...they stopped asking questions about her." Marchand hacked and coughed again. "And started asking me about *you*. I'd never heard of you, but they didn't believe me, so they started beating me again. They told me they had Jin, that she was your half sister, and that you were protecting Lauren. I think they were trying to check what Jin had told them against what I knew. That's when they started smashing my toes. The stupid jerks... I didn't know anything about you."

Great, thought Nathan. Voda has Jin and knows—at the very least—my name and connection to Jin. What else, he wondered, might Jin have given up under torture?

"Look," he told Marchand, "I'll be honest. I'm tempted to dump you at a police station and move on. From what I understand, you brought all this upon yourself by getting into bed with Voda. You put your stepdaughter's life at risk for the sake of money."

"Voda doesn't care about Lauren anymore. He tried to get her so he could make me talk. What he really wanted was something from my office."

"The coordinates to the location of the girl."

"How can you possibly know that?"

"Jin wrote me a note. She actually defended you, said you wanted out of Voda's world."

"It's true. I would've given it all up to keep Jin and Lauren safe."

Again, Nathan tended to believe him. What reason did Marchand have to lie at this point? His world had crumbled. There was no sense in tormenting the guy further. "I'm with you on that," he said, "although I don't think you can do much to help at this point. I'll be leaving you with someone from the FBI. If you cooperate, you might be able to strike a deal and avoid a prolonged prison sentence."

"I was already planning to tell them everything."

"That'd be your first smart move in a long time."

With Jin in Voda's hands, the situation became critical. Nathan had to consider his next moves carefully, yet his options were substantially diminished. Any action he took against Voda might result in Jin's death, if she weren't dead already. Meanwhile, Voda could be wringing classified information out of Jin—information that could be devastating not only to Harv and Nathan but also to the nation.

Holly needed to know about these new developments right away. He pulled out his cell and called her.

"Nathan, what's your situation?"

"Voda's men had Marchand. I have him with me. In a few minutes I'll be back with Grangeland and turn him over to her."

"Wait. He's not dead?"

"No, they'd been interrogating him. Voda has Jin as well. And he knows she's my sister."

"Nathan, I'm so sorry. Where did you find Marchand?"

"Some kind of furniture store near Montgomery Field." He gave Holly the address. "There are five more casualties. Two of them are Voda's, the others looked like mercenaries, probably coyotes. They were armed with AKs and tried to ambush me. Can you get some local agents over there right away?"

"I'll call the San Diego SAC as soon as we hang up. It's SDPD's crime scene, but I want some of our people there too." Holly paused for a moment. "I can't withhold this from Director Lansing. I normally report to the deputy director, but Lansing's given me a green light to contact him."

"Are you sure this won't compromise your new position in DC?"

"No, but withholding it definitely would."

"Holly, I'm still working independently. You understand that, right?"

She paused. "Yes."

"Grangeland's going to need some help taking custody of Marchand. He needs emergency care."

"Where is she?"

"The Rancho Bernardo Inn. Could you call her and let her know I'm coming?"

"Of course."

"Thanks. Tell her I can't walk through the lobby with Marchand. He's a mess. Ask her to bring Abrille and Lauren down to the valet area out front. I'll meet all three of them there. I'll leave Marchand nearby in a white Taurus that can be seen from the valet stand. Lauren and I will catch a cab and leave Grangeland with Abrille and Marchand. Oh, and when you call Grangeland, be careful of what you say. Lauren will be listening, and she doesn't miss much. I should be the one to tell her about her mom."

"Okay, I'll be careful."

"What's Abrille's legal situation at this point?"

"I'm still working on it," Holly said. "She's going to be admitted into the witness security program, where she'll be safe. I'm also arranging counseling."

"About that…," Nathan said.

"What is it?"

Nathan told Holly about the cache of alexandrites that had been implanted in Abrille's abdomen.

"Then this whole thing is an elaborate smuggling operation?" Holly asked.

"It looks that way. Are you in any position to make an inquiry with the San Diego medical examiner's office?"

"Sure. About what?"

"If the previous border murder victims were Bolivian orphans, like Abrille, then they might have a similar incision on their stomachs in roughly the same location—sort of like a fresh appendectomy. The slashing of the victims' torsos might've been done to mask the kind of wound Abrille has. The surgical staples would be gone, but they could've left tiny puncture marks underneath. If what I suspect is true, an extra quarter inch of skin will be missing around the wound. I don't know if the ME can determine that, but it's worth a look."

"I'm making a note…I'll make sure the ME's aware of it. So what are you going to do next?"

"Get Jin back safely, if I can."

"How?"

"I'm still working it out. Voda will want to recover the gemstones. They're worth a small fortune, and I'm willing to bet he's out of pocket on the deal. I think he's a middleman."

"He is," Marchand said from the backseat.

"Hold on, Holly. Marchand's talking." Nathan raised his voice and held his phone out so Holly could hear both of them. "Is what?" he asked Marchand.

"A middleman," said Marchand. "He's an independent buyer. He pays for the gemstones, then turns around and sells them to someone else for a huge profit. So, like you said, he's out serious money for any gemstones he loses. Plus, he'll lose credibility with his buyer if he doesn't deliver what he's promised."

Marchand's tone pissed Nathan off. The guy sounded indifferent. "Voda's been slaughtering young girls like cattle. How can you just turn a blind eye to that?"

"I never knew that!" Marchand protested. "I mean, I found out recently that he was using girls as couriers, but I never knew he was killing them afterward until it was too late. Get a clue. Why do you think I wanted out?"

"Let's assume I believe you," said Nathan. "Then why are you involved in Voda's world?"

"He launders money through my businesses."

"Are you telling me that was your only tie to Voda? Laundering his money?"

"Yes."

"Then how do you know about the girls and the alexandrites?"

"Voda was drunk one night and bragging about it, saying how brilliant he was. I even bought one of them from him. I gave it to Jin, but I didn't know anything about the girls being murdered. Look, Voda never told me every little detail of what he was doing. He's a very secretive man, and I wasn't about to ask how he got his money."

"It's easier that way, isn't it? You drive around in expensive cars while young girls are being butchered."

"That's a—" Marchand tried to yell and coughed more blood. "I just told you I didn't know about that!"

"Nathan," Holly said. "Let us interrogate him. You're too close to this."

"Okay. You're right. It just pisses me off."

"Me too. With Marchand's testimony, we'll bury Voda."

Nathan didn't say what he was thinking. "Thanks, Holly. I'll call you later."

He ended the call, wondering how he'd tell Lauren that Voda had her mom. He favored not telling her, but that would create trust issues further down the road. Nathan knew Lauren would feel betrayed if she wasn't told the truth right away. He'd need to choose his words carefully....

Ten minutes into his drive back to the Rancho Bernardo Inn, he felt his phone vibrate. He checked the screen. His father.

"Hi, Dad."

"Nathan, what's going on? I just stepped off the Senate floor. You said it's urgent. Are you okay?"

"I'm okay. I'm driving right now. Can I call you back in two minutes or less?"

"I'll be waiting."

Nathan looked for a place to pull over. Seeing none, he diverted into a small office complex and drove to a remote corner of its parking lot. He didn't want Marchand to hear the conversation with his dad, so he turned on the radio, cranked it to a medium volume, and climbed out. Fifty feet from the sedan, he made the call.

"It's me again."

"Nathan, what's going on? Are you in trouble?"

"It's not about me. It's about you. Do you remember Han Choon-Hee?"

There was a marked silence on the other end. "How do you know that name? Nathan, what's this about?"

"Dad, I don't know how to say this…Choon-Hee was pregnant when you left Korea."

"Pregnant? What are you saying?"

"I'm saying I have a half sister. Her birth name is Han Jin-Kyong, but she's using Jin Elizabeth Marchand now."

"Nathan…This is…difficult to believe."

"I know. I felt the same way when I found out. I'm going to read you a note Jin left me last night."

"Nathan, I assume you're serious about this. If you are, now's probably not the time—"

"That's the problem, Dad. I'm short on time. Look, this woman, your daughter, is mixed up with Hans Voda, a Spanish-born international criminal. He's on Interpol's ten-most-wanted list. It's a serious situation, and it might get a whole lot worse."

"What are we dealing with here?"

"I'll explain everything, but you need to hear this note first." Nathan removed the photocopied note from his pocket and read it aloud.

His dad listened silently, then spoke in a much softer voice. "I gave my dog tag to Choon-Hee the night before she disappeared. It was the last time I ever saw her."

Nathan heard the pain in his voice. "I'm sorry, Dad. It sounds like you two loved each other."

"We were going to be married. When I returned to the pub the following night, she was gone. No one would talk about her.

I waited all night. Later, I found out that North Korean sympathizers were rounding up any English-speaking citizens and smuggling them north across the border for money. I loved her, Nathan. She was the kindest, most giving person you could ever know. Three days after she vanished, the Chinese entered the war and all hell broke loose. I had to assume she ended up in a North Korean prison camp. I did everything possible to find her, but it was hopeless. I never knew she survived, and I certainly had no idea she was pregnant. We'd only been seeing each other for a couple of weeks."

"Well, Jin's in serious trouble, but her daughter's safe with me. The girl's name is Lauren, and she has our eyes. Nearly identical to mine."

"I'll bet she's beautiful."

"She is."

"Tell me about Jin's situation."

"That's the worst news: Voda has her." As briefly as possible, Nathan proceeded to summarize what had happened over the past eighteen hours.

Stone McBride had many faults, but being a poor listener wasn't one of them. He absorbed all the news, asking occasional questions. It took a few minutes. "Okay," Stone said at last. "How can I help?"

"I'm not sure, but obviously we'll do our best to keep this under the radar. It could create a nasty scandal for you."

"Nathan, I don't give a damn about any scandals. My only concern is getting Jin back and keeping Lauren safe."

Nathan was relieved to hear his father say that. "Still, this has to be hard on you, finding out you have a daughter. How will Mom react?"

"She knows about Choon-Hee. I told her about my life in Korea when we were dating. She'll be stunned by the news, but she'll be okay. We've been married for over fifty years. She knows

I don't hide anything from her, and I'd never conceal something like this."

"I didn't think you would."

"Do you have any theories on how Jin knows your old CIA call sign?"

"No."

"Are you sure there's nothing I can do to help?"

"I suppose a call to Cantrell might be in order, but you'd have to go through the DNI, wouldn't you?"

"Yes. Anything else undermines the chain of command. But there's no reason *you* can't call Cantrell."

"I might do that."

"But not now?"

"No."

"Then you're going after him?"

"He's murdering young girls."

"I'm taking the first available flight out there."

"Give me twenty-four hours. Lauren's safe with me, and Harv's on his way back from overseas."

"What's your plan?"

"I'm taking Voda out to the desert."

CHAPTER 28

Nathan waved at Grangeland and drove twenty yards past the entrance to the Rancho Bernardo Inn. He pulled to the curb and told Marchand to lie still and not sit up. As he walked toward Grangeland, the valet approached, but Nathan gave the young man a negative wave.

Grangeland had both girls in tow. Lauren looked alert, but Abrille's emotionless expression told all—the poor kid.

"I found your stepdad," he told Lauren. "He's in the back of the car, but don't go over there."

She looked at the sedan. "He's alive?"

"Voda's men had him at the furniture store. They beat him up pretty badly, but he'll be okay."

"What about my mom?"

He took Lauren's hand. "Lauren, we're pretty sure Voda has her."

She began crying.

Grangeland came closer and put an arm around her.

"She's going to be okay," Nathan said.

"You promise?"

"Yes, I promise."

Lauren wiped her eyes. "I hope you killed Voda's men."

He took a knee and kept his voice low. "Lauren, killing is not something to be proud of. Some of the men who hurt your step-dad are dead, but they were trying to kill me first, like in Tecate."

"What if Voda kills Mom?"

"He won't."

"Why?"

"Because we have his alexandrites."

"I don't understand."

"I'm going to force Voda to make a trade. He gives us your mom, we give him his alexandrites. He wants them back very badly."

"Bad enough to let my mom go?"

Nathan decided to tell a white lie. "Yes, absolutely."

Lauren wiped the tears from her face and hugged him. "I'm glad you're my uncle."

"I need to call Voda, to arrange to get your mom back. I want you stay with Grangeland, okay?"

"But I want to listen."

He shook his head. "Please stay with Grangeland. I'll be right back."

Lauren put her hands on her hips and cocked her head in a pouty manner that actually came across as charming, rather than bratty. Nathan walked down the sidewalk until he was far enough away to make the call.

Voda answered on the second ring. "You took your sweet time calling me back, *Mr. McBride.*"

Nathan winced inwardly at hearing his name, but kept his voice calm as he addressed Voda. "It seems each of us has something the other wants."

"Indeed we do."

"How about a trade? You keep the six hundred grand you offered and give me Ms. Marchand, and I give you ten beautifully cut alexandrites worth nearly two million dollars."

"I think that sounds more than reasonable."

"I choose the exchange location."

"I don't think I'll agree to that."

"Good bye, Mr. Voda." Nathan ended the call. It was a risky move, but given what Nathan had learned from Marchand, he believed Voda would call back. As sad as the thought was, Nathan knew that Jin was worthless to Voda in the long term. In Voda's eyes, she was nothing more than a five-dollar poker chip.

Ten seconds later, his phone rang.

"There's no need to be rude, Mr. McBride. You're acting as though you don't know how the game is played."

"So let's negotiate. I will choose the location. You may bring two men with you. I'll be alone."

"You sound confident."

"I haven't needed any other men up to this point."

"Do you expect me to believe you've been working alone?"

"Believe whatever you want. If you bring more than two men, I'll kill them."

"Spare me your threats. I'll bring two men, plus your beloved sister, of course."

Yeah, right, Nathan thought. "Now, before we go any further, I'd like to verify she's alive. I'll be asking her a random question in the event you've recorded her voice."

Voda sighed, leaving Nathan to listen through a brief period of silence. He realized he was holding his breath and calmed himself.

The calm was short-lived. Jin's voice put him on edge again. "Nathan, I'm sorry."

"What sports team was Lauren on in school?"

"She was on the cross-country track team, but she's home-schooled now." She spoke quickly now, almost under her breath. "Promise me, Nathan, you'll keep Lauren safe. *Please!* Don't let her out of your sight, no matter what."

"I won't, I prom—"

"Voda has insiders…" she began.

Nathan heard Jin grunt in pain, then nothing.

"Satisfied?" Voda sounded impatient.

"Yes. Her daughter won't be with me."

"That's fine. I have no interest in the girl."

"I'll text you within the hour with a precise location and time. When you arrive, look for a fluorescent surveyor's stake with a radio clipped to it."

Voda was silent for a few seconds, probably absorbing the fact that Nathan planned to take him to a rural location. "What's wrong with using phones?"

"I'd prefer to use the radios."

Another sigh. "As you wish. Just remember: stick to the terms, or the girl becomes an orphan."

The call ended.

Nathan had no illusions about the exchange and fully expected an ambush. Men like Voda didn't play by the rules—they made their own.

He returned to the hotel entrance. "The call went well," he told Grangeland. To Lauren he said, "We need to head over to my La Jolla home to pick up some equipment."

Grangeland looked back and forth between them, realizing—and apparently accepting the fact—that Nathan was taking Lauren with him. "Once my backup arrives," she said, "I'll make sure Marchand gets to the ER. I'll also make sure he's closely guarded in case he tries to slip away." Grangeland spoke with matter-of-fact confidence, one of the things Nathan liked best about her.

He took Lauren's hand. "How do you feel about helicopters?"

"Helicopters?" she asked.

"Are you okay going for a little flight?"

"I guess...Is it scary?"

"The most dangerous part of any helicopter trip is the drive to the airport." Nathan smiled. "Don't worry, I hardly ever crash."

"That's not very reassuring."

When Grangeland asked what he planned to do, he repeated his intent to make the exchange but avoided specifics. Again, she seemed to accept that he intended to work independently of the FBI. Together, they'd done it before. Grangeland gave him a quick hug and wished him the best, then embraced Lauren. Nathan and Lauren said their farewells to Grangeland and Abrille, then turned to leave.

"Come on," he told Lauren. "We need to take a cab over to First Security to get Grangeland's vehicle. From there, we'll head over to La Jolla."

Nathan told Lauren they should remain silent for the cab ride south, and they did. Watching Lauren along the way, he guessed that she was thinking about her mom. He and Lauren had survived some tight moments together, but Nathan feared that the worst was yet to come. He didn't believe for a second that Voda would simply trade Jin for the jewels. Nor would Voda expect Nathan to do anything but try to kill him and save Jin. He hadn't intended to bring Lauren to the exchange, but that had changed when Voda put Jin on the phone. She'd been firm about his not letting Lauren out of his sight. He also couldn't dismiss her warning about Voda's "insiders." Fortunately, the way his plan had been forming in his mind, Lauren would be 100 percent safe during the swap. As a bonus, she'd play a vital role in supporting the operation.

When they reached First Security and exited the taxi, Nathan realized he didn't have a surveyor's stake or any fluorescent spray paint, so they made a quick stop at Home Depot.

After arriving at his La Jolla home twenty minutes later, Nathan half expected to find an army of police and FBI agents waiting, but all was quiet. He attributed some of his unease to a reality check. The last eighteen hours had been mentally and physically draining. Remarkably, Lauren wasn't in bad shape. She'd held it together well, but he knew she was close to a breaking point. But then again, weren't they all?

He planned to make this stop as brief as possible. Angelica had left a note saying she'd gone to a movie, so Lauren didn't get an opportunity to meet her. Nathan turned her loose in the kitchen to make some sandwiches, then used the Google Earth program to get turn-by-turn directions to the exchange location he had in mind. Using the satellite view feature, he had no trouble finding the exact spot—it was clearly visible from the air. He wrote the directions on a Post-it note. Once they were on their way to Montgomery Field, he'd have Lauren text the info to Voda.

Outside, he coated the upper half of the surveyor's stake with the fluorescent pink paint, wincing at the horrid color. He set the stake aside and entered his basement via the garage. Nathan loaded a duffel bag with everything he'd need, including five stripper clips of armor piercing .308 ammunition in the event Voda's "two" men wore ballistic vests again. He realized he didn't have any subsonic armor piercing rounds in nine millimeter, so he took a few minutes to change the master plate in his rotary reloading press. It didn't make sense to use supersonic ammunition with a suppressor. A supersonic bullet makes a boatload of noise from the miniature sonic boom it creates. Nathan would best describe it as a giant bullwhip *crack*—a sound he'd tried hard to forget. He consulted his handwritten notes in the margin of his reloading manual and selected a power charge that would keep his rounds at 1,050 feet per second. Once the 9 mm reloading plate was in place, it didn't take long to generate the special ammo. Because of their lower velocity, the rounds wouldn't be as effective, but they'd penetrate better than standard ball ammo. He emptied all the SIG's magazines and loaded the new rounds.

They ate turkey sandwiches during the drive to the airport. Lauren asked all kinds of questions about helicopters, and Nathan did his best to answer them, but his mind was elsewhere—out in the desert—thinking about Voda and his men. Nathan anticipated facing a small army out there. So be it. He had lots of bullets.

It took some time to park the sedan, unlock the hangar's door, tow the Bell 407's sled out to the flight line with a electric cart, return the cart to the hanger, and then relock the door. As always, Nathan conducted a thorough preflight check before securing Lauren in the left seat. She was impressed with the checklist for starting the engine and commented on how easy driving was in comparison. She grinned when the ship vibrated and the main rotor began turning.

He brought the helicopter into a hover and told Lauren to remain quiet while he contacted the tower with his intent. He was given clearance for an easterly departure toward I-15. The weather conditions were ideal. Excepting the usual marine layer blanketing the coast, there wasn't a cloud to be seen anywhere. Flying directly north would be the fastest route, but that airspace belonged to MCAS Miramar. It wasn't a major detour going around to the east. He'd fly the I-15 corridor underneath Miramar's approach cone, then use the helicopter route above the freeway out to Victorville. From there, he'd make a left turn and fly deep into the Mojave Desert.

Although initially nervous about the motion and elevation of the helicopter, Lauren recovered quickly. She wanted to be the navigator, so Nathan gave her the chart and pointed out some delineated landmarks. She was a quick study and had no problem keeping track of their position. Nathan figured the flight should take around eighty to ninety minutes. He could make it shorter, but there was no need to push the Bell's engine.

By late afternoon, he was circling the area he'd first noticed during a long-ago flight up the Owens Valley. This area of the Mojave had always interested him. Abandoned mines and decaying buildings dotted the landscape—literal modern-day ghost towns. He started a gradual descent and studied a row of dilapidated buildings he'd once viewed from afar. It looked like a small subdivision from the sixties that had gone belly up long before being inhabited. As he'd remembered from his previous flight, some of the houses had been burned to the ground, their slabs the only evidence they'd ever existed. He didn't see any vehicles—the place looked deserted.

North of the ghost town, a pair of small mountains was connected by a rocky saddle that provided an ideal overlook for the entire area. Along with the peaks, the saddle offered an unobstructed view of the dirt track leading to the abandoned houses. He'd situate Lauren in the saddle. If Voda or his men suspected Nathan might have a lookout, they'd focus on the peaks, not the saddle. Tactically, it was the best place to put her. Camouflaged to be virtually invisible, Lauren would be able to see every building and report any approaching vehicles.

He kept his descent going and flew in a northeasterly direction. He'd set the ship down on the other side of the twin peaks in a deep, dry wash that would hide the helicopter's profile. There weren't any roads near the LZ, so no one would be able to see his helicopter, even from atop the peaks, unless they flew in by air.

Nathan checked his watch. They'd arrived with plenty of time to spare. Going overland, Voda wouldn't arrive for at least another two hours, maybe longer.

Lauren was blown away by his approach to the LZ. She seemed both frightened and excited and kept saying "OMG" over and over. Nathan reminded her he needed to concentrate. A huge dust cloud swirled as he set the ship down and brought it to idle. A few minutes later, after the main rotor had completely stopped, they climbed out.

Nathan told Lauren to leave her headset on the seat.

"That was seriously cool," Lauren said. "Will you teach me how to fly?"

"Sure, but I need to show you something important now, so pay close attention." Nathan pointed to a red switch. "If anything happens to me, and I'm not saying it will, you'll need to come down here, unlock the helicopter, and flip that red switch to the upper position. It's the emergency locator transmitter. The ELT has its own battery, so you don't have to turn the master battery switch on. Just flip the switch. The LED should turn solid red. Got that?"

"Uh-huh."

"The ELT talks directly to satellites, so after you activate it, just hide near the helicopter and SAR teams will come and find you."

"What's a SAR team?"

"Search and rescue. Okay, I'm locking the doors." He hid the helicopter's door key under a rock near the starboard skid and made sure Lauren knew exactly where it was.

Nathan grabbed the duffel from the luggage compartment and led her up the side of the wash and toward the gradual slope leading to the saddle between the twin peaks. With only five-hundred-foot rises, the peaks were little more than hills, but their rocky forms had profiles of rugged mountains. Vegetation was sparse, but he warned Lauren about the various kinds of cacti, telling her not to brush up against them. Everything in this desert stung, bit, pricked, or scraped. All the life forms out here were tough as nails.

After a few steps, Lauren asked, "Are there snakes?"

"Yes, but we have a better chance of winning the lottery than we do of seeing one."

"Seriously? I hate snakes."

"They're just trying to make a living—no need to hate them."

"What kind are they?"

"You don't want to know...."

It took fifteen minutes to complete the hike and reach the flat saddle that sat between the peaks. Again Lauren impressed him with her stamina. The view was beautiful. In every direction, a vast expanse of open desert stretched to distant mountains. In essence, they were inside a giant frying pan. Smaller hills, like the ones they stood between, dotted the landscape here and there, but the surrounding area was mostly flat, with occasional sandy washes running in a southerly direction.

Nathan saw an ideal spot to position Lauren. Two clumps of creosote bushes were about five feet apart. The bushes, although stringy and somewhat thin, would give Lauren perfect concealment. He set the duffel down and cleared the rocks away, checking unobtrusively for ants and scorpions and other unmentionables.

Next, he conducted a complete check of her radio setup, making sure everything worked, including the modified voice-activated lapel mike. He clipped the radio to her waist, making sure the frequency lock was engaged.

"Did you spray-paint these radios? They're cool-looking."

"I airbrushed them in desert colors. It's a flat finish so they won't shine in sunlight. Run the earpiece and mike wires under your shirt. It's probably best if you do that yourself."

"Well, yeah."

He clipped the mike to her shirt just under her chin, then put the field glasses around her neck and showed her how to focus them.

"Let's get you into your ghillie suit. You can skip the pants. The coat will fit you like a tent." He pulled it out of the duffel.

"I'm wearing that shaggy thing? It's totally ugly."

"It's not supposed to be a fashion statement. It's designed for a very specific purpose, to break up the hard edges of your outline."

"If you say so…"

He helped Lauren put the coat on. It hung down to her shins.

"I feel like some kind of crazy creature in this thing."

Nathan smiled. "You're a twelve-year-old female. You *are* a crazy creature."

"Hey, that was mean."

"Sorry, couldn't resist. Don't worry, Voda and his band of merry goons don't stand a chance against us. We're going to kick their asses."

"You're not supposed to use that word."

"What word, 'asses'?"

She rolled her eyes. "Duh."

"Put the ghillie suit's hood on after I leave. Have a seat right here where I cleared the rocks away. I'm leaving the duffel behind this bush, where you can reach it. You've got plenty of water. The canteens have camouflaged sleeves. Now listen up. Before I head down, let's go over some stuff. Your number-one rule is to move in slow motion. Everything you do up here has to be slow and measured. Don't make any quick moves. The human eye catches movement. We're going to use some landmarks for reference. See the access road leading into the ghost town?"

"Uh-huh."

The dirt road below the peaks provided the only way into or out of the ghost town. He pointed to where the road took a ninety-degree turn, approximately a mile from the town. "We'll call that 'the turn in the road.'"

"Okay."

"The houses down there are aligned on an east–west axis." He oriented her to the cardinal directions. "The ghost town is due south from this position. East is to the left. We're going to number the houses from one to ten and abbreviate them as H1, H2, H3, all the way to H10. The first on the right down there—the one on the west end of town—will be H1. See how houses four, seven, and eight are gone? We're still going to refer to them as H units. So H4, H7, and H8 are open slabs. Got that?"

"Uh-huh."

Nathan looked at his cell and saw one bar. He'd never experienced success with one bar showing, but tried it anyway. He called 411, but after two full minutes, it never connected. "It looks like there's no cell service out here, so the radios are the only way we can talk. Remember to make acknowledgment clicks unless I ask you a question. Since your radio is voice-activated, you'll have to press the transmit button to give me a click, but you don't have to press it to talk. I'll leave my cell with you anyway. It's set to vibrate, but it shouldn't ring. If it does, call me on the radio before answering it. It could be you-know-who."

"Voda?"

"Yes. *Do not* talk to him if he calls. Don't talk to anyone, not even Harv."

"I won't."

"I'll put my ghillie suit on later." Nathan conducted a quick inventory of his backpack to make sure he hadn't forgotten anything. Everything looked good. He assessed the weather. Temperature-wise, it felt like high seventies or low eighties. Before using his handheld wind indicator, he estimated the wind at around ten knots. He pulled the device out and took a reading. It showed a varying wind velocity between nine and thirteen knots. An amazing tool, the WM-4 measured wind speed, wind direction, temperature, relative humidity, and compass direction. It also calculated wind-gust speeds, as well as dew points and a few other things. He didn't need all that extra information. Wind speed and direction were his primary concerns.

The fluorescent stake stuck out of his backpack, but that didn't matter. Using a Velcro strap, he secured his ghillie suit to the backpack.

"Okay, Lauren, sit tight up here."

He started down the rocky slope, working his way through the creosote bushes and patches of cacti. The exposed faces of larger rocks and boulders shone with desert varnish. Halfway down, he stopped and looked back.

"I can't see you at all. Remember, no sudden movements. Do everything in slow motion. I want you to practice taking a drink of water. Okay?"

"Okay."

If Nathan hadn't known exactly where to look, he never would've spotted her, but he saw the right side of her ghillie suit move as she brought the canteen up. "Slower, Lauren. I want you to take twice as much time as you just did. Try again. I don't want to see any discernible movement."

She issued an acknowledgment click.

He watched her repeat the motion. "That's perfect. Good job."

Ten minutes later, Nathan entered the ghost town and looked around. The vacant slabs looked forlorn. Sticking up like punji sticks, stubbed copper pipes were all that remained of the plumbing. The metal had probably been salvaged for its scrap value. At various locations around the bare concrete, steel framing anchors designed to secure heavier posts had also survived the fires.

Nathan hadn't seen any signs of people, but he needed to verify that. He walked through the abandoned homes, thoroughly checking each one. They were small—approximately thirty by thirty feet—with hip roofs. All of them had the same three-bedroom floor plan. Most of them had incomplete or missing framing inside—in some places, only drywall had been removed, while in others, entire walls were gone. Perhaps campers or partiers had removed the lumber for firewood or bonfires.

Without exception, every window of every house had been broken by vandals, who'd either shot guns or thrown rocks. Numerous bullet holes were visible in the stucco surrounding the destroyed glass as well as the interior walls. Rocks were strewn about the concrete as well. Whoever had ruined these windows was either drunk, a lousy shot, or both.

Confident that the buildings were vacant, Nathan began looking for a tactical location where he'd be able to see the entire line of structures. He found a good spot—a large group of creosote bushes about sixty feet south of the road—and walked over. They were spaced in a way that would allow Nathan to conceal himself in the middle of them. He liked it. From this position, he checked to make sure he could see the top of the saddle where Lauren was hidden. He could. He shucked off his backpack and removed the radio he'd use to communicate with Voda. He also grabbed the surveyor's stake and hammer. Directly in the middle of the road, he used the hammer to drive the stake into the ground. It took several attempts to find a soft enough spot.

After the stake was rooted, he clipped the radio to it and returned to his hiding place. Looking back, he saw there was no way to miss its fluorescent form sticking up in the middle of the road. He verified his earpiece wire was securely plugged into his radio's jack, then tested the setup using Voda's radio. It worked perfectly. He could hear his own voice through the earpiece.

"Lauren, are you tracking me with the field glasses?"

"Uh-huh. I can see you perfectly."

"Good. I'm going to walk all over the place down here and create all kinds of false and confusing footprint patterns. Don't worry, it will only look like I'm confused. I'll be walking around in random directions, and I'll also walk backward on purpose. Keep an eye on the road and let me know if you see any vehicles."

His radio clicked.

Nathan spent the next fifteen minutes walking all over the place, forward and backward. He didn't think Voda's men would be paying much attention—if any—to footprints, but it was better to play it safe. When he finished, he got onto his hands and knees and backed away from the road toward the group of creosote bushes he'd identified. He smoothed his tracks as he went, then leaned over and blew on the sandy ground as a final touch. It wasn't perfect, but it looked good enough. The sixty-foot gap between his hiding place and the road looked undisturbed.

Now it became a waiting game. Nathan had no illusions about Voda. He didn't expect the guy to bring two men. Nathan believed he'd be facing at least four opponents, maybe more. In order to be prepared to fire on them, he used the spare time to measure distances to various landmarks with his laser range finder. The first distance he wanted was the base of the small twin mountains where Lauren was hiding. Aiming the range finder between houses three and five, he focused on a large rock that was shaped like an upended grand piano. The red digital display indicated 627 yards. Okay, he'd call that spot Piano 627. He believed it to be fairly level with his position. He swung the range finder up to

Lauren's position and read 1,210 yards. He looked for a landmark halfway up the slope beneath her and found a large, rectangular rock. He took a reading and got 851 yards. He'd call that location Rectangle 851. Because the slope up to the saddle was nearly constant, he'd be able to estimate intermediate distances accordingly. He took readings for the houses as well. The westernmost building from his current location stood 131 yards distant, the easternmost building 155 yards.

"Lauren, I'm going to take a practice shot for my wind and elevation corrections. Don't be alarmed when you hear the rifle report. Copy?"

"Okay."

Forty-five degrees offset to his target, Nathan took a cross-legged sitting position. He shouldered his Remington, rested his elbows on his knees, and leaned forward, finding his comfort zone. Since he always kept his scope zeroed at three hundred yards, he clicked an additional five hundred yards of elevation to line up on Rectangle 851, then added an extra twelve clicks to account for shooting at an elevated target.

Wind was a tougher call and always the biggest variable. Gravity was constant and never changed, but wind could push a bullet completely off target over long distances. Nathan knew the wind was coming from the northeast—his three or four o'clock position. He'd be shooting about forty-five degrees into a right-to-left crosswind. The current wind speed wasn't severe, but it was far from calm. Desert winds could be tricky, especially during a weather change, but Nathan had checked the report for the area and hadn't found any high- or low-pressure areas moving through. He estimated the wind hadn't changed since he'd taken a reading, and he didn't feel any significant gusts. For an eight-hundred-yard shot, he knew a pure crosswind of ten miles per hour would push his bullet around seven or eight inches—close to one minute of angle. Since the wind was blowing at a forty-five-degree angle, he dropped the correction in half. His scope employed one-quarter minute of angle increments, so he clicked his windage knob two times for a one-half MOA correction to the right.

"Okay, Lauren, stand by." He took in a full breath, blew half of it out, and steadied the crosshairs for the exact center of the rock. He knew he'd be able to see his impact, because the armor-piercing bullet would blast a sizable crater out of the desert varnish covering the rock face.

He thumbed the safety switch and began a gradual squeeze of the trigger, not knowing exactly when the rifle would discharge. It was a technique designed to eliminate trigger jerk, a common affliction among amateur shooters.

The Remington bucked, and its report hammered his ears. He reacquired Rectangle 851 and looked for the impact. A light-colored blemish now occupied the rock face, nearly dead center of where he'd been aiming. He clicked one additional windage correction. His elevation was low by almost eight inches. The rock must be higher than he'd estimated, so he clicked an additional elevation correction into the scope. He had little doubt Harv—who'd served as his spotter during their many sniping missions—would've nailed these corrections. Harv was much better at assessing this stuff.

Nathan cycled the bolt and ejected the spent brass. Since he wanted to keep five rounds in the rifle, he removed a fresh cartridge from a stripper clip. Using his left thumb to push the four rounds in the magazine down, he slid the bolt forward about halfway, inserted a cartridge directly into the breach, and closed the bolt. He now had one in the pipe and four in the magazine. He made sure the safety remained in the off position by checking it with his right thumb.

"Okay, Lauren. We're all set. You okay up there?"

"That sounded really cool. After the poof *sound, it crackled all around me."*

"It's the reverberation from all the rock faces in the area. It's a good effect. It makes it harder to locate the source of the shot. We're going to sit tight and wait. Keep drinking sips of water and practice making slow-motion moves. It's not super hot, but I don't want you to get dehydrated. If you have to pee, let me know. And don't worry...I won't look."

"*Awkward.*"

Awkward? Was that more kid lingo? Nathan smiled and settled in for the wait.

He looked across the road at the houses.

Collectively, these structures amounted to a sad sight—a testament to someone's broken dream. Maybe it hadn't been such a great idea to build ten houses in the middle of the Mojave Desert. If there'd been a common well with a storage tank and water-delivery system, he saw no evidence of it.

Despite the harsh nature of this landscape, Nathan liked it. He'd always felt at ease in a desert setting and didn't know why. He'd never tried to analyze it, because, quite frankly, he didn't care. He liked the desert, and that was that.

Thirty minutes later, Lauren's voice came through the tiny earpiece. "*I can see two cars, way far away.*"

"Copy that. Keep a close eye on them. Let me know if one of them stops and anyone gets out. If that happens, tell me how many men get out and where they go, okay?"

"*Okay. I think they're going pretty fast. There's a big dust cloud.*"

"Keep watching."

"*The one in back is slowing down a little.*"

The driver of the rear vehicle was probably hindered by the dust. "Are both vehicles still moving?"

"*Uh-huh.*"

"You're doing fine, Lauren. You're my spotter up there."

"*The car in back is going really slow now. I think they're SUVs.*"

"Don't worry about that. Just keep watching both of them. How close are they to the turn in the road?"

"*They're almost there.*"

Nathan stood but couldn't see the dust cloud yet.

"*Okay, they're turning. Wait! The one in back stopped. People are getting out!*"

"Good girl, Lauren. Let me know how many men you see and where they go. Can you see any guns?"

"*Yeah, they've got big guns. Okay, three people got out. They're running away from the road.*"

"Tell me what you see. Did they stay together?"

"*No. Two of them are running toward you through the bushes on your side of the road. The other one is running toward me!*"

"Lauren, don't move. He's way too far away to see you. Are your field glasses inside the hood of your ghillie suit?"

"*Yes.*"

"You're totally invisible. He'll never see you. Stay calm, okay?"

"*Okay.*"

Nathan knew what the three men were doing. They were moving into fire support positions. The mercenary or coyote heading toward Lauren was probably working his way toward the high ground to act as a spotter. Nathan had purposely placed Lauren in the low part of the saddle because tactically it wasn't the best position. If any of Voda's men headed for the high ground—like this guy was doing right now—he'd take up a position at the top of the closer peak, which was also a little higher than its counterpart.

"Where are the two guys who stayed on my side of the road?"

"*They're still running toward you.*"

"In a pure south distance, how far away from the road are they?"

"*I don't know. I guess, like maybe a soccer field?*"

"So they're running parallel to the road about three hundred feet south of it?"

"*Yes.*"

"Are they halfway here yet?"

"*No, maybe a quarter.*"

"You're doing great, Lauren. Where is the other guy? Has he started up the mountain yet?"

"*No, he's about halfway, maybe. It looks like he's going to the mountain next to me.*"

"Good call—that's exactly where he's going. You're totally safe. Just remember to make slow-motion movements."

"I will."

"Let me know when the man starts up the slope. Have the vehicles slowed way down?"

"Yes. How did you know?"

"They're giving the men on foot a chance to advance. How slow are the cars going?"

"Pretty slow, hardly moving. The guys running toward you are getting way ahead."

"Lauren, I'm going to relocate. Let me know when I'm the same distance from the road as the men running toward me. Do you understand what I'm asking?"

"Uh-huh."

Nathan got up and, in a crouch, ran to the southwest. The landscape sloped downward slightly. Sporadically spaced creosote bushes and sage scrub prevented him from seeing farther than fifty yards in any direction.

"Let me know when to stop."

"Okay, right about—there."

She'd called it pretty close. He'd run about one hundred yards from his previous position. "Tell me when the men are about a soccer field away from me."

"It's hard to tell, but if they keep going, it looks like they'll get to you in maybe five minutes. I can't tell…."

"Don't worry about it. Sit tight and don't react to what you see, okay?"

"I won't."

To Nathan's immediate right, a shallow sandy wash no more than ten feet deep and forty feet across stood between him and the approaching mercenaries. He looked for a place to hunker down and didn't see anything that would offer significant cover. He settled for a location just behind a trio of ankle-high barrel cacti. With his rifle secured behind his back, he pulled his SIG, checked for ants, and assumed a prone position facing the wash. Even though his human outline was completely camouflaged by the ghillie suit, he felt naked lying down on open ground. Since his rifle was wrapped in the same shaggy material, its silhouette couldn't be spotted easily. He waited, expecting that the new arrivals would be winded from their long run across the desert.

"Where are they?" he asked quietly.

"*They're almost there!*"

"Are they headed straight toward me?"

"*Yes!*"

"Stay calm, Lauren. Don't say anything more."

His radio clicked.

He heard them before he saw them. Their footfalls were also raising a dust cloud.

Like something out of a video game, two men—each carrying an AK in his hands—emerged from the landscaping and stopped running when they reached the dry streambed. They weren't wearing body armor.

Nathan froze, melding into the desert.

The men looked at each other, looked across the wash at his position, and then descended the bank quickly. The man to Nathan's left lost his footing and fell. He quickly regained his feet and resumed running with his comrade. Dressed in desert camo pants and tan T-shirts, these guys might've been difficult to spot had they not been moving. Although they possessed the correct color scheme, they were clueless.

From no more than twenty feet away, Nathan lined up on the lead man and fired two quick shots with the SIG. The man clutched his chest and dropped to his knees. Before the other gunman could react, Nathan double-tapped him as well. His arms flailed as he fell face-first onto the sand. The armor-piercing slugs had passed completely through the men. He saw exit wounds on the back of the man who'd done a face plant.

Given the distance, there was no possible way the other man heading toward Lauren could've heard the suppressed shots.

"Lauren, where is the other man?"

"That was unbelievable," she said in a whisper. *"I can't believe they didn't see you!"*

He wanted to remind her she'd just witnessed the death of two human beings, but her insensitivity wasn't an altogether bad thing right now. He'd rather have her in a state of admiration than in shock or disbelief. There'd be time enough for therapy later.

He calmly repeated his question. "Where is the other man?"

"He's almost to the base of the mountain."

"Where are the vehicles?"

"They're still pretty far from the ghost town, maybe halfway after the turn in the road."

"Okay, you're doing great. I'm going to relocate back to my original position. Sit tight and relax. Everything's under control. Acknowledgment clicks only, unless I ask you a question."

His radio clicked. Before moving on, Nathan conducted a quick pat-down of the dead men and was surprised to find they didn't have radios. Expendable, he thought. Voda had probably planned to use them as bait, hoping to get Nathan to reveal his position. In a full sprint, he returned to the group of creosote bushes where he'd taken the range-finder readings. He looked to the west but couldn't see the approaching vehicles.

"I'm back at my original position. Where's the third man?"

"He's at the base of the mountain, but he stopped running."

"What's he doing?"

"He's like, just standing there. I think he's resting."

"Keep watching. Let me know when he starts moving again."

"Okay, he's going, but he isn't running."

"Is he headed up the slope yet?"

"No."

Nathan assumed a cross-legged position again and shouldered his rifle. Out of instinct, he thumbed the safety, but it was already disengaged. He was huffing a little from the sprint, so he began a series of deep breaths.

He focused on a spot where he thought the man should appear.

The windows of the approaching vehicles would be rolled up, he hoped, against the choking dust. With a little luck, the occupants wouldn't hear the rifle report.

Sighting his rifle between H3 and H5 toward the base of the twin mountains, Nathan believed he'd see the man enter his line of sight within the next few seconds. As if on cue, the gunman appeared, moving from left to right, near the base of the mountain. As Lauren had indicated, the guy hadn't started up the slope yet.

Nathan shifted position slightly, giving himself better alignment toward Piano 627. If the guy kept going, he'd pass very close to that rock formation. Nathan reached up and clicked two hundred yards off his elevation knob. Since Piano 627 was nearly level with his current position, he also removed the additional clicks he'd put on for the higher elevation at Rectangle 851. Since the wind hadn't changed, he left the windage knob alone. He was now zeroed for a six-hundred-yard shot with a ten- to twelve-mile-per-hour wind coming from a three o'clock vector.

He placed the crosshairs on the man's right arm, just under the shoulder, and tracked him. Moving at a fairly even pace, the man was weaving his way through the vegetation. Nathan knew his bullet time to the target was just under one second, so he'd need to lead the target by approximately three feet—the distance of one stride.

He took a deep breath and told himself it was just business. He didn't relish killing this man—sniper work was never pleasant—but for motivation, he needed only to recall the image of the shirtless slob sitting next to Abrille, holding a can of beer. Given the right circumstances, Voda and his thugs would do the same thing to Lauren and countless other young girls.

He let half a breath out, placed the crosshairs out in front of the walking man, and began a gradual squeeze of the trigger.

CHAPTER 29

The report slammed Nathan's ears.

In just under two seconds, he cycled the bolt and reacquired the target.

The man had literally walked into Nathan's bullet. His mark was down, writhing on the ground as though covered with ants. Nathan had seen this before and knew it would end soon. It did. A few seconds later, the man stopped flailing and lay still. At least he hadn't suffered long.

"Lauren, you copy?"

"*That was* crazy."

"What are the vehicles doing? Have they sped up or slowed down?"

"*No, they're going the same speed. Super slow.*"

"Remember, no sudden movements up there. Stay invisible. Radio silence until you hear from me. I'm turning my volume down."

Click.

Given that the vehicles hadn't changed speed, Nathan felt confident that the men inside them hadn't heard his rifle report.

At a distance of a mile, a high-power rifle report sounded like a gentle *pop*, likely inaudible from inside a car.

That was the good news.

The bad news was that Voda probably wouldn't have sent a man to high ground without being able to communicate with him. Now that man was silent, it wouldn't take long for Voda to realize that his lookout man was down. The question was, how long did Nathan have until Voda knew? Estimating five minutes max, he started a mental stopwatch.

Guns reloaded, he stood and looked west, toward the oncoming vehicles. He still couldn't see them. He knew when the SUVs approached the town, someone in the lead vehicle would be using field glasses, so to avoid the possibility of being seen, Nathan settled into a cross-legged position again. He didn't expect the SUVs would simply roll into town. Voda was many things, but reckless wasn't one of them.

He unslung his Remington and used its scope to watch for the two-vehicle caravan.

His wait didn't last long.

Through the mirage effect in his scope, the lead SUV entered his line of sight. It looked like a Cadillac Escalade, and except for its windshield, its glass was darkly tinted.

A few seconds later, he saw the trailing SUV, also an Escalade. It too had dark windows. Both of them stopped about one hundred yards west of H1. For several seconds, nothing happened. They just sat there, and Nathan worried that Voda had already attempted to contact his lookout and received no response. Since there was nothing he could do about it, he pushed the concern aside. At least Voda wouldn't be able to see his dead lookout. The underbrush hid the body.

Moving slowly, the lead SUV resumed its approach, but the second vehicle stayed put. A wise precaution on Voda's part. At least he knew which vehicle Voda was in—the second one. Voda would never take the point and use himself as bait. He'd delegate that "honor" to one of his men.

Through its lightly tinted windshield, Nathan saw a single occupant, the driver. When it reached H1, he lowered his rifle and remained motionless.

Moving only his eyes, he studied the SUV as it rolled past and stopped about thirty feet east of his position, directly in front of the fluorescent stake. Its side windows were nearly black. There could be five or six additional men in there, but he wasn't concerned. Yet.

Again, the Escalade just sat there, unmoving.

Its driver finally got out and approached the fluorescent stake. The man was nicely dressed in a dark suit and armed with an MP5, a close-combat weapon. He grabbed the radio and tentatively looked it over, turning it in his hand.

Nathan pressed the transmit button. "Please take the radio back to Mr. Voda."

The man looked startled for an instant. Without responding, he climbed back into the Escalade and began backing up. Nathan shouldered his rifle and watched the Escalade recede. A minute later, it stopped in front of the second SUV and its driver climbed out.

Nathan watched through the scope as the man approached the driver's side of the second Escalade. Since he had two radios on his hip, he quickly confirmed that the tan radio he used to talk with Lauren was turned down. Without volume, the voice-activated system wouldn't work.

The other radio's earpiece crackled to life. "*Mr. McBride? Where are you?*" asked Voda.

"Please have your man open all the doors of your vehicles, including the tailgates."

"*I trust you brought my alexandrites with you?*"

"'Trust' isn't a word in your vocabulary. But to answer your question, yes. Please comply with my request and open all the doors. I'd like to verify that you only brought two men, as agreed."

Although Nathan wouldn't be able to see inside Voda's vehicles, Voda didn't know that.

"*All right.*"

Nathan watched the nicely dressed gunman systematically open all the doors and tailgates of both vehicles.

"*Satisfied? As you can see, I brought two men. I'm a businessman. I see no reason we can't complete this exchange.*"

"Same here. Please ask your man to get back into his vehicle."

If Voda had lost communication with the man on foot who'd been heading toward Lauren's position, he wouldn't be able to mention it without tipping the fact that he'd brought the extra firepower. And by now, Voda would expect his two other men— the men without radios—to be in place. Voda probably felt confident he was in the superior position tactically.

Voda's man complied and got in the lead SUV.

"Thank you," Nathan said. "I would like my sister to get out and begin walking toward the houses. Ask her to stop at the fluorescent stake where your man retrieved the radio."

"*I'd like to comply, but Ms. Marchand will have a difficult time walking.*"

"Why is that?"

"*I'm afraid she was less than forthcoming during her...visit with me.*"

"You smashed her toes."

"*I took no pleasure in it, but she was quite stubborn.*"

Nathan clenched his teeth but maintained a calm voice. "Then have your man drop her off."

"*What about my alexandrites?*"

"After I've verified my sister's identity."

"*You're asking me to risk losing my piece of the trade.*"

"Take a look around. Do you see any vehicles besides your own? Any men?"

"*Do you expect me to believe you and your sister are going to simply walk out of this desert on foot?*"

"Believe whatever you want. Have your man search the town if it will make you feel better. Once I'm certain of her identity, I'll drop a Ziploc bag containing your gemstones. You'll have ample opportunity to verify the contents."

"All right, we'll play it your way. No tricks."

"Please keep your radio on."

"Agreed."

Through the mirage-distorted image of his scope, Nathan saw the right rear passenger door of the second SUV open, and another gunman got out. He looked similar to the first guy but appeared to have trouble putting weight on his right leg. He could be the surviving gunman from the Ulric Street action. He reached inside the Escalade and pulled Jin out by her hair.

Nathan held his breath and was sorely tempted to shoot the asshole, but he couldn't see Voda, who probably had a gun trained on his sister. Now wasn't the time to act. Jin wasn't out of danger yet. He also realized Lauren was observing everything. If he acted hastily, he could get Jin killed in front of her daughter—not an option.

She limped forward and got into the front passenger seat. Nathan realized he'd never actually seen his sister before this. He couldn't see much detail because her disheveled hair concealed her face. He didn't like having the scope's crosshairs trained on her, but his finger wasn't anywhere near the trigger. Just to be safe, he moved the crosshairs off of her.

The Escalade started forward. As it neared H1, he got a better look at his sister. As with Marchand, she looked severely battered, one of her eyes nearly swollen shut. It looked like they'd worked her over pretty savagely.

The SUV rolled to a stop at the fluorescent stake, and Jin got out. Without warning, the driver spun the tires on the road as he sped backward. The open door clipped Jin and knocked her down. Twenty feet farther away, the driver slammed his brakes, which closed the passenger door. The Escalade peeled away in reverse again, leaving more dust.

Nathan had been sorely tempted to shoot the guy, but now the opportunity was gone. The dust was too thick. Given a shot, he probably wouldn't have taken it—tempting as it was. He needed to be patient and make sure Jin was totally alone before he took any action.

His sister painfully gained her feet and stood in the middle of the road, hugging herself.

Nathan's rage boiled at seeing her in this condition. He thought about the note she'd written, all she'd been through in her life. The heartbreaking story of Choon-Hee...Preserving Stone's dog tag all these years...Her love of Lauren and the beating she'd endured to keep her daughter—and him—safe. Jin was family, and it hurt to see her like this. He thanked heaven Lauren couldn't see the gory details. Yet.

Nathan forced himself to calm down. If he allowed his emotions to control his actions, he'd get not only himself killed, but Jin as well. Lauren would then be trapped in the middle of the Mojave, with no place to go. He'd shown her how to activate the helicopter's ELT, but that was little consolation. It would take time for SAR teams to arrive. How long, he didn't know. But a lot could happen in that span.

He took a few deep breaths, then settled in to assess his sister's condition more thoroughly. The first thing he noticed was her bare feet. On each foot, several toes were caked with blood. Thanks to Voda's medieval savagery, she wouldn't be able to run when the time came. She'd also likely be concussed and have trouble concentrating. One thing was certain: she'd never be able to walk to the helicopter. He'd have to carry her.

Resuming his examination, Nathan saw that his sister was tall, close to six feet, and her hair wasn't quite the jet black of Lauren's. It looked to be nearly the same color as his own—graying dark brown with a distinct hue of red. Her Eurasian cheekbones were cut and swollen from repeated blows. Nathan had seen other victims like this before, more times than he cared to remember.

Her blue jeans and T-shirt were spattered with blood. She tried to stand up straight but winced from pain. Although she'd been physically defeated, her dignity hadn't been broken.

Still hugging herself, she looked around, and her glance walked across his position. Like Voda, she was probably wondering where he was. Even if she'd known exactly where to look, all she would've seen was a large clump of creosote bushes flanked by a few barrel cacti.

Nathan didn't want Jin to hear him yet, so he kept his voice low. "Mr. Voda, are you still there?"

"*Yes, I'm here.*"

"Please back your vehicles out to two hundred meters."

"*I think I've been more than generous.*"

"I'm on foot, Mr. Voda, and it will take me several minutes to reach my sister. Please comply with my request."

Voda didn't respond, but both Escalades began backing away, and Nathan lost sight of them from his sitting position. Since the vehicles were moving slowly, he gave it a good thirty seconds.

Voda's voice came through his earpiece again. "*Okay?*"

"Yes, thank you."

"*My patience is running thin, McBride.*"

"Once I've verified my sister's identity face-to-face, you'll have your gems. Please be patient."

"*No tricks,*" Voda said again.

Yeah, right, no tricks…He was about to give Jin a command, but she spoke first.

Looking in the direction of Voda's SUVs, she called out, "We don't have much time."

Nathan remained silent.

"You're inside a clump of bushes at my ten o'clock position."

Without moving, Nathan said, "I'm impressed."

"Voda doesn't know you were a scout sniper."

"Did you give Harv and me up entirely?"

"No. All he knows is that you're my brother."

"Pretend you're still alone."

"I *am* pretending I'm alone."

Nathan now knew where Lauren got her feistiness. "Avoid moving your lips too much. They're probably using field glasses. Can you walk?"

"Not very well."

"Slowly work your way this direction and keep looking around. Stay near the road, though. I don't want Voda to lose sight of you."

She continued the act, hugging herself as though nervous. "Three men are on foot. They got out before we pulled in here."

"I'm aware of that. They're no longer a problem."

"Where's Lauren?"

Nathan put metal in his voice. "Who are you, Jin?"

She was clearly stunned by the comment. "What do you mean?"

"How do you know about echo five?"

"I promise I'll explain everything when this is over."

"If you want my trust, you'll tell me right now."

"Nathan—"

"Who *are* you?"

She looked toward Voda's Escalades. "DGSE."

CHAPTER 30

"French intelligence?"

She responded almost grudgingly. "Yes."

Nathan's mind went into overdrive. Things began falling into place, but he needed to be sure Jin was telling the truth.

"Your note. How much of it's true?"

"Can we discuss this later? We don't have the time."

"I'm making time. *How much?*"

"All of it. I've been working my way into Voda's operation for over a year. I'll explain everything, but not now."

Nathan emerged from his hiding place and walked toward Jin. Wearing the ghillie suit, he knew what he looked like. He flipped the hood back and kept going. In five more steps he'd enter Voda's line of sight.

Jin turned and faced him, her expression guarded.

Nathan walked up to her and stared into her blue eye. Her brown eye was nearly swollen shut. "Did you know Voda was murdering the girls?"

She didn't hesitate. "*No.*"

It was the truth—he knew it with certainty.

With a single word, Jin had proven herself in a way that ten thousand additional words never could.

"Where is Lauren?" she asked.

"She's in the saddle between those two peaks to the north."

To her credit, she didn't even glance in that direction.

Nathan pressed the transmit button on his radio.

"Voda, you copy?"

"*A desert-colored ghillie suit,*" Voda said. "*Well played.*"

"Do you remember what I said I'd do if you brought more than two men?"

"*There's no need for threats. I have two men, as agreed.*"

"You're a liar. I neutralized your three goons before you arrived with Ms. Marchand."

There was a marked silence. "*That wasn't necessary. They were only here to ensure my safety.*"

"Consider yourself uninsured."

"*Give me my alexandrites, as agreed.*"

Nathan removed a Ziploc bag from his hip pocket, held it at arm's length, and dropped it to the road. "Come and get them."

He tossed Voda's radio and earpiece aside and scooped his sister off her feet. "Hold on tight." Hauling her in a fireman's carry, he ran for the cover of H5, the closest standing house. He tried to minimized the bounce of his strides, but Jin cried out anyway.

"Sorry about the bumpy ride."

Through clenched teeth, she said, "I'll live. Keep going!"

"You think?"

Nathan heard it then, the unmistakable crackling of automatic-weapon fire. It sounded like distant firecrackers. Nathan dropped to his knees and laid Jin down. In a lightning-fast pattern, the road erupted toward Nathan as multiple bullets skipped off its powdery surface. He used his body to protect her from the maelstrom of slugs. As quickly as it had begun, the crackling ended and they hadn't been hit. Nathan looked west toward the vehicles, but the rising dust from bullet impacts obscured the SUVs.

"I guess I pissed him off."

"You think?" Jin said, mimicking him.

Nathan pivoted toward the road. "Stay down."

In a fluid move, he unslung his rifle and shouldered it. Without using the scope, he estimated a windshield-level shot, and he fired into the dust cloud. The discharge rocked him back. He chambered another round and fired again.

The roar of the lead vehicle's engine reached them. Within seconds the Escalade would penetrate the dust cloud and be upon them.

Nathan hoisted Jin again and resumed his sprint for H5. He reached down and turned up the volume on the tan radio he used with Lauren.

Her frantic voice screamed through his earpiece, "...*Why don't you answer me? Nathan!*"

"I'm here," Nathan said, still running.

"*There's another car coming down the road!*"

"A third vehicle?"

"*Yes!*"

"Where is it?"

"*It's almost to the turn where the other one stopped.*"

"Does it look like the others? A black SUV?"

"*Yes.*"

"Is that Lauren?" Jin asked.

"Yes. Lauren, keep an eye on the new arrival. I need to know how many men get out, and where they go."

"*Is my mom okay?*"

"She's fine. Keep watching the third SUV."

"*Okay.*"

Nathan glanced over his shoulder and saw the lead SUV penetrate the dust cloud. He'd hoped they'd make it inside H5 before being seen, but it didn't happen. The vehicle pulled off the dirt road and skidded to a stop at the western edge of the buildings. Another dust cloud swirled.

He set Jin down inside the house, steadied his stance against the jamb of the front door, and took aim at the driver's side. The door flew open, and the first gunman he'd seen earlier got out and used the open door for cover. Before the guy could bring his MP5 to bear, Nathan placed the crosshairs on the middle of the door panel and fired. The armor-piercing round easily went through the sheet metal and found its mark. Nathan reacquired the gunman through the scope. The man was on the ground in a fetal position, holding his stomach.

Voda must've seen his man go down. He drove his SUV off the road and raced toward the west side of H1, using it for cover. Nathan didn't have a shot from his position. The brush lining the road, coupled with the shallow angle, prevented a clear line of sight. Without leaving the cover of the building, he'd never get a shot. Voda and his man could now use the first three houses for cover as they advanced.

"Lauren, where is the third SUV?"

"It's past the turn in the road, and it's going real fast."

"Keep watching it."

By now, Voda and his other gunman would be out of their SUV. Both Voda and his cohort had leg wounds, and from what Nathan had seen earlier, Voda's man wouldn't be able to run very well, if at all. They'd both have to advance cautiously, and Nathan believed they'd stay together, at least initially.

"Jin, I need you to hunker down in the biggest bedroom's closet."

She began to protest.

"You're in no shape to help me. Take this." He pulled his SIG and offered it to her.

She shook her head. "Keep that. You're going to need it."

"Jin, you shouldn't be unarmed. You—"

"Keep it!"

Her white top was a problem. He shucked off his ghillie suit coat and tossed it to her, knowing it would mask her glaring white shirt. "I know your feet are bad, but if you get an opportunity, head up to Lauren's position."

"Nathan, go. Get moving, Marine!"

He ran through the debris littering the floor and peered through the rear door toward H1.

"Lauren, did you copy everything I just said to your mom?"

"*Yes.*"

"Where's the third SUV?"

"*It's almost to H1.*"

"Copy that."

He placed himself in Voda's head. With reinforcements coming, he'd probably sit tight and wait for the extra firepower to arrive, which was mere seconds away. He didn't have time to replace the two .308 rounds he'd just fired, which left him with three rounds left.

"*The car isn't slowing down,*" Lauren said.

Nathan knew then what they planned to do.

He stepped out of H5's rear door and began an all-out sprint toward H6. He couldn't allow Voda's new arrivals to flank him. There was nothing he could do for Jin right now. He hoped she'd take an opportunity to bug out if given the right circumstance. Dealing with the new arrivals had to take priority. If Voda's SUV made it through town, he'd be fighting this battle on two fronts. He sorely missed Harv's presence, but at least he had Lauren's eyes up in the saddle.

Nathan ran past the corner of H5 and angled toward the road, giving himself some cover from behind. The fifty-foot separation between H5 and H6 seemed like miles.

Nathan heard it then, the oncoming roar of the SUV's engine.

Lauren voice cut through his earpiece. "*Nathan, look out!*"

The stucco wall of H6 exploded at the same instant he heard the clatter of MP5 fire, dozens of slugs cratering the wall. Whoever had fired that burst hadn't missed by more than two feet. The gunman who had just opened up on him had to be positioned north of the row of buildings. There was no other way the bullets could've impacted where they did otherwise. Either Voda or his gunman was in the brush.

"I'm okay," he told Lauren, and scrambled farther south toward the road. A second barrage nailed the wall behind him, but he knew it was a desperation burst. The gunman no longer had a line of sight on him.

"Lauren, where did that come from?"

"He's in the bushes near H2."

Nathan was more than impressed. Not only did Lauren sound calm, she'd used his tactical designator for house number two.

"Good work. Let me know if he approaches H5."

"I will."

Nathan had the speed advantage and used it. Believing the newly arriving SUV would blow through town, he hustled back toward H5 and took a knee at its corner. Shouldering his Remington, he lined up on the approaching vehicle. Sure enough, it was barreling down the road, raising a massive dust cloud. A gunman behind the driver had his upper body extended out of his window, aiming his AK at the line of structures. Nathan had intended to shoot the driver, but this man with the machine gun became his primary threat.

The gunman saw Nathan and fired a burst.

Nathan ignored the exploding dirt to his right and steadied his Remington. He saw a tiny amount of heartbeat bounce in the scope, but not enough to matter at this distance.

Fully automatic AKs climb when fired, and that's exactly what happened next. In less than a second, the slugs impacting the ground moved up the wall of H5. The gunman hadn't held it low enough. Jin should be okay, since she wasn't positioned where the slugs hit the wall.

Before the guy could level his AK for a second burst, Nathan aimed slightly in front of the man's chest, and executed a controlled trigger pull.

The concussion of the rifle's blast shook loose dirt and dust from H5's roof. It rained down like mist. He cycled the bolt and lined up on the driver. In the right edge of his scope's image, he saw the man he'd just shot now hanging out the window like a rag doll, his head and arms dangling down. Nathan drove his next bullet through the lower-right quadrant of the windshield and scored another hit. The driver slumped to the right. He cycled the bolt, loading his last round.

Out of control, the SUV screamed past his position, clipped the corner of H6, and veered across the slab of H7. Sparks flew as the SUV's differential sheared the edge of the exposed concrete. The Escalade bounced, swayed, and nearly tipped over.

Nathan slung his rifle over his head, pulled his SIG, and took off in pursuit. He knew the SUV had enough momentum to carry it across H7's slab and into the vegetation north of the houses. If there were more gunmen in that Escalade, he wanted to neutralize them before they had a chance to recover from their jarring ride.

Running in a full sprint, Nathan followed the SUV into the brush. It hadn't slowed down, but it was turning to the left much faster than it could handle. Through a rapidly forming maelstrom of dust, he watched the Escalade roll. The man who'd fired the AK cartwheeled out of the window. The SUV rolled at least two more times before he lost sight of it in the billowing dust.

Nathan realized he had a solid tactical opportunity, but he had to hurry. Following the path of destruction, he squinted and nearly tripped over the body of the man who'd flown out of the window.

Thirty yards beyond H7's slab, he found the Escalade right side up but totaled. All its glass was broken out, including the back window. SIG in hand, he approached the hulk in a crouch and peered inside. The driver was dead, but the man who'd been in the front passenger seat clung to life by a thread, clearly out of the fight. Both of his arms were crushed, probably from being outside the SUV when it rolled. Semiconscious, he looked at Nathan with a resigned expression.

Despite what this guy would've done had their situations been reversed, Nathan knew that killing him wouldn't sit right with his conscience and decided to let the authorities deal with him, assuming he lived.

"Lauren, is this dust cloud heading toward the man hiding in the brush?"

"That was crazy! I've never seen anything like that."

"Stay focused and please answer my question. Will the dust cloud envelop the man hiding in the brush?"

"Yeah, I think so."

"Copy that."

His radio clicked.

Nathan waited until the dust completely cleared the SUV before falling in behind it. Working his way through the vegetation, he had to maintain a medium-paced jog to stay on the dust cloud's trailing edge. It wasn't as dense as a smoke screen, but it offered a good visual cone of concealment encompassing his ten-to-two-o'clock threat area.

"Lauren, keep your eye on me. Let me know when the leading edge of the dust reaches the man, then tell me when I'm around one hundred feet away from him. Did you copy that?"

"Yes, it's almost there…Okay, I can't see the man anymore."

"Don't worry about that. Pick a landmark beyond his position and use that for a visual reference. Let me know when to stop. When the dust clears, tell me where he is with a vector from my position. Due west will be twelve o'clock. Do you understand what I'm asking?"

"Yes."

"I'm going silent."

His radio clicked again, and he couldn't help but smile. Lauren amazed him—she'd make a fine operations officer someday. He hoped she'd get the distance right, or he'd end up running right into the guy's lap.

Nathan had always believed the best way to attack an enemy was to be unpredictable. Blindly following this dust cloud into his enemy's territory fit the bill. He didn't think Voda or his gunman would be expecting such an aggressive move.

Lauren voice broke his thoughts. *"I can't tell exactly, but I think you should stop now."*

Nathan clicked his radio.

He chose a large clump of creosote and dropped down. He knew the row of houses was off to his left, but he wouldn't be able to see them for several more seconds, until the dust moved through. At least the reverse was also true: if Voda had hidden himself in one of those houses, he hadn't been able to see Nathan's approach.

Time seemed to stretch as the dust continued to drift.

Through the thinnest parts of its nebulous form, he spotted the slab of H4 and knew he needed to go a little farther. He advanced another fifty feet and crouched on the northeast side of another creosote bush.

Nathan focused straight ahead, looking for any kind of motion.

"Okay, I can see him. He's at your...two o'clock."

Nathan clicked his radio again and waited for the last of the dust to clear.

An eerie silence fell over the landscape, touched only by the whisper of wind through the brush. Nathan remained motionless, focusing on the vector Lauren had supplied, but saw nothing.

It became a waiting game, and he took the opportunity to reload his Remington.

His ghillie suit pants still screened the lower half of his body, but his upper half held sharp lines. Although his 5.11 shirt was tan, it didn't offer more than color in terms of camouflage. As long as he remained frozen, he felt he wouldn't be seen. Slowly turning his head, he looked toward H3. Partially obscured by the brush, the black opening of its rear door loomed large. Voda could be in there, or in H2, or H1. Lauren hadn't reporting seeing Voda, but then again, he hadn't asked about him. But Nathan felt confident Lauren would relay any change down here, especially seeing Voda.

Knowing it involved some risk, Nathan needed to force things. In slow motion, he reached down and picked up a grapefruit-size rock. Keeping his arm as low as possible, he tossed it in an underhanded motion. The rock arced through the air and hit the middle of a creosote bush thirty feet distant—his intended target. Had the wind been blowing harder, the bush's movement wouldn't have been detectible, but its sudden shuddering made it stand out clearly from the other plants.

At first, nothing happened, but a few seconds later, Nathan saw something and slowly adjusted his position to the right for a better look.

There! Movement at his one o'clock position. Lauren had nailed the vector with near precision. The man was standing in a slight crouch, probably because his wounded leg prevented him from squatting. Nathan could see only a small portion of his opponent's upper body through the underbrush, but it was enough. It could be Voda, but Nathan gave it low odds. Voda would likely be sheltered inside one of the houses.

He tucked the SIG into his waist and in slow motion unslung his Remington, shouldered it, and placed crosshairs on the side of the man's chest. He saw it wasn't Voda. For a brief instant, he considered shooting lower, through the man's pelvis, but this wasn't the same situation as he'd faced at the wrecked SUV. This man was armed and in the fight.

He pulled the trigger.

The rifle's concussion hammered the surrounding area like a thunderclap, raising a new dust cloud. He needed to relocate. Fast.

He looked left, toward H3's rear door, and saw a chilling sight.

Standing in the opening of the H3's rear door, Voda had a scoped handgun lined up on him.

Nathan dived to his right.

Voda's gun boomed.

Nathan felt as though he'd been hit with a sledgehammer.

He fell to his hands and knees and tried to breathe.

When he sucked in a lungful of air, he coughed in a violent spasm and tasted blood.

There was something he had to do before he lost consciousness.

He unclipped the radio from his belt and yanked the wires free.

Falling to his side, he tossed it as far as he could.

He felt it coming, the sickening wave of oncoming darkness.

No. It can't end like this.

Lauren....

CHAPTER 31

Nathan felt something jar his leg. It annoyed him. He wanted to sleep. He opened his eyes and tried to focus. The world was gray.

"Welcome back, my gallant friend."

Where was he? A blurry image of a hand holding something in front of his face coalesced. Was it a Ziploc bag? He felt a hard surface beneath him, definitely not sand or dirt. His chest felt heavy and sore. What had happened? He'd been shot....

"This bag doesn't have any alexandrites in it. You can't begin to understand my disappointment, but I'll make it abundantly clear soon enough."

"Voda..."

"At your service."

Nathan coughed, and a million needles stabbed his rib cage. How long...Where was he? He focused on Voda. Dressed in slacks and a nice shirt, the man almost looked respectable.

"I have good news and bad news," Voda said. "The good news is that you're alive. The bad news is that *you're alive*."

Nathan looked down at his bare chest and spit out a mouthful of blood.

"That's a nasty bruise you've got there. Fortunately, I was using hollow points. A .44 Magnum packs quite a punch, wouldn't you agree? Your vest saved your life. You have some intriguing scars on your body. I can see you're no stranger to pain."

Nathan remained silent.

"You've done well to this point. You've managed to eliminate all of my men. Congratulations."

Nathan saw he was inside the living room of one of the houses. The gray he'd seen upon waking was the ceiling's unpainted drywall. His left wrist was handcuffed to a metal framing anchor sticking out of the slab. Half the manacle encircled his wrist, the other half was secured to the anchor through a hole designed for a bolt or heavy lag screw.

He didn't know which house he was in, but guessed it was either H2 or H3. He had a vague recollection of being dragged, but couldn't recall more that. Since Voda had a bad leg and Nathan weighed close to 230 pounds, he'd probably been dragged into H3, the closest house. He was fairly certain Voda had bashed him on the head at some point. He felt concussion symptoms.

Nathan looked at his manacled hand again.

"I see you've noticed the handcuffs. I pride myself on having the largest collection of antique handcuffs in the world." Voda smiled. "The wonders of eBay…I use these for special occasions, but I'm afraid they weren't designed with comfort in mind."

Nathan remained silent, realizing that anything he said would be pointless.

"You have caused me a great deal of trouble, but you can redeem yourself by telling me where my alexandrites are. I'm not beyond showing you some mercy. Although I promised you a slow death, I'm willing to reconsider…if you cooperate."

Voda backed up a few steps and picked up a four-foot length of broken two-by-four. It had a menacingly sharp end. He test-swung it a few times in the air.

"Why don't I give you a few minutes to think about things while I go find your sister? She couldn't have gotten far with all those broken toes." Voda turned to leave, then stopped. "She's remarkably tough, I'll give her that. She held out for hours before giving you up. A truly heroic stand."

Nathan spat more blood. "There's something I'd like to ask you, Voda."

"Oh, by all means."

"How's the leg?"

Voda's expression went dark, then a smile formed. He angled his head over his shoulder. "If you hear any screaming down the block, try to ignore it, okay?"

"How could you do it?"

He turned back. "Do what?"

"Rape and murder those little girls."

"I'm afraid you have me all wrong."

"Yeah, right."

"Believe what you want."

"Even if what you say is true, you're just as guilty as your perverted men."

"I'd love to pursue this philosophical debate with you, but it will have to wait. Don't worry, we'll have plenty of time together. When I return, I'll have your sister with me. Unless you tell me where my alexandrites are, I'm going to beat her to death while you watch. I have no doubt you're tough as nails, but watching someone else pay for your silence may be less easy to withstand." Voda shrugged. "If you still won't talk, I'll start beating you. You'll soon understand you're not as tough as you think."

"Give it your best shot, shit bird."

Voda smiled again. "Oh, before I go, there's something I owe you from our first encounter."

Moving with more speed than Nathan thought possible, Voda stepped forward and swung the two-by-four with both hands— like a lumberjack splitting a log.

Nathan's right shin took the impact. Shit!

He felt his bones snap.

Nathan clenched his teeth but didn't scream—he wouldn't give Voda the satisfaction.

"How's the leg?" Voda mocked. He tossed the piece of lumber against the wall out of Nathan's reach, pulled his scoped Magnum from his waist, and limped out the door.

With as much strength as he could muster, Nathan yelled, "Jin, Voda's coming!"

Fighting the searing agony in his shin, Nathan looked for a way to free himself from the framing anchor. Although the manacle around his wrist was tight, he still tried to pull free, but to no avail. The antique handcuffs were crude but thoroughly effective. The chain connecting the cuffs looked stronger than those of a modern pair, its links both bigger and thicker. Even if he broke his arm in the process, he'd never be able to get enough leverage to snap the chain connecting the cuffs.

His Predator knife was gone. He might've been able to use it to whittle away at the metal, but even if it worked, it would take too much time.

He looked around—too quickly. His world spun and a surge of nausea took him. Fifteen feet away, he saw his ballistic vest and ghillie suit pants. He hadn't realized he was barefoot until now. His boots and socks sat next to the vest. Voda was going to smash his toes, like he had with Marchand and Jin, or worse. Shit!

He clenched his teeth and tried to think. Even if Jin managed to ambush Voda, she'd never be able to defeat him in hand-to-hand combat, not in her present condition. Maybe she'd relocated to a house farther away, but with her toes all busted up, she couldn't have gotten far. Her window of opportunity to escape had been when Voda dragged him into this house. If she'd managed to limp her way into the brush, she'd be able to hide and make her way up to Lauren's position. The ghillie suit offered her good camouflage, and moving slowly because of her toes became an advantage.

If Voda returned without Jin, Nathan had his victory. He'd buy time for her and Lauren by holding out against Voda's torture for as long as possible. It was nothing he hadn't done before. At least he could cling to the small consolation of denying the bastard his treasure.

He looked around again, but Voda had clearly emptied Nathan's immediate area. There was nothing on the concrete he could reach, even if he laid himself flat and used his good leg. In frustration, he yanked his wrist against the handcuff and was rewarded with a stab of pain. He jerked his arm again—much harder—and felt his shoulder strain in the socket. He'd never be able to pull his wrist through this damned manacle.

What he heard next took him by surprise: the staccato clatter of an AK-47 burst.

The weapon had a distinct sound, much different from that of the MP5s that Voda's men carried. The burst had been short and controlled and had come from the far end of town. He was positive it hadn't originated from H5, where'd left Jin—more like H9 or H10. Had the man he'd left alive in the SUV rejoined the fight? Nathan thought that extremely unlikely. The guy had two crushed arms—there was no way he'd be able to hold an AK, let alone shoot it. Voda had said Nathan had killed all his men. Could a fourth man have been inside the SUV and crawled out a window before Nathan got there? No way. He'd arrived at the Escalade seconds after it had stopped rolling. There'd been only three men inside.

Unless Voda had another gunman out there, it must've been Jin who'd fired the AK. If so, she hadn't bugged out after all. As he pondered the possibility, Nathan felt conflicting surges of relief and concern. As much as he hated knowing Jin was engaging Voda, it gave him some hope.

Voda's handgun boomed, followed by another burst of AK fire.

What was happening out there? Nathan felt frustration and rage begin to build. He inwardly cursed for getting himself shot.

How could he have been so careless and sloppy? He should've anticipated Voda's appearance. Should've known Voda would send his gunman into the desert as sacrificial bait.

Voda's Magnum rumbled again. Good—he wouldn't have needed to fire a second time if he'd nailed Jin with the first round. A few seconds later, he heard more AK fire.

Shit! He was helpless in here while his sister fought his battle. In an act of pure rage, he yanked against the handcuff again. Pain shot through his arm like electricity. He growled and pulled harder.

"Nathan, are you in there?"

Nathan froze, his heart sinking. No, it couldn't be. What was *she* doing here?

"Lauren!"

She appeared from the direction of the rear door, still wearing the ghillie suit.

Crying, she ran up to him and hugged him. "I'm really scared," she said, still winded from her down-mountain sprint. She cringed at the expression on his face. "I'm sorry! I didn't know what to do!"

Her knee landed on his shin, and he cried out.

"What's wrong?"

"Voda broke my leg."

She put her hand to her mouth, stunned.

"Where's your mom?" Nathan asked urgently.

"I don't know!"

"Did you trigger the helicopter's ELT?"

"Oh, no, I forgot!"

"You forgot! What do you mean, you forgot?"

She cried harder. "Please don't be mad at me."

He hugged her with his free arm. "It's okay, Lauren, don't worry about it. You have to get out of here and go trigger the ELT like I showed you."

But Lauren showed no signs of leaving him. "I can help you."

"Voda could be back any minute. Lauren, coming down here was a very brave thing to do, but you have to leave. I'm handcuffed to this bracket, and Voda has the key. There's nothing you can do for me."

Outside, the Magnum boomed again.

The sound made Lauren flinch with fear.

For his part, Nathan felt a small measure of relief because the handgun report sounded farther away. He toyed with the idea of asking Lauren to go find a gun, but it was too risky. Voda might see her. The last thing he wanted was Lauren back in the hands of a proven child-murderer.

"Can't you break the handcuffs? Aren't you, like, super strong?"

"No, I can't break—" He stopped midsentence.

And in that moment, Nathan knew what he had to do.

"Okay, Lauren, you can stay. See that piece of wood leaning against the wall over there?"

"Uh-huh."

"Go get it. Hurry."

She ran over and back.

"I need a piece of broken glass. Go look under one of the windows."

Lauren returned a few seconds later. "Is this okay?"

He took it from her. It was about an inch long. "Perfect. Remember when you became the tough girl inside your stepdad's warehouse?"

"Uh-huh."

"I need you to be the tough girl again." Nathan used the shard of glass to slice into his wrist below the cuff. The cut wasn't deep enough to open any arteries, but it would provide a good blood flow for a few minutes.

"What are you doing! Trying to kill yourself?"

"No, the blood will act as a lubricant."

"A lubricant for what?"

"I'm going to break my hand, but I need your help."

"Break your hand? No way! Are you serious?"

"After I get this piece of wood in place, I'll need you to jump on top of it."

"That's crazy! Won't it hurt?"

"No, it won't hurt that bad." He pointed. "I need one of those socks."

Nathan considered using the two-by-four like a club and smashing his own hand, but the handcuff employed a ratchet locking mechanism, and if he missed his hand and hit the handcuff, the ratchet would lock down so tightly he'd never get his hand out, short of amputating it. He needed to act quickly and not give Lauren a lot of time to think.

Nathan placed his manacled wrist on the concrete next to the framing anchor and shivered. This was going to be bad. He had no illusions about it. The damage might even be irreparable, but he had no choice. The trick, however, was convincing Lauren to do the dirty work.

With his hand facing sideways in a karate-chop position, he tucked his thumb into his palm and placed the end of the board directly on top. He used his left foot to anchor the other end of the lumber. The downward force from Lauren's weight should dislocate his thumb, and the ensuing momentum should shear the carpal bones apart—a very crappy deal.

"Okay, Lauren. I need you to stand next to this board, jump up in the air, and land on top of it. You have to drive your feet down at the same time you land, like you're jumping on a trampoline."

"I can't do that!"

"Lauren, you have to. If you don't, Voda will kill your mom, then come back and kill me. I'd rather have a broken hand than have your mom and me dead."

She was crying. "I can't. I can't!"

"Lauren, look at me. You're saving my life. Do you understand? You have to hurt me to save my life. Your only other choice is to run away and never come back."

"But if I do that, you and Mom die."

"That's right. Be the tough girl. Spies have to do difficult things. Do it!"

"Are you sure?"

"Yes. I'm sure. Hurry, Lauren. Do it!"

Nathan folded the sock a couple of times and put it in his mouth.

Lauren's face reflected the horror of what she was about to do, pleading for a reprieve.

He gave her a smile behind the sock, and a nod.

"I'm sorry. I'm sorry...!"

Lauren jumped into the air and stomped down with eighty-three pounds of momentum.

His world went red.

CHAPTER 32

Nathan's mind registered the event but had difficulty processing it.

He felt his thumb rip free from the socket a split second before his bones crunched like dry pasta. A sickening wave of agony fogged his vision, but this was only half over.

Screaming behind the sock, Nathan bit down, put his good foot against the anchor, and yanked his arm with all his strength. He had to pull free before the swelling set in.

The manacle held.

No! Not in this marine's world!

Near unconsciousness, Nathan tapped a dark part of his soul. Spiraling inward to a place he'd spent half his life trying to forget, he whipped his head back and forth in a frenzy and pulled. Hatred, bitterness, and a desire to kill every living thing on the planet emerged from inside him like an exploding sun.

Pain chewed into his brain as the carpal bones ground and compressed against one another. He felt everything in horrid clarity.

He screamed through the sock and pulled harder.

And harder.

He pulled until his shoulder reached the separation point, and then gave it even more.

In a final spurt of effort, Nathan sucked air through his nose and yanked with everything he had.

With a sickening, liquid sound, his wrist literally extruded through the manacle.

Nathan tumbled backward and slammed against the living-room wall.

His vision grayed again, then began to tunnel inward.

A low whistling in his ears got louder and louder as he teetered on the verge of blacking out.

He fought to stay conscious.

And lost the battle.

Nathan...

The voice sounded distant, echoing from a deep well.

Nathan...

He felt his body shake.

Nathan...

"Nathan! Are you okay?"

He opened his eyes. Lauren's face was inches from his.

Reality slammed home. He was still in the living room of H3. The throbbing in his hand instantly became a brutal reminder of the horror he'd inflicted upon himself.

Lauren's voice pulled him through the haze. The room came into focus.

She hugged him. "I'm sorry I hurt your hand."

He heard himself panting and struggled to control his breathing. "I'm sorry you had to see that part of me."

"What do you mean? What part?"

He knew then that the dark place he'd visited had been completely internalized. She hadn't seen or heard the inner battle he'd waged, nor did she know about the vicious monster living in his soul. And he'd never share that aspect of himself with her.

Nathan looked at his hand. Aside from the blood, it didn't look too bad. The bones were crushed, but it wasn't horribly deformed.

"Are you going to help my mom now?"

"Yes, but first I need you to hide. Go into the bedroom on the east side of the house and get in the closet."

"What are you going to do?"

Nathan squinted at the throbbing in his hand and leg, but managed a smile. "Don't question orders. Good spies never question orders."

"I *knew* you were a spy!"

"Guilty as charged, but you can't tell anyone, ever."

"I promise I won't."

"Go on."

Lauren left the room.

Keeping his pulverized hand elevated, he hopped on one leg to the front door, each labored bound sending a jolt of fire along his broken shin. With slothlike slowness, he peered to the east, along the row of houses.

His stomach turned.

Limping along the road, Voda had Jin by the wrist, dragging her. The ghillie suit coat he'd given her was gone. Although Voda was a good fifty yards distant, Nathan could see a red stain on Jin's shirt. It looked as though she'd taken one of Voda's bullets—a .44 Magnum hollow point. If that were true, Jin's body had absorbed a massive amount of destructive energy, putting her at serious risk of bleeding to death. Even if the mushroomed bullet had missed critical organs, she wouldn't survive without medical care.

Estimating he had fewer than ninety seconds before Voda arrived, Nathan struggled his way back into the living room and put the two-by-four against the wall where Voda had thrown it. He sat down next to the framing anchor and placed his body between it and where Voda would enter the room.

"Lauren," he whispered loudly, "Voda's coming. No matter what you hear, stay put and don't make a sound. You're safe in there."

He decided to give Voda some additional confidence. As loudly as he could, he yelled, "Voda, you can have your alexandrites. Leave my sister out of this and I'll tell you where they are!"

Nathan's body began an uncontrolled shiver as the adrenaline rush wore off.

"Voda! Can you hear me? I said you can have your gems!"

He heard Voda's voice, muffled in the distance. "It's too late for that. You had your chance."

He repeated his order. "Lauren, stay in there and don't make a sound."

A minute later, Nathan heard Voda before he saw him, recognizing the sound of Jin being dragged across the concrete. Red-faced from exertion, Voda pulled Jin into the living room and dropped her arm. She lay still, unmoving except for the heaving of her chest as she breathed. The bullet wound appeared to be high on her shoulder. Nathan prayed that her brachial artery hadn't been clipped. If it had, she probably would have been dead by now.

Nathan faked a jerk against the handcuffs and cursed.

"I see you're still feisty. There's no fun in beating your sister when she can't feel it, so I might as well begin with you."

"Stop," Nathan pleaded. "I said I'd tell you where the gemstones are. I can't tell you if you kill me."

"I have no intention of killing you. At least not yet."

"You're a sick asshole, you know that?"

Voda shook his head dismissively as he retrieved the two-by-four. Holding it like a baseball bat, he moved in. "What are you smiling at?"

"I was just thinking about how I'm going to continuously bash your head on the concrete until your brains drip out of your ears."

Voda actually laughed at the comment. "I must have busted your *cabeza* worse than I thought." He took a menacing step forward. "I'll just have to wipe that stupid grin from your lips."

"Yes, of course you will."

Using his good leg, Nathan sprang up. Headfirst, he lunged forward, catching Voda completely by surprise. Like a linebacker, Nathan drove all his weight into his target's midsection.

They fell to the concrete, Voda landing on his back with a grunt.

Nathan's pulverized hand smacked the floor. Fresh agony erupted, threatening to overwhelm him. But face-to-face with Voda at last, Nathan regained his focus quickly. Before Voda could twist away, Nathan used his good knee like a piston and rammed his wounded leg.

The man cried out and cursed.

Time wasn't on Nathan's side. Half his body had been rendered useless. The longer this went on, the more likely Voda was to gain the advantage. One way or the other, this was a brawl to the death. Knowing it would make his own concussion worse, Nathan head-butted Voda and felt the man's nose collapse. His vision reeled for an instant.

Voda let out an animal-like shriek and tried to knee Nathan in the groin. Nathan was no stranger to hand-to-hand combat and had already anticipated the move. He closed his legs before Voda's knee could penetrate.

Nathan took advantage of Voda's dazed state. Using his good hand, he gripped Voda's hair, lifted the man's head up, and drove it into the concrete.

For a split second, Voda's body went stiff.

With iron determination, he hefted Voda's head again and slammed it down.

Nathan repeated the move. Harder. Then did it again. And again, each impact sounding like a watermelon being dropped. For every girl Voda had murdered, Nathan cracked the man's head onto the concrete. Over and over and over, until Voda stopped breathing.

At long last, completely spent, Nathan rolled onto his back.

Time drifted, and he felt an eerie warmness wash over him. Despite the pain, it felt good to lie there, but Jin needed immediate attention.

"Lauren, you can come out now."

"I'm here."

He turned his head and knew she'd witnessed what he'd done.

"Lauren, what you just saw...Are you okay?"

"I'm okay," she said with conviction.

Nathan knew she hadn't passed judgment.

"It will be our secret."

"Forever."

Lauren took a tentative step forward and saw her mom. She rushed into the room and knelt beside Jin. "Mom!"

Nathan rolled onto his good arm and felt for car keys in Voda's pockets. Nothing. "Lauren, there's an Escalade on the west side of H1. Go see if the keys are in it. Drive it over here. I'll take care of your mom and stop her bleeding."

"I don't want to leave her!"

"Lauren, if we don't get her to a hospital, she'll die. Go on, run as fast as you can."

She looked conflicted.

"Don't question orders. Get going, now!"

Lauren looked angry but ran from the room.

Using one arm, Nathan crawled over to his sister. Next to his ballistic vest and boots, he saw his belt. He found his shirt under the vest, folded it into a compact square, and, using his good hand and teeth to tighten the belt, secured the compress against her shoulder wound.

Jin didn't react to the pressure with any signs of pain, and he saw why. A swollen contusion above her left ear seeped blood down the side of her face. Voda had bludgeoned her with something, probably the Magnum.

"Jin, can you hear me?" He gently shook her arm, trying to revive her, and got no response. "It's over. Lauren's safe."

He shook her arm again. Nothing. He checked one of her eyes. Unconscious. Even though she couldn't hear him, he talked to her anyway. "You've got a bullheaded daughter, you know that? You aren't going to die, Jin—you can't, Lauren needs you. *I* need you. There are so many things I want to say, I don't even know where to begin."

Nathan heard the sound of an approaching vehicle.

"Don't worry, Lauren's a good driver. You can't die, Jin. You have to hang in there. *You are not allowed to die....*"

EPILOGUE

Nathan awoke and tried to focus. Where was he? In a bed at Sharp Hospital. He looked around, then down at himself. The lower half of his left arm was bandaged and secured in a sling, and his right leg—from the knee down—held a fiberglass cast. His mouth felt like a dry lake bed. He knew he was recovering from surgery to repair his broken carpal bones. The orthopedic hand specialist had told him he was going to need months of painful therapy to get his motion back. He'd also been warned he might need follow-up surgery down the road to remove scar tissue, but the surgeon thought he'd make a full recovery.

He stared at the ceiling, trying to recall everything he could from yesterday's battle in the desert. He'd been through some harrowing moments in his life, but pulling his broken hand through that handcuff—compounded by his fear for Lauren if he failed—was near the top. He remembered fashioning a pressure bandage around Jin's shoulder. Lauren had driven the SUV up to the door, and they'd struggled to get Jin into the backseat. The rest came in foggy patches. Lauren must've driven to the outskirts of Victorville and gotten help. He remembered being wheeled into an emergency room. Harv and Grangeland had arrived sometime later, in the early evening, but the exact time eluded him. He had a loose recollection of Harv talking on the phone, making arrangements for his and Jin's immediate transfer down to Sharp, but beyond that, things weren't too clear. Morphine tended to do that.

"Harvey said it was okay if I came in."

Lauren's voice startled him. She was sitting in a chair near the window. She had a clean change of clothes on—an outfit that Nathan had never seen before.

"You have lots of balloons," she said. "Can I take some to my mom's room? She doesn't have as many."

"You can have all of them." He elevated his bed and reached for the plastic cup of water on the tray.

"I'll get it." Lauren held the straw to his lips.

Plain water had never tasted so good.

"How's your mom doing?"

Lauren fought back tears. "She doesn't remember who I am."

Nathan put his good hand on her shoulder and gave it a gentle squeeze. "Lauren, brain injuries can have that effect. I'm sure she'll remember you, but it might take some time. Your mom's concussion was more severe than mine. That's why I asked my mom and dad not to put any pressure on her. She needs time to sort things out. So what do you think of them? Your grandparents?"

"They're really nice. I like them."

"I think you charmed the senator, but don't let him spoil you—I like you just the way you are. Are they still in the waiting area with Harv?"

She nodded. "Do you think my mom will be like the guy in the movie who got shot in the head and couldn't remember anything?"

"I know the movie you're talking about: *Regarding Henry*. That was totally different. The bullet scrambled his brain and he couldn't even talk. That's not what happened with your mom. She just got knocked on the head really hard. You shouldn't blame yourself for *anything* that happened. None of it was your fault."

"But I forgot to trigger the ELT in your helicopter. You said if anything happened to you, I was supposed to do that."

"Lauren, I'd like you to tell me the truth."

"What do you mean?"

"You didn't just *forget*, did you...." It wasn't a question.

She shook her head. "I saw Voda drag you into the house, and I knew I had to help you. Are you mad at me?"

"What you did was incredibly brave, Lauren. Not one in a million kids your age would walk into a situation like that. No, I'm not mad at you. I never was."

"Are you sure?"

"Yes, I'm sure. Do you remember the causality pyramid we talked about?"

She nodded.

"What do you think would've happened if you'd gone to the helicopter first? Remember, it was half a mile away, in the opposite direction."

"I wouldn't have helped you in time."

"That's right. We wouldn't be talking right now, and your mom would be dead."

She looked at his bandage. "I'm sorry about your hand."

"For a second there, I thought you weren't going to jump onto the board."

"Your hand made a terrible sound. I can't believe I did it."

"I can. You're a very brave girl, and you saved my life. Your mom's too."

They fell silent for a moment.

"Remember when you told me your mom didn't love your stepdad?"

"Uh-huh."

"Your mom never told you that, did she?"

"No, I could just tell."

"That was very intuitive on your part."

She didn't say anything.

"It means you sensed it. Are you really serious about wanting to be an operations officer someday?"

"You mean, like, a spy?"

Nathan shook his head. "We don't use that term. The most important part of being an *operations officer* is keeping secrets. What I'm going to tell you must be kept secret. You can never tell anyone, ever, not even your mom."

"Okay."

"Before my surgery this morning, Harv and I had a long phone call with someone who's high up in the intelligence community. Very high. I'm not going to tell you who it is, and you shouldn't ask, but this person knows secret information about your mom."

Nathan had actually been returning Director Cantrell's call. She'd left an urgent message on his phone the night before. They'd done the usual dance, and Cantrell hadn't been forthcoming until Harv had insisted, telling Cantrell that Jin had used Nathan's old CIA call sign. That, and Harv's reminder of a debt she owed Nathan and Harv, got the director's undivided attention. Still, Cantrell hadn't revealed everything, but it had been enough for them to get a clear picture.

"Haven't you always suspected your mom had a secret life before you were born, but she could never talk about it?"

Lauren nodded.

"I'm going to tell you a story about your mom, because it will help you understand her better. Before you were born, your mom was a hero in North Korea. She carried out many successful missions all over the world and was at the top of her game. But she was married to a high-ranking government official who was jealous of all the attention she got. He also drank too much, and when he got drunk, he would abuse your mom. Now, I'm not talking about your *real* dad, who your mom mentioned in her note—this was someone else. Your real father didn't marry your mom, and I'll tell you why in a second. Well, the abuse got worse and worse.

It went on for years, until one night, when he was super drunk, he tried to kill your mom."

Lauren's eyes widened in shock.

Nathan nodded. "And he nearly succeeded. Fortunately, your mom was a trained operations officer. She fought back and accidentally killed him in self-defense. Even though there were witnesses, it didn't matter. Your mom was in big trouble. She'd killed an important person in the government. She went from hero to criminal in an instant. She was arrested and jailed without a trial."

"But she didn't do it on purpose."

"It didn't matter. North Korea's government didn't care and wasn't fair about it. Anyway, this is where your real dad stepped in to help your mom. Your father saw what was happening to your mom as a real injustice, especially after all she'd done for her country. He couldn't stand to see your mom spend the rest of her life in a prison labor camp. So, at great risk to himself, he faked some papers, freed her from prison, and smuggled her out of the country. I don't know this for sure, but they probably posed as husband and wife for the trip. Lauren, it sounds to me like your real father was a good man. Soon after he smuggled her across the border into South Korea, your mom was pregnant with you. Unfortunately, your dad's role ended there. He couldn't do anything more for Jin without exposing himself as a traitor. If he'd been caught helping your mom, he would've been executed. He gave your mom some money, but it wasn't much. There were, and are, very few wealthy people in North Korea, and your father wasn't one of them.

"Here's where the debt comes into play. See, once she knew she was pregnant, Jin wanted to make the best life for herself and her baby. That meant getting into the US and living there, but that's not easy to do."

"Why not?"

"There are thousands and thousands of people each year who want to enter the US and become citizens, but they have nothing to offer in return. The US can only take in a small number of people each year. Well, your mom was different from a lot of people who want to get into the US. She contacted the US embassy in South Korea and told them who she was and that she had a gold mine of secrets to offer. She had information about the inner workings of North Korea's spy program and details of the missions she'd carried out. Some of her work was quite famous in the espionage world, including the theft of an antimissile system's plans and specifications. She had quite a reputation. In the covert world, it's all about what you know....Well, Jin knew a lot. The US was impressed and agreed to offer her asylum, but it came at a pretty high price."

"What did she have to do?"

"Two things. First, she had to tell the US everything she knew about all the espionage missions she'd ever conducted—her method of training, locations of camps, her contacts. Everything. And second, at some undisclosed point in the future, she'd have to perform one final mission for the US. She didn't want to agree with the second part, but she was going to have a baby soon—*you*. She didn't have a lot of options. She was faced with being a single mother in a foreign country right next door to North Korea. She'd never feel safe there, especially given her unique-looking eyes. They were hard to miss."

"So she said yes?"

"That's right. To give you a better life, she struck a deal and the US set her up with a new identity and brought her over. I think she chose La Jolla because I lived there. Remember, she knew who my father was but never told anyone. I don't know how she learned about the echo five reference, but someday I'll need to find out."

"What does 'echo five' mean?"

"It's something from my past, and it's top secret. Very few people in the world know about it. But back to your mom. Think about it, Lauren. What would it be like living that way? Knowing that out of the blue, you'll get a phone call from the US government someday and have to drop everything and go on a potentially dangerous mission…"

"It sounds awful."

"I'm sure it was, but she did it for you. Remember the part in her note about running, about how she said she didn't want to run, how she didn't want that life for you? She wanted you to have a good life, and if she ran from her obligation, it would mean running for the rest of her life. She didn't want that. You told me she used to cry all the time. It was from being under pressure. Her unpaid debt took a heavy toll on her over the years. The important thing for you to know in your heart is that your mom loves you. Everything she did was for you."

Lauren was quiet for a while, and Nathan let her absorb what she'd just heard. He knew this wasn't easy on her, but she deserved the truth, deserved to know what kind of woman her mom was.

Nathan took another sip of water. "Lauren, there's something else you need to know. When I first met your mom, in the ghost town, I asked her if she knew Voda was murdering the girls. I guess I needed to know that for myself. She said no, and I believed her. I still do. The triggering event was when you fell down in your stepdad's warehouse and saw the dead girl. Everything changed after that. You told your mom, she told your stepdad, and things spiraled out of control from there. But none of this is your fault. You did the right thing telling your mom."

"I wish I never saw the dead girl."

"I understand why you feel that way, but here's the good thing: we burned Voda's operation to the ground. If you hadn't seen the dead girl, more girls would've been murdered, and Abrille would have been one of them."

"Were all the girls Voda used killed?"

"I'm not sure," Nathan said. "I had a talk with Holly, and the FBI's working with French authorities to piece together the fate of the other girls, the girls we saw on the passports. Holly thinks most of them were flown into France. She's trying to track them down. She thinks Voda killed at least six of the girls. He probably had a local buyer for the gems. But it's important for you to know that both your mom and your stepdad *didn't* know what Voda was doing. I think they knew he was smuggling alexandrites, but they didn't know how he was doing it. And they certainly didn't know he was using the girls as human couriers until you fell down in the warehouse. It's amazing where one little fall can lead."

"Yeah, that's for sure."

"You asked me if I believe in evil....Well, the answer is yes. But the reverse is also true. I believe there are good forces working against evil. We aren't meant to understand such things, but when you saw the dead girl, a complex chain of events was set into motion."

"It's that causality thing again, right?"

He smiled. "Right. You helped save the lives of countless other girls. You should be proud of that. Don't ever second-guess yourself about it."

"I won't."

Ironically, second-guessing was exactly what Nathan had been doing to himself. About Voda. He would have preferred not to talk about it, but that was a form of denial, and he'd long ago learned to face certain truths about himself head-on. And if he were going to have an ongoing, familial relationship with Lauren, he needed to be forthright with her as well, especially about something as important as this.

"I'm going to tell you something personal, okay?"

Lauren nodded, eyes wide.

"I killed a lot of people yesterday, and unfortunately, you saw some of them die. I'm not proud of what I did, and I certainly don't feel good about it."

She nodded, then said, "But they were trying to kill us first."

"I wish that made it easier, but it doesn't. But here's the point." Nathan spoke softly. "I didn't have to kill Voda. After I bashed his head on the concrete a few times, he was out of the fight."

"You wanted to kill him."

Nathan locked eyes with her. "Yes, I did, and it's a power-ful feeling I never want you to experience. It can be dangerous, Lauren, like an addictive drug."

"I wish you didn't feel bad about it."

"If I didn't feel bad, I'd be no better than Voda."

Lauren went quiet again, then nodded slightly. Nathan knew she understood.

"Okay," Nathan said, lightening his tone. "Enough of that. Is Harv still out in the waiting room?"

"Do you want me to go get him?"

"Please."

Lauren left the room, and Nathan stared at the ceiling again. Half a minute later, Lauren returned, holding Harv's hand.

"How are you feeling, partner?"

"I'm okay. A little sore here and there, but I'll manage."

"Harv said he's taking me out to lunch," Lauren said.

"A date? And you didn't invite me? I hope you'll at least bring me something. The food in here is good, but I'm jonesing for a Caesar salad with extra dressing."

Lauren wrinkled her brow. "Jonesing?"

"Craving," Harv answered. "I think that could be arranged."

"Harv, help me into the wheelchair. I want to visit Jin."

"Do you think that's wise?"

"Yes, I do."

"All right."

Getting out of bed didn't hurt as badly as he had thought it would. His hand throbbed, but that was to be expected. His bro-ken leg held a dull ache, but it felt tolerable. As Harv had told him on many occasions, he'd been through worse.

When Lauren turned to open the door, Harv handed him something and he nodded a thank-you.

Jin's room was several doors down. Nathan immediately saw the two men sitting in chairs. CIA or FBI or both. He nodded and they nodded back.

Lauren held the door open while Harv pushed him inside. Lauren followed them in. Jin's room was identical to his, but Lauren was right: it didn't look as cheerful. It needed more color. As with Nathan, Jin had her arm secured in a sling. A thick bandage covered her shoulder. The back of her bed was about halfway up. On the opposite wall near the ceiling, her muted TV was tuned to a news channel. She turned her head when they entered. Her swelling and bruising still looked bad, but the cuts had been cleaned.

Her expression remained guarded.

"Hi, Jin. I know all of this is difficult for you, but I want you to know you're not alone. You have a family that loves you, and we're going to help you get through this."

"I…"

"You don't have to say anything. My name is Nathan McBride, and I'm your brother. And this little girl is your daughter. The man behind the wheelchair is like a brother to me, so he's your family too. His name is Harvey Fontana, but we call him Harv. Your father's a US senator."

She didn't say anything.

Harv rolled Nathan up to Jin's bed. Lauren approached too, but didn't say anything.

"I want you to look at our eyes."

Jin did, and a smile formed.

"That's right, they're nearly identical. I don't want you to worry about anything. I'm going to take care of Lauren until you're back on your feet. She'll be safe with me. Harv will help too, won't you?"

"Indeed I will."

"I want to give you something. Maybe it will help trigger some memories." He gently placed his father's dog tag on the bed.

Jin looked at it, then picked it up. She turned it over in her fingers, looking it over closely.

"That was our father's when he was stationed overseas. You gave it to me two days ago. The drop of blood on the back is yours."

"I gave this to you?"

"As proof of who you are."

She didn't say anything.

"Head injuries can cause loss of memory, but they're usually short-term. I've seen it before. Now, this big girl here needs her mom, more than she ever has. I'm certain by the time you're up and about, you'll be remembering some bits and pieces. You may not remember everything, but you have very strong memories of Lauren, and I'm willing to bet they'll begin to surface within the next few days or so. Like I said, I've see this before."

"I'll try," Jin said.

"For now, you need to rest. You've got a difficult and painful surgery ahead of you. You need a new shoulder joint."

"Lauren said I was shot?"

Lauren took a step forward at hearing her name.

"Yes, the three of us were in a life-and-death struggle. I don't know how much Lauren told you about it, but you saved our lives. You bought time by taking a bullet for us."

Harv nudged his leg.

Jin kept turning the dog tag in her fingers.

"Harv is taking Lauren to lunch and bringing me back a Caesar salad. Is there something he can get for you?"

Jin looked up at them. "I like...macaroni and cheese."

Lauren glanced at Nathan quickly with hope in her eyes.

"All right, mac and cheese it is."

Lauren leaned over and gave her mom a kiss.

"We'll see you in a little bit."

Harv wheeled Nathan toward the door, and Lauren held it open again. When Lauren's back was turned, Nathan looked back at Jin.

What he saw brought a smile.

Jin mouthed the words "Thank you."

Nathan winked and was gone.

Out in the hall, Lauren seemed energized. "Mac and cheese is her favorite food!"

ANDREW PETERSON

"Given your reaction in there, I gathered that."

"Nathan," Harv said, "you *do* realize you left a two-million-dollar piece of hardware sitting out in the desert?"

"I trust you dealt with that while I was indisposed?"

"You trust correctly. I found the key. Try not to do it again."

"I'll remember that...the next time I'm faced with a similar situation."

Lauren asked, "Do you really think my mom's going to get her memory back?"

Harv stopped pushing his chair and turned it to face Lauren. He looked up at Harv, and they exchanged a silent understanding. Harv knew the score.

"Yes, absolutely."

"You promise?"

"Yes, I promise. Marines keep their promises."

Avoiding his injured hand, she leaned over and hugged him.

"Can I call you Uncle Nate now?"

He took a deep breath and looked at Harv, who had his arms crossed.

"Lauren, I think you've earned it."

334

ACKNOWLEDGMENTS

There are many people I wish to acknowledge and thank. Writing a novel is a solitary endeavor, but it stops there. After it's written, the process transforms into a collaboration and the people who contribute their effort and expertise are equally important. I have a lot of faults, but a lack of loyalty isn't one of them. I'm deeply devoted to those who've helped and supported me over the years.

Ed Stackler has been my freelance editor from day one. Ed helps me with every aspect of writing—from plotting to polishing. Without Ed, I'd be lost. He's not only a terrific editor, he's a valued friend.

My agent, Jake Elwell, is a gem. He believed in me when others didn't. Jake once told me he's in the "futures" business. Simply stated: he's my guy. I look forward to his continued guidance and friendship.

At Audible.com, Steve Feldberg is solidly influential in my career. Steve took a chance with me, and for that, I'll always be grateful.

Dick Hill is an amazing audiobook narrator, and I'm blessed to have him on the team. He's the voice of Jack Reacher—what more needs to be said?

My editor, Alan Turkus, is a joy to work with and being part of Amazon Publishing's new serial project is an honor. I hope I'm worthy.

Bob Mayer. Ridley Pearson. Steve Berry. If I hadn't attended their classes, I wouldn't be published. They are three of the most generous, sharp, and dynamic people in the industry.

There are people I can call in the middle of the night when I need a friend. Laura Taylor. Rebecca Cantrell. Tom Davin. All of them keep me grounded.

Thank you to Douglas W. Reavie, MD, FACS, for allowing me to use him as a character in the book. Doug is not only the best plastic surgeon in San Diego, he's a kind and generous man who donates many of his hours to charity. It's an honor to consider him a friend.

A special thank-you is owed to Andy Harp. Semper Fi, my friend.

My family is the foundation of my life, especially my wife, Carla. Without a doubt, you are—and always will be—the love of my life.

ABOUT THE AUTHOR

Photograph by Carla Martinez, 2010

Andrew Peterson is a San Diego native who holds a degree in architecture from the University of Oklahoma. An avid marksman who has won numerous sharpshooting competitions, he has donated more than 2,000 books to American troops serving overseas and wounded soldiers recovering in military hospitals. The author of *First to Kill* and *Forced to Kill*—the first two thrillers in the Nathan McBride series—Peterson lives in Monterey County, California, with his wife, Carla, and their three dogs.

Visit Andrew's website at www.andrewpeterson.com, and follow him on Twitter at @APetersonNovels, and on Facebook at www.facebook.com/Andrew.Peterson.Author.